Gabe Hartman is an award-winning, workaholic soap opera writer who prefers friends with benefits that don't interfere with his deadlines. After his mother dies unexpectedly, he returns to his small hometown to settle her affairs, then get back to work ASAP. He schedules the memorial, arranges the burial, but makes no plans to fall for anyone, especially not a married man.

Owen Greene is open-hearted, good looking, and blessed with a charmed life. He's passionate about all things farm-to-table and isn't afraid to pursue what he wants—experience optional. When Gabe stumbles into his chaotic farmers market booth, the sparks are instant.

Gabe wants to do right by his mother and get back to work. Owen wants Gabe. Their chemistry? Unavoidable. Between messy estate finances and a fake-date crash course in emotional vulnerability, they just might stumble into something real. If only Gabe could come clean about a secret of his own...

Fall in love with this warm, witty MM rom-com about unexpected connections, complicated timing, and kissing the guy who makes your heart trip.

ROM-COM FOR

DUMMIES

Tom Diggs

A NineStar Press Publication
www.ninestarpress.com

Rom-Com for Dummies

First Edition, August 2025

ISBN: 978-1-64890-888-0
Also available in eBook, ISBN: 978-1-64890-887-3

CONTENT WARNING:
This book contains sexually explicit content, which may only be suitable for mature readers. Depictions of infidelity, grief/death of character's mother, and mention of past school shooting.

To R.I., my teacher

Chapter One

Gabe Hartman was a first-class liar. It made sense he would become head writer on a soap opera.

If Tomorrow Never Comes had been around for decades. It was created in the late fifties by the legendary Aurora Helms, one of the doyennes of soaps. She had the vision to recognize bored, postwar, suburban housewives who needed the fantasy of romance and drama to keep them going until their husbands returned home in the evening after work. Aurora had created a kingdom of daytime dramas for the networks. *If Tomorrow Never Comes* was not only the feather in the cap of her reign, but also her last remaining soap still on the air. The fans couldn't imagine a world without their hour of escape to Harmony Hills. The poor municipality had survived fires, plagues, serial killers, cult suicides, and Russian invasions. As of late, the show's plots had become more tame and socially conscious, thanks mostly to Gabe Hartman's sensibilities as head writer. He had grounded the show in salt-of-the-earth storylines that appealed to its down-to-earth audience, mostly from rural areas and red states.

Aurora Helms was in her nineties now and popped into the

Manhattan offices of *If Tomorrow Never Comes* once a year from her estate in Connecticut. The staff performed a dog-and-pony show for the reigning "Queen of Soapland." She spent a quick morning dispensing worthless advice and questionable anecdotes about the "Golden Age of Harmony Hills." She bragged about getting now-famous actors from the New York City theater community to act in the early years of *If Tomorrow Never Comes*. Actors who would go on to become the greatest actors of their generation were allegedly cast as extras and "day players." No corroborating record of any of this existed, but Gabe had trained his staff to listen politely, chuckle adoringly at her jokes, eat cheese, and drink sherry with her. She loved sherry. She waxed about her dreams of owning a cable network that played nothing but reruns of her soaps; no one had the heart to tell her cable networks devoted to soaps rarely succeeded. At some point, Aurora would have closed-door meetings with both the suits and the executive producers. Eventually, she would get tired and be limo-ed back to Connecticut while the staff returned to business as if she had never been there. Did she even watch *If Tomorrow Never Comes* anymore? Did it matter? As long as the show stayed on the air, her coffers kept filling.

The staff always complained about Aurora's visits, but Gabe would have none of it. He was extremely vocal about his gratitude. Because of Aurora, he had been gainfully employed and living comfortably as a writer in New York City for over a decade. What other writers could say that? This year, he won his first Daytime Emmy due to Aurora's creation, and he amplified his gratitude in his Emmy acceptance speech.

Gabe was good at his job and had always been well respected at *If Tomorrow Never Comes.* He had the unique talent of all great head writers: he made the writing staff feel like they were equally involved in a collaborative process. Gabe, however, always had the final say. He also had the best ideas. Everyone was always impressed with what he came up with.

But Gabe had a dirty little secret. None of his ideas were original. He was a world-class liar and a world-class thief. Morality was of no use to Gabe when it came to getting the job done.

Gabe's secret weapon was his hometown, Concord Valley, a small borough Upstate. The people there were nice enough, but nothing else was of interest for Gabe, especially having grown up there as a young gay boy on the verge of his sexual emergence. That said, Concord Valley was where Gabe got all his best ideas for *If Tomorrow Never Comes*. Or more accurately, *stole* all his best ideas.

Every great idea he got for his soap came from someone's real life story in Concord Valley. The love triangle between the beautician, the plumber, and the nun...Gertie, Phil, and Concetta in Concord Valley. The child misdiagnosed with autism who simply needed an ocular aid...the Waverly child in Concord Valley. The bad girl who returned to town and ran the cafe...Mildred in Concord Valley. Concord Valley as a town was the perfect population to inspire Harmony Hills-sized storylines.

Even though his dear mother still lived there, Gabe seldom went to visit. Concord Valley was the kind of place gay boys leave and never look back. That was the lie Gabe told himself. He went home for Christmas and birthdays, and he called his mother almost daily when she unwittingly fed him his latest storyline updates. Deserted by Dad decades ago, Gabe considered his mother one of his closest friends. He was planning to check in with her that night as he might have a couple of new storylines that needed developing.

His deception had one more layer. Gabe was such a professional liar, he never told anyone in Concord Valley he worked at *If Tomorrow Never Comes*. For all they knew, he worked in Manhattan at some aimless job in a nebulous megacorporation. Visits home would be easier if they didn't know. He wrote for *If Tomorrow Never Comes* under the pseudonym, George Sample. Since soap writers are basically invisible, there was little chance of anyone ever learning the truth. The daytime writing awards were never shown on the televised part of the Daytime Emmys. There might be a still photo of Gabe floating around on the interwebs, but the image would be labeled George Sample and not Gabe Hartman. A "Gabe Hartman, soap writer" online search would yield fruitless results. Gabe was confident he had safely set up an impenetrable secret life. As long as the networks were broadcasting soaps, Gabe was guaranteed a healthy career as a writer for soap operas.

One of Gabe's jobs as head writer was to keep track of the weekly ratings. Erin, the show's fabulous writer's assistant and Gabe's work spouse, was the first to retrieve the ratings and make copies for all of the upper-level management production team.

Gabe headed to Erin's cubicle next to the copy machine in the supply room. Erin had been an intern from NYU during her undergrad years. Not only did the staff adore her, but Erin was also a super fan of the show. She was offered a full-time gig the moment her internship was over. Gabe couldn't imagine the place without her.

The supply room was abuzz with the whirr of script pages being printed and the organized chaos of ZipExpress overnight delivery envelopes getting prepped for drop off. The staff writers mainly worked from home. They didn't need to come into the Manhattan office every day. As the sole writer's assistant, one of Erin's jobs was to put the finishing touches on several overnight packages for the out-of-town writing staff.

Erin had also already organized and highlighted the ratings in a neat pile. Gabe admired her competence and efficiency, a rare find in anyone, especially someone so young.

"How do we look, Erin?" he asked.

"Not great," said Erin. "Down another two hundredths of a point. You want a look?"

"I trust you. Not too precipitous."

"Steady but sure. The fans want more shirtless dudes, Gabe."

"Take a number."

"You should read the fan mail." Erin held up a pile of letters.

"Above my pay grade. Wait! These ratings were from the week the plot revolved around the men's swimwear competition. Guess our dudes need to work out more."

"You can't expect good actors to be gym rats. I still say the cannibalism storyline could be a Sweeps Week winner."

"You're nuts. Short of hardcore porn, I'm not sure what would spike the ratings."

"What about a simple romance?"

"Right…"

"Or better yet, hide a romantic comedy in what might have been a tawdry storyline. Who doesn't love romance? Add a few jokes. The combo is incredibly sexy. Some daytime drama sleight of hand."

He considered Erin's rom-com idea charming, but quaint.

"Not sure how that would work…on the air or in life," said Gabe. "We'll see what the producers have to say. Speaking of, how are the Douglasses today?"

"Higher than the ratings."

"Not saying much. Wish me luck. Thanks for these." Gabe grabbed the pile of ratings. "You make the shitty parts of my job look easy."

"I bet you say that to all the exploited underlings. Want me to join you with the Douglasses?" asked Erin.

"I'm wearing my big-boy pants. I can handle a couple of drunken producers."

"I always admire your detachment."

"That's what they pay me for."

Gabe glanced at the actual ratings numbers and tried not to blanch. They'd recently been sliding so low, this week's two-hundredth percentile decline was inconsequential compared to the previous hemorrhaging. The consistent slide was not good for *If Tomorrow Never Comes*, let alone soaps in general.

Gabe understood soap operas were no longer a sustainable business. *If Tomorrow Never Comes* produced five hour-long television shows per week with full casts, sets, and costumes, not to mention writers and all the salaries below the line. Its producers had been clever and resourceful. Lots of repurposed sets and double casting with an occasional twin storyline. Gabe did his best to consider costs when he crafted his story arcs. The days of soap opera location shots in Paris were over. Daytime drama eventually wouldn't be able to outrun destiny. Ultimately, the industry could only support a handful of high-end soaps, and the chances *If Tomorrow Never Comes* would be among them were pretty slim. The miracle was soaps had lasted this long. Unlike Gabe, the numbers never lied.

On his way to the Douglasses' office, Gabe bumped into the soap's favorite on-again-off-again-on-again couple, Suzy and Cameron. They had both started on the show over twenty years ago right out of Juilliard and were now considered soap legends, if one believed everything they read in the soap opera trade magazines. They had been married and divorced from each other (and others) so many times they put Elizabeth Taylor and the Gabor sisters to shame. As was the custom on *If Tomorrow Never Comes,* veteran actors were no longer referred to by their professional actor names, but by their Harmony Hills character's names. Suzy's real name was Heidi Arbuckle; Cameron's childhood friends still referred to him as Lachlan Davenport, but there was already a Lachlan Davenport in SAG. At *If Tomorrow Never Comes,* they were called Suzy and Cameron.

"Got our latest script, Gabey Baby?" asked Suzy. Something in her tone always oozed sexuality. She was always *on.*

"It's been a few months since our last divorce," reminded Cameron. "And you never wrote us a breakup sex scene."

"Don't be crass, Cammy," said Suzy. She gave him a playful slug to the shoulder. "Mmm, someone's been working out."

"Those new script pages? Let's have a tiny peek," said Cameron.

If Gabe hadn't bumped into Cameron at a notorious after-hours gay bar a few years ago, Gabe would have never guessed he was gay. Gabe knew Cameron knew Gabe had a crush on him, but Gabe had impeccable boundaries at work. Cameron, on the other hand, would flirt with a broom if he thought his career would benefit.

"C'mon, dude." Cameron hummed his words seductively. "Give us a preview."

"You know that's not how this works," said Gabe, subtly shielding their declining numbers from them both. Actors, as a rule, were insecure. The slightest indication of trouble could undermine their fragile egos. They would take the ratings to heart as a report card of their work and be convinced they were about to get canned. Gabe and the producers went out of their way to keep the actors sheltered from reality. Being a world-class liar, Gabe made sure none of the actors had a clue their ship could gradually be sinking. "I promise you both fabulous storylines in our new story cycle."

"How about a May-December romance for me?" asked Cameron.

"You're a little long in the tooth to be May in that one," said Suzy.

"And far too young to be December," said Gabe.

"Flattery will get you everywhere," said Cameron. "Almost everywhere." Cameron tapped the tip of Gabe's nose with his index finger, a condescending gesture Gabe found insufferable.

"I think you both need to be caught in a torrid love triangle with either an amnesia twist or with a neurodivergent third," said Gabe.

"Can't I play a neurodivergent amnesiac twin?" asked Suzy. "I've still got my classically trained chops."

"And give me enough shirtless scenes to finally win an Emmy. Please?" asked Cameron. He had been nominated five times without ever taking home a statuette.

"Who needs an Emmy when you get most of the fan mail?" asked Suzy.

Gabe loved when actors spun into the butter, impaled on jealousy. They could be such children.

"Cameron," said Gabe, "I was thinking you would be the perfect actor to shatter the glass ceiling with a bisexual polyamorous storyline. Think our audience is ready to see that side of you?"

Gabe's joke made Suzy laugh from her gut. Her raised eyebrows screamed "typecasting."

"Better run that by the suits," said Cameron. Gabe slightly regretted putting Cameron in his place, but it was an appropriate comeuppance for the condescending nose flick.

"Speaking of," said Suzy, "we don't want to be late for our costume fitting... Come on, stud. He was kidding, Cam. Geez, you're too sensitive." Suzy grabbed Cameron's arm for a hasty retreat.

Gabe tidied up the pile of ratings but got easily distracted by Cameron's ass as he walked away, perfectly round and dimpled in all the right places. Cameron was undeniably a handsome man but would no doubt make a terrible boyfriend. Too needy. But that ass... Gabe was convinced

Cameron had a secret boyfriend stashed away somewhere. He hoped so, for Cameron's sake.

Other than an occasional fleeting Cameron fantasy, Gabe never came within a mile of mixing business with pleasure. He often fantasized about letting romance into his life and being swept off his feet. How nice, he wished, to have a handsome someone at home to bear witness to his life, yet give him all the space he needed; a wealthy someone who was fully self-sustaining, yet not afraid to offer Gabe boundless generosity; one who was sexy and would offer Gabe sensuous pleasures without limits, yet with full satisfaction in the bedroom.

Gabe's mystery date fantasy always got superseded by his impending to-do work list. Romance tripped up his efficiency. As long as work consumed his attention, he had no time for a pesky boyfriend underfoot. Getting laid had never been a problem. Depending on the app, sex had become compartmentalized. Why ruin a functional circle of regular hookups with old-fashioned intimacy or the tawdry cliche of an office romance?

Gabe admired the economy of the hookup apps. Adjust the filter to whatever one is in the mood for and see who's around. When his regulars were unavailable, he auditioned potential newbies for understudy and replacement casts. Gabe had no illusions. As long as everyone assumed the world was full of flakes and refugees from the island of broken toys, disappointments were at a minimum.

Gabe checked the app on his phone. No new messages. He checked to make sure the app's sound was on. The ritual of sex was always initiated with a *drrroot,* that unique sound specific in pitch and length, a sound every gay man could identify. Pavlovian. A tap led to a quick chat followed by a few provocative pics and an even quicker discussion of intentions, sexual positions and peccadilloes, hosting options, boundaries, diseases, and vaccines. Whoever came up with the idea of a "dating" app for gay men was a genius. Now that HIV was undetectable on a bad day, everyone was acting like it was the seventies again. Gabe was glad he had been spared the world of sexually transmitted diseases. He basically played safe and rarely ventured outside his trusted circle of favorite regulars.

Once in a while, his instincts were off and he'd cross paths with a weirdo, but he trusted his gut enough to know when to cut and run. If 10,000 hours made someone an expert, he was a hookup expert a few times over. If Gabe had an hour-long break and the timing was right, he could use the app to take the edge off a day and be ready for his next work meeting with time to spare. Even though his prolific sex life was one of volume and optimization, he secretly hoped romance would someday find him again.

He had never been lucky in love. Once upon a time, there had been a boyfriend, charming Nicholas, early on when he moved to New York after college. At that age, long-term meant six months. They started out innocently enough, but when the boyfriend wanted an open relationship, Gabe cut his losses and got out. He didn't want to end up like his mother.

Around the time of the Nicholas breakup, Gabe landed the gig at *If Tomorrow Never Comes*. Television gigs are a workaholic's dream. Gabe had no time for the rituals of courtship, let alone a long-term relationship. No time for romance shenanigans when you're creating five hours of video content a week, fifty-two weeks a year. Gabe barely had time to grieve the end of his relationship with Nicholas when he was thrown into the world of Harmony Hills. In the last decade, Gabe had survived a half dozen teams of executive producers.

The Douglasses were the current EPs, a husband-wife team. On a real show, they'd be called showrunners. They got praise for all the show's successes and blame for all the show's failures. They got paid fuck-you money, but the burnout rate was extremely high for executive producers on soaps. They rarely lasted more than two years before getting fired. The Douglasses were nearing the end of a two-year tenure. Due to the stress of the declining ratings, both Douglasses had developed a drinking problem. The drama behind the cameras sometimes outperformed the scripts they shot.

Gabe stood outside the fancy executive producer's office, gathering his thoughts. All memories of Cameron's ass and plans to hook up with a sexy, detached regular were filed away until after the uncomfortable conversation he was about to have. Gabe had spent his adult years knocking on this executive producer's hard oak office door.

"Who izzz it?" Doris Douglass was already slurring her words.

"Gabe Hartman." He listened for any sign of movement or tidying up. None.

"You might as well bring uzzz the bad news..." Thomas Douglass was even more sloshed. "Enter!"

The Douglasses' office was less slick than the fancy offices of network executives. Executive producers were expected to stay late into the night; they needed an office that emphasized comfort. Thomas sat behind the mahogany desk with his legs propped up, no shoes, but his expensive socks were on display. Doris was stretched out on a plush loveseat, a former set piece, looking too exhausted for someone who arrived at work less than an hour ago.

Gabe was immediately overwhelmed by the heavy smell of liquor.

"We already know what you're about to tell us." Thomas stood up from the desk chair, attempting not to wobble.

"The ratings sucky suck, suck, suck..." said Doris.

"They're not as bad as you think," said Gabe. He neatened the pile from Erin in preparation for a softened landing.

"Who are we kidding! They're almost on life support," said Doris, clutching the side of the loveseat to support her sitting upright.

"We all hear the death knell in the trades." Thomas made his way to the middle of the room. He was remarkably well-balanced considering all the half-full bottles of booze on the coffee table.

"They hired us to save the show," said Doris, releasing a gassy burp.

"Classy," said Thomas.

"Sorry," said Doris.

"No worries," said Gabe.

"We have another problem," said Thomas.

"This involves you," said Doris. "We both consider you the master troubleshooter."

"The consummate professional. You have a rarability. Rare. Ability," said Thomas.

"What Tom means is we admire you and consider you part of our team," said Doris.

I hope so. I am part of the team. "What's our latest problem?" asked Gabe.

Thomas leaned against the mahogany desk for support. "Bad news, good news. Bad news first: we have to scrap the whole school shooting story."

"But we shot the whole story arc!" said Gabe. "It's in the can and starts airing a week from Monday. And it's great! Our best work in years!!!" Gabe had been inspired by the recent Concord Valley lockdown and school shooter threat.

"Preaching to the converted, kiddo," said Thomas. "However, whoever wrote it, coincidentally wrote fifty percent of the exact same details as last week's school shootings in both Texas and Florida."

"Our audience—and the world—would consider that whole storyline in poor taste," said Doris.

"Where's the good news in this?" asked Gabe.

"Even though we have to rush a whole new story to take its place, like yesterday, we got word from casting they are scouting a major young talent specifically for this storyline."

"Only he won't be expensive."

"But he will become famous," said Thomas. "The actor we're courting is that good."

"And when they sign him, things are going to happen fast," said Doris. "This is where you come in. We're going to need you to come up with a new storyline for a brand new character ASAP."

"We want something hip and fresh," said Thomas.

"This could be exciting," said Doris.

This could be a lot of work. Gabe hoped he appeared excited.

"You don't have to do anything this minute," said Thomas. "They haven't signed him yet. But you need to start brainstorming."

"You're going to need to drop running, kiddo," said Doris. "There will be zero turnaround on this."

"I appreciate the heads-up," said Gabe.

"Make him someone American women will want to have sex with," said Doris. "Sex on the washer-dryer. On the spin cycle."

"What the hell is that, Doris?" asked Thomas.

"The kind of guy you'd cheat on your husband for," said Doris.

"Make him someone you, Gabe, you would want to fuck," said Thomas. "You're not offended I assume you're queer?"

"Technically, I'm gay, but all good."

"Nobody says queer anymore. That's a microaggression, Tom. He could sue us," said Doris.

"He's not gonna sue us. *Queer* got reclaimed, Doris. Don't be old-fashioned. And this is showbiz. We're all artists having queer sex on washing machines!"

"If only," said Gabe.

"Bottom line," said Thomas. "Start thinking about a character and a storyline that will make Harmony Hills the most sought-after real estate on the daytime schedule. Crisis is opportunity and...something."

"Crisis is opportunity and danger," said Gabe.

"He'll think of something, dear," said Doris. "He always does."

"You always come up with the best storylines," said Thomas. "So simple, refreshing, and real. I don't know how you do it."

Gabe made a note to himself: *Call Mother tonight and get the latest gossip from Concord Valley. And turn* that *into a rom-com.*

"Bottom line: we trust you," said Thomas. "I mean you <u>did</u> win the show's one and only Emmy." The alcohol couldn't disguise a tinge of resentment. Gabe was glad he had made a fuss about the Douglasses in his acceptance speech.

"We don't want to take any more of your time, kiddo," said Doris. "You've got the next masterpiece to conjure."

"The main takeaways," said Thomas. "The new kid takes Harmony Hills by storm!"

"I have my marching orders," Gabe said as he made his way to the door, walking backward. "Do you want these?" Gabe held up the pile of ratings. "It's Wednesday."

"Leave 'em on the credenza," said Thomas.

Gabe double-checked the space. The office never had a credenza. He put them on the end table by the door.

"We'll let you know when casting is official," said Doris. "You—we'll—have to work fast."

"Faster than fast," said Thomas. "If the ratings keep falling, this character might be the last new citizen who arrives in Harmony Hills. Stakes are through the roof right now."

"I won't let you down," said Gabe as he closed the door behind him.

He could hear Doris on the other side of the door: "Should we have offered him a drink?"

Thomas replied, "Kids today can't hold their liquor."

Gabe's eavesdropping was interrupted by a jarring ironic, old-fashioned dial phone ding-a-ling sound coming from his cell phone.

"How's the drama in soapland?" asked a familiar female voice from his past.

"Same ole, same ole," said Gabe, getting as far away from the Douglasses' door as fast as he could. "I should have majored in alcohol counseling." Gabe finally found a more private space to talk. "Hey, Jess, to what do I owe the pleasure?"

Gabe hadn't spoken to Jess in months, maybe over a year. Not since she had coerced him to her apartment in Astoria for a rainy afternoon of crafting.

"Congratulations are in order. You remember our vision boards?" asked Jess.

"I am permanently scarred."

"I love it when you go faux-cynical on me." She cleared her throat. "You are talking to the newest editorial assistant at NewLibrary Books.

"Congratulations!"

"I know, right? A major imprint. I am officially retired from the cater-waitron world. Even though you'll pretend not to remember, I put the big five publishing company logos all over my vision board."

"No recollection."

"You're blocking, Vito. How is my new position about *you*, you may ask? Well, in order to get the job, I convinced them my contacts were made up of Emmy-winning talent and writers ready to publish their memoirs and spill all the behind-the-scenes tea of a leading soap."

"Hardly leading. And I signed an NDA."

"Forget the soap. I'm sure you have more than a few other stories to tell."

"Yeah, like the one I was assigned today. We're getting some new hot talent—probably a second-tier clothing store underwear model, but still, a new character is coming to Harmony Hills. Hurray!"

"What's a Harmony Hills?" asked Jessica.

"You *wish* you lived in Harmony Hills."

"You're not getting it, Gabe. This is your chance to escape Harmony Hills. Start pitching me brilliant ideas. I'm your ticket out of there. A rising tide, circles rise together, and all that."

"Not so loud. And who says I want to leave?"

"You did. Once upon a time. Your vision board revealed as much. You know deep in your heart you want to be a legit writer with a *Times* bestseller. That was definitely on your vision board."

"Stop with the vision board. Look, I'm at work. If we could talk about something else—"

"Duck into some place you can speak freely. There must be a broom closet nearby."

"Gonna put you on hold for a second."

They had known each other since the first week of freshman year of college when they both tried to get into the popular History of Semiotics seminar. In spite of their aggressive gumption, neither made it off the waitlist. The next year, when they no longer suffered from the freshman scheduling curse, they both got into the seminar but dropped it the second week when they agreed the professor was far too pretentious. But their aggressive gumption had bonded them forever.

Gabe popped his head into the supply room. "Hey, Erin, I'm going to go out for a while. If anyone needs me, I'm a text away."

"How was the meeting?" asked Erin.

"They were pretty pickled before I got there. And they're wanting me to write a fancy new storyline to replace the whole school shooting storyline."

"Shit!" said Erin, aware of the work that would take.

"I'll catch you up when I come back."

"I'm telling you, a rom-com. Could be big," said Erin.

"That's what *she* said."

Gabe headed out the door.

"Where were we?" said Gabe, returning to the Jess call out on the sidewalk.

"As long as I've known you," said Jess, "I have seen you sell all your dreams short."

"How can you say that? I won an Emmy!" Gabe was aware his voice was rising in volume and pitch. He didn't want to come across as arrogant to eavesdroppers. He lowered his voice. "I am perfectly successful and happy here at my soap job."

"Who do you think you are talking to? You have been threatening to quit since day one. You moved to New York to be a successful writer of fiction, essays, and memoirs."

"I'm indirectly doing that on the soap. I make more money here than I ever would have as a freelancer. That world is incredibly hard to crack."

"That's what you're not hearing. My new job gives you the entrée into publishing you always wanted."

"I'm in the middle of too much right now to do a complete career pivot."

"I'm only asking you to consider a pitch. I'll even write the book proposal for you. It's all done by AI now anyway. Will you at least think about it?"

The sound of *drrroot* from Gabe's hookup app announced an incoming message.

"I have a call coming in."

"Are you still on those sex apps?"

"Technically, it's a dating app."

"How many dinner dates have you been on? No protein diet jokes, please."

"Dating apps are efficient. You should try it."

"Meaningless sex is bad karma for those of us who want a sustained relationship."

"How's that involuntary sexual abstinence working out for you?"

Another *drrroot* sounded.

"That's no doubt a dick pic," said Jess. "Are you checking it?"

"No."

Gabe lied and swiped once to get to the app, twice to see a respectable eight-inch, cut erect cock next to a comparable can of shaving cream from a profile that read "FunGuy."

"Well?" asked Jess.

"Got to go."

"That good, huh?"

"Yep."

"You ever once consider letting one of your fuck buddies in a little?"

"Some of them find their way in with no problem."

"You ever want to let them get to know you beyond the bedroom?"

"Sex with me has never been limited to the bedroom."

"I'm being serious. You never once met a guy on your hookup app who was both hot *and* nice? You never consider, maybe, going out to dinner and a movie with him and getting to know him before you jump his bones?"

"That's not what the app is for. Who has time for all that? The return on that investment would be marginally low."

"It's called friendship. You should try it sometime."

"I've never been at a loss for friends."

"But ever since I've known you, you've been willing to settle for second best on those apps."

"I make choices based on expediency. And the fewest number of subway stops."

"You gotta dream bigger, kiddo," said Jessica. "I don't want you to die alone. You don't want to die alone."

Another *drrroot* came from his phone.

"More pics?"

"He'll think I've lost interest if I don't respond."

"Go!"

"Bye—and congratulations!"

"At least think about my offer?"

"I'll think about it. Oops, going through a tunnel."

"Asshole. I love you."

"Same, same."

Gabe hung up and swiped to FunGuy in the app. He searched for red flags in his profile. Gabe was not into dudes in open relationships. Could get complicated. Nothing disgusting like golden showers, scat, or unpleasant like fisting. On the surface, FunGuy presented as safe enough for a sexy, seductive chat at least. Gabe typed in his usual:

> *Gud2Go: Mmmmm. Nice. Horny?*
>
> *FunGuy: Always*
>
> *Gud2Go: wya*
>
> *FunGuy: Pics?*

Gabe sent his usual three pics: the obligatory headless torso with some ab definition, the butt shot, and the dick pic—all well above average, even for New York City.

FunGuy followed up by sending him twice as many pics. Effusive photo sharing was a red flag for Gabe. But the guy looked fine, if overly earnest. Mid-thirties, decent body, an obligatory headless torso, and lots of shots in the middle of prior sexcapades. Too many pics made for an unclear narrative.

> *Gud2Go: DDF?*
>
> *FunGuy: Same. Nsa, first time safe, condoms okay?*
>
> *Gud2Go: Y*

Gabe prided himself in not wasting time with too much small talk or fully spelling out words. He wrote for a living; breaking the rules of grammar mechanics was his foreplay. Gabe didn't fully commit until he was certain FunGuy wasn't an ax murderer and he was serious about hooking up.

FunGuy: *The app says you're nearby.*

Gud2Go: *258 feet, if you can believe the Chinese satellite. Host?*

FunGuy: *Yes. Give me a sec to clean...deep.*

Gabe didn't want to know all the sordid details. Spontaneous hookups usually ended up a blow-and-go anyway. *Please don't smell bad.* FunGuy's profile claimed he was a "side." *Why bother cleaning deep?* Unless his profile needed an update...

FunGuy: *I'll send the address when I'm ready.*

Gud2Go: *K*

Gabe didn't expect a one-off experience to be satisfying. That's what his regulars were for. He needed to get his rocks off to balance his chemicals. Casual sex was more about science than psychology. No matter how bad the sex or unpleasant the dude was, if Gabe needed to feel secure, all he had to do was reach out to his mother for loving emotional support. No one could be expected to meet all one's needs.

Gabe headed to a nearby coffee shop where he planned to wait a few minutes to see if FunGuy would flake out or come through. Crossing the busy street, another call came in. He didn't remember giving the phone number to FunGuy. He saw a number he didn't recognize. The 845 area code, Upstate New York, could be Concord Valley, but he didn't know the number.

"This is Gabe Hartman."

"Gabe, hey—"

Gabe couldn't place the voice...scratchy...maybe an older man.

"Who is this?"

"Arthur—Arthur Quinn."

It took a second for the name to register. "Arthur! The bookstore Arthur."

"And cafe. The Quinn & Ink."

"*That* Arthur? How are you?"

Arthur Quinn was one of his mother's friends. Arthur had moved to Concord Valley long after Gabe had moved away. He opened a bookstore on Concord Valley's town square, the only bookstore in town. His mother may have attended a book club at his store and played canasta or bridge with Arthur. She spoke about him frequently.

"Well, son... It's your mother. She passed."

"Is that good? What kind of test did she take? I didn't know she was enrolled in a class."

"No, son, she passed away. Today, probably this afternoon."

The information hit Gabe hard. He stopped where he was on the sidewalk in front of the coffee shop.

"What do you mean she passed away? She was healthy...she was... she was..."

"As far as we could tell, she was expected at Minnie Norman's for an early luncheon, and she must have crawled into her favorite chair for a nap."

"The recliner? Her Chairvana?"

"Yes. Her happy place. She fell asleep, and she never woke up. When she didn't show at Minnie's, Minnie called me and asked if I could check on her. I found her in that chair with a smile on her face. She must have gone peacefully during a nap."

"That's BS! No one dies peacefully in their sleep. That's a myth. She likely had a heart attack." Gabe knew full well about the lie of "dying peacefully in your sleep" from his soap research.

"Maybe," said Arthur. "The coroner took her to the morgue, and you being the next of kin, I thought I'd best catch you up. Your work must give you time off for bereavement. Best let personnel know before you head up here."

"Human resources..." Gabe was having a hard time processing any feelings except numbness. He didn't know what to say.

"Right. I'm sorry to be the one to pass this on," said Arthur, "but Minnie thought it best you heard the sad news from one of her friends rather than someone at the county morgue."

"I'm sorry I snapped at you."

"That's all right. No one prepares you for the passing of a parent."

"I appreciate you letting me know. Where did you say she is?"

"The county morgue."

"She wanted to be cremated."

"They'll know where to send you for all that."

The familiar *drrroot* announced FunGuy was ready.

"What was that?" asked Arthur.

"A message. I'm kind of in the middle of something right now."

"You take your time. She's not going anywhere. I didn't mean that as a joke, but for logistics."

"I understood."

"So you'll be making plans to come Upstate?"

"Yeah...this wasn't on my calendar."

"We're never ready for death, kid."

"I'll look for you when I get to town."

"Please stop into the bookstore and cafe. And if you need anything—Do you have anything you can write my number on?"

"If this is your number, my phone picked it up. It's automatically put into my contacts."

"That's right. Thank goodness for modern times."

As Gabe hung up, he swiped directly to the hookup app, more out of habit than intent. He wasn't ready to accept the news of his mother's death yet.

FunGuy: *Ready*

Gud2Go: *That was fast*

FunGuy: *I'm good*

Gud2Go: *No, I'm gud*

FunGuy sent him a map and the address with instructions on how to get in the building.

What am I doing? I need to arrange travel and time off from work and...

Gabe made the decision to pursue sex with a stranger first. After that, he would take responsibility and face the bad news. Right now, he wanted to avoid thinking about how overwhelmed he had become by Arthur's call. This was a new level up for being a liar. Lying was now a survival strategy.

He was two blocks away from FunGuy's place. As long as he didn't start to cry, he'd be fine dwelling in his promiscuous persona for an hour or so. *Get my rocks off, take the edge off the day, and then deal with the fact I'm now an orphan.*

FunGuy's apartment was every cliche about a New York apartment: fourth-floor studio of a fifth-floor walk-up, exposed brick wall, the futon/sofa that made the room smell of thatch, and posters on the wall of a world map, a framed photo of Samuel Beckett ripped from a magazine, and a photo of Dorothy Parker. Gabe was working hard not to feel his feelings. He didn't notice he and FunGuy had several of the same books on their bookshelves.

Rob, an aspiring fiction writer, was nice enough. Recently moved to New York from a small Midwest liberal arts college Gabe hadn't heard of, he had performed on NPR on *the Moth* a few years ago. Rob reminded Gabe of himself; he projected his sadness and loneliness onto Rob.

To get through this hookup, Gabe created a game for himself: everything he said would be a lie. He couldn't be the "Grieving Gabe" whose mother died. He told Rob his name was Leo, he was a legal secretary at a financial firm downtown, and he was visiting his sister uptown who worked at Sloan Kettering.

"You want some tea? Water?" asked Rob.

"Let's get on with it. I have to get back to work soon."

"Cool."

The sex was insignificant, well-rehearsed, and learned by rote from porn. "Leo" lied and said he didn't like to kiss, which inspired Rob to fall directly to his knees where he worked efficiently. Gabe regretted the lie about kissing; he could have used a make-out session, but he was terrified the mindless kisses would devolve into weepy, grieving kisses.

Lies were always a turn-on for Gabe. He had no trouble getting and staying hard. Rob gave competent head, too enthusiastic at times, like he was performing in a music video about head. Gabe usually loved it when a guy craned his neck backward to eyeball him during a blowjob, but with Rob, the eye contact was all too performative. Gabe pretended his oral technique was much better than it actually was. He could see his fake moans were turning on Rob. He channeled Meg Ryan in the famous deli scene from *When Harry Met Sally*. At one point, he got so loud Rob asked him to quiet down. Rob had a neighbor with early onset dementia who would start to sing "Beautiful Dreamer" off-key whenever she heard the sounds of people having sex.

In the middle of the blowjob, Gabe's memories of his mother arose: random fragments of her at the stove, decorating a Christmas tree, in her garden planting bulbs...

"You okay?" asked Rob.

Gabe could see his erection was losing its fullness.

"Sorry." Gabe grabbed his own cock and brought it back to full attention in no time, willfully thinking about anything but his mother. "All good."

"Indeed," said Rob, returning to his too-earnest efforts.

Gabe continued a more muted Meg Ryan act and came shortly thereafter.

Gabe was surprised Rob swallowed. He, himself, reserved swallowing for only a few pineapple-eating regulars.

"I'll have what she's having," said Gabe.

"I'm negative and on PrEP," said Rob, not catching the Meg Ryan reference.

"It said on your profile. Same."

An awkward pause followed. Was Rob expecting Gabe to recipro-cate? On a strategically placed red towel, Gabe saw Rob had already shot his substantial load.

"Guess I was horny," said Rob in a humble brag.

"Fuck yeah," said Gabe.

While Gabe was getting dressed, a family photo caught his eye on Rob's nightstand: two parents and two other siblings.

"Where do your folks live?" asked Rob.

"Upstate. I'm the middle child." Gabe preferred his fake identity to reality.

"Me too," said Rob.

"I see," said Gabe, referring to the photo. "It sucks."

"Could be worse."

"Much worse."

When Rob asked if he wanted to hook up again, Gabe continued his lie with a "Sure, put a gold star by my name."

On the way back to work, Gabe could no longer hide behind the lie. All the repressed feelings finally poured forth. On the sidewalks of Man-hattan, he wept a river of tears. No one around him cared that everything in his life was now seen through the lens of loss.

More importantly, who would feed him his storylines?

Chapter Two

Everyone at work had a dead parent story. If Gabe heard, "It comes in waves," one more time, he would scream. Human Resources explained he could take a full week off for bereavement, but only if he intended to do no work. With too much to do with the new storyline, Erin could keep the day-to-day writing flowing while he was away, but she was only aware of half of what he did in a day. Most of the writers worked remotely, a lifestyle Gabe wasn't wired for. However, taking time off wasn't really an option in the world of television production—but he had to attend to the logistics of his mother's passing. He turned down the bereavement time-off in lieu of working remotely with Erin as his liaison.

"I'll hold down the fort," said Erin. "And I'm sorry about your mom. I hear losing a parent is intense."

"Have you lost a parent?" asked Gabe.

"Grandparents. And a pet budgie—my folks lied and kept replacing it, but I knew."

"That's terrible."

"And one of our plots from the early nineties."

"That's why we hired you."

"Not because I'm eye candy? I still have abandonment issues over that budgie. I will never let my parents forget."

"Milk that guilt, girl."

"I've got you something." Erin handed him a paperback, *Death for Dummies.* "My rabbi said the hardest parts about dying are the logistics. No one prepares you for the workload, and you still have to grieve."

"Very thoughtful. Thanks." Gabe slipped the book into one of his bags. He was next heading to the rental car office. "Do you have my Concord Valley address for overnighting packages?"

"It's already in my computer."

"You're good. You think you can handle the Douglasses?"

"The liquor cabinet is fully stocked. That should get them through lunch. Start with the expensive stuff, and when they're blotto, refill with the cheap stuff."

"You're the best."

"I still can't believe how your school shooting sequence so closely matched real events. You're psychic. A Cassandra."

"School shooters act pretty much the same these days. And with frequency. Looks like we have a shitload of work ahead for us. I'll be calling you constantly."

"Putting your mother to rest should be your first priority. Follow what the book tells you."

"With all the funerals and memorials we've written on the show, this one should be a piece of cake."

"I have a feeling real ones are kinda different."

"Fewer actor egos involved."

"Maybe you'll meet someone at the memorial service and have a fling."

"Everyone I know in Concord Valley is over seventy."

"Work on your daddy issues," said Erin. Her generous hug cracked his professional demeanor for some grief to surface.

"Here comes a wave," said Gabe, swallowing his tears. "God, I hate crying in front of people. No one cries pretty."

"Our little secret," she said, wiping a tear from his cheek.

"It shouldn't take but a couple of days. See you Monday?"

"The logistics of death take as long as they take. Call or text me anytime."

It's always an ordeal to get out of New York City, but once Gabe got on the Taconic State Parkway, he could feel the city stress leave his body.

His phone buzzed the familiar *drrroot*. Gabe didn't even bother to look. He imagined an effusive thank-you from Rob for yesterday's fun. He didn't want any more distractions until after his mother was put to rest, so he deleted the app.

The buzz of a regular text message vibrated his phone. Gabe hoped it wasn't a distraction.

> **Douglasses**: *May her mammaries be a blessing. Memories. We meant memories. Spell-check...*

> **Gabe**: *I knew what you meant. *prayer hands emoji**

Everyone had become super nice to Gabe once they found out his mother died. Lots of tiptoeing, avoiding, not knowing what to say.

Gabe marveled at how effortlessly the rural landscape changed as he made his way to Concord Valley. He loved this drive. The appearance of hills blended into gentle mountains that jutted into more substantial mountains. He passed a cafe where he and his mother often stopped when she would take him to the city for a show or a museum. The cafe currently had a for sale sign in front. *I'll have to let Mother know about that. She's not going to be pleased.* Then it hit him: no more mother to tell favorite bits to anymore. He was having a hard time referring to her in the past tense. Her death was still too new, too big, too difficult. His brain was off to visit her, but his heart knew better.

He had never been to Concord Valley without his mother there. Who would he be now?

One of the soap staff writers had once written the line, "You're your father's son, but your mother's child." *Damn waves of grief.* He flicked another tear into the wind. He was terrified of what might come next.

He kept creating scenarios about her last moments from the scant information Arthur had provided. He imagined her in Chairvana, the reddish-brown leather recliner she loved to fall back into with one grand plop, never bothering with the hand lever on the side. He imagined her drifting off to sleep that afternoon. He envisioned her waking to the surprise pain of a heart attack, maybe a stroke. She would have gasped and grabbed her arms as she succumbed to the pain, dying sad, alone.

Guilt was the hardest part of Gabe's grief. He had not been there in her time of need. Forget the unpredictable nature of her death. After all she had done for him as a single mother, he could have at least provided comfort during her time of death. He imagined her reaching out to someone, anyone—as she took her last breath.

Gabe got off at the Concord Valley business loop exit, but he wasn't yet ready to walk through his childhood home alone. He pulled off at the exit's rest stop and thumbed through *Death for Dummies*. He glanced at the many to-do lists throughout the book. When he got to the appendix, he found a timeline of duties. "If you discover the dead body, first decide what to do with it." He found no advice for how to wander sadly through an empty childhood home. Gabe set his GPS for the county morgue, relieved he could delay his return to his home for another hour at least.

"Our job is to hold the body until you tell us what to do," said the associate at the morgue. She had a pale complexion, which made sense. "But we do make referrals."

This woman is showing up as a future character in Harmony Hills. "She wanted to be cremated," said Gabe.

"We can help you with that too. It's done at the same facility with roadkill, but we'll coordinate her cremation so no animal ashes get mixed in. We clean after each one."

"The same people burn roadkill?"

"A team from the state penitentiary. Your mother will be taken care of by professionals."

"Thank goodness," said Gabe.

"I would be remiss if I didn't invite you to view the body. Optional, of course, but there's some closure that comes from seeing them dead.

Cuts through any pesky denial."

"It sounds morbid. Not an inconvenience?"

"It's what we do. Wait a moment, and I'll have them set up a viewing."

Gabe was terrified. He had seen many fake dead bodies on the soap. How different were they from real life? The soap's makeup artists were top-notch.

"Come say goodbye to your mother, Mr. Hartman. This way."

She led Gabe to a curtained space with barely enough room for the body on a gurney under a white sheet. She calmly rolled down the white sheet to reveal the face of Gabe's mother, ashen and empty of life, not the woman who lived in his memory. As the associate continued to take off the sheet, it was clear to Gabe that his mother was not wearing clothes.

"You can stop there," said Gabe.

The associate understood. Gabe wanted to treat the dead with dignity.

"Feel free to take a photo."

"What?"

"This could be the last time you ever see her."

"Not how I want to remember her."

"We're always here for you," she said, starting to cover his mother, rolling the sheet up, her face almost disappearing forever.

"Wait," said Gabe.

She had been right about the closure. Seeing his mother like this cut through any magical thinking. Gabe got out his phone and took a few pictures.

"That'll do. Thanks. If you can pass on any contact information regarding cremation services..."

Before he finished the sentence, she handed him an envelope. "It's all in here."

Back at the rental car, Gabe checked the *Death for Dummies* appendix timeline for his next task: consult the family attorney.

Gabe was happy to keep postponing the return to his mother's home.

Roger Cohen was the only attorney he'd heard of who lived in Concord Valley and most likely the family attorney. His name was familiar, but everyone in Concord Valley came with a vague familiarity. If this was that Roger Cohen, he was his mother's age, long past retirement, and a cross between Colonel Sanders and Burgess Meredith. Attorneys in small towns rarely retired. He found Roger's office address near the town square and set his GPS.

Concord Valley embraced the quaintness of its charming town square as part of its brand. Looking for a place to park, Gabe saw the square was full of vendors' booths. Signs for a Green Farmers Market pointed to the center of the square. Gabe didn't expect to see this many people. He couldn't remember ever attending the Thursday afternoon Farmers Market, but his mother had referenced it from time to time. Eventually, he found a place to park in front of the Cohen Law Office, a block off the square.

"May I help you?" asked a receptionist at the front of the nicely remodeled storefront. She was young, pretty, and blonde, dressed too fashionably hip for Concord Valley.

"My name is Gabe Hartman, Amelia Hartman's son. I was wondering—"

"Oh dear, sweet Amelia Hartman! I heard. My condolences."

Gabe responded with a tight, grateful smile. He did not want to invite a hug from an effusive stranger.

"Thank you. My mother and I never discussed a family lawyer, but I was wondering if Roger Cohen was her— I mean, *our* family lawyer."

"He may have been everyone in Concord Valley's family lawyer. Wait here a minute, please."

Gabe made up a narrative for the receptionist as she walked briskly behind a partition in the rear of the storefront: *a divorcee from Albany who needed a new start, or an abused wife from Saratoga Springs in the witness protection program who had snitched on a mafia don. Too pretty to stay where she was, this woman's story had potential.*

Hushed voices came from the rear, the receptionist's soprano notes mixing with a baritone hum. As they got louder, Gabe could decipher, "The son?"

"Yes. Gabe."

"He's out there right now?"

"But no appointment."

They both appeared from behind the partition. Roger Cohen was not the octogenarian Gabe expected, but a handsome man in his late twenties with sandy hair.

"Gabe! I'm Roger Cohen." He extended his hand for Gabe to shake. "My condolences."

"Thank you. It's still a shock." Roger's handshake was tender but firm.

The receptionist nodded empathetically.

Gabe found this Roger Cohen somewhat of a turn-on. *Where were you when I was growing up here?* Maybe his friends were right: a fling while he settled his mother's estate might be in the cards. Would that be a conflict of interest if his mother had already paid the retainer? Roger's cologne seduced him with its subtle musk notes.

"Is something wrong?" asked the young lawyer.

Am I coming across as pathetic, lonely, and vulnerable? Focus on settling Mom's estate, dude.

"I'm sorry. I was expecting someone older," said Gabe.

"You're probably thinking of my grandfather. Also Roger Cohen. He and my grandmother retired to Florida a few years ago. When Bethany and I graduated from law school, the timing was right to pass along the business."

"We're still in our learning curve," said the former receptionist, now wife/partner and attorney named Bethany in Gabe's mind.

"How expedient." Gabe found a ring on Roger's hand and took a breath to recalibrate his projected Roger narrative. "Good for you both. Look, I arrived in town an hour ago, and I'm beginning my grieving process. But I wanted to check in and do my due diligence," said Gabe.

"As you should," said Bethany.

"We weren't expecting you so soon," said Roger.

"Aren't you working in advertising somewhere in the city?" asked Bethany.

"Something like that." With a multitude of moving pieces, Gabe was challenged to keep his lying skills honed.

"Your mother was proud of you," said Roger.

"So proud," echoed Bethany.

"Like I said, I'm trying to settle her affairs. Be the responsible son."

"Of course. And you've come to the right place. We—or my grandfather—had taken care of all her filings. We're still finding our way around this place. It might take a few hours for us to prepare everything."

"I know Concord Valley is a small town where people like to pop in," said Bethany. Her tone was cool and professional, not what Gabe expected in Concord Valley. "But we should set up an appointment to do this properly. With all our information in front of us."

"Of course," said Gabe. "My apologies. Billable hours and all that. Let's call this our meet-and-greet. This is all happening so fast and unexpectedly, I have no idea what I'm doing."

"Who can plan on the unforeseen?" said Bethany, boundaries set, in compassionate maternal mode.

"We do have a free window later this afternoon," said Roger.

"Could you come back in a few hours? We'll need to gather all her paperwork and look over all her files."

"Sure," said Gabe. "Is there a place around here where I can hang out?"

"Not ready for the old homestead, huh?" asked Bethany.

"Not yet."

"Arthur Quinn's bookstore and cafe would be the place." Roger pointed to a building on the other side of the square. "He was part of your mother's inner circle, right?"

"I guess."

"If I may," interrupted Bethany. "I know your mother was a devout volunteer at the Thursday Farmers Market. The one happening right now."

"A volunteer? She never mentioned it."

"We never really know our parents until they're gone," said Bethany. "She took great pride in all her volunteer work. Her passing was literally yesterday. I'm pretty sure they didn't find a replacement for her."

"Not that you could ever replace her," said Roger.

Roger's words hit Gabe hard. He could barely defend himself against the next wave of consuming grief.

"If you're up for it," said Bethany, "you might want to do her volunteer gig, keep you busy while we get organized. Carry on her legacy and all?"

"Great idea," said Roger.

"Who would I see?"

"Charlize Burton is in charge of the volunteers," said Bethany. "She and your mother basically ran the place. Find the lady in the scooter with the clipboard who looks extremely important."

"I think I might know Charlize," said Gabe. "Familiar name."

"She'll find you something to do. Let's check in again after you're done."

Gabe left the offices of Roger Cohen feeling impatient. This day was not going as planned; everything always took longer in small towns. Gabe was curious about the by-products of grief. Was grief triggering him to look at every man as a potential sex partner? Was this a normal reaction to his newly orphaned loneliness? He had almost hit on Roger Cohen. Navigating the loss of his mother was *terra incognita*. At least he was getting lots of ideas for future storylines and new characters.

The Thursday Green Farmers Market was bustling with activity. In addition to local produce, crafts and food carts sold their wares. Families with strollers, local chefs in search of produce in season, and gossiping locals were everywhere.

Charlize was larger than life. She had lost a foot to diabetes but was skillful on her scooter. "There he is!" She scootered in and squeezed the air out of Gabe in a monster bear hug. "I can't tell you how much I miss your mama—our hearts are empty. She was my feet and legs."

Gabe couldn't remember ever having met Charlize. He went into professional-liar mode. "It's been forever, Charlize."

"Don't kid a kidder. We never met. I know you through pictures your mama made me look at."

Relieved he wasn't expected to know her, Charlize would also make a great character on the soap, but tricky to finesse with the politically correct crowd. Gabe was intrigued to know how a woman with a disability and a thick Southern accent ended up wrangling the volunteers at a farmers market in Upstate New York.

"I've come to do her volunteer gig."

"Hell, yeah! You're your mother's son: goodness through and through."

"Hardly."

"She was a control freak, but I doubt she had the foresight to arrange a sub. I'm guessing she didn't wake up yesterday morning and think, I'm gonna croak this afternoon; I better line up a sub for my farmers market gig. Don't want to piss off Charlize. Too soon for dead mama jokes?"

"Never."

"If you can't laugh at death, what can you laugh at?

"Exactly. What do you need me to do?"

"Put on this vest." Charlize threw a bright yellow synthetic vest at Gabe. "You'll look like an overstuffed crossing guard, but people find yellow vests intimidating. You walk around with this clipboard and troubleshoot."

"What do I write on the clipboard?"

"Whatever you want. It's part of the costume. Clipboards make people think you're official. Your job is to make sure everything is aboveboard. I'll give you a heads-up. The knife sharpener is acting pissed off today."

"That's not good."

"Especially considering he's a felon. Sex offender. Nothing with kiddies—habitual rest-stop sex. Where men lie down to have sex in a public rest stop toilet is beyond me, but never mind. Keep an eye on the knife sharpener."

"Why is a sex offender permitted—?"

"Hush! Your mother. She believed everyone deserves dignity and a second chance. Casually stroll the grounds. Pay careful attention to the new vendors."

"How will I know if they're new?"

"They will be sticking out like sore thumbs. We got a couple of 'em today right next to each other. There's a big sturdy fellow, a real chunky monkey from the city—they're always from the city—selling what he thinks are heirloom strawberries. You know how city folks are: clueless. They think it's their birthright to try their hand at farming. Keep an eye on him. And there's a new baker next to him—she's on the young side but on the up-and-up. Pop-up bakery booths come and go. One decent banana bread recipe does not make a full bakery. Keep an eye on them. They're bound to make all kinds of mistakes today."

"This is exciting."

"Your mother had a great phrase she would use when dealing with any trouble. She would say, 'It would—'"

Gabe overlapped. "It would be helpful if..."

"Cut from the same cloth! Remember, you're on the Helping Committee. Have a good time, but be *helpful*, Gabe. We're grateful to have you here, kiddo. And remember, no free samples while you're wearing the vest. Your mother was a firm believer in solid boundaries."

"Was she?"

"She learned from experience. Make your mama proud. Off you go!" said Charlize as she scootered back to her perch behind the entrance table. "Let's touch base at four o'clock, and I'll train you on closing protocols."

"Aye-aye," said Gabe, saluting Charlize with the clipboard.

Gabe began his walk-through. The place buzzed with small-town joy. Each section was clearly marked. The arts and crafts were mostly textiles and gifts for women of a certain age. He gave a friendly wave as he passed each booth. The knife sharpener was stationed at the end of the row. Gabe was curious as to why every market had one. He could never remember to bring dull knives to a farmers market. But there he was, earnestly sharpening one of many sets for people who did remember. The knife sharpener looked up briefly from his work and gave Gabe a nod. Gabe acknowledged him. He wasn't as angry as Charlize led him to believe. Gabe's life in Concord Valley might have taken a similar turn had he stayed, acting out a repressed sexuality at rest stops. Everyone had a story behind the veneer. Telling them was why he loved being a writer.

The next two rows were for produce, certified organic in the first row and non-certified in the second. The certified farmers' booths were packed with consumers, comparing prices and the quality of lettuce and early spring fruits and vegetables. The prices were hardly a bargain, almost the same as his favorite Saturday morning market in Union Square, but he expected New York City prices to be outrageous. Gabe understood why his mother enjoyed this volunteer gig. The warm, earnest vibe wrapped around him like an earthy enchantment.

At the end of the second row, Gabe understood what Charlize had warned him about, regarding the two new vendors. A young brunette woman, probably in her early twenties, had a simple display of banana breads, some with nuts, some with chocolate, some with both. Everything was individually wrapped, some by the slice and some by the loaf. Not a bad display, but limited. The young woman's brand was "Attractive Girl Next Door Tries Her Hand at Baking" and by the looks of it, she had already sold more than half of her inventory. Gabe was impressed.

The booth next to her was a different story. Gabe didn't know how to take it all in. The vendor was leaning over and working out of a car he had backed up to the tarp on the far side of his booth. His head and torso were hidden by the interior. What exactly was he selling? All Gabe could see of the man was the backside of a pair of dusty jeans and a thin line of an underwear band. The sign on the booth's table read, "Heirloom Strawberries," not something Gabe had ever seen at a farmers market or even the fanciest gourmet food catalog. The table had about a half-dozen cardboard cartons of sad-looking, tiny strawberries, nowhere near heirlooms.

"Excuse me," said Gabe, approaching the booth. "Is there anything

I can help you with?"

Gabe was not prepared for the appearance of the man who turned around. A warm pearly smile, cerulean-blue eyes, and a chin dimple announced to the world this was a fiercely good-looking man. His clothes looked more like a costume of a man playing a farmer than an actual farmer. He wore an untucked work shirt with the suggestion of a tank top underneath. Gabe was comfortable being around good-looking actors on the soap, but this man took his breath away.

"Oh...so..." Gabe started to say. "Hi, I'm...Gabe." Gabe cringed at his own awkwardness.

The handsome man extended his hand. "Owen."

Gabe tried not to swoon at the firm, confident handshake of this gorgeous man.

"It looks like... What's going on here?" Gabe was confused by the disconnect. Here was a fiendishly good-looking man failing miserably at the farmers market. "Is this your booth?"

"Yeah. See, I bought this farm, and I wanted to try my hand at a farmers market. I brought everything I could harvest today."

He may be adorable, but he hasn't a clue. Gabe instantly adjusted the narrative in his mind from flawless beauty to city slicker to failed country mouse.

"You never farmed before?"

"That obvious?"

"I'm not trying to shame you. I need to know where to start. First off," said Gabe, "these are not heirloom strawberries."

"They're not?"

"Where did you pick them from?"

"By the side of the driveway. They were everywhere."

"They're wild strawberries. They're like a common weed around here."

"No wonder nobody's buying them."

"Heirloom strawberries are usually grown in greenhouses during peak strawberry season. Let's forget about the strawberries. Throw them out. They'll make you sick to your stomach. Rabbits won't even eat them."

Owen slid the cartons into a garbage can under his table. "The people I bought my farm from mentioned heirloom produce being grown on the land. Do you think they lied?"

"It's possible you can grow other heirloom plants there, but not that. That's real estate language they use to seduce wealthy city folks to buy their farms at inflated prices."

"I'm not such a unique story, I guess. Maybe I should pack everything up and head home."

Gabe could see he was deflating Owen's dreams. The girl selling banana bread was entertained by Owen's naivete. Owen's vulnerability, however, was attractive to Gabe, which made him want to help him even more.

"This is not necessarily a lost cause, my friend," said Gabe. "You said you harvested some other stuff? What else have you got in your car?"

Despite his despondency, Owen grabbed some produce from the trunk. Gabe paid special attention as Owen's shirt rode up to reveal a tanned lower back with perfectly sculpted side sinews. Owen turned around to reveal an armful of reddish stalks with green leaves.

"Could I sell these? It's the only other produce I brought. Rhubarb?"

"Sure, you can. I don't see a lot of rhubarb. None of the other booths are selling it. *The Times* did an article on rhubarb a couple of weeks ago. It's still got some buzz. Let's give it a go. Did you grow it?"

"No. I mean yes. Rhubarb grows all over the land I bought, and it looked ready for harvest. You figured out I haven't a clue, right?"

"Oh, yeah. But you're charming, and you have a beautiful smile. You just might get away with it." Owen's smile grew even more at Gabe's compliment. Gabe wasn't sure if flirting was acceptable in his capacity as a volunteer.

"Can I say they're heirlooms?" asked Owen.

"Nobody cares about heirloom rhubarb," said Gabe.

"Can I call it organic?"

"Do you have organic certification?"

"Not that I know of."

"In that case, no. Do you have any more poster boards or a black felt tip pen?" asked Gabe.

Owen instantly produced half a poster board and a marker.

"May I?" asked Gabe, taking them both.

Owen bowed and gestured his approval as Gabe crafted a sign for the rhubarb. "Nice calligraphy," said Owen. "'Best Rhubarb in the State'?"

"It would be hard to prove either way, but since you're the only rhubarb vendor at the market, I think you'll be fine. Price it fair; see how it goes."

"Thanks for your help."

Gabe walked away a few steps but turned around with one last thought. "Oh, and—what's under your work shirt? A tank top?"

"Yeah."

"Formfitting?"

"Kinda."

"It's such a warm day... I'd lose the work shirt and stand there in your tank top with your best country boy 'aw shucks' grin. Merely a suggestion."

The girl at the banana bread snickered quietly.

"I've yet to make a full set of rounds," said Gabe, "but I'll check on you in a few minutes."

"Hey, thanks, dude. I owe you."

Gabe walked away as Owen unbuttoned his shirt. He didn't want to turn around. He had spent too much time at one booth, and he was afraid he would be tempted to gawk inappropriately at disrobing "Adonis of the Rhubarb." He didn't want to be accused of workplace harassment while volunteering at the farmers market. Ogling would not have made his mother proud.

Gabe was grateful to turn the corner to check on the food truck row when his OG telephone ring announced a call from Jessica.

"Do you have my pitches ready?" asked Jessica without formalities.

"You would not believe my life since we spoke."

"I hope it's filled with interesting anecdotes for the creative nonfiction you'll be pitching."

"First, my mom died."

"Oh, no. Gabe. I'm so sorry…"

"I'm fine. Completely unexpected. But I had to drive Upstate to settle her estate."

"Sounds exhausting. Let me know if you need everything. How are you holding up? The grief comes and goes in waves."

"Currently it's low tide. Besides, I met this guy."

"Of course, you did."

"So, I'm helping him set up his booth. I'm volunteering at the farmers market."

"You're volunteering at a farmers market? Your mom died—"

"I know, but it's very Concord Valley. Stay with me. There's this hot loser—

"Are you saying the guy's hot and a loser? That's not a thing."

"This guy could be the exception."

"I consider you a hot winner."

"Not hot like this guy. He is chiseled from chisel."

"Yummy. You don't think you're hot?"

"I'm pasty and thin. I avoid the sun. I don't work out. I'm the equivalent of a bottom-feeding flounder in the gay community."

"No selling yourself short, darling. And don't let your internalized self-loathing get in the way of a happy life. Your core insecurity—"

"I love being reduced to a social pathology."

"Dude, you are hot, and I'm sure your stock rises exponentially in Podunk Valley."

"You should see this guy. Oh my God! But he was trying to sell wild strawberries as heirlooms!"

"And you naturally saved his ass. That is classic meet-cute."

"What are you talking about?"

"Your life as a rom-com, baby. You're thrown together and you save his butt. Classic meet-cute."

"He was drowning and clueless."

"And hot. Adorbs!"

"I don't even know if he's into guys."

"Everyone's into guys these days. Your gaydar is finely tuned. You're a writer. This is a classic rom-com setup. Pay attention to what's in front of you."

"Burying my mother is in front of me."

"You're the king of dissociating and multitasking. Don't let this opportunity pass you by. They say your life doesn't start until after your parents die."

"Who are 'they'?"

"Oprah, *Redbook* at the dentist's office, morning-commute shock jocks—where we learn everything in life. Do me a favor. If you recognize any more tropes, spilled coffee or orange juice, a shared disaster, trapped in a vehicle together, read the tea leaves and go for it."

Gabe's phone buzzed for an incoming call.

"That's my job. Gotta take this call."

"I'll want an update later. Meet-cutes often end with a kiss."

"I'm not kissing a virtual stranger."

"You've had sex with guys whose names you don't know."

"Later." He clicked to the incoming call. "What's up?"

"Three items," said Erin. "Number one: How are you?"

"Fine. Thanks for the book. Super helpful."

"Great. Two. Have you been to your mom's home—former home, sorry—yet?"

"She still technically owns it, I think. And no. I've been putting that one off."

"I get it, but, FYI, you need to work through that trauma-slash-guilt-slash-whatever ASAP. Your first ZipExpress package should be arriving at around six p.m. at that address, and you need to sign for it."

"Will do. What's item number three?"

"The Douglasses want to chat on teleconference. Ready to be patched in?"

"Give me a second."

"Take your time."

Gabe took in the whole farmers market. The food truck row looked perfectly self-sufficient. A long, orderly line at the empanada truck, the gourmet yogurt booth was doing healthy business, and the delicious aroma of seafood paella made Gabe hungry for a real meal. He could imagine his mother savoring this gig. She loved nothing more than to be part of a wholesome community in action. He inhaled to reclaim his composure then exhaled, surrendering to the inevitable. "I'm ready, Erin."

"I'm at their door." He heard knocking on his end of the line. "They usually mess up the conference call device. All the red lights confuse them."

A couple of awkward clicks later, he could hear Thomas say, "Is this contraption on?"

"The red light says yes, Mr. Douglass. Doris and Thomas Douglass are both on the line, Gabe."

"What's up?" asked Gabe.

"How's it going, kiddo?" Doris's voice was scratchy but full of empathy.

"Grief is a bitch. But I'm about to go into a meeting with Mother's lawyer," said Gabe. *How easily the lies flowed some days.*

"The reading of the will?" asked Thomas. "Any bastard siblings around to contest it?"

"I hope not. What's going on?"

"Good news," said Doris. "We signed the fabulous actor we were courting. We got him!"

"That was fast," said Gabe. "May I ask who we got?"

"A young Tisch kid by the name of Barrett Hodges," announced Thomas.

"I know Barrett Hodges," said Gabe. "I saw him in some Off-Broadway play a few months ago. He's the real deal. This is great news. How did we sign him?"

"He's a friend of Cameron's," said Doris.

"That makes sense. Cameron was in the same show." Gabe did the relationship-math in his head. Was this Cameron's special friend? Had

Cameron finagled a job for his secret boyfriend? Gabe was impressed by Cameron's clandestine manipulations. And Barrett was incredibly talented.

"After he graduated from Tisch last spring, he immediately got that theater gig, which paid nothing. He wisely took the first independent film role he was offered—in Bulgaria—to fill the coffers, pay off student loans. I don't know what these kids need money for these days. But he hated traveling and wanted to stay in Manhattan."

Yeah, to be with his boyfriend. Gabe was happy someone got to spoon with Cameron's splendid ass at night. "We're lucky to have him," said Gabe.

"We're lucky to have you too," said Doris. "Who better to draft his storyline thumbnail ASAP than you? HR wants you to start right now with a character name for the contract. What do you have for us?"

Gabe was momentarily distracted. At the coffee truck near the end of the row, his tank-topped protégé was ordering coffee. Even from a distance, Owen was yummy in his white tank and tight jeans. Something about Owen might inspire him. Owen handed money to the cashier in the coffee truck with his strong arms.

"Gabe?" asked Thomas. "Do you have a name for us?"

"Did we lose you, Gabe?" asked Erin.

"Still here. Reception's not great up here," he lied. "How about...?" He couldn't stop looking at Owen's muscular, strong arms. "How about Armstrong for a last name?"

"Nice," said Doris as ice clinked in cocktail glasses. "I like where this is going."

Owen made his way back to his booth. *His ass could definitely give Cameron's a run for its money.* From a distance, Owen had the whole package. Except common farming sense. He was also awfully confident leaving his booth unattended to grab coffee.

"We still need a first name," said Thomas. "This will be who he's contracted to play. They need to put his character's name on the contract today."

Can't use Owen. But a name beginning with O. A classic O name.

"How about Oliver?" asked Gabe.

A moment of silence. Gabe imagined the Douglasses looking at each other to second-guess each other's reactions. No one ever liked to be responsible for an untested decision in film and television.

"Oliver Armstrong is...perfect!" exclaimed Thomas.

"Perfect!" Doris enthused.

"Good job," said Erin.

"Listen, I got to run," said Gabe.

"Family lawyer. We know," said Doris. "Good luck!"

"To Oliver Armstrong!" More clinks of toasting cocktail glasses ended the call as Gabe headed to Owen's booth.

When he rounded the corner, he saw Owen folding up the table at his booth.

"What happened? Are you giving up already?" asked Gabe.

"I sold out. Thanks to you," said Owen.

"Oh. Need any help?"

"I'm good." Owen had no trouble lifting the folded table sideways into his car. He moved like a sexy, sinewy ballet dancer. "I couldn't have done it without you. Can you wait here for a second?"

"Sure."

Owen made his way to the food truck row. Gabe tried not to stare, but Owen was too good-looking not to witness how beautifully he moved through space.

"I think he likes you," the girl selling banana bread said, snapping Gabe out of his reverie.

"Huh?" Gabe turned around. He hid the shame of having been caught gawking. "Why would you say that?"

"He forgot your name and asked me who that good-looking guy was," said the girl.

"He must have been talking about someone else."

"Nope. He meant you."

"I'm glad he was able to sell the rhubarb."

"I hate rhubarb," said the young woman.

"Me too," said Gabe.

"Sorry if that was too junior high 'my friend likes you' and all."

"All good. Thanks, I guess?" Gabe wasn't quite ready for this moment and did all he could to conceal his delight at discovering Owen's hookup potential. He scanned her booth for something to change the subject. She had one last slice of banana bread in plastic left. "Looks like you had a pretty good day too. Can I buy your last piece?"

"Sure," she said, handing him her last slice. "One dollar. Do you think my pricing is too low? That price point feels like I'm at a kid's bake sale."

"Depends on how good the product is," said Gabe, balancing his clipboard as he handed her a dollar from a pocket. He ripped open the plastic and took a bite. "Oh, my God. That's amazing!"

"Right?" said the girl.

"Two fifty easily. Maybe more. You're an amazing baker." He inhaled the rest in another bite. Gabe had forgotten to eat all day. "It's exceptionally good. Some surprising flavor notes. What did you put in it?"

"Dunno. I didn't make it. He did."

As the girl pointed, Gabe turned around, only to bump—SMACK!— directly into Owen's outstretched arms as he precariously balanced three iced coffees that were catapulted directly above them into the air. As the cups spun, their lids came off, sending the light brown contents onto the two men below. Gabe was able to shield some of the coffee and ice with his clipboard, forcing everything to ricochet onto Owen, drenching his thin tank top and dying him completely in brown mocha.

The girl tried to stifle a belly laugh.

"Oh, my God! I am sorry. I'm sorry. I'm sorry," said Gabe.

"I shouldn't have snuck up on you."

"Do you have any towels? I'm mortified."

"Don't be. I still have the other shirt you made me take off." Owen ripped off the tank top to expose his magnificent torso that must have been curated by a gym trainer for years. The iced coffee stimulated Owen's nipples to full attention. Gabe hoped he had not let out an audible gasp, but he couldn't be sure.

Owen wiped his torso with the tank top, and threw the mottled shirt at Gabe. "Use this to clean up with. Looks like I got the worst of it." Owen made his way to his car to put on his work shirt. "Taking this off was another of your good ideas."

"One of those iced coffees wasn't for me, was it?" asked Gabe.

"To thank you for your other good ideas."

"Glad you didn't get hot coffee," said the girl.

"I feel terrible. What should I do with this?" Gabe said, not knowing where to put the coffee-stained tank top.

"I'll take it. Forget about it." Owen grabbed the shirt unceremoniously, convincing Gabe any goodwill had all but disappeared.

"This is like *Notting Hill*," said the girl.

"That was orange juice," said Owen. "It's a lot cuter in the movies. Yuk. I feel sticky and gross and yuk..."

"I need to keep making my rounds," said Gabe. "If you can think of anything else I can do for you before I go?"

"I just need to get my bearings," said Owen, buttoning up his work shirt.

Not to prolong the awkwardness, Gabe turned on his heels. He was relieved to see all the booths were packing up as the market officially ended in five minutes.

He returned to Charlize at the entrance, ready to retire the yellow vest, not completely free of coffee stains.

"What happened to you?" asked Charlize.

"Don't ask. Where do you want me to put the vest?"

"I'll take it, darlin'," said Charlize. "But you still have clean-up duty."

"I have to clean the place?"

"Each vendor brings their trash down here to me in large plastic bags, and you load them all into a pickup truck. After that, you drive to the sanitation and waste management facility."

"Can't I just take the trash to the dump?"

"That's our fancy new name for the dump. Tell Andy at the booth you're from the farmers market. He'll take care of you."

"My mother did a dump run all by herself?"

"We always got her a helper."

"Hey," said a familiar voice. Gabe turned around to find Owen.

"This chunky monkey is your helper," said Charlize. "Off to the dump, boys!"

Gabe and Owen didn't say much as they loaded up the truck with the big black garbage bags from all the booths. They didn't say much either for the first part of the trip until Gabe pulled over.

"What are you doing?" asked Owen.

"I haven't been to the dump since I was a kid," he said, checking his phone for directions. "Do you know the way?"

"I'm along for the ride," said Owen with a shrug.

Gabe placed the phone on the dashboard for directions and returned to the road. "That's the way! Sorry about the coffee."

"Water—or caffeine under the bridge. So," said Owen, attempting small talk. "You grew up in Concord Valley?"

"But I don't live here anymore. Being gay here was tough. And boring." Gabe waited to see if the banana bread girl was on track and Owen would open up about his own sexuality.

"It's tough lots of places. It must be easy to spot an outsider when you see us, yeah?"

"Look, I'm sure you were good at whatever job you were doing before you cashed out to move here."

"You don't have to be good at anything when you work for the family business."

"But. There's a literacy and a learning curve to living in agricultural communities."

"I can see that. I like how you put that."

"I don't know what you're up to buying a farm, and it's none of my business, but I share this as a former local: farming is a lot harder than you think."

"Duly noted. What did you escape to?"

"New York City. I needed a bigger canvas to paint on."

"You're an artist?"

"I'm speaking metaphorically. I'm a writer." Gabe was so disarmed by the handsome man next to him, he had unintentionally let his guard down.

"Cool. Have I read anything you wrote?"

"I meant...I want to be a professional writer." Gabe caught himself telling the truth. "I work as an administrative assistant in a boring job."

"Pink Collar Ghetto?"

"Something like that. By the way, your banana bread was out of this world. Did you make it? Like from scratch?"

"Of course. You had a piece?"

"Before the coffee explosion. Delicious!"

"Thanks. I've always been a weekend baker."

"What did you put in it?"

"Love?" Gabe appreciated his earnestness. "I get it. It's a cliche: gay man sells banana nut bread at a farmers market in a pop-up booth."

Gabe finally got the sexuality-confirmation he was looking for. "No more than a city slicker who tries his hand at farming."

"Touché. Maddy, the young lady selling it, is my assistant."

"You have an assistant?"

"I'm no slouch."

Gabe took a moment to process Owen's privilege, to be able to buy a farm and bring an assistant.

"Any other assumptions I can confirm?" asked Owen.

"Wealthy family?"

"We're more than comfortable but we're not Forbes Top Fifty."

"I have no idea what that means." But he knew exactly what that meant.

"How about your family? Are you visiting them this week?"

"Funny you should ask," said Gabe. "I'm here because...my mother died last night. I'm here for all that."

"I'm sorry for your loss, Gabe." Gabe had never heard Owen say his name before. The warmth of his voice and depth of his empathy invited a wave of grief in Gabe. He tried to push his sadness down, but tears welled in his eyes. Gabe felt Owen squeeze his arm. His affectionate touch offered Gabe gentle comfort.

"Do you want me to drive?" asked Owen.

"I'm fine." Gabe sniffed away the tears. "You still have both parents?"

"Yep. Want one?"

"Not with that tone as a recommendation. Ah, here's the entrance."

Gabe slowed down as Owen read the signs. "It looks like you pull up to the red line. Must be the scale and how they weigh us."

Gabe pulled up, and a short man stepped out of the small booth. He had almond-shaped eyes, a gently rounded face, and carried an air of innocence.

Gabe rolled down his window. "Are you Andy? Charlize told us to tell you we're here from the farmers market."

"Where's Amelia?" asked Andy.

"She's not here today. She's um... Did you know my mother?"

"You're Amelia's son? She got me this job. Where's Amelia?"

"She...um. She's..."

Owen leaned across the seat. "Hey, Andy, I'm Owen," he said sweetly.

"You Amelia's son too?"

"I'm his friend." Owen squeezed Gabe's shoulder to let him know he would handle this.

"Amelia got me this job," said Andy. "She saved my life. Where's Amelia?"

"She passed away last night. She's not coming anymore. Do you understand?" asked Owen.

Andy's eyes widened as he started to cry. He thrust his arms into the window of the pickup truck and grabbed Gabe for a clenching hug.

"I'm sad. I'm not happy. I want to cry. I feel sad," said Andy through tears and kisses on Gabe's cheek.

"Me too, Andy," said Gabe as Owen rubbed Andy's arm until he loosened his grip.

"Hey, Andy," said Owen, "we need to drop off our stuff, and you've got a line backing up..." That was enough for Andy to let go.

"She saved my life..." said Andy, stepping away from the truck.

Gabe drove about fifty feet toward the actual dump and stopped. He took a breath.

"That was intense," said Owen, seeing the tears welling in Gabe's eyes. "I'm not crying, you're crying. What's that from?"

"*Starsky and Hutch*?"

"I think Charles Dickens."

"Ben Stiller and Owen Wilson."

"I'm pretty sure it's *A Tale of Two Cities*, Miss Pross. But you're the writer."

"I don't have the bandwidth for this conversation. I'm grieving my mother and I have a hot, sensitive guy I have a crush on sitting next to me."

"Wow and thank you."

"More a fact than a compliment."

"Back at you."

"And today I learned my mother was a super-volunteer at the farmers market and was also a social justice warrior who helped people with disabilities craft sustainable lives—a lot to unpack."

"She sounds like a lovely lady."

"She was great. And I'm certain that quote is from *Starsky and Hutch*."

"Search it online."

"Can we settle the debate later and complete the dump run?"

Gabe put the truck in drive and headed to the dumping area.

"Want some gum?" asked Owen.

"Why not?"

He handed Gabe a stick of mint chewing gum. As he put it in his mouth, all he could think about was Jessica's words on how meet-cutes led to kisses. They had survived spilled coffee, been forced together into a road trip, and now the gum, in case a kiss was looming.

They were currently the only people at the dump's pit. They stood at the lip of the pit and tossed the odd twenty black garbage bags into the big pit below where they would be crushed and compacted when enough had been collected to create a block of landfill. To get to the bottom of the pit, one had to go down an incline steep enough to separate the dangers of the pit from the rest of the dump. Gabe and Owen grinned at each other as they worked, silently smacking their gum. Gabe had to admit he had come to genuinely like Owen. Naive about farming, but a good-hearted fellow.

"This is it," said Owen, getting the last black plastic bag from the truck.

"Let me take that one," said Gabe.

"I've got it," said Owen.

"No, no, I—"

Both men held onto the bag as they simultaneously heaved the heavy plastic container with such force, it caused the other man to lose his footing and slip over the lip and trip down the incline into the pit of the dump. Wiry Gabe was the first to hit bottom, luckily landing on his back with one of the soft plastic bags cushioning his fall. Owen was not far behind, tripping as he arrived at the bottom and landing on top of Gabe, looking shocked to be face-to-face, a fraction of an inch within touching noses. Gabe could feel the warmth coming off Owen's skin.

Gabe could no longer deny he was in the middle of the world's longest meet-cute. He looked into Owen's eyes to see the sexiest combination of kindness and vulnerability. He leaned in for a kiss and was met with equal enthusiasm. The kiss lingered longer than either could have imagined. It wrapped Gabe in great comfort, and he would have kept the kiss going if reality hadn't interrupted them.

"You boys all right?" yelled a woman from the lip of the pit above.

Owen popped up first. "We're fine," he yelled back, picking himself up to hike up the incline.

"It's not safe down there," yelled the woman.

"Or sanitary," said Gabe, following Owen up the incline.

"You okay?" asked the woman when they returned to the lip of the pit.

"Couldn't be better," said Gabe with a wink to Owen. They got in the truck and headed to the town square.

They both gave Andy a wave as they drove by his gate booth. Andy, however, was focused on his discussion with the currently entering client and didn't notice them leaving.

At first, they were all beaming smiles. No words were necessary. Jessica was right: time to take a risk and try an old-fashioned dating situation. Their romance would be long distance, but worth the drive for such a kind, great-looking guy. Gabe fantasized about how great the sex would be. He tried to imagine all the excuses he could come up with to visit Concord Valley. But he was getting ahead of himself. Sometimes the hot guys aren't the best lovers. But that kiss! Fireworks went off in Gabe's heart.

"What are you thinking?" asked Owen.

"Umm..." Gabe was embarrassed to be caught in the middle of his schoolboy rhapsody. "I was thinking about that kiss. Too bad it got cut short."

"I'm not sure how I feel about our first moment of intimacy being on top of garbage."

"First?" asked Gabe. "So you want there to be a second?"

"Sooner than later," said Owen without missing a beat.

"What's the rest of your day like?" Gabe had already forgotten about the Cohens. Instead, he was deciding how he could end up at Owen's place as he hadn't yet made an appearance at the scene of his mother's death. He wouldn't stay long. First times with hot guys usually don't last more than an hour or two. He imagined going two, maybe three rounds with this sexy guy. At some point, Gabe would have to bow out to work on the script he received by overnight express.

"There's something I better share with you first," said Owen.

"Undetectable? I'm cool with that. I'm negative on PrEP."

"Me too. Same. It's that I'm in a relationship. I'm married. To a man."

Gabe slammed on the brakes and pulled over to the side of the road with a dramatic screech.

"Of course, you are." *How could I be so stupid?* "Of course, you are..." he whispered in defeat. His dating fantasy of Owen vanished instantly.

"Is that a problem?"

"When were you going to tell me this?"

"I didn't expect you to kiss me."

"We literally had four meet-cutes! And you're not wearing a ring."

"Rings send mixed signals in an open relationship. So, this: us—" He gestured in an awkward circle to symbolize Owen and Gabe as a couple. "—not a problem."

"Not for the dudes in the relationship. What about the outsider?"

"I don't care who my husband sees. He doesn't care either."

"I do," said Gabe. He was surprised at how Puritan he sounded. "Look, I'm as sex-positive as anyone, but my number one rule is I don't get involved with married men. End stop."

"Even if the married men both consent?"

"I imagine your open relationship has a few rules, right?" asked Gabe. "Let me guess. Don't ask, don't tell. No diseases. And one more minor detail." His words oozed sarcasm. "Oh, yeah. Don't fall in love."

Owen's lack of response was confirmation.

Gabe went on. "In my experience, an open relationship is an abundant life for the dudes in the relationship, but crumbs for the third. And that wouldn't be good for my self-esteem."

Gabe's self-awareness landed strong and true. Owen was at a loss for words.

"A pleasure to meet you, Owen," continued Gabe. "I wish you the best of luck with your farm. If your crops fail, you can always fall back on your baking skills. I'll drop you off at your car, and you can have a funny story to tell your confidants about how a sex-crazed local guy hit on you on a pile of garbage at the county dump."

"That is reductive and not an accurate assessment of what happened. This whole day has been more than a you-hit-on-me moment. Being around you has been the most sexy, satisfying foreplay from the moment I laid eyes on you."

"Stop. No more." Gabe raised his palm to Owen's face to silence him. "Enough." He put the truck in drive and headed to town. They rode in silence for a while.

"Such a great kiss," said Owen. Gabe didn't want to engage him any further. "The best kiss I ever had. Ever. No hyperbole. Sparks flew." While he may have been speaking the truth, Owen's sensual tone was pure manipulation.

"Maybe you rolled onto a battery at the dump. Can we ride in silence, please?" If Gabe bantered with Owen, he might be opening a door he couldn't close.

"You know you felt it too," said Owen. "We've got natural chemistry. Come on, dude. You rarely experience this with someone. Please don't walk away."

"I don't have many boundaries with sex and dating. I need you to respect this one."

"I don't get it. Why not try it once? And, if you don't like it, don't do it again."

"You think I haven't? This is personal, historic, and loaded. And not your business. I don't want to have this conversation with someone I barely know and will most likely never see again."

"You don't know that. If it's meant to be, destiny will undermine you. At least tell me why you're blocking the possibility of dating a potential soulmate."

"I don't need to justify, argue, defend or explain my choices. I'm a grown-up."

"You get sexier and hotter with each word."

"And I do not need any distractions with low-hanging fruit."

"Aren't you even curious to see how low it hangs?" Gabe was getting turned on by Naughty Owen. As much as the answer was "Yes!" he couldn't submit. After all he had said before, surrender would have shown a weakness of character.

"Where are you parked?" asked Gabe when they got to the town square.

"You can drop me off here. I'll walk. I don't even know your last name."

"Let's keep it that way. Listen, Owen, I like you. I find you incredibly attractive, a great kisser, and a lot of fun. We even have terrific chemistry. I'll give you all that. And I would love to have sex with you. Even date you, in another context. But in spite of my worst intentions, I still have a moral compass and I choose to follow it. Please accept that we're never going to see each other beyond this...moment."

"Never say never."

"Sometimes never is never. Can you at least respect that? For me."

"For you. For today," said Owen. "How do meet-cutes work? Boy meets boy. Boy loses boy. Maybe boy gets boy once more in the future?"

"Only in the movies," said Gabe.

"Nice to meet you, Gabe," said Owen leaning in for a platonic peck on the cheek.

"Same."

"See you again soon, I hope," said Owen as he slammed the car door and shuffled away, more deflated even than when he was covered in iced coffee. Gabe let him get the last word in as he, too, secretly hoped their paths would cross again. If he took the logistics of death into consideration, he had too much on his plate to put any energy into starting a new relationship, let alone a long-distance one with a married man.

His OG ringtone revealed a local number he didn't recognize. "Hello. Gabe Hartman here."

"This is Bethany at Rob Cohen. Listen. We're still rounding up your mother's paperwork. It might be more complicated than we first thought. Can we reschedule for tomorrow morning?"

"Sure. Does ten o'clock work?"

"Perfect. And if you could look through her mail and bring in any tax or land information documents, that would be helpful."

"Is there something I should be worried about?"

"We don't have enough information to make an informed opinion at this point. Nothing to worry about yet. See you tomorrow."

Gabe hung up. With one phone call about legal logistics, he was able to refocus his life after the Owen detour. The purpose of his visit was to take care of his mother's estate. He had no time for an affair with a handsome transplant. He needed to focus on lawyer meetings and planning a memorial service.

Gabe dropped the pickup truck keys off with Charlize who was barking orders at the last of the booths being taken down. "Always a few slow pokes. How'd it go?"

"Uneventful," he lied.

"You never know whether those new city slickers are going to be divas or know how to read the room."

"He was helpful." No need to add to Charlize's gossip mill. "We met Andy."

"Your mom saved his life. His family was going to lock him away in an institution. She found him that job and some government money in addition to available transportation resources for him to get to and from work."

"She did all that?"

"She was a great lady. You gotta let people surprise you sometimes, Gabe. Come here." Charlize grabbed him for a hug and clung to him for an extra-long time. Even though Gabe was uncomfortable, he leaned into it. "God, I miss her."

She finally let go.

"Me too," said Gabe.

"Thanks for covering her shift today. We'll find someone else for next week. See you at the memorial. It's Saturday, right?"

"News to me."

"You may want to check in with Arthur before you plan anything," she said, pointing in the direction of the bookstore on the square. "He may have already put some plans for a memorial service in motion."

"Thanks for the heads-up."

"Assume good intentions, kiddo. You don't have to do the service all by yourself. If somebody wants to help, let them. That's what your mother would have done."

Gabe needed a time-out from all the Concord Valley small-town hempen homespun. He got in his car to check on the next item from the *Death for Dummies* to-do list: plan the memorial/funeral service. Before overwhelm could kick in, Gabe headed over to Arthur's bookstore-cafe.

Arthur Quinn's bookstore-cafe was called Quinn & Ink. The logo had a feather quill pen spelling out the name Quinn, in case one missed the reference. Gabe didn't know Arthur at all. Arthur had retired to Concord Valley after Gabe had gone away to college. He was one of his mother's buddies, but he had never been around when Gabe came to visit. Arthur had taken his retirement savings and invested it in a storefront on the square. He was a widower from Albany; when his wife was alive, they took day trips and were often lured by the charms of Concord Valley. They moved to Concord Valley where Arthur satisfied a lifelong dream: to open the first and only bookstore in town.

"Forget the romance of running a bookstore," Arthur had been known to say. "I thought I would sit around talking about books all day. But it's retail. My feet are killing me at the end of the day."

The bookstore was everything one wanted from a small-town bookstore: four front tables with current trendy reads and bestsellers, fiction and nonfiction, hardcover and paperback. And a table for tourists of local hiking trails, restaurant guides, and local lore and authors. Gabe didn't see any novels, memoirs, or books of merit by local artists. Concord Valley would never be confused with a bastion of literary inspiration. The store had a cafe toward the rear where a few people sat and read while a lone barista, a teen from the local high school, cleaned coffee cups and restocked the coffee bar. Gabe was happy to see his hometown had embraced modern times enough to support one small independent bookstore with an espresso machine. If Arthur's bookstore had been around when Gabe was growing up, he would have made it his second home.

Gabe figured Arthur was the old guy beyond the cash register struggling with changing the receipt paper.

"Let me help you with that," said Gabe approaching the counter.

"Would you? This is the hardest part of my job. My arthritis—"

"Are you Arthur Quinn?" asked Gabe.

"In person."

"Nice store," said Gabe, easily dropping the cash register receipt paper into its place. "I'm Amelia Hartman's son."

"Of course, you are!" Arthur gave him a handshake. Gabe was

surprised at how firmly a man with arthritis could shake. "Amelia used to help me change the receipt paper. She struggled with it, too, but was better at it. Technology is a young man's game."

Gabe was amused at the thought of changing cash register receipt paper being technology.

"It must have been a shock," said Arthur. "My call yesterday."

"Feels like I've lived a thousand lives since then."

"Death forces us to grow up real fast. I hope you don't mind. I took the liberty to plan a memorial for your mother here at the store. If you feel I've stepped on your toes and want me to cancel—"

"No. That's great news. Thank you. I can't tell you what a relief—" Out of nowhere, Gabe's tears came. "I'm sorry."

"Come here, son." Arthur took Gabe by the shoulder, hugging him as they walked to an empty table in the cafe. "Never apologize for missing your mother. Can we get this young man some water?" Arthur signaled the barista with a gentle gesture. "She was a great lady."

"She always spoke highly of you and this place," said Gabe.

The barista brought over a bottle of water for Gabe.

"I wasn't sure if you knew her current circle of friends. We have our phone tree. I was able to contact them all with a few phone calls. Easy. And since Amelia and I were kind of dating," said Arthur.

"Yeah?" Gabe's tears were instantly distracted by this major piece of new information.

"When she wasn't out there saving the world. I mean, we weren't aggressively sexual. A lot of smooching, second and third base when we were feeling frisky. But not, you know. She was helping me get up the courage to ask my doctor for that purple pill. Is this too much information?"

"A bit..." Gabe took a sip of the water the barista had handed him.

"Sorry. We were going to out ourselves to you as a heterosexual couple on your next visit. And here we are."

"All good," said Gabe.

"That's why I took the initiative to plan her memorial...as her boyfriend. I imagine you have a lot on your plate. Since I have the place here, we can save on renting a space. I'll shut down the shop on Saturday for a 'private party.' Wait. She never told you we were dating, did she?"

"Not outright. She referred to you as her 'nice gentleman friend.'"

"I guess that was her way of telling you. How did you tell her when you had a new boyfriend?"

"Didn't have many occasions." Gabe took another sip of the water.

"At the risk of sounding like a two-bit therapist, how does her having a boyfriend make you feel?" asked Arthur.

"As long as she was happy."

"She was," said Arthur with such confidence, Gabe was assured his mother lived a full life of friends and purpose when he was not around.

"That's why you were the one to call me yesterday," said Gabe, putting all the pieces together. "Thank you for taking care of the memorial service. I wouldn't have known where to start."

"I figured. I've had some practice burying a loved one..."

"What can I do to help?"

"If you can make sure the ashes get here."

"I'm picking them up tomorrow. I'll make sure they don't mix her with any roadkill."

"Amelia said you were funny. And, unlike your mother, well-organized. Oh, if you could say a few words at the service, that would be great. Your mother said you were an aspiring writer. I've set aside a place in the program for you."

"I'll do my best."

"That's all we can do."

"Thank you, Arthur."

Back in his rental car, Gabe could no longer put off the inevitable: a return to his mother's house, the house he grew up in. Outside of a handful of apartments in New York City, this was his only real home. He had lived there for eighteen consecutive years, from birth to escape. The house stood alone on a stretch of isolated road outside the main part of town. The lots were large and next-door neighbors more than a stone's throw. Gabe and his mother had argued over whether their house could be called a Victorian farmhouse (Gabe's side of the argument) or a

Victorian cottage (his mother's side). It had once been the estate of a modest gentleman farmer. Through the years, the arable land became a burden to farm. By the time Amelia put down a deposit, the house was in slow disrepair. Amelia and Gabe only farmed the quarter-acre garden in the backyard. Over time, they gave up that, but Amelia always enjoyed tending her flower garden around an aspen tree in the backyard.

Gabe's last visit was during Christmas and New Year's, a few months ago. How much could have changed? Except everything.

Golden hour was waning as he approached the handsome, square facade of the house. The sight of the slightly peeling white paint and green shutters offered him calming emotional support, undercut by pangs of terror. He had already seen her dead, partially covered, nude body at the morgue. He was surprised at the range of feelings emerging: guilt over not having visited more frequently, shame over not having asked more about Arthur when she brought him up, and sad terror at not having the courage to walk through "their" house as "their" was no longer applicable.

Gabe parked the car and went to the mailbox, still significantly dented from the last group of bored teens joyriding with baseball bats and nothing better to do on a Saturday night. He skimmed the letters, a couple from government officials with rice-paper address windows. He would remember to set them aside with anything else he found for the meeting with the Cohens tomorrow morning.

He was amused at the absurdity of thinking he had time for a fling with Owen; he didn't even know his last name, thank goodness. Otherwise, he might be tempted to troll him on social media. He was annoyed Owen was taking up head space and tried to banish any thoughts of him. But remembering him shirtless and that kiss... *Stop!*

He proceeded to the front porch.

He got out his key, but he didn't need it. Whoever had taken his mother's body away didn't have a key. They didn't lock the door behind them. Any looter could have gotten in. But in Concord Valley, crime clocks were set back fifty years. Gabe's anxiety increased as he pushed open the front door and let himself in.

"Anyone here? Hello!" Gabe figured his mother died with good karma and would be spared any indignities after her death.

He set his bags by the front door, turned around, and took in the house he grew up in, for the first time without his mother around. The notorious Chairvana caught Gabe's eye. The scene of the crime. Forever haunted. He would have to get rid of it. Another item for the to-do list. At least the EMTs had returned the chair to its neutral position.

He didn't feel any lingering ghosts. Existential questions emerged, like, if his mother had any premonitions when she woke yesterday, it would be her last day on earth. And if she hadn't known, is there anything she wouldn't want the world to discover? He anticipated finding hidden sex toys and instant photos of Arthur getting to third base. Gabe was already planning a backyard bonfire.

He headed to the dining room work table. The dining room table, rarely used for meals for as long as Gabe could remember, was more often a home for Christmas decorations or piles of papers that may or may not have been organized, like today. This was how his mother lived when Gabe wasn't around.

Gabe picked up a friendly letter from a nearby pile. He recognized another pile of her recipe cards. Yet another pile contained letters similar to the rice-paper-window envelope from the mailbox. Each pile shared a theme, at least. He put the letters from the latest mail in their corresponding piles as his OG telephone ring announced a work call from Erin.

"I finally arrived at the crime scene," said Gabe.

"How is it?" asked Erin.

"Dusty. And not as tidy as when I left a few months ago."

"And emotionally?"

"I was scared at first, but I'm fine. There's a lot of clutter. She must have hidden it all when I came for visits."

"Scared you'd judge her?"

"And I would have."

"Has the overnight arrived yet?"

As if on cue, a knock on the front door grabbed his attention.

"Maybe." Gabe turned around. On the other side of the lace-curtained window stood a woman in a ZipExpress uniform. "As a matter of fact..."

"Cute?"

"If you're into girls."

"Not so loud," said Erin.

Gabe opened the door.

"I'm not a girl," said the ZipExpress woman. "I'm a womyn—with a y."

"I meant, if you're into hostile lesbians," said Gabe as he signed for the envelope.

"That's not funny," said the ZipExpress gal, handing him the envelope with a twinkle in her eye. He had read her correctly. ZipExpress gal could be joked with. "Sorry about your mom. She was cool."

"Thanks," he said, closing the door. "Erin, you won't believe the day I had!" Gabe plopped into a chair at the dining room table, his first moment of relaxation all day.

"How's the grieving?"

"Tell your rabbi thanks for the book. This trip would have been a nightmare without it. Real-life death logistics make planning a funeral on a soap a breeze."

"Those pesky emotions... Was I right? Please know you're missed and loved."

"Same. Like a favorite younger sister, not a jilted ex-lover."

"No need for explanation," said Erin. "I hope you have some energy left for the night you're going to have. Have you opened the overnight package yet?"

Gabe picked up the envelope. "Are all our packages this thick?"

"That's what she said. And yes. You're holding all the work you do on a regular day. You do impressive work."

"I must be good," he said, carefully ripping the paper zip pull off and taking a peek at the contents. The many-colored page sets for various states of revision were organized neatly by Erin with familiar color-coordinated tabs.

"They don't give Emmys to slouches."

"They actually do, but—"

"Actually, shut up," said Erin. "Besides the revised pages to fix, the Douglasses want a one-page for the Oliver Armstrong story arc by ten tomorrow morning. And of course, they want a paper copy. Their wet brains don't understand you're out of town."

"How hard is it to open a shared document?" asked Gabe.

"Have you met the Douglasses?" said Erin. "I'm creating a document right now for us to share."

"Great. I'm pretty sure my mom didn't have a working printer."

"I'll take care of the hard copy on my end. You worry about writing a great story for Oliver Armstrong."

"I'll see what I can come up with."

"By tomorrow morning. This is shooting next week."

"I keep forgetting how fast this is happening."

"Got a thumbnail?"

"Sure."

"I'm ready to take notes. I'll share the doc when we're done. Go."

These were the moments Gabe would have called his mom to get the latest dirt on Concord Valley he would turn into Harmony Hills storylines. He browsed across the piles of letters picking one up randomly. Junk mail from a sustainable farming nonprofit.

"Well?" said Erin. "You're taking too long."

"How does a sustainable farming storyline sound?"

"Kind of dull. But kind of current. How would that look on screen?"

"Think like a red-state country girl. Imagine Oliver-slash-Barrett's first appearance, all sweaty and dirty, coming from working in the fields in tight jeans he needs to get out of ASAP."

"You meant thirsty sustainable farming. That works."

Gabe could feel his own tumescence rise as he worked with the visual of Barrett, switching to a fantasy of Owen posing in tighty-whities. "We can repurpose the old holiday market set as the Harmony Hills Farmers Market where Oliver can have a booth."

"Who doesn't love a farmers market?"

"Or a sexy sustainable farmer. His produce isn't the only delicious display at his booth."

"Where are you with the rom-com idea?" asked Erin.

Gabe's mind flashed to a memory of Owen covered in coffee, taking his shirt off to clean up the coffee mess.

"A farmers market scene," said Gabe, "gives us lots of options for meet-cutes. I'm tempted to go with spilled coffee from a coffee truck. Coffee stains read well on a television screen."

"Fabulous!"

"Also playing with the idea that he's a Sunday baker."

"That's fun too. I love a man dusted in flour. Dude, are we moving forward with the rom-com idea?"

"Do you think Barrett and Suzy will have chemistry?" asked Gabe.

"She's the Queen of Daytime," said Erin. "She can fake chemistry with a loaf of bread."

"Which they might knead together."

"Hot. And you want to leave Oliver open to some mystery for a crisis plot point down the road. What's his secret mystery?"

"He's in an open relationship with a girl in another city. A girl we never need to see. No budget for her."

"Yet. Dude, you are cracking this story wide open!" said Erin.

"Making shit up and getting paid for it: what we do," said Gabe, relieved how easily they had outlined a workable story without his mother's help.

"The Douglasses will love it. I think introducing him with a light, down-to-earth rom-com touch will be a lot of fun."

"What actor doesn't enjoy playing sexy and complicated and selfish?"

"Thanks for giving the rom-com idea a try."

"If it pops the ratings, I'll make sure you get promoted."

"Big *if*. You write it, and I'll make sure a hard copy gets to the Douglasses tomorrow."

"You're the best. I better get to work on the revisions. I'll put them in the mail tomorrow. I have to drive to a ZipExpress office in the next town."

"Not one person in Concord Valley knows you write for *If Tomorrow Never Comes*?"

"And we're gonna keep it that way. I have many good reasons for them not to know."

Gabe's phone buzzed, announcing a call from Jessica.

"I have a call coming in. Better take it."

"Check in tomorrow." Erin clicked off.

"Hey, Jess."

"How are my pitches coming along?"

"You're nonstop." Gabe went into the living room and lay on the sofa. A coffee table piled with magazines and newspapers separated him from the storied lounger.

"How are the ghosts of your childhood?" asked Jessica.

"I'm in the presence of one right now." Chairvana gave off the aura of hallowed ground. "Death sucks."

"Tell me about it. I lost my dad when I was a kid. How's your hot loser rom-com honey?" asked Jessica.

"More like a cold rom-com fail."

"Too bad. Did you at least get a kiss?"

"I'd be lying if I said no."

"Yay! Why the 'fail'?"

"I don't remember pasting any pictures of dating married men on my vision board."

"You and your freaking standards."

"Believe me. This guy was absolutely lovely and delicious, and *aaarrrggghhh*! But I wouldn't want to share him."

"I have never heard you talk about someone like this before."

"Other than he's *married*, he was—everything."

"Was the kiss before or after he told you he was married?"

"Of course, before. In my defense, he was not wearing a ring."

"Everyone feels stupid when they fall in love."

"Who said anything about love?"

"Whatever you want to call it."

"I liked him. That's all. This is what always happens when you let someone in."

"You can't use this as an excuse to remain eternally jaded. If you like this guy, why not be friends and hang out—go to dinner, see a movie."

"That sounds like dating."

"Friends do that too."

"I put a kibosh on the whole shebang. I don't even know his last name. Boy meets boy; boy loses boy."

"Rules of rom-coms: boy always gets boy a second time."

"Not this time. You should have seen Righteous Gabe in action."

"At least you're off those apps."

"How do you know?"

"I haven't heard a *drrroot* once on this call."

"I wonder if anyone uses them up here. I might have to do some research."

"Such bad karma."

"By the way, a gay man's dating app memoir would be a great book. I'll pitch you that."

"Yech."

"What? Your new corporate job has already turned you into a sex-negative homophobe?"

"The straight girl book market does not want to read about your thousand annual hookups. That's not an exaggeration, is it?"

Gabe didn't correct her vast undercount. "Is the whole straight girl book market made up of sex-negative homophobes?"

"Honestly, they'd be jealous. No one buys a book because they want to feel envy. There should be a word in English for straight people who feel jealous about how easy gay guys get laid."

"Sounds like that word is pronounced 'J-E-S-S-I-C-A.'"

"Ha ha. I'll forgive you because you're grieving. But I'm not going to stop bugging you until you give me one decent pitch. By midweek?"

"I am extremely overwhelmed at the moment, Jess."

"Promise me, and I'll hang up."

"I have a eulogy to write."

"One pitch?"

"One pitch. I promise," said Gabe.

Gabe hung up and put the phone on the coffee table. He glanced at the lounger, remembering how his mother loved to take mini breaks from life's business to rest peacefully in her favorite spot. He kept wondering if she knew yesterday would be a day of lasts: her last meal, her last look at a flower, her last smile. "You poor, beautiful lady," he whispered as softly as a prayer. He closed his eyes, intending to rest for a few minutes, but slept through till morning.

Chapter Three

G abe woke up to sunrise streaming across the sofa. The panic of already running behind struck him before he even got off the sofa. His disorientation was doubled by the fact he hadn't bothered to go upstairs and unpack. His bags were still leaning against the door. He couldn't bring himself to venture into his second-floor bedroom. He had no problem going into his mother's room upstairs. She had moved the television in there. He turned it on and used it for white background noise while he performed his morning ablutions in her bathroom. He didn't even go into his room to change. He had a few hours before he had to be at Rob Cohen's office. He was too busy to face whatever awaited in his bedroom.

He made his way into the kitchen and brewed some coffee. Grateful his mother always had a fully stocked refrigerator and pantry, he had breakfast while looking over the revised pages from Erin. He scribbled a few notes for the production crew. Erin had written out instructions for how to return the pages with his notes overnight via ZipExpress. All Gabe had to do was find a ZipExpress office where no one recognized him, to preserve his anonymity as a soap writer.

Roger and Bethany requested he bring any documents that looked like they might be related to her estate. Except for her checkbook and a couple of piles of IRS-looking letters on the dining room table, not much looked relevant.

Gabe loved his childhood home, but as his mother got older, she was less interested in doing housework and more interested in saving the world. The kitchen floor was slightly sticky, and the whole place needed a good cleaning, accentuated by a few new water spots on the ceiling. The house could use a fresh coat of paint inside and out.

With the soap opera paperwork completed, Gabe planned his morning appointments. He hoped he could keep his grief at bay and stay focused—and most importantly, not get distracted with thoughts of Owen. That was over and done with. On the way out the door, he said goodbye to Chairvana, his problematic family member, his unwelcome companion.

The ZipExpress office in the next town offered Gabe perfect anonymity. While he was there, no one called out his name or offered condolences. The young woman behind the desk seemed friendly but detached. His first task complete, he returned to the Concord Valley town square for his meeting with the Cohens.

Roger and Bethany sat Gabe at a big oak table in the back conference room at their office. The paperwork they had prepared was in a short, neat pile with a single document on top.

"This doesn't look good," said Gabe.

"No," said Roger. Bethany sat next to her husband shaking her head with great seriousness. "The good news is you're the sole surviving descendant, correct?"

"As far as I know. Did she even have a will?"

"Not exactly," said Bethany "We discovered some notes that look like they were from a meeting with Roger's grandfather, maybe a brainstorming session for a will she might write later on."

"She was easily distracted when it came to business, money, and numbers, and she wasn't keen on follow-through. Too busy saving the world to balance her checkbook."

"Or pay property taxes, evidently," said Roger, looking over a spreadsheet from a file.

"I also found these," said Gabe, handing the envelopes to Bethany. "All from the county tax board. They were unopened when I found them." The potential exhaustion ahead was coming into focus for Gabe.

"What was her primary source of income in retirement?" asked Roger.

"Some social security," said Gabe. "Her modest teacher pension. She barely eked by."

"I don't mean to insult the dead," said Roger. "But..."

"But she was clearly living beyond her means," said Bethany.

Gabe admired how Roger and Bethany overlapped but never seemed to interrupt each other.

"How would you describe the state of your mother's house?" asked Roger.

"It isn't in complete disrepair, but, eventually... Let's cut to the chase."

"You want the long, diplomatic version?" asked Roger.

"Rip the bandage off," said Gabe.

"She owned the house, but she was in arrears with her property taxes," said Bethany. "She left some modest middle-class debts, credit cards mostly, a few thousand dollars, but nothing outrageous."

"You make a decent salary, right?" asked Roger.

"I save a little while living in New York City," said Gabe proudly. "Why?"

"As the sole descendant," said Bethany, "you inherit her estate and all her property-related debts."

"Shit," said Gabe. "Won't the bank or someone eventually foreclose?"

"It's more complicated," said Bethany. "This is about taxes, not a mortgage. There's going to be outstanding interest, penalties, the taxes themselves, and who knows what other charges. It all becomes a lien on your house."

Gabe had a hard time processing all the terms at once. From his soap work, he knew a lien was never a good thing. He was not prepared for this conversation.

"Since you will technically own the house," said Bethany, "you will also be responsible for taking over the back taxes."

"Which might be inching toward six figures," added Roger.

Gabe's exhale was painfully audible. First grief and now anger at his mother's fiscal irresponsibility. Too many feelings to process.

"Roger and I want to protect your credit rating," said Bethany. "What do you know about liens?"

"The state can go directly into my checking account and take money." Gabe had written liens into several inheritance plotlines on *If Tomorrow Never Comes*. He loved liens as a high-stakes plot device: potential financial ruin. He did not love liens when it came to his own life. "Can't I decline the inheritance?"

Roger and Bethany were empathetic to Gabe's naivete.

"Not this kind," said Bethany.

"What happens if I put the house on the market as is?" asked Gabe. He hated that he was starting to sound desperate.

"Any potential buyer would have to buy the debt. Concord Valley is not a hot real estate market right now. The nicest properties linger on the market for a while, and a lien adds zero curb appeal."

"What are my other options?" asked Gabe.

"If your mother had come to us for counsel," said Roger, "we would have advised her to set up a revocable living trust and transfer the property to her trust."

"That way," said Bethany, "the state couldn't dip into your savings. A trust protects you."

"Is it too late to set one up?" asked Gabe.

"It's too late for your mother, but maybe not for you; we don't know," said Roger. "It's a matter of timing. There's probate, which usually is slow, but you don't want to be too slow here. We need to work fast to protect you. First, you need to set up a trust."

"Problem is, we're not trust attorneys," said Bethany.

"Where do I find a trust attorney?" asked Gabe.

"We're one step ahead of you," said Roger as Bethany handed Gabe a slip of paper.

"We checked a few legal databases and, luckily, there's a semi-retired trust attorney who lives on the outskirts of town. He hasn't been here long. Here's his contact information."

"Greene Associates?" asked Gabe looking over the paper.

"We've never met him either," said Roger.

"I imagine he's some older bored guy," said Bethany, "who would be happy for the diversion. Lawyers never retire; instead, they put out a shingle."

"Give this Greene guy a call," said Rob. "Ask him what he thinks about the timing and let us know what we need to do."

"We feel this is your best shot," said Bethany. "In the meantime, I'll call the tax board and see what I can do to slow down their processing. We know a few tricks."

"Tell Greene you need to work fast," said Roger. "We'll give him a heads-up."

Outside Cohens' office, Gabe's resentment toward his mother swelled as he tried not to freak out while dialing Greene's number.

"Good morning," said a young female voice.

Gabe was expecting an older fellow's voice. "Oh...hello. I was given your number by an attorney in town, Roger Cohen."

"I'm Mr. Greene's associate. What can I do for you?"

"My mother, Amelia Hartman, passed away recently, and I want to set up a revocable living trust. For me. There are issues with taxes and a possible lien. The Cohens said Mr. Greene might be able to help."

"That was his specialty," said the woman. "He's semi-retired now."

"Would it be possible to set up an appointment?" asked Gabe. "The sooner, the better."

"Ironically, he's got a lot on his plate since he tried to retire. I'm looking over his book...busy afternoon ahead..."

"It's extremely time sensitive," said Gabe.

"Any chance you can stop by in the next fifteen minutes?"

All Gabe had on his to-do list for the day was check in with Arthur, pick up the ashes, and be home at eleven o'clock. He loved nothing more than watching *If Tomorrow Never Comes* as it broadcast in real time. His watch read 10:15 a.m.

"Perfect."

"He's working out of his home."

"Is the address I have on Linden Road current?"

"Yes. What was your last name?"

"Hartman."

"See you in fifteen, Mr. Hartman. FYI, he has a standing appointment at eleven o'clock he can't miss."

"Same. On the way."

Mr. Greene's house was a ten-minute drive from the square. In a dozen blocks, Concord Valley went from in-town smaller homes on alphabet-lettered streets to country farmhouses on streets named after trees.

Gabe couldn't put his finger on where he had seen Mr. Greene's house on Linden, a clean, crisp light olive-green Victorian farmhouse with white shutters and black Italianate touches on the eaves. Gabe took a photo of the house and messaged it to Jessica.

> *Gabe*: Where have you seen this house before?

He pulled in behind a fancy SUV and a hybrid parked in the driveway. The quiet stillness of the place struck Gabe as he climbed the shiny, newly renovated steps to the front porch with the picturesque hanging swing.

> *Jessica*: The house from your vision board! OMG!

Could it be the same? A picture of a similar house was smack dab in the center of his vision board.

> *Gabe*: A coincidence.

Gabe rang the doorbell. The front door synthesized both vintage and restored looks which Gabe found magical. He touched its sleek, white wooden boards. The home was strong and clean, solid. If he believed in falling in love and love at first sight, he would have fallen in love with this house.

Footsteps approached the door. Gabe cleared his throat and stood straight to prepare a good first impression for his potential new trust attorney.

The door swung open.

"Oh, my God! Boy meets boy once more!"

"No..."

Gabe was unprepared for the reappearance of Owen.

"Destiny is a bitch. Guess 'never' doesn't mean '*never*' in our case."

Owen was even more handsome standing before him dressed in classic upscale comfort. Seeing Owen in soft woolen gray socks without shoes, Gabe's knees buckled a little.

"What are you doing here?" asked Gabe.

"I live here," said Owen.

"I'm supposed to meet a retired trust attorney by the name of Greene."

"Owen Greene?" He extended his hand. "That's me."

Gabe shook Owen's hand in a daze of confusion.

"Gabe Hartman. I'm sorry. I was expecting an old, retired guy."

"That's me too. Old—to someone in their early twenties. And I'm retired—semi-retired—from my law practice."

"You told me you worked for a family business."

"My dad is the founding partner of a white-shoe corporate law office in the Financial District. As you can see, I would prefer a life where I don't have to wear shoes."

Gabe was furious at fate's practical joke. At the moment, he couldn't appreciate Owen's charm, good looks, and self-deprecating humor. "This isn't happening." Gabe turned around and walked away.

"Gabe, come back. My assistant said your issue was time sensitive. Right, Maddy?" he called into the house.

"That's what he said on the phone," said Maddy, appearing in the background.

Gabe turned around to see Maddy, the girl from the banana bread booth. His phone buzzed another message from Jessica, which he didn't bother to look at. He was too overwhelmed by the circumstances in front of him to respond to Jessica's text.

"Clearly we need a reboot after yesterday. Don't let your pride get in the way. Come on in. You remember Maddy?"

"I made tea," said Maddy.

"I seem to be the only person in town," said Owen, "who knows how to set up revocable trusts. Maddy does most of the paperwork. Oh—and I do have a hard stop at eleven o'clock."

Owen's business jargon cut through Gabe's petulance. "Gorgeous home," said Gabe, reluctantly crossing the threshold.

"It's too overly designed for my taste. I was in charge of the outside, though. I had the original wood taken off and re-treated to last another generation. The exterior should outlive even Maddy here. I didn't want to be one of those outsiders who comes in and doesn't give back to his new community."

"Great karma."

"The whole place is too grand by half. I want to up my farming game. Have a seat in the parlor here."

Gabe tried to hide how impressed he was at the scope and taste that had gone into the renovation and interior design choices. "I didn't see any wild strawberries outside."

"He pulled them all up," said Maddy, handing Gabe a cup of tea, "Thursday night when he got home. In the dark."

"Don't tell him that," said Owen.

Gabe smiled at Owen hiding his shame.

The parlor was a lovely blend of contemporary modern with historical references. The renovation must have cost a fortune.

"It's like something you'd see in a glossy design magazine," said Gabe, caressing the intricate wooden detail on the back of the Victorian loveseat.

"Good eye," said Owen.

"The place was featured in several magazines a while back," said

Maddy at the French pocket doors separating the parlor from the rest of the house. "You want these open?"

"Closed," said Owen. Maddy left the two men alone in the parlor. "So, Gabe Hartman, son of the benevolent but fiscally challenged Amelia Hartman...the Cohens already called to give us the heads-up. But I better take some notes." Owen put on a pair of designer frames and got out a pen and a yellow legal pad. Gabe could now envision Owen in the role of brilliant attorney.

"I was told you were the trust expert," said Gabe.

"With us, it always comes down to trust, doesn't it?" said Owen, looking up from his notes.

Gabe gazed into his eyes. He was secretly re-enchanted by his favorite memories of the day before.

Gabe snapped out of his reverie. "Yep. Trust. A trust."

Without missing a beat, Owen continued, "It's also about probate court. I take it your mother didn't have a living trust."

"Not in her bandwidth."

Owen scratched a few notes and simultaneously asked, "How goes the grieving?"

"Too busy."

"I hear it can be overwhelming. This is also about taxes, yeah?"

"Predictably...uh-huh."

"It usually is." Gabe was grateful for Owen's neutral tone, void of any sense of shame. Owen checked his watch.

"If this is a bad time?" Gabe asked.

"We're good. Roger Cohen referred you, yes? Nice young couple—offices on the square..." said Owen, scribbling a few more notes. "He's adorable and she's super smart; she no doubt runs the place. So... This is what I'm gonna do. I'll get titles and deeds from them—at some point I'll need signatures, mostly done electronically. Keep reading your emails. I'll need to see what's in the will."

"There might not be an official will."

"Oh," Owen added that to his notes. "In that case, there might be some issues with timing and probate. I'll coordinate your mom's paperwork with the Cohens. They'll know how to stall the IRS, and I'll figure out how to speed up probate."

"You might want to bribe them with a loaf of that chocolate banana nut bread."

"You're funny."

"I'm serious. It's transformative."

"Thank you," said Owen. "Banana nut bread." He jotted into his notes. "Team Gabe Hartman has your back, my man."

"Why are you being so nice to me after yesterday?"

"Look, I'm sorry. I should have told you I was married up front. I was blinded by the fact that you are—how do I say it—my type." Before Owen code switched to full-on dithering teen, he pulled back. "But you have boundaries. Which I will respect. I don't know if I made this clear, but I enjoy you. You were kind and helpful at the market."

"Except for the coffee."

"Except for the coffee. The least I can do is help you over this speed bump like you helped me. In spite of everything, I enjoyed hanging out with you yesterday. While you're in town, I'd like to try to see where a friendship might go."

"Doesn't hiring you as my trust attorney color our friendship? Money changing hands is not good for friendship. By the way, how do you like to be paid?"

"Hugs and kisses? Too soon?" Owen could tell it was. "Sorry. Let's talk about options. I can do this pro bono."

"Thanks, but I'm not a charity case."

"I had a feeling. Why don't we do this the old-fashioned way? Barter."

"I don't think I have anything to offer."

"Agree to disagree." Owen stood up with his legal pad, checked his watch, and swung open the sliding doors. "Come with me," Owen said over his shoulder, as he slipped into a pair of orange garden shoes by an umbrella stand and continued out the front door.

Gabe was taken aback by Owen's swift confidence and kept up as best he could as Owen headed around the outside of the house.

The backyard was at full capacity with a dozen wooden planters filled with rich topsoil constructed in three rows of four, all tidy and neat, more a work of abstract art than a functional farm at this point.

"I wasn't expecting to find all this," said Gabe. "Is this where the rhubarb was planted?"

"A field down the road. There's some fennel I was going to harvest and sell at the market next week."

"Nobody in their right mind buys fennel. It's invasive and grows wild. Forget about the fennel."

"That's why I need you—to constantly remind me I know nothing about farming. But that doesn't mean I can't have a passion for it, hence the planters, a pet project I started. I want to keep the goals simple my first year and focus on these planters."

"Did you build these?"

"The carpenters did the first few, training me as they went. I'm a fast learner. I'm proud of how they turned out. But I don't know what to put in them."

"Your heirlooms."

"I knew you were my guy. If you could mentor me through the first year, be my farm consultant, in exchange for my legal services, we'll call it even."

"But I'm not here much."

"Ever heard of texting? And when you *are* here..."

Gabe took a moment. "Is this some kind of legal scam?"

"Trust issues much?" asked Owen. "Why not help each other out during a time of transition and develop a friendship in the process?"

"What kind of consulting do you expect from me?"

"Well, can you teach me to drive a tractor?" asked Owen. "They don't make them with automatic transmissions."

"I don't recommend learning stick shift on a five-thousand-pound tractor."

"First matter of business: What heirlooms do you think I should plant?"

"That's a no-brainer with these planters: tomatoes."

"Great idea. Can I do organic heirloom tomatoes?"

"Probably an overreach for year one. Plant a season of regular heirloom tomatoes and see how they do."

"Great. I'll buy some seeds."

"Too late in the season. You want to buy starter plants. Henderson's is a farm that sells the best starters around here."

Owen flipped over the legal pad page and jotted, "Henderson's. What do you mean 'best'?"

"If you go to a big box store nursery, their plants are mass-marketed and not always healthy."

"More trust issues?"

"Everywhere you look. This is for real. No trust issues at Henderson's. Mrs. Henderson will let you know which two plants grow best next to each other. And which need to avoid cross-pollination."

"I am clearly getting the better end of the deal here. What heirloom tomatoes do you recommend?

"If you're planning on selling at the farmers market, I recommend considering a variety of colors. The Black Cherry and Black Krim do well up here. And there's the Chocolate Stripe heirloom."

"A tomato with chocolate flavor notes?"

"Can you imagine? No! It looks like it has a chocolate stripe."

"Aren't tomatoes fruit and not a vegetable?"

"First of all, vegetables don't exist in farming. Everything that bears fruit is a fruit; therefore, everything, in reality, is a fruit. The word vegetable was invented for grocery stores to separate sweet and savory produce. Stick with me, kid."

"I intend to. I figured it's dirt and seeds—"

"*Soil* and seeds."

"I mean, how hard can farming be?" asked Owen.

"I don't mean to be critical, Mr. Darcy, but you might want to check your pride at the county line. Did you catch my reference?"

"Yes, Elizabeth. Did you look up the Dickens 'crying/not crying' reference yet?"

"You mean the *Starksy and Hutch* reference?"

"Look it up," said Owen.

"Later. We good?" asked Gabe.

"Number one rule of friendship: friends trust each other enough to call each other out and tell each other the truth—and know they won't be abandoned. We're more than good."

"Okay. The truth is people around here went to college and got four-year degrees in agriculture. Not unlike law school, but with a lower return on their investment. No one takes anyone seriously who moves here and thinks they're going to be a successful farmer with no farming experience."

"The real consultant is coming out!"

"Farming is a livelihood for most people around here, not a passion project. It's a hard life and a real struggle for most small farmers to eke out even a meager living. You know what I'm saying?"

"Note to self: Don't be a privileged asshole. Stay humble. Respect. Shoulders of giants."

"Was I too harsh?"

"I appreciate the honesty. Any other favorite heirloom tomatoes?"

"Uh, yeah." Gabe was impressed how easily Owen had moved on and embraced the role of inquisitive student. Everything he had found attractive about Owen yesterday was amplified today. Such a shame he was married. "Some gorgeous orange and blonde heirlooms are both beautiful and delicious." *Like you.*

Owen jotted more notes. "Didn't know I'd get a master class in heirloom tomatoes. Where did you learn all this?"

"In the second grade. This is an agri-community."

"Will Henderson's have Early Girls?"

"Sure, but Early Girls are not heirlooms. Do you even know what an heirloom tomato is?"

"No idea."

"It's about the seeds. Heirloom plants are true seeds that have not been crossbred for over forty years. Oh my God, you don't know anything about farming, do you?"

"That's why I need a friend like you. To remind me to stay humble."

Owen jotted "forty years" onto the legal pad.

"If you want classic red heirlooms, ask for Brandywines. They're my favorite."

"Brandywines it is. Gabe's fave." Owen jotted and checked his watch again. "Sorry to cut this short, but—"

"One last thing: when you plant the tomatoes, make sure you plant basil and marigolds around them. Write that down. Super important."

"Basil. Marigolds. Thanks for this, Gabe." Owen led Gabe toward the front yard.

"We good?"

"We're great," said Gabe. "I didn't embarrass myself once today. Did I?"

"There's plenty of time for that."

One of Gabe's eyelashes came loose and caught between his upper and lower lashes.

"I think you have a... Here. Let me..." They stopped walking. Owen reached up and caressed Gabe's eyelash free with his right thumb. Their eye contact was concentrated and intense. Gabe's heart raced faster as Owen's face got even closer, their lips less than an inch apart. Gabe could feel the warmth of Owen's breath on his cheek, and he didn't mind. He was overcome by Owen's sweetness and gentleness. *He's a married man. No more kissing. Under any circumstances. Do. Not.*

"Got it," said Owen, holding the lash in front of Gabe. "Make a wish."

Gabe closed his eyes and made a wish. He tried his best not to wish on Owen and living happily ever after, but he was not successful.

"Got it?" asked Owen. Gabe nodded and opened his eyes. "You deserve all your wildest dreams."

"Careful there... My wildest dreams..."

Before Gabe could undercut the moment, Owen blew his eyelash into the breeze. "I saw the eyelash-wish ritual once in a movie."

"What kind of movie?"

"Something with Meg Ryan or Julia Roberts?"

They continued to the front where they found Maddy on the porch.

"Your eleven o'clock will be starting soon," said Maddy.

"Leave your contact information with Maddy. I'll start filing your trust issues after my appointment. Friend-slash-consultant?"

"Gabe and Owen two-point-o." They shook hands. *Boy meets boy again. Destiny...*

Gabe checked his phone as he made his way home. At a stop light, he responded to Jessica's last message.

Gabe: *That was the house of my trust attorney.*

Jessica: *Trust attorney? Someone had to wear his big-boy pants today.*

Gabe: *Same house on my vision board.*

Jessica: *That's how VBs work. Like the time I put an Oscar on my board and ended up adopting a cat named Oscar. #wheresmypitch*

Gabe: *#later #driving*

He made his way onto his front porch, aware of chipping paint, wishing he could afford the exterior treatments Owen had done. He walked past the lounger with a quick salute and headed upstairs. Even though he had yet to enter his old bedroom, he summoned the courage to ascend the stairs, knowing the comfort of his mother's bed awaited him. In the upstairs hallway, he gently shut the door of his bedroom and headed to the warm embrace of his mother's room.

Like Owen, Gabe had an eleven o'clock appointment that morning that he didn't want to miss. One of his favorite guilty pleasures was to crawl into his mother's bed and watch *If Tomorrow Never Comes* under her sheets. Every sick day in high school and at least once every visit home, watching the show as it broadcast in "real world time" was one of his favorite activities and the closest he got to connecting his bifurcated identities.

Gabe clicked the remote, slipped out of his shoes, and slid between the sheets. He had missed the pre-credits sequence. The *If Tomorrow Never Comes* theme song had just started. Gabe's secret pleasure was watching the soap he helped create with Harmony Hills storylines observed from their origin in Concord Valley. The event was clandestine and delicious.

Gabe had missed the cold open. He was always curious as to what was being broadcast. Today's show had been shot a few weeks prior, due to a holiday, actor contracts, and union rules. The theme song was beginning its fade-out as his pen name, George Sample, Head Writer, scrolled across the screen. When the director's name faded in, he knew exactly which episode he was watching. They had tried to give one of the younger actresses a twin storyline in hopes of getting her a Daytime Emmy nomination. But the actress wasn't up to the task. One of the twins was from Texas, and the actress kept confusing a Texas accent with Brooklynese. Her performance was train-wreck bad. The decision was inevitably made to write the Texas twin off the show. This was the episode where the Texas twin leaves in search of their birth mother, an adoptee storyline Gabe had borrowed from the prior mayor of Concord Valley. In three episodes, it would be reported the Texas twin met with a grisly end, killed by an errant bullet in a drug deal gone bad.

Gabe relaxed into one of his mother's pillows to wait for the two minutes' worth of commercials to finish. Her scent lingered on her pillows, reminding him of how comfortable it felt to be around his mother. Now that she was gone, her pillow smell was the last remaining evidence she had ever existed. *How long did scent remain and how could I preserve it?* He hugged one of her pillows closely as a grief wave crested and hit his shore. He dried his eyes on the pillowcase and inventoried his morning: liens and potential financial ruin, the return of yummy Owen and his unrequited crush.

He regretted keeping everything a secret from Jessica, but he wasn't ready for her snarky ripostes.

Today's to-do list was endless. He had yet to face Arthur and the ashes. He needed to be home in time to sign for his weekend's pages by six. And when was he going to write the killer memorial service speech for tomorrow? He grabbed the copy of *Death for Dummies*, but he didn't have the bandwidth for timelines and to-do lists. He put the book away.

Gabe got out his phone to check his hookup app. *I might need a few distractions to get through the next few days.* The Texas twin's cringy accent and campy acting distracted Gabe. He put away his phone and forgot about launching his favorite app. Getting lost in the foibles of Harmony Hills was enough to tamp down his grief and dispel his feelings for Owen. The wish he had made on his eyelash would have to wait. For now.

*

Later that afternoon, Gabe tapped the bell in front of the glass window at the crematorium on the other side of town, an address he got from the morgue associate.

"What are you doing here?" asked Gabe when the same associate from the morgue appeared behind the glass.

"I volunteer here so I can be close to my honey," said the familiar face. "He works in cremation."

"Didn't you say cremation work was done by prisoners?"

"Prisoners make the best boyfriends. The conjugals are quick and intense, they're not underfoot all the time, and they appreciate a real woman," she said with authority.

"Sounds much more reliable than a hookup app."

"Don't knock it till you've tried it. How are you going to be paying for this?" she asked.

Gabe handed her his paperwork and a bank card, which she processed with a swipe.

"Honey!" she yelled to the back, "I need the ashes of Amelia Hartman. You need any help finding them?"

A handsome, yet rugged man in an orange jumpsuit appeared behind the woman. "I always need your help, darling." Gabe hastily grabbed and hid his credit card.

"Give us a sec," said the woman with a twinkle in her eye, disappearing behind a curtain with the man in the orange jumpsuit.

It took them longer than Gabe expected, but eventually the woman re-appeared, a bit flushed, with his mother's ashes. Her lipstick was slightly smeared. Gabe was more focused on the black rectangular box in her hand. She unlocked the glass window and slid the box to Gabe.

Gabe picked up the box of ashes. "It's heavy."

"People always say that. She came in at six pounds and change. You want her accessories?"

The woman handed him a sealed baggie with small fragments of gold and silver.

"Some people try to pawn them, but there's a limited market for gold and silver filings. There is, however, a whole cottage industry around making jewelry with this stuff. No one's contacted you yet?"

"Not that I know of."

"Wait until the obit gets published. That's when the death circus comes to town. Heads-up about the obit: newspapers will milk you for every penny. They charge you by the word. I suggest using one small local paper and keeping the obit short and sweet."

"Thanks for the heads-up." If he had checked *Death for Dummies*, he would have already added "draft obituary" to today's to-do list. "What happens if I don't publish an obituary?"

"There's no law that says you have to, but some long-lost relative always makes a stink if you don't. Like it's some birthright. You end up doing it. I mean, she is your mother, right? Dude! Write her an obit, for God's sake. Or pay someone to do it for you. There must be templates online."

"I need some help back here!" said the man in the orange jumpsuit, his head reappearing through the curtain.

Something wasn't right about the label. "Excuse me," said Gabe pointing to the label. "Why does the label say 'Monka' on my mother's box of ashes? Her name was Amelia Hartman. You sure this is my mother?"

"Of course, it's her!" said the man in the orange jumpsuit as he returned to the office, his volume and tone frightening Gabe. Gabe was curious to know what crime the man had committed and what reentry employment program he worked under.

The woman sensed Gabe's fears. "It's all good, boys. Monka was this dog who was supposed to die of stomach cancer and get cremated this week. Monka's owner prepaid for everything, and we had already made a box for Monka. But Monka was misdiagnosed and survived. He suffered from indigestion, not stomach cancer."

"I had already labeled it," said the man in the orange jumpsuit, getting grounded and settling down. "But Monka lives."

Gabe snickered at the absurdity.

"What are you laughing at?" asked the man in the orange jumpsuit, his anger resurfacing.

"Calm down, sweetie," said the woman.

"I'm sorry," said Gabe. "Monka is a funny word. Words with Ks are funny."

"You forgot to change the label, honey," said the woman.

"Sorry," said the man in the orange jumpsuit. Gabe was relieved everyone was now smiling.

"You 100 percent sure this is my mother?" asked Gabe.

"No dog named Monka is that heavy," said the man in the orange jumpsuit. "That's human ashes all right. A six-pounder."

"You gotta trust, babe," said the woman to Gabe. "You gotta trust."

Gabe set the box of his mother's ashes in the passenger seat and protected it with a seat belt. Treating her ashes like they were an animate object was as silly as his new relationship to Chairvana, but he was learning death made him do the inexplicable.

Even though having ashes next to him in the car was borderline creepy, he opened the lid of the black box. The external box was made of thick cardboard; inside, the ashes were contained in a strong plastic bag. Everything was gray with shards and splinters of bones mixed with the ashes. He was tempted to open the bag and touch them, but he didn't like the idea of having mother residue on his fingertips. The ashes experience proved somewhat disturbing. He would drop them off at the bookstore where they could live for the night.

His phone buzzed with a new text from an 838 area code he didn't recognize.

Unknown: *Progress at probate.*

Then another text buzzed.

Unknown: *Not looking like a total disaster. You're still in it.*

Gabe assumed it was from Owen and tread lightly.

He responded to the message with a thumbs-up and a thanks that was auto-replaced by a prayer hands emoji, which he sent anyway.

Owen: *Banana nut bread—wise move.*

Gabe: *You must have a good consultant.*

Owen: **smiley face emoji* #worldclass.*

Gabe didn't mind texting with Owen. He would keep their correspondence light, polite, and professional. His mind drifted. *Owen would make a great boyfriend. Stop! Friends. We're just going to be friends.*

"Who's Monka?" asked Arthur when Gabe handed him the big black box of ashes at the Quinn & Ink.

"Long story. It's Mom. Trust me."

"We can't have Monka stealing focus from dear Amelia." Arthur conveniently found a new label and covered up "Monka," then wrote, "The Divine Amelia Hartman" in perfect cursive.

"She would have liked that," said Gabe, grateful for Arthur's attention to detail. "What can I do to help with the memorial?"

"How's your eulogy coming along?"

"Good. I'll finish it up tonight." The facile liar was always waiting in the wings. Gabe hadn't started the eulogy. He was banking on his well-honed skill of writing under pressure, thanks to the soap. "I also need to start drafting her obituary."

"I hope you aren't insulted by this, but—" Arthur handed Gabe a letter envelope with a couple of folded pieces of paper. "Some of her friends took the liberty of writing a first draft of her obituary."

Gabe's text message buzzed, but he ignored it.

"Do you need to get that?" asked Arthur.

"Later."

"Izzy, our editor at the local paper, was fluent in obit jargon and phrasing, and I knew all your mother's latest volunteer roles. We took a stab at a draft this morning. Why don't you look it over and add what we left out. Izzy will be at the memorial. You can return it to her at that time. She'll run the obituary gratis."

"Arthur, you are a lifesaver. I feel like I should be helping more."

"Everything has fallen into place. The phone tree took care of letting people know the when and where of the memorial service. Let me show you the program. You can scan for typos and whatnot."

Arthur handed Gabe a prototype of the program. Gabe was charmed by its quaint simplicity. A flattering xeroxed ten-year-old photo of his mother adorned the front. One fold to open. Nothing too fancy. He scanned the order of speakers, his name was a third of the way through. He approved: less pressure to open or close. The selected songs were perfect, all songs his mother loved and had sung to him as a boy.

"Who chose the music?" asked Gabe.

"Amelia, I suppose," said Arthur.

"She would love this. Looks good, Arthur." Gabe handed the program back. "I need to ask a favor. Could you please keep the ashes here tonight?"

"A bit much for you, huh?"

Gabe nodded.

"I can keep them here for the night. But you'll want them after the service to broadcast them."

"Broadcast?" asked a puzzled Gabe.

"That's what they call spreading the ashes when they do it at sea."

"Do you think she wanted to be broadcast out to sea?"

"Amelia wanted to stay right here in Concord Valley among friends. She couldn't imagine her ashes being anywhere else. She told everyone she wanted her ashes placed in her flower garden by the aspen and live forever near the home she loved."

Gabe didn't have the heart to tell Arthur, had his mother lived, she would have lost her beloved home.

"Looks like you have everything taken care of," said Gabe.

"There is something else. Come sit with me for a second."

Arthur led Gabe over to the cafe section of the bookstore and found an empty table where they could have a private conversation.

Another text message buzzed Gabe's phone.

"You sure you don't need to get that?" asked Arthur.

"I'm with you right now. What can I do for you?"

"When your mother and I were dating," Arthur said, getting out his phone, "we promised each other, if the other person died first, we would start dating as soon as we could. Like today."

"Isn't it a little too soon...?"

"Spoken with the luxury of youth. When you don't have too much time left, 'you want to get back on the horse ASAP.' I'm quoting your mother."

"I can hear her saying that."

"Here's the problem: I've never dated, in the traditional sense. And I hear these days you need one of those apps to meet ladies. I found one I hear is friendly to older fellows, but I need you to teach me how to set it up. I want to get where I only have to swipe right. Or is it left? I get confused."

Gabe chuckled. "You want me to help set up your dating app?"

"I already downloaded it. I need help with my profile."

"It would be an honor." Arthur handed him the phone. "That's...an interesting photo." Arthur had chosen an image one might find on a widower's Christmas card. Arthur is wearing a questionable Christmas sweater and standing by the hearth.

"All I could find. I need to come up with a good profile name."

"And a clever description," said Gabe, comparing Arthur's site to his hookup site: not much difference. Gabe started typing.

"What are you...?" asked Arthur.

"How about this for your profile name: 'The Silver Fox'?"

"I like that."

"Matches your pic. And your description reads, 'There may be snow on the roof, but there's still a fire in the furnace.'"

"You've done this before."

"Maybe. Next, the app has several prompts, all optional, but they help narrow your profile down. First, you're 100 percent straight, right?"

"Oh, yes. I wouldn't know much about all the new combinations."

"Next: tribe?" Gabe could see Arthur was perplexed. "What type of woman are you looking for?"

"A nice, older gal who hasn't declined too much. Someone to mitigate the loneliness."

"Not one of the choices. But you're technically a Daddy."

"More a Granddaddy."

"Here's the one." Gabe clicked a box. "Mature. Next, UC?"

"I did not attend the University of California, although I would have enjoyed Berkeley in the 1960s."

"Different. UC... Um... It's about your private parts, Arthur. Are you circumcised? Cut or uncut?"

"Of course, I'm circumcised. How unsanitary!"

"Let's not go there."

"Why do they need to know that? Do women today consider the tip of the penis attractive from an aesthetic point of view? Or is it covert antisemitism?"

"It's generational. Moving on. DDF?"

"So many new terms."

"Oh, brave new world. Are you drug-free, Arthur?"

"I've taken a statin for cholesterol for some time now. That's all."

"A 'no' to drugs. When were you last tested for any STIs?"

Arthur looked confused.

"Sexually transmitted infections?"

"Oh. Hmm. After a weekend pass when I was stationed in Korea in '54, we once had a syphilis scare, but no one had it. The next platoon over—they were the rascals."

"N/A," wrote Gabe. "I don't think we need to go on with these questions. But I do think you look better right now than the photo you chose. Can I take a new picture?"

"Do you need me to show you how..."

"I got it," said Gabe, already looking through the phone's camera lens. "Look natural." Gabe was already clicking shots of Arthur as he spoke. "Do you have any favorite Amelia stories to share with me?" Gabe continued to take pics of Arthur. Gabe wanted Arthur to tell him a story about his mother to get him to loosen up.

"So many. Your mother... She used to love to come into the bookshop, take a classic off the shelf, and sit for hours, reading. I don't know how she did it. I used to flatter myself and think she was here to be near me. When I asked her what she was up to, she said she didn't think she'd read enough books in life—too busy working and raising a kid—and she needed to catch up."

"That sounds like my mother," said Gabe. "All done." Gabe handed the phone to Arthur with a fabulous new profile picture already in place.

"Who's that handsome devil?" asked Arthur.

Arthur's phone vibrated with a *drrroot*.

"Whoever he is, he's got some rizz. That's what the kids are calling *allure* these days. And a potential lady friend already. You know how to use the chat feature?"

"Like texting?"

"Exactly. Watch out for scammers. Make Amelia proud."

"What do you think of this one?" Arthur held up his phone to show Gabe a picture of a slightly overweight woman in an unflattering one-piece at the beach.

"She responded too promptly, which means she was lurking, which means she's lonely."

"Aren't we all?"

"Not *that* lonely. Red flag: that pic is too revealing in all the wrong ways. You can chat with her for practice, but you want to play the field before any coffee dates."

"Should I invite her to the memorial service?"

"Absolutely not. And if anyone asks you if you're *looking*—"

"Of course, I'm looking."

"Not that kind of looking. Looking means looking for quick sex."

"I would never. What kind of person—?" asked Arthur with a sweet touch of innocence.

"You'd be surprised." Gabe scared himself at the glib, sneaky sleaze of his response to Arthur's question.

Arthur's phone vibrated with another *drrroot*.

"That should keep you busy," said Gabe. "I'll see you tomorrow. Call me if I can do anything. And thanks for keeping the ashes."

Arthur didn't respond. He was fully engaged with his two new lady friends.

"Arthur?"

"Huh?"

"Thank you for everything."

"No. Thank *you*."

Outside the Quinn & Ink, Gabe checked his texts. Two from Owen.

Owen: Why basil and marigolds with heirlooms?

Owen: Did you look up the source of "I'm not crying, you're crying" yet?

Gabe: Driving. When I get home.

Owen: Stop texting and driving. It's against the law.

Gabe: I know a fancy lawyer.

Owen: A fancy, humble lawyer.

Gabe typed, "*And good-looking*," but he deleted it. He wanted to practice restraint and decency. Instead, Gabe put an emphatic heart on Owen's last text, an appropriate button to their exchange.

When he got home, he greeted the lounger, "Honey, I'm home!" Then he headed to the kitchen to see what he could round up for dinner. His mother had been the queen of leftovers, and he found several stacks of plastic containers in the refrigerator. As long as the leftovers passed the smell test and showed no visible signs of mold, he figured they were safe for consumption.

His phone buzzed while he was gathering his supper. He put Erin on speaker.

"Did you get my revisions?" asked Gabe.

"You followed my directions beautifully."

Gabe opened a container of marinated string bean salad and ate it—nice and vinegary, the way his mother liked them. "So many typos. Since when is the character called Laura Lee 'Laurel Leaf'?"

"Revenge for paraphrasing lines?"

"They all paraphrase. I was watching today from the house. I barely recognized the scenes I wrote."

Gabe opened a container with a piece of meatloaf. He was famished and didn't bother to warm it up.

"Otherwise, how was it?" asked Erin.

"Good riddance Texas twin... Did we get new numbers today?"

"You want the good news or the bad news?"

"Better get the bad." Gabe got a spoon and dug into a container of potato salad, his mother's recipe with egg, relish, and mustard.

"What are you eating?" asked Erin.

"The last of my mother's leftovers. It's too surreal. How are the numbers?" Gabe asked, finishing the potato salad.

"We had a slight dip."

"Not good."

"I delivered them to the Douglasses while one of the suits was visiting. Ring and run."

"That couldn't have been good. What was he visiting about?"

"I don't have the details. I overheard something like 'big changes might be coming.' And they weren't about to share them with an underling like me."

"Could be about the Oliver Armstrong storyline."

"The Douglasses could be given their skates soon," said Erin. "Hence, the drinking."

"They drink during the good times too. Best not project too much." Gabe opened a container of fried rice, gave it a whiff, made a face, and threw it in the trash.

"When can we expect you back?" asked Erin.

"The memorial is tomorrow, but I still have a lot of loose ends. And there's a hiccup with the house and some legal stuff. I'm planning to be in the office midweek next week at the latest. You said you had some good news." Gabe returned the leftover containers to the refrigerator.

"The Douglasses love the new sustainable farm rom-com storyline."

"Thank God!" Gabe didn't have any other ideas if they had hated it.

"Did tonight's overnight package arrive yet?" asked Erin. A loud knock at the door punctuated the sentence.

"How do you do that?" asked Gabe on the way to the front door.

"I have innate tracking instincts. Is it the same angry lesbian?" asked Erin as he opened the door to the same angry lesbian.

"Did she call me an angry lesbian?" asked the same express delivery woman from the night before, handing him the envelope and an electronic signature device.

"Did I forget to tell you? You're on speaker," said Gabe as he signed.

"Oopsie," said Erin.

"I'd rather be known as your favorite delivery gal," said the former angry lesbian.

"Done."

Gabe closed the door gently behind her.

"Is the angry lesbian gone?" asked Erin.

"Don't mess with my favorite delivery gal slash angry lesbian," said Gabe.

"I love her and I love that you both get each other. New subject line—colon—good news. The Douglasses love the sustainable farm rom-com storyline, and they want to see a first draft of week one scenes on Monday morning, written by you, no pesky staff writers. That means you have a busy weekend ahead. Can you handle it?"

"I'll have to." Gabe sat at the dining room table and ripped open the envelope. His workload was piling up. "I may ask you to handle all the other shooting revisions. I need to focus on Oliver Armstrong."

"At your service. The beauty part is they don't need anything before Monday. That gives you a whole weekend. Let's keep sharing documents, and I'll take care of the Douglasses' obsession with hard copies."

"Perfect. I'm playing with the idea Oliver is also a part-time lawyer, and he puts out his shingle for some cash flow. And to be of service."

"Sounds right. Our fans would want to know how he makes money while his crops are growing. A lawyer who is also a gentleman farmer could be sexy in a rom-comy way."

"He is. I mean, he will be. I better get started on it."

Gabe was approaching the point of overwhelm: probate and tax issues, a eulogy, fresh new pages, revising old pages. Was he forgetting something?

He was still bothered he hadn't ventured into his old bedroom. Something always stopped him. He had no clarity around it, and he was exhausted. He was entitled to a reward.

Gabe grabbed his phone and went directly to the app store. He typed the first three letters in search of his favorite hookup app; it popped up, and he downloaded it. He entered his ID and password and got ready for some action to distract him from his overwhelm.

He had never hooked up with a guy in Concord Valley. His hometown had always been a sexless place to him. When he came home for visits, he was always a well-behaved, asexual virgin boy. But that was when his mother was alive. Now that he was alone in his childhood home, he was overcome with guilt, downloading his go-to sex app. But he was fiercely lonely and twice as horny. Time to reinvent his hometown. He owed himself the chance to discover the other horny gay men in town.

"What kind of person does that?" Arthur's question echoed in his head as a challenge. *"You'd be surprised."*

Gabe's guilt got the best of him. He put his phone aside and straightened up the dining room table.

He then picked up the pile of recipe cards.

The top card was a recipe for brownies. The handwriting was in cursive and not his mother's. The card was old-fashioned with an illustration of a potbellied stove and an adorable kitten at the foot of the stove. "From the kitchen of Mabel Quinn." Mabel must have been Arthur's first wife. Had his mother known her? Had they exchanged recipes? Had Mabel insisted Arthur date immediately after she had died? Arthur recognized this brownie recipe as one of his favorites, clearly one of Gabe's mother's most referenced cards, stained in places with butter and chocolate smudges.

Gabe's phone buzzed from the table. "Hey, Jessica."

"Where's my pitch?"

"I thought I had until after the memorial service," he said, adding another item to the list of overwhelming activities.

"I was kidding. How are you holding up?"

"Hanging in there," said Gabe, exhausted.

"Loved the lawyer's house."

"Gorgeous. And the house wasn't bad looking either."

"*Ba-dum-bum.* Did your married hot loser make a reappearance?"

"I set a boundary and I intend to keep it," said Gabe.

"Please! All bets are off when the gods of rom-coms are at work. If your internalized self-loathing would keep it down to a dull roar, you might be able to tune into the destiny they have in store for you. If he reappears, take that as a sign."

Gabe did not intend to tell Jessica how prophetic her words were. He was banking on the assumption she would never have the opportunity to meet Owen.

"Think about it." she went on. "If you hadn't rejected the hot loser, you might have had a convenient FWB-NSA—whatever other letters you call it."

"DL Discreet?"

"Thank you," said Jessica. "All I want for you is something classy to help you get through the grief. You deserve someone nice. Who cares if he's married? If you're never going to see him after this visit...?"

"This conversation is exhausting. Everything is exhausting. Especially all this death business," said Gabe in full surrender.

"You don't have to do everything at once," said Jessica. "I hope you haven't cleaned out her house."

"I wasn't planning on it," said Gabe. He needed to keep on reading *Death for Dummies,* which grounded and guided him.

"Not this trip, huh?"

"Honestly, I don't have the bandwidth."

"Wait until everything is settled." Gabe was grateful to have Jessica in his life.

"You think I could pay someone to take care of it?" he asked.

"Estate sale people usually throw everything out that doesn't sell."

"I want to save some of her belongings—for her legacy."

"Get ready for all the emotions that come up as you go through stuff," said Jessica. "I suggest throwing out as much as you can."

"This is surprisingly hard." Gabe exhaled. "I'm sitting here in the dining room with some of her recipes. There's a ton of information in them. I've never heard of some of the ingredients. Can you even get oleo-margarine anymore?"

"I think oleo-margarine is now just called margarine," said Jessica.

"Correct. I'm poking around online. It had to be rebranded when there were issues with high levels of trans fats. There are all these nuanced details about America and cuisine and communities of women in these cards. I can't throw them out."

"Do me a favor," said Jessica in business mode. "Find a chunk of time this weekend, twenty minutes, and journal about her recipe cards. Sketch out some ideas. See if you have something to say. I hate to jinx it, but there might be some narrative hidden in those cards."

"Right after I write a eulogy," said Gabe.

"Eulogies are easy."

"Please don't suggest I write from the heart."

"I was going to suggest starting with an AI app, but whatever."

"Isn't that cheating?" said Gabe, straightening the recipe card file.

"It's your mom; of course, write it from your heart. Where is the memorial going to take place?"

"Her boyfriend's bookstore. He's a sweet old geezer."

"The eulogy will be easy. Start with a few sentences about how much you love her—it's a bookstore, right?—compare her to a few of your favorite heroines in literature and conclude with how much you'll miss her. You'll slay."

"You're good."

"Or use that as a generative prompt on the app."

Gabe's phone buzzed. "Listen, I have a call coming in. It could be about the memorial service. I better take it."

"Journal, baby, journal. Call me this weekend if you want to spitball."

Gabe clicked to the new call. "This is Gabe."

"Hello, friend."

"Who is this?" asked Gabe politely.

"Owen, your fancy, humble lawyer. Boy calls boy. What are you wearing?"

"Shut up." Gabe giggled. "I didn't know we were phone friends."

"You implied there might be a call. In your text? I'm doing a follow-up. Is it okay that I called?"

"I guess. Let's see how it goes before we become official phone friends though."

"On probation. I like a challenge. I called because I have two legit questions and a third not so legit."

"I'm intrigued."

"First, why plant marigolds and basil with tomatoes? You weren't pranking the newbie, were you?"

"No. This is genuine farming." Gabe headed to the living room and made a face at Chairvana before plopping onto the sofa. "They say the basil improves the taste, but that's projection."

"Basil improves everything," said Owen.

"Exactly. The marigolds give off a scent that deters aphids and hornworms but attracts pollinators. You won't need pesticides. But the real scientific reason: the basil and marigolds will take on any root diseases before they can get at your tomatoes. Basically, they protect the tomato's root system. I'm a little rusty with all the science, but Mrs. Henderson will know more."

"You know a lot about plants," said an impressed Owen.

"I'm a country boy," said Gabe. "It's in my blood. Next question?"

"I'm not crying, you're crying."

"You are a dog with a bone."

"I got your bone, baby."

"Cut that out," said Gabe, but he loved being flirted with.

"I had a hunch you would drag your feet. So I took the liberty to—"

"Of course, you did. Are you on Wikipedia?"

"Never. 'DigitalCultures.com' is my citation. And yes. You were correct. In the 2004 film *Starsky and Hutch,* the line was said by Ben Stiller to Owen Wilson."

"And not Charles Dickens," said Gabe, smug and righteous.

"I'm sending you a couple of related memes."

Gabe's text message buzzed with several gifs and memes. "Oh my god, there's a whole crying-not-crying subculture out there. Well, I'm glad we settled that. And how big of you to admit defeat."

"I'm not done," said Owen. "'DigitalCultures.com' goes on to say, and I quote, 'but the true origin looks to be the 1859 Dickens novel, *A Tale of Two Cities,* in which Miss Pross says, 'I'm not crying, you are.' There. I'm glad that's settled."

Gabe paused for a moment before he added one last thought, "That's not exactly the quote verbatim."

"You won't even give me a minor victory? C'mon! Let me surprise you once in a while."

"Oh, you're full of surprises."

"You too. More to come, I hope."

"I'm impressed you were correct about Dickens. I'll give you that, Owen."

"Oh, I like it when you say my name. I get goose pimples."

Gabe loved the way Owen flirted with him, but he needed to stand his ground.

Neither spoke for a full three seconds.

"Our first awkward pause," said Gabe. "This phone friend

experiment might be a failure.”

“Oh, well. How was the rest of your day?” asked Owen.

“Busy. Can I share something with you?”

“Please.”

“It feels strange and uncomfortable being in the family house without my mother.”

“The house you’re creating a trust for?”

“The very one. It’s my second day here, and I still haven't slept in my bed in my old room.”

“Have you hung out in your bedroom at all?” asked Owen.

“Barely. It’s weird being here without her.”

“It may be related to your new adult orphan status.”

“Like a syndrome?”

“Too fancy. A phenomenon maybe. I don't have any experience in this area.”

“Every detail is loaded and heavy right now,” said Gabe. “Can we change the subject?”

“Of course.”

“I’m scared to ask, but what was your third less-than-legit question?”

“Oh. Would you mind if I attend your mother’s memorial tomorrow?”

“Why would I mind?” asked Gabe. “Sure. Please come. But why do you want to be there?”

“I want to hear your eulogy,” said Owen. “You said you wanted to be a writer. I want to be supportive.”

“Then you better let me get off the phone, or it will never get written.”

“Wait! Before you hang up. Did we redeem ourselves? Aside from the one awkward pause. Any chance we can officially become phone friends?”

“Sure. You give good phone.”

“No complaints. Do you see this as a forty-slash-sixty phone-to-text relationship?”

"I was thinking more twenty-slash-eighty. To start." Gabe could feel himself smiling. "I enjoy you, Owen. More goose pimples?"

"You know it. Gabe. I enjoy you too." Owen's hushed voice was like a soft caress against Gabe's ear. Sweet comfort for his exhaustion.

Gabe's phone announced a *drrroot*, and his joy instantly jolted to shame.

"What was that?" asked Owen.

"A text, work-related," he lied. Gabe was embarrassed Owen had discovered him using the app. He felt worse about lying, especially since their friendship had been developing authentically. "Better start that eulogy. See you tomorrow."

Gabe hung up before Owen could say goodbye or the next *drrroot* could interrupt them.

Why did he care so much what Owen thought of him? They weren't in a relationship. *The guy has a husband... He never mentioned him. Nothing was done wrong.* Image maintenance was always elusive once Gabe got to know someone. *Another reason to avoid intimacy*, Gabe lied to himself. *Why do I feel guilty? Shake it off, dude.*

"So much for decency and restraint," he whispered to himself before responding to the app.

Chapter Four

The next morning, Gabe woke up, once more on the sofa.

"Good morning," he said to Chairvana before making his way to the kitchen for his new morning coffee ritual. The tension of an oppressive to-do list returned, but he was relieved to find a legal pad with the eulogy he drafted the night before. He went over his speech while the coffee brewed. *Not bad.* He proofed and tweaked it one more time. *I hope the tone is appropriate for the event. Too late for changes now.*

Under the speech, he found some notes: *meet-cute, spilled lattes, accidental kiss, heirloom tomatoes, basil and marigolds, need a lawyer, texts and phone buddies.* Gabe structured the Oliver Armstrong scenes around the major events in his relationship with Owen. *Write what you know.*

A faint *drrroot* sent him searching for his phone.

He had missed a few early morning texts. One from Owen asking about the time of the service. Gabe checked his watch: 10:30 a.m. He still had a few hours to kill.

Another *drrroot* and he went to the app where several blank profiles had opened their chats with a cliched "Hey." One caught his eye. It opened with a "Howdy," a more authentic introduction, considering where he was. *A local hookup might be a good way to pass the time before the memorial. Find someone age-appropriate, 28-32, somewhat in shape—under 200 pounds and not "stocky."*

Rural areas were populated by fearful gay men, probably dating or married to a woman, terrified their secret double life would be exposed. Lots of discreet, down-low, NSA descriptions attached to pictureless profiles. Gabe was getting turned on by all the anonymity: the less committed, the better.

> **Gud2Go**: *Howdy2U2*
>
> **BlankProfile**: *Looking?*
>
> **Gud2Go**: *Yep U?*
>
> **BlankProfile**: *rn?*
>
> **Gud2Go**: *I have to shower.*

Gabe considered the logistics of location. He could not imagine hosting an anonymous hookup in his mother's house. The only stranger he could envision in this house would be a realtor.

> **Gud2GO**: *You host?*
>
> **BlankProfile**: *yep rare*
>
> **Gud2GO**: *wya*
>
> **BlankProfile**: *discreet*
>
> **Gud2GO**: *same wya*

BlankProfile sent the address and a map. According to the directions, he lived in a cabin down a dirt road. *This hookup could either be an interesting rural adventure or my last day on earth.*

BlankProfile: *What are you into*

Gabe skillfully negotiated a menu of generic options no dude could resist. His goals: play safe and get his rocks off. Writing everything out horned Gabe even more.

Gud2Go: *b there in 20*

Gabe gulped the last of his coffee, showered like a speed freak, threw on some clothes that would be easy to take off, grabbed his suit to change into before the memorial, and headed out to meet *BlankProfile*.

Gabe almost left the eulogy behind. He ran back into the house for the legal pad. He tucked the envelope with the obituary behind the last page of the legal pad and followed the map *BlankProfile* had sent him.

On a scale of Dull-to-Sexy, the guy was a solid six. He didn't live on a dirt road, but in a respectable model home in what might someday be a respectable middle-class subdivision, if the meth-heads didn't get there first.

The guy said his name was Joey Dakota, but Gabe didn't believe him. Joey Dakota was a name worthy of a porn star. Gabe told Joey Dakota his name was Austin DeFranco, the name of an actual porn star who had once auditioned unsuccessfully for *If Tomorrow Never Comes*. After Joey and Austin negotiated a morning of not-too-awkward sex, they got down to business. Joey smelled slightly of body odor, which gained in strength the longer they went at it. Gabe found Joey's sour scent strangely alluring in a punishing way. He had a feeling Joey had never hooked up with a dude before. He exuded the nervous tentative-ness of inexperience. At one point, Joey confessed his wife was out of town on a church trip. (He hadn't bothered to take off his wedding ring.) Gabe's sadness and respect for Joey grew, for he would have been living a similar life had he stayed in Concord Valley. They ended up playing everything safe, for the wife's sake. Gabe was gentle and kind and atten-tive, which encouraged Joey to gain confidence (and BO) as the sex built to its inevitable conclusion. Joey, the consummate host, offered Gabe a shower, which he took. He didn't want to carry the smell of Joey's sweat and sex into his mother's memorial service. After the shower, he went to his car and changed into his memorial clothes.

"Could I bum a ride to town?" asked Joey. Gabe's watch read 11:30. He tried to think of a reason why not, but couldn't.

"Sure. You ready?" asked Gabe.

"We're outta here." In the dirt driveway, Joey took in Gabe's car. "Nice wheels."

"It's a rental."

The ride to town was the most awkward part of their morning. Gabe asked Joey to find a good radio station to cut through the silence. Joey scanned the AM stations. Bible thumpers and conservative talk shows reigned.

"Try FM," said Gabe. "Something basic." Joey found a classic rock station. *That'll do.* They rode to town listening to Led Zeppelin's "Whole Lotta Love."

"You okay?" Gabe asked.

"Uh-huh," said Joey.

"My name's not Austin," said Gabe. "I sometimes use a fake name until I trust a guy. I'm Gabe."

"K..."

Joey didn't add any more to the conversation after that. Pink Floyd's "Comfortably Numb" played them the rest of the way to the town square where several cars and trucks were parked around the Quinn & Ink. A smattering of people were chatting in front of the bookstore; no one Gabe recognized.

"Where can I drop you?" asked Gabe.

"McFarland's," said Joey, pointing to the dive bar in the next block. Gabe had never been inside McFarland's, the seediest place in town. His mother used to say nothing good ever came out of or went into McFarland's.

"A little early to start drinking," said Gabe.

"No such thing."

"Happy hour somewhere?"

Gabe parked between McFarland's and the Quinn & Ink. Joey got out without a thank-you. Neither pretended a second hookup would be in their future.

"See ya," said Gabe, but Joey had already disappeared into McFarland's.

"Who was that?"

Gabe turned around to find Owen faking a smile. Gabe was not ready to face him, not like this.

"Some guy who needed a ride." Owen cocked his head but said nothing. "Are you judging me?"

"No. You trying to see how low you could punch?"

"You *are* judging me."

Owen shrugged, pretending not to care. "How was he?"

"None of your business."

"I personally think hookups can be very revealing but, ultimately, counterproductive. The shadow-self personified. I can think of several better ways to meet people."

"I don't recall asking for unsolicited advice," said Gabe. He didn't like how that came out.

"Was he the 'work-related' text from last night at the end of our call?"

"Owen. Drop it. This is not what we do."

"Sorry."

"Oh, my God," said Gabe. "Are you jealous?"

"I'm not jealous. Of course, I'm jealous! I assume he's not married," said Owen.

Had Owen seen Joey's wedding ring? Oh my God! I slept with a married man! I don't do that. In Gabe's mind, having sex with a closeted guy married to a woman wasn't the same as sleeping with a gay man in an open relationship. Gabe rationalized his morning with Joey as an act of charity. Joey was clearly working through something, and who better to help than a kind man like Gabe? Besides, Gabe wasn't going to hook up with Joey a second time. From what he could tell, Joey was more likely curious than gay. *Why am I in the middle of a fantasy argument with Owen in my head when he's standing right in front of me?*

"I don't sleep with married men," Gabe lied. "I have a question for you." Gabe grabbed the legal pad with his eulogy and locked the car. "How come you never talk about your husband around me?"

"Kevin? There. What do you want to know about *Kevin*? You need to talk about Kevin?"

Gabe appreciated the movie reference. "Whatever you want to tell me. Does Kevin know about me?"

"I told him all about you. Not about the legal details—attorney-client privilege and all that—but about your farming advice. He agrees with you. I need to put down my pride and be more humble with local people."

"Common sense."

"Kevin has a lot of common sense. Like you. They say you're attracted to your opposite." Gabe appreciated and resented him for being open about everything, especially his attraction. They headed toward the bookstore. "What else? Kevin is successful. He's a consultant. An expert in his field. He specializes in fundraising and development reorganization for multimillion dollar nonprofits."

"Fancy," said Gabe. He had no idea what Kevin did, but it was definitely a more grown-up job than writing imaginary stories about a fake town in a soap opera.

"Maybe you'll get to meet him."

"Did you tell him about our kiss?" asked Gabe.

Owen paused. "No."

Gabe couldn't tell if Owen was telling the truth.

"I figured, since we're not going to be a real couple, and he's on a need-to-know basis in an open relationship... Did you want me to?" Owen was making more hand gestures than usual. "No. I didn't tell him."

Gabe had never seen Owen this flustered. He believed him.

"We can change the subject if you want," said Gabe.

"Are you ready for your speech?" asked Owen. They were standing outside the bookstore about to head in.

"I better be. Thanks for coming." Gabe gave Owen a hug which he held for a second. "Be a true friend. Tell me if I still smell like cheap sex."

Owen sniffed him discreetly, whispering in his ear, "No, you smell like cheap soap."

"As long as you can't smell my fear and low self-esteem," Gabe whispered back.

"You're going to be great. Knock 'em dead, tiger!"

His phone went *drrroot*.

With the awkward hookup sound, Owen released them from the hug. "You're a hot commodity. Already lining one up for after the memorial service?"

"Probably the last guy telling me how amazing I was," said Gabe.

"Out of respect to your mother, you might want to silence your phone for the service."

Gabe flipped off the sound as Owen opened the door and guided them both into the bookstore.

The Quinn & Ink had been transformed into a lovely memorial chapel. The shelves around the cafe were masked in black fabric. Chairs were arranged in gentle angles that led the eye to a modest podium in front of an ersatz altar. Flowers surrounded the box of ashes beside a lovely blown-up photo of Amelia Hartman. This picture was taken more than a few years ago when she still had the sparkle of youth in her eyes. The cafe tables had been pushed aside for grazing nibbles, sweets on one side, savory on the other, beverages in the middle.

"Can I get you something to drink?" asked Owen.

"Water would be great," said Gabe.

Owen made his way to the beverage table, leaving Gabe to take in the crowd.

The Quinn & Ink was overflowing with people. Gabe recognized only a few by name. Andy from the dump was chatting with Charlize, still on her scooter and successfully navigating the crowded shop. Gabe was grateful they hadn't seen him as he wasn't ready to expend the energy it took to engage them.

"Are you ready for your moment?" asked Arthur, coming up behind him.

"Ready as I'll ever be."

"We changed the order of the service. You're going closer to the end."

"Fine by me," said Gabe. "Great turnout."

"Your mother showed up for many people. Paying last respects is the least they can do. Who's the handsome gentleman you walked in with?" asked Arthur. "Someone important?"

"Very. He's my attorney."

"I hope there's potential for more than that." Arthur gave him a wink.

"He's already taken. I don't date married men." *There's the winning argument. I have no intention of ever* dating *Joey Dakota.* "I had no idea how many people my mother influenced."

"Amelia had her fingers in a lot of pies. Some are from her teaching days. You were aware she founded the Comadres Teacher's Mentoring Program in the county schools here, right?"

"I read about that in her obituary."

"Interesting what we learn about our parents after they pass. Your mother touched a lot of people's lives. We all do."

"Before I forget..." Gabe handed him the envelope with the obituary. "Will you make sure the obit finds its way?"

"I'll make sure Izzy gets it. She's over there. I can introduce you if you want."

"The Izzy by the beverages?" asked Owen, joining them and handing Gabe a bottle of water. "Very dynamic. Editor of the *Concord Gazette*."

"Arthur," said Gabe, "this is my attorney. And friend. Owen Greene. Owen, this Arthur Quinn."

"Quinn & Ink Arthur. My pleasure," said Owen, shaking his hand.

"Arthur was my mother's...boyfriend? Lover?"

"Best friend," said Arthur.

"I'm sorry for your loss," said Owen. "Arthur, can you please wait on introducing Gabe to Izzy until after the service? I can tell Gabe's nervous, and she's a force of nature." Gabe was surprised at how insightful and protective Owen was and how easily he read his emotional state.

"Of course," said Arthur. "And about that dating app you showed me, Gabe, will there always be this many gals responding to me?"

"You're only fresh meat once, dude," said Gabe.

"Wait!" said Owen. "You set him up on a dating app? You're relentless."

"He asked," said Gabe.

"He's very skillful," said Arthur.

"So I hear..."

"When you say 'fresh meat'?" asked Arthur.

"It's a gay term related to the penal system," said Gabe.

"Ignore him, Arthur," said Owen. "He's a mess of nerves right now."

"We should start," said Arthur. "I'll gather everyone." Arthur left them alone.

"You're like a sex-positive version of your mother," said Owen.

"According to Arthur, she was a pretty sex-positive version of herself."

Gentle acoustic music in the background indicated the service was starting.

"You want a companion during the service or would you rather sit alone? Some people prefer to fret in solitude," said Owen.

"Please join me," said Gabe.

"Is this 'Somewhere Over the Rainbow'?" asked Owen as Gabe chose their side seats in the front.

Gabe pretended to look at his speech. "Yep. My mother's favorite song."

"The Eva Cassidy cover?"

"How did you—? Yeah, her favorite version."

"Great taste," said Owen. "I mean, it's universally accepted as Judy's song, but Eva Cassidy owns it." Gabe's mother had frequently said those exact words. "It's unfair she died young...both of them."

"You would have liked my mother."

"I'm sure. And I would have made sure she created a revocable living trust early on," said Owen. "It's all going to work out, kiddo."

Gabe leaned his head on Owen's shoulder for an unguarded moment. He briefly relaxed and forgot he was at a memorial service. "Thank you for being here," he said. He took a full moment before straightening up and returning to a memorial-service mindset.

"Need a program?" asked a middle-aged woman handing Owen a program as she sat beside him. "I'm Minnie Norman. Such a loss."

"My mother was supposed to have dinner with you," said Gabe.

"She never made it. She loved my potatoes au gratin. You know the secret?"

"Gruyere and heavy cream?" asked Owen without missing a beat.

"Why, yes," said Minnie.

"If she hadn't already died, those potatoes would have given her a heart attack," Gabe whispered in Owen's ear as Arthur made his way to the podium and Eva Cassidy changed keys for a high note in the final verse. "Why, oh, why can't I?" echoed Gabe.

If Gabe had been in charge, the service would have been more polished. He would have had one rehearsal at least. Cues would have been picked up, and readers would have been asked to practice their selections and pronounce all their words correctly. When Gabe finally put aside his judgment and perfectionism, he could see the provincial memorial service for what it was: something beautiful, earnest, and charming. Arthur's voice cracked with emotion as he read, "Do Not Stand At My Grave and Weep," and Charlize overemphasized every emotion in her reading of "She Is Gone." The service unfolded in a perfectly Concord Valley way.

With the first chords of "My Way," Owen whispered in Gabe's ear, "You're after this song. You ready?" Owen's warm, soft breath made Gabe tingle. Owen gave Gabe's hand a supportive squeeze before letting go. Sitting by Owen's side gave Gabe a sensual comfort. But he couldn't walk to the podium and make a speech about his mother sporting an erection. He tried to mentally will any tumescence away.

"Which version of 'My Way' is this?" asked Owen.

"Nina Simone," said Gabe as the percussion picked up.

"Not Sinatra?" asked Owen.

"Mother preferred a woman's voice with these lyrics."

"Couldn't agree more."

When Nina was finished, Gabe took his legal pad and walked to the podium. He took a moment to look across the crowd, grateful for the full room of friends his mother had made through the years, most of them from after he had moved away. His eyes met Owen's handsome, supportive smile, which he matched with his own.

"Ladies and gentlemen," he began, "friends and family, we gather here today to say our final goodbyes to a remarkable woman, my beloved mother. Her absence leaves an unfillable void in my heart, but I'm here to celebrate her life, a life shaped by her generous spirit.

"It is appropriate we celebrate her life in a bookstore.

"My mother was a woman of extraordinary grace and resilience. She faced life's trials with the strength of Jane Austen's Elizabeth Bennet. She possessed a keen wit, a sharp intellect, and a strong sense of independence.

"Like Emily Brontë's Catherine Earnshaw, my mother's life proved love knows no boundaries. As a single mother, she embraced her role with a fierce devotion, showing me love and passion, in all their forms, are boundless.

"Like Virginia Woolf, my mother found solace and a deep understanding within the human psyche. She lived her life with an unyielding spirit, demonstrating how the mind should remain untamed and free to explore all possibilities of existence. And like Virginia Woolf, she left us far too soon.

"My mother's journey, much like the epic adventures in Homer's *Odyssey*, was filled with trials, tribulations, and a relentless quest for self-discovery. She showed me that the path to understanding ourselves is an ongoing odyssey, and if embraced with courage and perseverance, can lead to profound personal growth and enlightenment.

"William Wordsworth once wrote, 'The best portions of a good man's life are his small, nameless, unremembered acts of kindness and of love.' My mother embodied this sentiment in her compassion and generosity, often leaving an indelible mark on all who came in contact with her.

"As we bid farewell to Amelia Hartman, let us remember her not with sorrow, but with the understanding that her life was a masterpiece, a work of art filled with wisdom and grace.

"May her memory continue to inspire us to live with a profound appreciation for the beauty of the human experience. In this way, we can ensure her legacy endures, Rest in peace, dear Mother. You are now a part of the great stories of the past, but your story will live on in our hearts forever."

Several people applauded but ceased when they remembered they were at a somber event. Gabe walked to his seat next to Owen in sweet quietude.

"I was unprepared for that," said Owen. "You're such a great writer. Smart...beautifully orchestrated..."

Gabe was happy to have impressed Owen but more pleased he had done right by his mother.

"Your mother would have been proud," said Minnie Norman sotto voce, leaning across Owen to squeeze Gabe's arm. "Your mother was goodness through and through."

The service continued with another song, a time for anyone who wanted to come to the podium to speak, which went on far too long, and a sweet, concise benediction by Arthur. The final song was a recording of Joan Baez singing, "Let it Be."

"Your mother had great taste in music," said Owen.

"She was something else," said Gabe.

"There he is!" said a voice Gabe didn't recognize. "Wonderful eulogy!"

"Here comes Izzy. Excuse me for a sec," whispered Owen, leaving Gabe alone with the editor of the local paper.

"What a glorious send-off!" said Izzy, wrapping Gabe in an unexpected hug. "If you keep up those wordsmith skills, I might offer you an internship at the paper."

"Thank you," said Gabe, watching Owen get co-opted by a stranger and absorbed into the crowd.

Izzy was short, strong, oddly shaped, and slightly off-balance. If she had been a cartoon, she might have played a talking tea pot. *Potential future character for Harmony Hills.*

"Did you bring your handsome boyfriend?" asked Izzy. "Us journalists are known for being observant and asking probing questions."

Gabe added *"an editor with bad grammar"* to her Harmony Hills character profile.

"Owen is only a friend. And my lawyer. Thank you for writing a beautiful obituary for my mother."

"The details were mostly Arthur. I'm still in shock. I don't know how we'll continue without her. My sadness is making me ridiculous. Of course we'll go on, but you know what I mean."

"I know exactly what you mean. Arthur says you'll run the obituary for free, but I insist on paying for it," said Gabe.

"Don't be ridiculous. Your mother organized a series of bake sales to keep the newspaper afloat during some of our darker days. It's the least I can do."

"She was something else," said Gabe, adding another item to the list of surprises about his mother. "I want you to know how much I appreciate your kindness."

Gabe's phone buzzed an incoming text message.

Erin: *Call me when you get a chance.*

"You have to excuse me," said Gabe, pointing to the text. "My job."

"Of course," said Izzy. "I better work the crowd. I'm also running for mayor. Your mother was my campaign manager."

"Of course she was."

Another hug from Izzy before she moved onto the next circle as Owen materialized by Gabe's side.

"I don't think I've made an appropriate fuss over your gorgeous speech," said Owen, "A privilege to hear: deliberate, measured, and eloquent."

Owen had a way of making Gabe feel seen. "I wondered if the literary tone would land."

"It's a bookstore. You crushed it."

"I was originally going to write anecdotes from my childhood, but the thoughts alone made me bawl like a baby... I wouldn't have been able to get through that kind of eulogy."

"You wrote that speech all in one night?" asked Owen.

"I'm pretty good with a deadline," said Gabe.

"Have you ever considered writing for television? They're always looking for people who can write to a deadline. You want me to make a few calls? I might know some people."

"I'm good, but thanks," said Gabe, amused at Owen's oversimplified idea of how to get a television writing gig.

"I was proud of you," said Owen, initiating their second hug of the day.

"Cut it out, you two love birds," said Arthur approaching them.

"Quick question," said Gabe, smoothly separating from Owen. "Was Mabel Quinn your wife?"

"Yes. Why do you ask?"

"I came across my mother's recipe cards. And her name was on one of them."

"Her brownies?"

"How did you know?"

"Mabel's brownies were legendary. Your mother and Mabel were close. A whole group of them would share recipes. They talked of opening a restaurant together someday. But that didn't happen."

"We should bake together," said Owen to Gabe. "I love to make sweets. Let's bake something tonight. Unless you have other plans already."

"No telling what this one has up his sleeve," said Arthur to Owen with a nudge to Gabe.

"It's not his sleeve I'm worried about," said Owen.

Gabe wasn't sure he liked Owen and Arthur ganging up on him, even in a loving way.

"Arthur," said Gabe, "the memorial was perfect. Unfortunately, I have to take off right now for a work call. Can you please hold onto the ashes for now? I'll pick them up on Monday."

"And Arthur," said Owen, "no booty calls, no matter what your mentor here says."

"Arthur? Booty calls? Naughty boy!" said a middle-aged woman approaching them, wagging a finger at Arthur. "We'll see you Monday morning?" she said to Owen.

"I better head out. I need to start setting up for Monday," said Owen to the woman.

"I don't think we've met," said Gabe.

"Gabe, this is Mrs. Lomax," said Owen. "She's bringing her second-grade class to help me plant my heirlooms."

"Adding the visit to the tail end of our Monday morning field trip," she said.

"I'll have my assistant contact the school early Monday morning with all the details. I can host your group up until eleven."

"Perfect! The kids need to return to school by then for their morning snack anyway. You're a lifesaver," said Mrs. Lomax.

After gracious goodbyes and thank-yous, Owen and Gabe finally made it outside where they stood awkwardly on the sidewalk, unsure of what to do next.

"I'm glad you were here today. And you're hosting a field trip on Monday?" asked Gabe.

"I wish you could accuse me of pure altruism. Her last name is Lomax, which is also the last name of your probate judge. She mentioned enjoying the banana bread I took him."

"Impressive move, Esquire."

"You're not the only one with some moves. Also, I have a world-class mentor who has advised me to stay humble."

"You're totally teachable."

"What other lessons have you got?" asked Owen.

"Check out my online video on How to Maintain Boundaries with Oversexed yet Underappreciated Attorneys," said Gabe.

"I like that I'm underappreciated," said Owen. "I better start getting ready if I'm having forty third graders over Monday morning."

"And I need rest, but first, a work call."

"What office makes demands during bereavement time on a Saturday morning? Besides a law office."

"It's stupid. But I'm the one who knows the data."

"Constant contact, dude. Seriously, you crushed it in there. Pulitzer-worthy."

One last hug. Gabe chuckled as Owen walked away. He would have walked with him, but his car was parked right beside his. And they had already hugged three times today. A fourth would have been too much...and Gabe didn't trust himself. He lingered in front of the Quinn & Ink, pretending to read messages until Owen's SUV drove past him with an acknowledging wave from its driver.

A moment later, Gabe's phone buzzed a message.

> **Owen**: *Were you pretending to read work messages so we didn't have to negotiate a third awkward hug at our cars?*

> **Gabe**: *Fourth, but who's counting? Srsly I have a work call.*

Having a friend tuned into his wavelength surprised Gabe in how it made him float, until Owen's SUV turned the corner, and Gabe got grounded in the fact he actually had a work call to make.

"You picked a helluva week to be away," said Erin.

"I didn't exactly pick the week my mother died."

"I misspoke. Forgive me."

"Of course. What's up?"

"I have major information," said Erin.

Gabe's text message buzzed.

"Do you need to get that?"

The text was from Owen. "It can wait."

"You know how yesterday I overheard whisperings of 'big changes' coming? Today, the Douglasses were having a major screaming match."

"What did you hear?" said Gabe, now in his car.

"They're moving *If Tomorrow Never Comes* to LA. The whole organization: the sets, the actors, us— We're moving to Los Angeles, Gabe."

"Oh...you were right... This is...major."

"Is this good or bad?"

"If you were worried about cancellation, it's a vote of confidence. If you work on the show because you want to live in New York, it sucks. Ah! The timing of the Barrett Hodges hiring makes sense now. They needed to sign him before they announced the move. It would be extremely expensive for him to get out of his contract if he didn't want to move. This has not been announced yet to anyone, right?"

"Top secret. They must have thought no one was in the building when they were arguing."

"Any idea when it will be announced?"

"I heard Doris yell, 'Latest possible date,' at one point. They might have been discussing when to tell people. How does all this affect us?"

"It doesn't right now. But as soon as the cat's out of the bag— Excuse me. Wait a sec. Shh, shh."

A couple from the memorial approached his car and tapped his window. Gabe rolled it down.

"Lovely eulogy," said the woman.

"Don't interrupt his call, dear," said the man.

"Thank you for coming today," said Gabe. "Excuse me, I'm talking to a friend." Gabe gave them a grateful wave before rolling up his window.

"What was that about?" asked Erin after the couple had moved on.

"Some locals who attended the memorial."

"Why didn't you say you were on a work call? Why the secretive act? You don't want them to know you work for—? Oh my God! Do you steal their stories or something?"

"Moi?"

"I'm onto you, Gabe. That's your secret, isn't it?"

"Maybe...upon occasion...I might have..."

"Hold on! A secret polygamist in Concord Valley? Really?"

Only Mr. Blickstein, but he ignored her. "Stay on task, girl. I appreciate the heads-up. This is huge news. But there's nothing we can do openly until there's a formal announcement."

"And it could fall through," said Erin.

"Not likely. This has more than likely been in the planning stages for some time. Moving out West makes good business sense. Produce all the soaps in one studio: consolidate.

"Why not move the others to New York?" asked Erin.

"The top-rated shows are all made in LA. I wonder how Aurora fits into all this?"

Another text message buzzed Gabe's phone.

"Who's leaving you all those messages?"

Gabe checked. "My trust attorney."

"Are you stealing his story too? Oh, my God! Your attorney is Oliver Armstrong!" Gabe admired her brilliance. His silence confirmed her assumptions. "You are! Is he also trying to be a farmer?"

"God bless the good citizens of Concord Valley." Gabe grabbed his legal pad for some notes. "But I'm going to need your help if we're going to get away with the rom-com idea. I've got the boy-meets-girl meet cute that leads to an awkward kiss."

"He kissed you?" Silence from Gabe. "You kissed him!? You Jezebel!"

Gabe's lack of response told her not to press it. "We've got the boy-loses-girl when she finds out he's got a girlfriend."

"Make her a wife," said Erin. "A wife provides higher narrative stakes."

"So true. What comes next?"

"The fun and games. Once boy-loses-girl, every time they accidentally meet, it's another opportunity for verbal foreplay. The rom-com audience can't wait for them to get down to the business of love. You haven't slept with your attorney yet, have you?"

"And I'm not going to," said Gabe. "So a soap rom-com should take much longer than a movie for them to finally get down to business. What marks do I have to hit?"

"In the old films, potential lovers would call each other on the phone or send emails. Today they text a lot. Like your attorney is texting *you*. Send me screenshots of everything, please."

"You are relentless. Texting and emails won't work on a soap. We'll have them call on the phone."

Gabe's phone rang its old fashioned "ding-a-ling" sound: Owen's number. He sent it to voicemail, hoping it had been muted from Erin's end.

"Was that him calling?" asked Erin.

"Mind your own business. Tell me some other tropes."

"The fake date, the fake boyfriend or girlfriend. Have them attend a wedding together. Or a funeral—oh my god! How perfect is this trip?"

"Stop! But keep going."

"It's all about creating tests for their relationship. Establish some allies, and make sure they both have enemies, internal or external. Pride is a good one. Or prejudice."

"Pride it is," said Gabe, remembering Owen's handsome smile as he jotted notes.

"And have them do fun stuff together. Create activities that will reveal their talents. You're going in the farming direction. Have them garden, or he needs something specific she does. Maybe she needs his legal services. OMG! Gabe. This is what's happening to you right now in Concord Valley, isn't it? Wait! Was there a school shooting recently in Concord Valley?"

"They prevented it from happening."

"You are such a story thief," said Erin. "I love it! Wait. Is this even legal?"

"I'll ask my lawyer. Ha ha. No one ever wrote an original story, Erin."

"Fair enough. Here's the key to successful rom-coms: you have to put off the sex for as long as you can. Once they do it, the audience knows something bad will happen next. Boy loses girl."

"I thought he already lost her."

"The first time, but the second time, it feels like he loses her for good. Until he gets her back in the last reel."

"Such a cheesy format."

"A cheesy, comfortable format that has worked since the Romans invented it."

"So we hold off on the consummation," said Gabe, jotting the note.

"Is that advice to yourself?" said Erin, one last attempt to get information.

Gabe didn't take the bait. "Thanks for brainstorming with me, Erin. The full arc will be in your hands Monday morning with the first week of Oliver's scenes. If we're moving to LA, there will be a lot of moving pieces. Keep paying attention."

"You better answer those texts."

He hung up and immediately listened to Owen's voicemail.

"I'm at Henderson's. Dude, you are worth every penny of your consulting fee." Gabe chuckled. "I took your advice and led with humility and gratitude.

"Mrs. Henderson gave me a master class in tomato root rot, fungus, and how to test for pH in the soil. You were right: these people are smart. I have loaded up the SUV with heirlooms and instructions on which plants get planted next to which. I also got basil and marigolds like you suggested. And marigolds? Who knew there were so many varieties?

"I am having the time of my life. I couldn't be doing this without you. Thank you. And I'm still thinking about that eulogy. Can I commission you to write mine? That's a weird ask, but you know what I mean, he said, taking his foot out of his mouth. Call me."

Gabe checked his text messages. Two photos. One, a selfie of Owen with his arm around crusty Mrs. Henderson. Gabe double tapped a thumbs-up onto the picture. The other photo, another selfie of Owen looking inside his luxury SUV, filled with starter plants: tomatoes, basil, and marigolds. Owen is glowing, slightly sweaty, with a blissful expression. Gabe double tapped a heart onto the picture and called Owen back.

"What took you so long?" asked Owen.

Gabe recognized the ambient background noise of driving in a car.

"I told you I had a business call. I'm calling to say how great all your plants look."

"You sure that call wasn't your trick in the double-wide wanting more?"

"No one says 'trick' anymore. And he lived in a respectable sub-division. I have no intention of making Mr. Joey Dakota a regular."

"Is anointing regulars your MO?"

"Few are chosen. And stop asking about my sexploits."

"Can't a girl live vicariously? I have half a mind to go straight to McFarland's and ask Joey Dakota about your lovemaking prowess."

"I would hope you have more pressing things to do," said Gabe.

"Joey Dakota doesn't even sound like a real name," said Owen. "It must be a hookup name."

"Porn star," they said in unison.

"Jinx. You owe me a soda," said Owen. "What name did you use?"

"Austin DeFranco, one of my favorite porn stars."

"I prefer vintage porn," said Owen. "Guys with names like Chad, Tex, and Sky."

"I can't imagine you watching porn."

"We have to learn somewhere. You must be losing your mojo, Gabe. Your hookup app is awfully quiet."

"You made me silence it."

"As any mature, self-respecting gay man at a funeral would. Out of curiosity, when was the last time you went on a real date?" asked Owen.

Gabe took a moment to think about the question.

"You still there?" asked Owen.

"Still thinking."

"Don't take too long. I'm almost home."

"Me too."

"That long ago, huh?" Their conversation had shifted. Apparently, neither man knew what to say next. Gabe grew thoughtful and quiet. "Listen," said Owen, "I didn't mean to upset you."

"I'm not upset. I'm... It's been a long day," said Gabe. "It's been a while since I've been on an old-fashioned date, that's all."

"This is more than a thirty slash seventy phone buddies convo. BTW, we're great on the phone."

"Promise me you'll never say the word 'convo' again. Or BTW. Let's talk later. I still have work to do."

"And I've got a full load I need to dump somewhere."

"You did that on purpose."

"Maybe. Bye."

Gabe headed home. He was content the eulogy had been a success, but happier because his friendship with Owen was shaping up to be an unexpected pleasure. He had forgotten about his hostile relationship with Chairvana, until he bumped into it as he entered the house.

He took a picture of the offending recliner and texted it to Owen.

Gabe: Scene of the crime. The deathtrap.

Owen: Get rid of it.

Gabe: Do they have to know she died in it?

Owen: She wasn't murdered in it. Donate it to a thrift shop. I'll make the call for you. Maddy will, actually. I'm pretty useless.

*Gabe: *heart emoji**

*Owen: *blushing emoji**

Gabe: Stop bothering me. I'm working.

Owen: You initiated.

Gabe: Oopsie.

Gabe went to the kitchen and gnoshed on more leftovers as he constructed Oliver Armstrong's story arc. All he had to do was remember his favorite bits with Owen, translate them into a hetero Harmony Hills version, and each section fell into place. His notes from the Erin conversation guided the progression. The writing of the scene flowed naturally, and the dialogue unspooled easily. He would make sure Erin got promoted when they moved to Los Angeles.

During the day, Owen would periodically text Gabe a stupid farm meme. *When you realize the new guy may not be as experienced as he says* with a picture of some disaster on a farm. Or a scarecrow in a field:

This job isn't for everyone, but hay, it's in my jeans.

Gabe: *Those memes make Hee-Haw look like Harvard.*

They texted sporadically for the next few hours. Owen initiated. His stupid farm memes shifted to classic house pet memes. Gabe always responded. He enjoying having a buddy to reach out to, someone paying attention to him.

Gabe was hitting a wall and needed a break from the rom-com story arc. Mabel Quinn's brownie recipe caught his eye. He craved something sweet. He committed to making the recipe, as long as he could find all the ingredients in the kitchen.

His mother's kitchen was always well stocked with baking ingredients. She had all the dry ingredients, even the suggested dark brown sugar. Vanilla was with the spices—easy. Eggs and butter in the refrigerator. Still good. She had died only three days ago, though it felt like years. The only ingredient he couldn't find was the chocolate—nowhere in the cabinets. The recipe called for chocolate wafers. His mother worshipped chocolate. It had to be somewhere in the house. She never skimped when buying chocolate. Her guilty pleasure was to nibble on chocolate while sipping on a cordial.

The liquor cabinet was located next to the lounger. The chair had become hallowed ground. Gabe tried not to lean against it as he explored the liquor cabinet. Inside the cabinet, he discovered a motherlode of chocolate. Not his mother's typical big box store haul, but a pile of expensive chocolate. *No wonder you couldn't afford to pay your property taxes. You spent everything you had on chocolates.*

Gabe gathered and organized all the ingredients neatly on the kitchen table.

His phone buzzed again. *Why hook up with a closet case when I have a gorgeous man texting me?* Owen's next two memes returned to the farm motif: *Who needs swag when you're a tomato* against a perfect beefsteak red, and a cow with an engorged udder saying, *Eyes up here, please.* He figured Owen was bored and responded with a basic smiley face emoji. Text bubbles floated next to Owen's name, but no text came.

Gabe initiated the next thread.

> **Gabe**: *Still thinking about how great my eulogy was?*

> **Owen**: *Was I too effusive?*

> **Gabe**: *Was my self-loathing too noisome?*

> **Owen**: *If I don't get to say convo or BTW, you don't get to say noisome. You can't help but exude charm. You get some rest?*

> **Gabe**: *Nope*

> **Owen**: *Your attorney recommends some self-care.*

> **Gabe**: *Does this count?*

Gabe took a picture of the brownie ingredients.

> **Owen**: *Quelle mise en place. WTF! You're making Mabel's brownies? We were going to bake them together.*

> **Gabe**: *We never made a plan to bake brownies. I'm in for the night.*

> **Owen**: *We can bake in our pjs, take social media pics, and make our own memes! I want to see this house you're fighting diligently to abandon.*

In his vulnerability, Gabe couldn't think of a good excuse fast enough. A baking party could take their friendship to the next level and inspire him with more details for the Oliver Armstrong storyline.

> **Owen**: *If I were a stranger (or a regular) looking for a quickie, you wouldn't hesitate.*

Gabe dialed his number.

Owen answered, "Was that too mean, thirty slash seventy? Are you breaking up with me?"

"Not yet," said Gabe. "You can come over, but know the place is not in great shape."

"As long as it's not the set for *Hello, My Name is Doris*. I love to bake. And I love baking with friends even more. And you're a friend who's pretending he's not lonely and sad. I sat right next to you at the memorial service, and you didn't cry once. Suppressing your emotions is exhausting. You don't have to keep it together with me. I know you're escaping into your work with meaningless sex. So, tonight, I want to be a good friend and keep you company. I'll be a comfort if you'll let me."

Gabe was deeply moved. He sniffed away a tear and cleared his voice.

"Gabe? You 'Starsky and Hutching' on me?" asked Owen.

"Dickens," said Gabe. The word got caught in the lump in his throat. He couldn't contain how overcome he was by Owen's kindness.

Gabe pushed through his feelings and gave Owen the address. After he hung up, he hustled to hide any evidence of *If Tomorrow Never Comes* paperwork. He put everything in the overnight delivery envelope and stashed it under his mother's bed. By the time he got downstairs, he could hear Gabe's SUV in the driveway.

"That was quick," said Gabe, opening the door.

"It's a small town."

Gabe reached out to shake his hand, which confused Owen.

"That's not who we are. Come here."

Owen held Gabe in a hug a half beat longer than their prior hugs.

"This is who we are," said Owen in mid-hug.

The hug came to an organic ending and they separated.

"That was nice," said Owen. "By the way, nice place."

"You don't have to say that. She was having a hard time keeping it up. And a harder time hiding everything that needs fixing."

"She was too busy saving the world. I wish my place were this size. Mine's too big for one person."

"Doesn't Maddy live with you?"

"She has her own place in town. For privacy."

"Yours or hers?"

"Exactly. Maddy is an extremely competent assistant, but Kevin hired her. That tells you everything you need to know."

"She's his spy?"

"She keeps him informed. He's convinced my farming dreams are a phase. I think he's more worried I won't grow out of it. Be careful what you tell Maddy. Let me get a look at this place." Owen took in the living room and the shotgun, open-concept layout, going all the way from the front door to the rear of the kitchen. "The design has a lot of potential. It would make one of those great homes that gets converted to a restaurant."

"Maybe that's what Mom and Mabel were dreaming of."

"Can't you see it? Intimate, farm-to-table seasonal cuisine, simple wildflower bouquets, eclectic tablecloths—nothing too fancy."

"I hope someone with that kind of imagination wants to buy it."

"The good news is most homes in Concord Valley are zoned for business and residential," said Owen. "You'll sell this place for sure. It's got great character. It feels cozy and lived in. This house exudes love. Wait!" Owen froze in front of the recliner. "Is that...the infamous lounger?"

"The one and only."

"Why is it even still here?" asked Owen.

"If you saw my to-do list..." said Gabe.

"Its energy is sucking all the life out of the room," said Owen with a psychic flare. "Like it did your mother. It's the Jeffrey Dahmer of living room furniture." Gabe had to laugh. "No wonder it's haunting you. Can you grab a sheet or something to cover it up? I'll have someone pick it up on Monday."

Gabe opened a living room coat closet and found a large blanket on an upper shelf, which he unfurled over the chair. Owen helped him tuck in the corners.

"Much better," said Owen.

"You want a tour of the whole place?" asked Gabe.

"How about we cook first, then a tour when the brownies are in the oven?"

"Sounds good. You are aware we've been hanging out a lot together?"

"Is that bad?"

"Not necessarily. But aren't you worried we'll run out of topics to talk about?" asked Gabe, his guard down. Gabe didn't like feeling this vulnerable.

"That is not what I'm worried about with you."

"What *do* you worry about?"

"That is something I will also share while the brownies are cooking."

"Ooh, suspense. Fair enough. This way, sir." Gabe led Owen to the kitchen where he had gathered all the ingredients.

"Beautiful!" said Owen. "So well organized. And gourmet chocolates? Posh!"

"Here's Mabel's recipe," said Gabe, showing him the recipe card.

"I love this card! Such a lovely illustration."

"Doesn't everyone's mother have a set of recipe cards like this?"

"Not mine. Mine doesn't cook."

"Who taught you to love baking?"

"We had a great cook on staff."

"I forgot who I was dealing with," said Gabe with a touch of snark.

"You do not get to do that. I had many privileges...but living in a home filled with love wasn't one of them."

"Sorry. I hope you got to lick the mixer blades."

"Of course. Do you have aprons?"

"Only a few." Gabe found the hook with his mother's aprons. He handed Owen one and donned another.

"On the shoulders of giants," said Owen, tying the apron. "We must look adorable."

"You do."

Owen kissed Gabe's forehead.

"What was that?" asked Gabe.

"That was a two-friends-cooking-brownies-looking-adorable kiss. Not a sexual kiss. A blessing."

"Keep your pants on, dude. This is serious work. We need to concentrate."

"If you insist. Why two pans?"

"I did a little reconnaissance today…" said Gabe, moving on from the warm kiss still on his forehead. "Since we have an abundance of ingredients, why don't we make two batches, and you can serve them to the class that's coming to your farm on Monday morning? I already called an old friend who works at the school. They'll be cool with you serving the kids brownies as long as there are no nuts."

"You're your mother's son: a kind and generous spirit."

Gabe smiled.

"Skillful work with parchment, Mister," said Owen.

"Thanks. I have a crafty side," said Gabe.

"You're very crafty," said Owen, looking over the recipe card. "It's pretty straightforward. Why don't you preheat the oven and start on the dry mix. I'll melt the butter and chocolate. And we'll join forces at the mixer."

"Sounds good."

They worked in silence at first. The air was full of too many feelings and too much subtext, and this was neither the time nor place to parse any of it.

"Tell me about your cook," said Gabe after setting the oven at 350 degrees, then sifting the flour, cocoa powder, and salt into a large bowl.

"Her name was Luisa," said Owen at the microwave. "She came to the States after some Central American coup. She had been a cook for one of the top governors. My mother liked to brag to her friends about her." The microwave dinged, and he switched a blue mixing bowl of half-melted butter for a yellow mixing bowl of chocolate. "I think she had been trained at the Cordon Bleu or something ridiculously fabulous. She would hate how I'm melting the chocolate and butter right now." The microwave dinged, and he switched bowls one more time.

"The recipe calls for a double boiler," said Gabe.

"But who has time for that?" said Owen.

"The kids won't know the difference."

"As long as the butter doesn't explode. And I don't want to mess up this pricey chocolate."

"You probably know as much about baking as I do about gardening," said Gabe.

"Except you don't have to be reminded to be humble," said Owen.

"The dry mix is done," said Gabe.

"Mine too," said Owen, returning to the table with the melted chocolate and butter. He had somehow managed to get a dab of melted chocolate onto the tip of his nose.

"You have a little...um." Gabe tapped the tip of his own nose to indicate where Owen should wipe.

Owen wiped his nose but only got some of the chocolate off.

"No, it's— Let me." Gabe stepped in and took his thumb to smear the rest away.

"Get it all?"

"Uh-huh." Gabe licked the chocolate off his thumb. "Yummy."

"So I've been told. Stop slacking, you scamp," said Owen. "I'd love to flirt the night away, but we can't dawdle or the chocolate will get hard."

That's not the only thing that could get hard. "Where are we in the recipe?" asked Gabe.

"We have to mix the wet together first," said Owen, looking over the card. "These cards are mini works of art."

Gabe set up the mixer.

"You start on your butter and sugar. And I'll crack the eggs," said Gabe.

While Owen ran the mixer, Gabe cracked the first egg on the rim of a small glass bowl. A few tiny fragments of eggshell fell in with the egg whites. He struggled to pick them out with his fingers. He could feel Owen watching him.

"Let me show you something." Owen stopped the mixer. He walked behind Gabe and reached around him like a golf teacher demonstrating a putting stroke. Gabe could feel his bulge lightly pressing into his backside. Owen took Gabe's right hand from behind. "Pick up half an eggshell." He guided Gabe's hand with a gentle caress. "Now use the shell to scoop the little pieces up one at a time." Owen guided his hand to easily lift out one of the tiny pieces of eggshell. The small piece of shell clung to the large piece like a natural magnet. "Beautiful." Owen let go of Gabe's hand and stepped back. "There's something in the eggshell that draws the smaller pieces to it."

"Like attracts like?" asked Gabe.

"Luisa never used those words, but yeah. America is evidently the only country where people crack eggs on the sides of bowls, which leads to pieces falling in with the egg whites. Luisa taught me to crack eggs on the counter. Like this." Owen took an egg and gave it a good whack on the counter. The egg white fell flawlessly into the bowl.

"Like this?" Gabe took the egg and copied Owen, surprised at how cleanly it broke.

"Fast learner."

"I'm teachable," said Gabe proudly.

"Yes, you are, sweet Gabe Hartman." Owen gave Gabe a look over-flowing with kindness.

"You ever considered opening a restaurant?" asked Gabe, changing the subject.

"One dream at a time, my man. Restaurants are hard work."

"Farms are no cakewalk."

Owen turned the mixer on again. "Eggs ready?" asked Owen. Gabe handed him the eggs for the wet mix, no shells. They had a natural work-ing rhythm, a collaboration in the kitchen. "Now the melted chocolate." Gabe handed it to him, which turned the mixture a rich, deep brown. Both men admired the alchemy. Their expectations were high; the recipe had the potential to be an astonishing success.

"Uh-oh," said Owen." The recipe says 'fold in' the dry mix."

"Why the uh-oh?"

"You never saw *Schitt's Creek*?" asked Owen.

"I know that scene," said Gabe. He had basically lifted the "fold the cheese" scene for an *If Tomorrow Never Comes* scene.

"It's iconic, went viral with memes, gifs, and everything. It's now a cultural reference," said Owen.

"It's such a dumb scene. All they had to do was look online. What did Luisa teach you about folding in?"

"Circle and cut with the spatula. Don't stir. It's about adding air to the mix."

"Then that is the way we shall do it."

Gabe grabbed a spatula as Owen added the dry mix to the bowl. Gabe folded the mix like he had seen the actors on *If Tomorrow Never Comes* do. Circle and cut until the ingredients were all mixed together. While he was doing this, Owen took a handful of chocolate wafers and chopped them on a cutting board. Gabe was impressed at Owen's skill with a knife. Gabe was discovering much to admire in Owen tonight.

They worked in silence. They worked with peace of mind. They were thrumming.

"Shall I?" Gabe broke the silence, indicating he was ready to spread the mix into the two pans. Owen found a second spatula and evened out the surface of one pan while Gabe filled the other. Owen spread a handful of chopped chocolate across the top of one pan, and Gabe, the other. "Ready for the oven?"

They each grabbed a pan and then put them in the oven. Gabe made sure the oven door was closed completely.

"Twenty minutes?" said Owen, reading the recipe card and setting the timer on his phone.

They took off their aprons, and Gabe went to the water faucet to rinse off his hands. Owen joined him. Their fingers occasionally brushed against each other as the last bits of chocolate melted into the warm water. Eye contact would be a mistake right now.

"We work well together," said Owen. "That's rare with two dudes in a kitchen." Gabe read his response as a criticism of Kevin.

"We're fun people," said Gabe. "Let's hope they taste good. How about I give you that tour of the house?"

"Is there any more to the downstairs?" asked Owen.

"We think there might have been a maid's quarters off the kitchen over there, but the prior owner had the downstairs reconfigured. The original architectural integrity is long gone."

"This open concept design was done—when—forty years ago? Way ahead of its time. The place feels both big and cozy."

"Come see upstairs."

"You still haven't spent the night in your old room, have you?" asked Owen as Gabe led him up the stairwell.

"Not yet," Gabe shrugged, "I don't know why."

When they got to the second-floor hallway, Owen asked, "The room with the closed door?"

"Uh-huh."

"Can I have a look?"

Gabe opened the door for him. He still didn't dare enter, but he bent over the threshold for a proper onceover as Owen walked around. The double bed and desk set barely fit in the small room.

"Is this how the room was set up when you were in high school?"

"And before. And after—whenever I'd come to visit."

"It looks like a perfectly normal, tiny Victorian bedroom to me. Do you feel like the room's haunted?"

"It's not that. I don't know how to hang out here...how to occur in this space...now that she's gone. It's weird."

"Maybe you need to reinvent it. Maybe it becomes your writing room or something. You have no problem going into her room though?" asked Owen, crossing the hall into his mother's bedroom.

"I hang out and watch television on her bed all the time."

"Find any hidden sex toys?"

"Not yet."

"Did you check the bed?" Owen headed to the bed.

Gabe didn't want him to discover the hidden ZipExpress envelope and discover his livelihood.

"Already looked. Nothing there," said Gabe. He was relieved when Owen flopped onto the bedspread.

Gabe sat on the edge of the bed. He didn't want this to devolve into a compromising situation. If any sexy physical shenanigans commenced, they would certainly be interrupted by the timer for the brownies.

"I'm sorry we got off on the wrong foot with the kiss," said Gabe. "I was too aggressive. I should have done more research before I made a move like that."

"No need to apologize. It wasn't unwanted. Our friendship is all the richer because of it."

"Come clean. When you were at the microwave, did you put the dab of chocolate on your nose when I wasn't looking?"

"Maybe."

"I knew it!" he lied. He slid down on his mother's bed and lay next to Owen. "To be clear: we are not having sex in my mother's bed."

"Too Oedipal?" Owen took his hand. His honesty allowed Gabe to feel comfortable with this level of contact.

"You said—earlier tonight you were worried about something with me."

"Yeah. You still haven't told me the last time you went on a date."

"These days, work keeps me too busy."

"You use that excuse a lot. When was your last real date? And app hookups don't count."

"The last date-date? A while back I was in a relationship. We went on several dates before we made our relationship official."

"When was that? A few years ago?"

"More like seven. Maybe more," Gabe lied. It was over ten years.

"So...at best, you're rusty; at worst, you have forgotten how to date."

"Why is my dating history important to you?"

"You're flat-out boyfriend material, Gabe. It's selfish of you to deny the world your Gabe yumminess. You're good-looking, fun..."

"I don't think so."

"The self-effacing act is adorable, but you come off as disingenuous. In reality, you're a hot, sexy guy. You're smart; you're a fabulous writer... Your potential is off the charts, dude. Why waste it settling for the crumbs? I saw the mullet you hooked up with today. You're better than that."

"His mullet had almost grown out..."

"Unless you're with someone who loves you dearly, you're selling yourself short." Gabe felt like he was talking to Jess. "I know you don't want my advice, but you need to get your dating mojo back."

"And how does one do that?"

"First, you need to reenter the dating world, and I'm going to teach you how."

"Are you going to start sending me instructional dating videos instead of corny barnyard memes?"

"The corny barnyard memes will keep coming. I'm going to take you on a practice date, a fake date."

"On a fake date, do we eat fake dinner and see a fake movie?"

"So you *do* know how to date. But the movies here suck. It'll be more like dinner and a video. And I'll pick the video."

"*The Notebook*?"

"Please! Something classy. I want you to start dating people who challenge you and bring out the best in you. Like me. I can see how much you need connection. Think about it: instead of getting your discreet NSA DL rocks off, you can get love <u>and</u> get laid. What a concept."

"You like your projects, don't you?"

"If I can't have you—" Owen got up on one elbow and looked him in the eye. "—I want you to have someone amazing, someone nice, but someone you can complain about to me. Someone I can diss and be jealous of, but secretly approve of. What do you say?"

Owen waited for a response.

Gabe feared the velocity with which Owen was moving with their friendship, one that included a future with some commitments. Gabe enjoyed Owen, but he barely knew him. He hadn't considered much of a future with Owen beyond this current week in Concord Valley.

And yet fake date ranked high on Erin's list of rom-com tropes. Accepting Owen's proposition might add a few days of content to the Oliver Armstrong storyline.

"Fine," said Gabe. "When would we go on this fake date?"

"Are you busy Monday night?" asked Owen.

"I don't think so."

"Of course you're not. Nothing happens on Monday night in Concord Valley. I'll find a nice restaurant that's open on Mondays. Leave the rest to me."

"What's the dress code?"

"What do you wear to a hookup?"

"Something you can easily take off."

"Not that. Let's say country club casual."

"Your privilege is showing."

"You know what I mean."

"Smell that?" The aroma of brownies had wafted to the upstairs bedroom. "So comforting."

"Remember to bake brownies when your realtor has an open house," said Owen.

A *ripple* sound effect came out of Owen's phone. "Time to check on them."

Owen popped off the bed and headed downstairs to the kitchen, the aroma leading the way. Gabe followed him.

Back in the kitchen, Owen opened the oven door. "Oven mitts?"

From a nearby drawer, Gabe pulled out four multicolored hand-made potholders, old and worn brown in places over the years.

"Please tell me you made these," said Owen.

"Guilty. The last loop was the hardest."

"They're fabulous!"

Owen took one pan of brownies from the oven, and Gabe got the other. They stood over them looking at their glorious work.

"Perfect shine," said Gabe.

"Too perfect. One more step." Owen moved over to the wooden cutting board and brought the whole brownie pan down hard with a *slam-whack*! The loud sound scared Gabe.

"Why'd you do that?"

"I wanted to get the classic brownie crack all over the top. Look. Now it's perfect."

"Another Luisa trick?"

"You know it. Your turn."

"Whack it, huh?" asked Gabe.

He took his pan and brought it down hard: *slam-whack*!

"Gorgeous," said Owen. "And the brownies aren't bad either."

Gabe grinned.

"Too bad we have to let them cool. You better take them with you." said Gabe.

"You're kicking me out already? Am I one of your 'cook 'n go' regulars?"

"More like a bake 'n shake," said Gabe.

Owen grabbed a spoon, scooped a piece of brownie out, and placed it on a plate.

"When it cools," said Owen, "text me what you think. I have a hunch we made a scrumptious treat tonight."

"Thanks to Mabel," said Gabe.

"And Amelia and Luisa," said Owen.

"I wish I could figure out what to do with my mother's recipe cards. I love reading them."

"I wish there was a museum you could donate them to."

"Unfortunately, there's no Ordinary Housewives of America Museum." Gabe picked up a pile of recipes and looked through them. "It's kind of astonishing. These extraordinary, ordinary women, figuring out how to create community and navigate their tough farm lives, sharing recipes to make the world a sweeter place. Finding their strength in shared generosity. I find the cards nostalgic and enchanting and lovely."

"It sounds like there's a potential history-slash-recipe-book-slash-memoir-slash-love-letter in those cards," said Owen. "You should write about that. Preserve your mother's legacy."

"Maybe I will. If the muse hits me."

"Can I help clean up?"

"I got it, and you've got a fake date to plan. Let's wrap the brownie pans in tinfoil. You can borrow the potholders."

"You would let them out of the house?"

"I know, right? The family heirlooms. I made plenty."

They covered the brownie pans and piled them diagonally in a brown shopping bag with the potholders so they wouldn't smush.

"That was the best." Owen kissed Gabe on the forehead at the front door. "Are we good?"

"We're great."

"Even though I'll see you Monday, we're still on the thirty-slash-seventy plan."

After Owen left and Gabe cleaned up, softly smiling at Owen's goodness the whole time, Gabe sat down in the kitchen, opened his computer, and created a new document named, "My Mother's Recipe Cards." The moment he began typing, past images of his mother poured forth onto the screen. Long forgotten memories of her in the kitchen, always a wooden spoon in hand for tasting one of the simmering pots, always a stovetop full of cooking pots, always a kitchen warmed by the heat of love.

His text message buzzed.

> **Owen**: *Have you tried the brownies yet?*

Gabe pinched off a taste, still warm.

> **Gabe**: *OMG!*

> **Owen**: *Transcendental. Orgasmic. Interrobang Brownies!?*

> **Gabe**: *A shame to waste them on the kids.*

> **Owen**: *We made magic tonight. What are you wearing?*

> **Gabe**: *Thin on patience. Leave me alone. I'm writing about the recipe cards. You inspired me.*

> **Owen**: *I'll leave you alone, author. Write on! Goodnight, John-boy.*

> **Gabe**: *Goodnight, John-boy.*

Gabe took another taste before returning to his writing, thinking, *Yep, we made magic...*

Chapter Five

Gabe was well rested when he woke up on Sunday morning. He had spent the night in his mother's bed, still warm with memories of Owen and a hint of brownies aroma still in the air. He would dedicate the day to writing. He loved what he had written about his mother's recipe cards the night before. He wasn't clear about the form yet; it was all too exploratory at this point to share with Jessica.

Sunday would be all about Oliver Armstrong. His plan was to finish the first part of his story arc and, when that was done, work on script pages. He filled the coffee maker and opened the document while it brewed. He checked his text messages for the latest from Owen.

Their thread was unchanged from the last shared meme and his thumbs-up response emoji. Maybe Owen was still asleep. Gabe returned to the Oliver Armstrong doc. The synopsis tracked exactly like his time with Owen. Gabe had written up to Owen's purchase of heirloom tomatoes, marigolds, and basil. The next sequence would have Oliver baking something with Suzy.

Gabe paused. He had to decide how much to deviate from the truth. If anyone close to Owen, like Maddy, followed *If Tomorrow Never*

Comes, he didn't want them to connect Oliver's storyline to Owen. He considered substituting the heirloom tomatoes with some other heirloom crop, like heirloom beets. But clunky, dirty beets added zero romance to the narrative. He was sticking with the wild strawberries for the meet cute. Heirloom peaches had some potential for sexy, sensual fun, but *If Tomorrow Never Comes* didn't have any orchard sets. He left it as strawberries, rhubarb, and heirloom tomatoes for now.

Next, he jumped into the cooking scene. He could easily change brownies to chocolate chip cookies or a chocolate silk pie, anything with melted chocolate for wiping and licking chocolate off body parts. Too many sexy food scenes and soap operas start to get too kinky for Middle America. He kept the slamming of the brownies to get the surface to crack. Suzy could do one of those Julia Roberts boisterous cackles when Oliver did it.

It was time to outline the fake date section. Many actors had told him performative romance was great fun to act. Gabe planned for clever conversation over dinner, good wine, vulnerable confessions, returning to Oliver's house for cuddling up with a romantic film. Gabe appreciated how easily the story spooled out. Both Gabe and the audience would want this section to go on forever.

The fake date would last a full week in soap opera time. Gabe would flesh out all the details after he and Owen had their date tomorrow night.

Gabe checked his text messages to see if he had missed one. Nothing new from Owen, but chat bubbles billowed by his name, so he must have been composing one as Gabe was checking messages. Gabe waited for the chat bubbles to cease and the text to arrive. The bubbles stopped, but no message came. In a few seconds, the chat bubbles re-appeared.

He must be composing something lengthy. Gabe returned to Oliver's story document.

"Cuddling and a romantic film" were the last words he had written.

Gabe wrote *In the Mood for Love* into the story arc, one of the greatest romantic movies ever made, a film that never stopped seducing him. While Oliver and Suzy watched the video, Oliver would confess his love for Suzy at the same time the man in the film does. This would inspire her to throw aside her moral compass, and they would finally and fully consummate their relationship. This was where Gabe would stop writing for now. The network would end up picking a rom-com title they owned, some cheesy Hallmark-esque rom-com to save money.

Gabe checked his texts again. No chat bubbles and no memes or messages from Owen. Something was up. Second thoughts on Owen's part? Gabe tried to edit and block any negative Owen scenarios in his head. *Maybe Kevin called mid-text, maybe he's having a hard time finding a restaurant open on a Monday, maybe he had a heart attack.* Gabe hated that he had become obsessed. *Find something constructive to do.*

Usually he would finish an outline by celebrating with a hookup, but he didn't want to jinx the fake date. Instead, Gabe opened a new document and drafted dialogue directly into script pages for Oliver's first week of scenes, unheard of in the process of writing soaps as writing dialogue and script pages was relegated to staff writers, only after weeks of parsing outlines and story arcs. Without knowing the timing of the LA move, Gabe took the initiative and went ahead putting dialogue on the page. He wanted to keep it as close to reality as he could recall. Writing Oliver script pages might be a fool's errand, but Gabe enjoyed recalling his Owen time so much, he didn't care if the dialogue might never be used.

All he had to do was remember the events at the farmers market and give Suzy the roles of ally and future lover. The pages unfolded more like mental dictation than writing. The farmers market scenes fell into place with unusual ease. The entire sequence, from meet-cute to regretful kiss fit perfectly into a one-week schedule of scenes.

Gabe finished the section by midafternoon. He checked his text messages. More chat bubbles by Owen's name. Gabe fought his impatience and swiped the hookup app closed. He needed to get to the ZipExpress in the next town before the last pickup at 5:00 p.m.

As Gabe headed up the stairs to retrieve the ZipExpress envelope under his mother's bed, he caught the sound of a car on the driveway.

Hoping for a surprise visit from Owen, he ran to the door to discover Arthur carrying the box of ashes.

"I hope you don't mind my dropping in unannounced," said Arthur. "I was passing by and wanted to make sure you got these." Arthur handed the black box to Gabe.

"No problem. Thanks," said Gabe trying to hide his disappointment at it not being Owen. "I'm always amazed at how heavy they are. You said she wanted them in the garden?"

"I told her the usual custom was to broadcast them out to sea. But she wanted to stay here."

"She loved this place," said Gabe.

"Especially her flower garden around the aspen tree," said Arthur.

Gabe had plenty of time to put the ashes in the garden before the ZipExpress office closed. "Would you like to join me?"

"Right now?" asked Arthur.

"Why not?"

"I thought there would be a ceremony for the ashes," said Arthur.

"How many more ceremonies does she need? You can say a prayer if you like."

"I don't believe she was religious," said Arthur.

"She hated religion," said Gabe. "We can frame the 'broadcasting' with two short meditations. Let's do it."

Gabe led Arthur around to the backyard. They stood beside an aspen tree surrounded by a small circular flower bed with newly emerged jonquils on the verge of blooming.

"She preferred jonquils to daffodils," said Arthur.

"She preferred their sweet scent to the earthy daffodils," said Gabe.

Gabe opened the box of ashes and undid the twisted wire gathering the plastic. "A few minutes of meditation?" asked Gabe.

"Sounds good."

They both closed their eyes and listened, leaning into the gentle ordinariness of early afternoon: occasional birds, the faraway river sound of traffic, all the ambiance of being outdoors in a small town.

"Good enough?" asked Gabe.

"Perfect. I'll bear witness. Proceed."

With the wire off and the plastic fully open, Gabe took the box and gently tilted it into the circular garden. He was extremely deliberate at first, treating the soft white-gray ashes like a sacrament.

"You don't have to be that careful with her," said Arthur. "Not at this point."

Gabe gave the box a steeper tilt, and the ashes cascaded into the garden in gray puffy splotches. He continued circling even after completing one full circle of the aspen. The ashes landed in gray patches, sometimes gathering in small heaps. "Do you think I should level them or leave them?" asked Gabe.

"You don't want to get your mother on your shoes. The wind and rain will blend everything together eventually," said Arthur. "Keep going."

Gabe continued his circumambulations until the black box was empty. Some of the ashes had drifted onto the jonquils giving them an elderly appearance.

"The broadcasting of Amelia Hartman's ashes is complete," said Gabe.

"Lovely. Let's end with another moment of silence."

Both men bowed their heads in a final moment of silent reverence.

"You're a good son, Gabe," said Arthur when a respectful amount of time had passed.

"I don't know about that."

"Any idea what's going to happen to the house?"

"That's where Owen Greene comes in. Hopefully the estate gets figured out next week, and I can return to the City. By the way, did Mother and your Mabel ever consider opening a restaurant here at the house?"

"They talked of opening a catering company when Mabel was alive."

"Owen thought the place would make a good, homey restaurant. They shared so many recipes. Just curious."

"A restaurant may have been part of their dream if the catering company took off. But time was not on their side."

"What should I do with the ashes box?"

"Demystify it, kiddo. Recycle it."

They walked to the side of the house where Gabe tossed the box into the recycling bin.

"How's the dating app working out for you?" asked Gabe.

"Not my forte. Too many desperate lonely hearts out there."

"You figure out who's crazy real fast."

"In my experience," said Arthur, "the trick is to fall in love with your best friend."

"Is that what happened with you and Mabel?"

"And your mother. And there's another trick."

"Tell me."

"Once you get the call for an adventure," said Arthur, "you better take it."

"What happens if you refuse?"

"Nothing good," said Arthur. "People act like desperate fools when they're lonely, Gabe."

"The student has outgrown the teacher."

"What a miracle whenever any two people find time to connect in this crazy world. You and that Owen seemed to be getting along. I think he fancies you. Maybe he's your call for adventure."

"He's a great guy," said Gabe, "but...how often will I be here once the house is sold? Oh yeah, and he's married."

"Ah, destined not to repeat the sins of your mother. Probably for the best. Thanks for including me in the ashes ceremony," said Arthur as Gabe opened the car door for Arthur. "You brought your mother home today. Forever she will stay."

As Arthur drove away, Gabe checked a clock: plenty of time to make it to the ZipExpress office in the next town before the five o'clock pickup. He checked to see if Owen had left a text. Still, the chat bubbles, but no message.

Do not obsess. Go about your day.

At the ZipExpress office, the young woman at the desk recognized him from Friday.

"Hey, George."

"How do you know...my name?"

"The computer says George Sample is the name on the account."

"I'm surprised you remembered. That's all."

"I take great pride in remembering all client names."

Gabe leaned in conspiratorially. "In my line of work, we need to keep our identities confidential. I know you understand."

"Of course, Mr. Sample," she whispered.

Gabe was grateful the place was empty. At yet, the young woman had awakened his anxiety.

Still shaken as he headed home, he was tempted to go onto his hookup app, but he came to his senses and swiped to his text messages instead. A full day with no messages from Owen didn't track, not after they'd had such a great time making magical brownies the night before. The timing was far too soon for boy-loses-boy.

Gabe steeled himself before picking up the phone.

"Thirty slash seventy!" said Owen as if nothing was amiss. "How's your Sunday?"

"Busy," said Gabe "Lots of writing got done. And Arthur Quinn came by with Mother's ashes. We broadcast them in her garden out back."

"Sounds intense," said Owen.

Gabe listened for signs of detachment in Owen's voice but heard none.

"No memes today?" asked Gabe.

"I figured you would appreciate some space. A good idea if you got all that writing done."

"Very thoughtful of you."

"Plus, I had to get ready for the forty third graders coming tomorrow morning."

"That's right."

"At one point today, I started a message to you, but something came up. I'm super excited you got some writing done."

"Thanks. I'll tell you all about it tomorrow. What time are you picking me up? Unless you need to reschedule?"

"Not on your life, dude. I found the best place for our fake date. I flew recon to check the place out. Prepare to be wowed. Be ready by seven."

Gabe was relieved his worst fears had not come to pass. The fun and enthusiasm he had taken for granted and found attractive in Owen were back.

"Oh, and did I see a VCR or a DVD player at your mom's place?"

"Both."

"I love your mom! Never give up on analog. I found the greatest romantic film ever made to share with you. Get ready for a wonderful romantic adventure tomorrow night!"

My call for an adventure.

"A wonderful fake romantic adventure... I missed you today," said Gabe. The words came without a filter.

"Me, too."

*

Monday morning, Gabe's phone woke him from his mother's bed. He didn't recognize the number but answered it anyway.

"Morning," said Gabe, clearing his voice, still heavy with sleep.

"This is Maddy, Owen Greene's assistant. I hope I didn't catch you at a bad time."

"What's up?"

"First, I've got the trust and probate paperwork. I'll need your wet signature on both. Can you swing by this morning, say, ten o'clock?"

"Sure."

"And second—" A banging on Gabe's front door interrupted Maddy. "—Owen said you needed a pickup service for a recliner? They said their window was between eight and ten this morning."

More banging at the door. Gabe's watch read 7:30.

"They're early," said Gabe. He threw on jeans and a sweater before heading to the front door. "How much is this costing me?"

"Owen took care of it. Including a tip. See you at ten!"

The banging on the front door continued. "Anybody home?"

"Coming!" said Gabe at the front door where he met two men, one short but muscular, holding a clipboard, and the other tall and lanky, both ready to remove the offending lounger. In the driveway was a large truck open at the back.

"We have an order here to take away a recliner," said the short guy with the clipboard. "Can we see the piece of furniture?"

Gabe invited them in and removed the blanket covering Chairvana.

"Easy parcheesi," said the short guy, handing the clipboard and a pen to Gabe. "If you sign at the X, we'll take this puppy off your hands."

The taller fellow circled the recliner. "This is one of the nicer ones. Still work?" Before Gabe could respond, he plopped into the chair for a full recline. "Comfy."

Gabe was horrified. The taller guy's silhouette eerily resembled his mother's.

"Get off the merch!" said the short guy, taking the clipboard with his signature. "Protocols, dude. It hasn't even been cleaned yet. No telling what all it has seen." Then, to Gabe, he said, "Nothing personal."

"None taken." Gabe withheld any disclosure.

The tall fellow levered the recliner to its upright position, and the short guy threw the clipboard onto the lounger. Getting on opposite sides of the chair, with a shout of "One...two...three," the men easily lifted it and headed to the front door.

"You've done this before," said Gabe, opening the front door. "Do you need anything else from me?"

"Good to go," said the tall man.

With that, Gabe's traumatic relationship with the infamous Chairvana was removed from the house. The two men hoisted it into the truck, retrieved the clipboard, and headed off to their next pickup.

Gabe moved other furniture to fill the cavity where Chairvana had been. The room instantly looked less empty. A stranger would never have known a recliner had been there. Another grief-action completed, void of ceremony or sentiment.

Gabe immediately texted Owen a picture of the empty space where the chair had been, followed by the praying hands emoji.

Owen responded with exclamation marks on the picture, and a message:

Can't talk rn. Kids everywhere. Beaucoup energy. Herding... *kitten emojis*

Gabe was about to respond with a laughing-to-tears emoji when a call from Erin came in.

"I'm here with the Douglasses," said Erin. "They've read the outline. Are you good for a conference call?"

"Patch me through," said Gabe.

"Gabe!" said Doris.

"Hi, Gabe!" said Thomas. "We love the storyline you created for Barrett," said Thomas.

"Love, love, love it!" said Doris, more hyper than her usual drunken self. "When we pitched your rom-com-on-the-farm idea to the suits, they went bananas. Or tomatoes in this case."

"Did Erin share the farmers market script pages?" asked Gabe.

"Who needs staff writers? You met the challenge and then some!" said Doris.

"I found a comma splice, but other than that, no need for revisions," said Thomas.

"We want you to keep doing it all," said Doris as if she were delivering good news instead of a stressful situation.

Gabe was glad he had gone ahead with those pages for the first week and was ready to write Oliver's second week.

"We can easily weave the Oliver scenes with the other non-Oliver scenes already in the can," said Thomas.

"The farmers market meet-cute," said Doris. "Love the 'Oh, by the way, I'm married' cliff-hanger. Classic!"

"The old inevitable surprise," said Thomas.

"I can work on week two as soon as I get off the phone."

"Atta boy!" said Thomas.

"Your muse awaits," said Doris.

Gabe waited for a ten-count after the called ended before calling Erin.

"Helluva Monday," said Erin. "Man, you worked hard."

Gabe went to his computer and shared the scenes. "I need real notes. Be ruthless."

"Nothing much to revise. Considering you lived it."

"Not going there," said Gabe. "Feel free to tweak. And see what kind of set the production team can put together. If it's too cheesy, get lighting involved."

"They could repurpose the Christmas Fair set," said Erin.

"They always do. And make sure costumes know Oliver's a sexy farmer. No loose overalls," said Gabe.

"I am your eyes."

When the Erin call ended, Gabe was finally able to sit on the sofa and take in the living room without Chairvana.

Things are changing fast on all fronts. He checked his watch and headed to Owen's house.

He got there a few minutes before ten. The children were in the back, sounding excited, like they were at a huge birthday party. Gabe parked behind the two school buses in front.

"Right on time," said Maddy at the front door. "I printed out your documents. Come on back, and you can sign them."

She led Gabe past the parlor where they met the first time. The open-concept downstairs was immaculate and spacious. Gabe glanced out a side window: children were giggling and running around the yard. Maddy led Gabe to a side room that served as an office where she had prepared two clipboards, each with documents to sign.

"Here's the trust document," she said, handing him a clipboard. "Sign here. Great brownies, by the way."

"You had one?" He traded clipboards.

"They were the best. That document is a request to hasten probate. Yeah, Owen saved a few brownies to deliver to Judge Lomax with these documents. His wife is somewhere in the yard right now. The teacher. We may have timed the paperwork perfectly. Want to say hello to Owen?"

"Sure..."

"You guys are having dinner tonight, right?" Gabe tried not to show his discomfort with her casual reference to their fake date. "I made the reservations."

"Where are we going?" asked Gabe.

"I think he wants to surprise you. Let's spy on the field trip and see Owen in action."

Maddy led him to the mudroom door on the side of the house. She quietly opened it so they could hide behind a screen door without Owen seeing them.

Gabe took in a sea of smiling children eating brownies. Owen spoke to them as a gentleman farmer, dressed in muddy work pants and layered flannel shirts. He was surrounded by marigold and basil plants. "Does anyone know why we plant tomatoes near basil and marigolds?"

One child blurted out, "Smell;" another said, "They're pretty;" and another replied, "Tastes good."

The planters were now filled with tomato starter plants. Owen must have spent a fortune at Henderson's. No wonder Mrs. Henderson went out of her way to help him.

"All of those are good answers. You all are exceptionally smart. We're actually protecting the roots of the tomatoes. If any root diseases live in the soil, they will infect the basil and marigold roots first and protect the tomatoes. When you're finished with your brownies, let's have each team grab one basil plant and one marigold to put in each of your planters. If you do this, your tomatoes will be protected and grow into super strong plants."

Gabe found Owen's kindness extremely moving as he generously passed on his newly acquired knowledge to the kids. Owen's warm heart glowed as he worked with the children.

"Do you want to say hello to him?" said Maddy.

"I don't want to be in the way," said Gabe.

"I'll never hear the end of it if I let you leave without saying hello." Maddy cleared her throat as she opened the screen door. "Mr. Greene, look who's here!"

The moment Owen saw Gabe, his whole countenance softened.

Gabe was beaming back at him as he gave Owen a strong thumbs-up.

"Hey, Gabe," said Mrs. Lomax from the side.

"Good morning, Ms. Lomax," said Gabe.

"Hey, kids!" said Owen. "See that man at the door?" All the kids turned around toward Gabe and Maddy. "That's Mr. Hartman, my farming teacher. He made your brownies."

The kids let out a collective cheer.

"Looks good, kids," said Gabe. He waved a quick goodbye before returning to the house. "He was having the time of his life out there."

"A far cry from his heirloom stupidity," said Maddy. "Any questions about the docs?"

"I was planning to stick around until I could put the house on the market. Think probate will take more than a week?"

"Probate takes forever—much, much longer than a week," said Maddy.

He needed to be in the office as the future unfolded for *If Tomorrow Never Comes*.

"The two most important elements when dealing with the law are paperwork and patience," said Maddy as she led him to the front door. "Owen seems to think, however, the trust paperwork is working in your favor."

"That's something."

Maddy checked her watch. "Excuse me. I have to check in on the field trip out back. Don't forget. He's picking you up at seven."

*

Work took precedence over anticipating the fake date. Mason tuned in to Monday's episode of *If Tomorrow Never Comes* from his mother's bed. The actors improvised more than usual in this episode. Afterwards, he spoke to Erin who set up a productive conference call with the costume team. They were all on the same page: Oliver would wear a tight T-shirt, easy to strip off when it gets spilled on, dusty tight jeans with ripped knees and a mud smear. Erin later called with good news about repurposed set pieces for the farmers market set. The Oliver Armstrong shoot was coming along.

After lunch, his text message buzzed with information from Maddy.

Maddy: *Docs filed. I'll keep you posted.*

She attached a photo of a blissed-out Owen and several third graders climbing all over him with evidence of having eaten brownies smeared on their faces. Gabe sent thumbs-up on the picture. He didn't want to give too much away with a heart emoji, but the picture filled his heart.

Gabe drafted new script pages for the next sequence where Suzy would need Oliver's legal help on a trust. Legal jargon never tested well. Gabe constructed the scene around Oliver adding a deck to his new house. He wanted an activity to show off his guns, a physical detail Suzy would appreciate and create a context that would lend itself to double entendre and sexual innuendo. He was satisfied enough to share the writing with Erin and put the document aside.

With his job duties completed, he returned to his jottings about his mother's recipe cards. Flipping through the cards, he became curious that many of the recipes were from other cultures, many international dishes. Her cards were a complete circumnavigation of the globe: Greek spanakopita, Polish pierogi, Mexican tamales, Russian borscht. She highlighted and underlined the country-of-origin for each dish. This was how his mother, who rarely left provincial Upstate New York, traveled the world. With so many revelations, Gabe was starting to think there just might be a book here.

He shared the document with his raw, unfocused musings with Jessica, adding a note asking for some feedback, and ending with "Let's talk tomorrow."

He had spent enough time writing. He now needed to put in some serious time obsessing about his fake date, starting with what to wear.

When he left New York City on Thursday, Gabe had not expected to stay long. He only brought a few changes of clothing. He hadn't planned on a dating wardrobe. He didn't want to buy anything new. That would feel too desperate.

As much as he dreaded it, he would have to venture into his

bedroom closet to see the inventory of clothes, still there from senior year of high school. He made his way into his bedroom with its Currier & Ives and Audubon prints on the walls, unchanged for as long as he could remember. The worn bric-a-brac bedspread and pillows evoked nostalgia. He had spent a majority of the nights of his life asleep in this room, yet the room contained no signs of his identity.

In the closet hung a few pairs of slacks, three Oxford button-down shirts, and a small pile of sweaters on a shelf, one wrapped in a plastic bag. He grabbed the plastic-bag and pulled the sweater out.

During his junior year, he wanted a cashmere sweater, but his mother couldn't afford to buy him one. Gabe decided he would buy one for himself and took a job at a fast-food restaurant, a hybrid rip-off of a famous pizza parlor and an even more famous burger joint. The organization would eventually get sued by both the pizza parlor and the burger joint, but not before Gabe saved enough of his salary and purchased his classic high-end preppy navy-blue cashmere sweater. Ironically, he had never worn it. He was terrified country moths would devour the wool. The sweater had spent its life protected in a plastic bag, tucked away in his closet. He had been waiting to wear it on a special occasion. What better occasion than tonight?

Gabe grabbed a white oxford shirt and the most pressed pair of khakis he could find. He was relieved he still could fit into clothes from high school. As a gay teen in Concord Valley, he considered these clothes the pinnacle of good taste. Today, he understood them as the conservative uniform of the closeted gay teen Gabe had left behind.

Gabe's phone announced another call from Erin.

"What's up?" Gabe put her on speaker.

"Checking to make sure"—Erin's words overlapped with familiar rapping on the front door—"your favorite express mail gal has appeared."

"Coming!" Gabe raced down the stairs to the front door.

"Don't you look swank?" said his favorite package delivery gal, handing him the envelope and the signing tablet.

"Is tonight the big date?" asked Erin.

"Clearly," said the favorite ZipExpress gal.

"How does he look?" asked Erin.

"Handsome. Leaning conservative, but there's some real potential here. He looks like someone who doesn't know how hot he is."

"He's great at pretending," said Erin.

"I'm standing right here," said Gabe. "I have too much to do before he gets here."

"Mañana," said his favorite ZipExpress gal as he closed the door.

"You might want to hide your work," said Erin. "If you don't want him to find out your secret."

"Best. Assistant. Ever," said Gabe, stashing the pages on top of the rest of the gourmet chocolate stash inside the liquor cabinet.

"FYI: everything Oliver Armstrong is falling into place. Word is Barrett and Suzy both loved your pages. The Armstrong schedule has been keeping the Douglasses the busiest they've ever been. They even missed happy hour to stay focused. Don't forget: they start shooting Wednesday with Monday as the first airdate."

"I wish I were there."

"Don't you have a date to obsess about? Go primp!"

Owen tapped on the front door promptly at seven.

"You clean up nice."

"You too." Owen was dressed casually, yet perfectly for a fun date, fake or not. He wore a beautiful floral print shirt, light blue slacks, unobtrusive belt, and colorful two-tone blue loafers, no socks. Owen offered Gabe a small bouquet. "From your garden?" asked Gabe, giving the flowers a whiff. "Do you bring flowers on all your fake dates?"

"When I want to impress the guy."

Gabe gave him a friendly peck on the cheek. "Goes with the shirt."

"Maddy tells me this shirt brings out my eyes."

"Blue on blue," said Gabe.

"Is that cashmere?" Owen stroked his sweater. "Soft."

Before their physical intimacy went any further, Gabe pulled away. "Let me put these in water so we can be on our way."

Gabe looked uncomfortable when Owen opened the door of his SUV for him.

"You didn't like that?" asked Owen when they were both in the car.

"I appreciate the kindness, but it's borderline heteronormative. Does that make me the 'girl' in this situation?"

"Not at all. I erred. Sorry." Owen was mad at himself.

"A prompt apology. That's sexy."

"Yeah?" said Owen.

"Like this car, sexy and comfortable."

"What do you drive?"

"Rentals. I don't need a car in Manhattan."

"If you did?"

"Something sensible, like a pre-owned, compact SUV."

Owen laughed as he drove the car away from town.

The sun was shifting from sunset to golden hour, casting a magical spell on the nature around them.

"Gorgeous evening. Handsome man in my car. I am having it all tonight," said Owen, regaining control of fake-date conversation topics.

"When are you going to tell me where we're going?" asked Gabe.

"I find an element of surprise to be sexy," said Owen.

"Or a power play."

"You are one smart, distrustful dude. Would you let me lead the dance for a while? And I didn't mean to reinforce the idea that you're taking the traditional female role in this dynamic," said Owen.

"Is this what normal people talk about on a date?"

"No. The first part of a date should be small talk, like, how was your day? How *was* your day?"

"Busy, but a good day." He was not going to confess one of his goals was not to obsess about their date. "You?"

"I got the car cleaned," said Owen.

"It has that new car smell," said Gabe.

"And I hosted some adorable third graders this morning."

"That was lovely."

"I had a blast. What were you doing at the house?"

"Maddy said she needed wet signatures on some documents," said Gabe.

"Did she?" asked Owen, sounding skeptical.

"Why did you say it like that?"

"No one needs wet signatures anymore," said Owen. "Everything is electronically signed."

"Why would she want me to see you with the kids?" asked Gabe. "She even sent me a cute picture of the kids climbing all over you."

"Ulterior motives. I think she's trying to get us to hook up."

"Why would she care?"

"She personally doesn't. But she works for Kevin... I think Kevin wants me to hook up with someone. That way, he can feel less guilty about his extracurriculars. Friends tell me he's enjoying our open relationship a little too much."

"Is this your idea of small talk?"

"Be careful what you tell Maddy. That's all."

They drove in silence for a while.

"How much farther is this place?" asked Gabe.

"Not too. If you're interested, I have prepared a brief speech on the history and origins of romance and dating. I did some research. Purely academic. Do you want to hear it?" asked Owen.

"If you took the time, counselor, go for it."

"Do you know who invented romance and dating as we know them today?" asked Owen in an elevated professorial tone.

"The Romans?"

Owen made a wrong-answer buzzer sound. "Catherine the Great."

"The sex-with-a-horse lady?"

"Urban legend. Never happened. Catherine the Great invented dating as a way to audition appropriate husbands. She needed to find someone with the skills to fit in at court."

"Like which spoon to use for the borscht?"

"More like, don't embarrass her by talking while he had food in his mouth, and could he keep a conversation going with foreign diplomats," said Owen. "Ironically, she ended up marrying a man who used the right salad fork in the dining room but never figured out how to consummate in the bedroom."

"That explains why she hooked up with the handsome stallion."

"She never hooked up with a horse!" said Owen.

"I hear she was quite a thoroughbred herself."

"Stop." Owen chuckled.

"I get it. Catherine the Great invented the idea of romance that has evolved into our social construct of dating rituals."

"That's one way to put it."

"But social constructs are designed for one group to maintain power over another in America, usually to prop up and sustain capitalism."

"Capitalism, heteronormativity... You are hopeless when it comes to small talk," said Owen.

"I'll behave."

"No, I love it. The first rule of dating is to be yourself. Besides, small talk is over because"—Owen pulled into a nondescript driveway—"we're here."

"Where?"

All Gabe could see was an old Victorian cottage slightly bigger than his mother's house. The place had no signage, only some light coming through the windows. A few diners could be seen drinking wine at scattered tables in the front dining room.

"This is supposedly one of the best kept secrets in Upstate New York. The restaurant has no name, but it's a farm-to-table restaurant that serves food solely sourced from their farm. There's one seating and it's prix fixe. You game?"

"Sounds amazing."

The restaurant's decor was cool and contemporary with a few Victorian touches. The eclectic feel exuded a hip sweetness. The dining room was incredibly relaxed. One might confuse the servers with the diners. The place was designed for the diners to feel like they were eating in a fine cook's home.

Gabe and Owen were seated by a side window. They became enchanted by the waning golden-hour light bouncing off the hills of the surrounding farm. "This place is so romantic," Gabe said without challenge or irony.

"The food will have to go the distance to match this view."

"Are we still in the small-talk phase of the fake date?" asked Gabe after a server poured wine.

"We're way beyond that. We've entered the getting-to-know-you phase." Owen picked up his glass for a toast. "To fake dates, real friends, and farm-to-table."

"To lovely new friends. Cheers."

They clinked glasses and sipped.

"That's delicious," said Gabe. "You think these grapes are sourced here?"

"Their press says everything. Rieslings grow well up here. I consider Rieslings one of the most underrated wines." Owen took another sip. "Mmm. This one is nice and dry. So, what do you want to know about me?"

"We're jumping in, huh? Got it. Umm... So, have you ever tried any hookup apps?"

"Once. When Kevin and I first tried out our open relationship, we both were on the apps. I'm pretty sure he still uses his."

"And you?"

"It was a disaster, like ordering intimacy from an online delivery service: every choice was commodified. And you have to learn this whole other language."

"That's the fun of it. We've got to keep up with the kids, Grampa."

"When did we stop being 'the kids'?" asked Owen. "And when did we all agree on the term 'side'? And the sex..."

"I'm glad you at least got to the hooking up part," said Gabe.

"Technically, I have stayed true to my wedding vows."

"Owen..."

"I couldn't believe the amount of false advertising! I'm just not wired for it."

"You get literate real fast. Stocky means clinically obese, add at least ten years to anyone's age over thirty. And check an ID for anyone who claims to be twenty-one or under. Profiles are a game of 'Two Lies and a Truth.' And your job is to figure out the one truth."

"I hear versatile actually means bottom," said Owen.

"Not necessarily," said Gabe.

"Oh?" asked Owen.

"I put versatile, and I am. I never know what the chemistry will be until I'm with the dude. That way, the rhythm and the roles naturally fall into place."

"Literally, fall into place," said Owen with a smirk.

"Depends on if I trust the guy and all that."

"I'm authentically versatile too, but I've always topped. Honestly, Gabe, I didn't get a lot of play on the apps."

"I find that hard to believe," said Gabe.

"I found it empty and depressing," said Owen.

"No! Hooking up is meant to be fun!"

"I wish I had your attitude. But no one gets to know anyone. And no one ever spends the night anymore."

"True. It's about doing the deed and moving on to the next thing," said Gabe. "You have to think of it like a diversion, like tennis."

"But there's no attempt at intimacy."

"Intimacy is overrated."

"You don't really believe that, do you?"

"When you don't know someone, sex for the sake of sex can be liberating."

"It reduces sex to a game."

"As long as everyone knows the rules," said Gabe with a shrug. He took a sip of wine. "Mmm, this Riesling is good."

"Can I see your profile?" asked Owen.

"Never," said Gabe. "And it's not a trust or power issue. Looking at a hookup app would not fit the vibe of this fabulous place. And I don't want you judging my scrawny torso."

"I'm sure you have a lovely torso," said Owen.

"Stop imagining me naked. Shh! Here comes our first course."

The server set an overflowing platter in the middle of the table and announced: "The raw spring vegetables were picked a few hours ago by Chef, with reserve gouda, soft camembert, sharp cheddar aged with Irish whiskey from our dairy with roasted rosemary nuts from our orchards. The salume is a Finocchiona, aged in the Tuscan style with toasted fennel, black pepper, garlic, and red wine. Enjoy." The server returned to the kitchen.

"This is such beautiful food," said Gabe. "I love how it looks randomly tossed onto a platter, and yet..."

"Yet there's deliberate storytelling involved. Knowing every piece was picked a few hours ago, how could it not be delicious? The word 'Tuscan' prepares the palate to be transformed by romantic tasting notes."

"You should run a restaurant."

"I want to be the 'farm' part of a farm-to-table."

"You could be both. You're such a talented baker."

"I love all culinary adventures," said Owen, taking some cheese, then looking around the dining room. "Sometimes these places feel like they're auditioning for a Michelin star, but not this place. If I did run a restaurant, this is the kind of place I'd want. Limited seating and one menu made up of whatever I picked from the garden."

"You better learn to garden first."

"I would put a big community table in the middle of the dining room and have a few two- and four-tops scattered around it."

"Sounds like you've thought this through."

"So many dreams; take a number. Only twenty-four hours in a day," said Owen, before nibbling on a pink radish. "Oh my god, this is good. And I hate radishes."

"Radishes are easy to grow, and a super-short growing season. Sometimes as little as twenty days." Gabe took some cheese. "The whiskey is smooth in this cheddar."

"Are you having a good time so far?" asked Owen.

"I always have fun with you—even when we're rolling around in a dump."

"Me too," said Owen. "So what would it take to get you and me in a full-on relationship? We kinda are, you know."

"No, no, no. We are friends. This is still the getting-to-know-each-other part, right? We're still on a fake date, right?"

"Absolutely. But seriously, what would it take for us to become an actual couple?"

"Divorce Kevin, for starters."

"Probably not going to happen. Let's say you learn to trust me, and you figure out I'm not on some power trip. Then what would stop you?"

"Wouldn't that break the first rule of an open relationship? Don't fall in love."

"True. What I want to know is why you won't get involved in any open relationship with anyone. What's that about?" asked Owen, then continued to graze on a purple heirloom carrot from the starter platter.

Gabe took a generous sip of wine. "It started way before I was born. Once upon a time..."

"Yay! More storytelling."

"My mother fell in love with a married man. The cliche was cinched when he promised her he was going to leave his wife. Someday."

"Was he a creep?"

"I never met him, but I don't think so. My mother always claimed they were in love. I think he set her up in the house up here."

"Was he from here?"

"From what I gathered, he lived in someplace like Islip with his other family, worked in the City, and met up with my mother on business trips to Albany. Their trysts had to take place far from his other life. My mother was always sketchy on the details."

"Sounds exhausting."

"I know, right? Cut to: my mother eventually gets pregnant."

"With you?"

"Correct. The way my mother told it, the morning he was supposed to ask his wife for a divorce, he died of a double cardiac arrest. Fitting, as he left two families destitute, broken-hearted."

"Had you been born yet?"

"I came along a few months later. She raised me as a single mother in the house he left her. But she never got over him. Until Arthur Quinn, that is."

"Concord Valley is not a bad place for a childhood."

"For a gay kid being raised by a single mom, Concord Valley was a terrible place. The only culture is agriculture. It's changed a bit, but rural agricultural communities always lean conservative, not at all welcoming when you're growing up gay. I didn't know one single out gay man here."

"No hairdressers? Florists?"

"None. Gay boys are wise to get the hell out of poor farming communities. When people don't have a lot of wealth, gossip becomes currency. I didn't want to make my mother's life miserable. Leaving town was the best solution."

"How did you survive when you lived here?" asked Owen.

"I was the classic 'best little boy in the world.' Avoid shame at all costs. I erased my true self."

"When gay kids erase themselves, they usually take on a different identity. We get good at lying."

If you only knew. "I did whatever I could to fit in. I focused on farming, did a lot of 4-H projects, joined Christian clubs, went to Christian summer camp, dated a cheerleader, and played the least amount of sports I needed to get by. It served me well, as long as I didn't pop a boner in the locker room. I didn't come out to my mother until after I graduated from college. She was always loving, but she didn't know how to talk about it."

"That explains a lot."

"What about you? Did you have a tragic gay youth?"

"Much different. I was shipped off to a progressive boarding school where we were encouraged to pop boners in the locker room. As a political act."

"Lucky."

"In many ways. My parents were grumpy when I first came out. Until Kevin came along; he is the perfect son-in-law. But why are we talking about me? You are great at deflecting. We were discussing your former Concord Valley identity that doesn't serve you anymore. Now that your mom's gone, there's no need for defensive strategies."

"Look, it's lovely to be here with you, but the reason I feel tentative about committing to a friendship here is because I never feel like I belong here. And now that my mother is gone, I don't belong to anyone here anymore." Gabe didn't think this was the time to share that he had no plans to return to Concord Valley after this visit, especially if the soap moved to Los Angeles.

"I hope you feel like you belong with me and my heirloom tomato project."

"Of course. But...the hardest part about being here—" Gabe stopped. Unexpected emotions caught in his throat. "I'm talking too much. I don't want to ruin the evening."

"Nothing you could say— Tell me."

"The hardest part about being in Concord Valley now is...I miss my mother so much." Gabe hated that his eyes were filled with tears. Owen reached out for his hand with a sweet tenderness Gabe had never known from another man. Gabe swallowed another incoming wave of tears. "I wasn't ready for her to go... I never got a chance to say goodbye."

Owen took a thumb and wiped away some of the tears that surfaced.

"I wish I could have shown her..." Gabe hadn't lied all night, but he did not want Owen to find out he wrote for *If Tomorrow Never Comes*. He chose his words carefully. "I wish I could have shared the fullness of my life with her. Made her proud. She did the best she could with what she had, which wasn't much."

"From my perspective, I'd say she did a great job. I'm sure she was proud of you."

"She'd be even prouder if I don't get involved with a married man. It's the family mythology I want to rewrite."

"But we're not comparable. Your father wasn't in an open relationship."

"Someone's going to get hurt. It's inevitable. More than likely, it'll be me. I don't want to be someone's something on the side."

"My man, you are not capable of becoming that." Owen leaned in and gave Gabe's hand a squeeze. "Aren't you even curious to see where we would end up?"

"Don't push it, Owen. Please." Gabe took his hand from Owen's.

"Thank you for sharing all that," said Owen. "You're much better at dating than you let on."

"Did I surprise you?"

"Every day. I'm surprised how easily you let down your guard to let me in. I'm surprised how honest you are."

"When I want to be. I wish I could let you in more," said Gabe.

"Vulnerability is very sexy on you."

"If this is the getting-to-know-you phase, I'm afraid of what comes next."

"Besides the entree? If someone shared all of that with me on a first date…"

"I hope you would run for the hills. That's a bit of an overshare for a first date. Don't you think?"

"True. More a third-date disclosure. But perfect for our fake practice session."

The server had arrived at their table with two plates. "Our entree tonight is our baked free-range lavender chicken with homegrown polenta milled by our river pond with a flash-fried broccoli-cauliflower-Romanesco salad."

"This place has its own mill and a river pond?" asked Gabe after the server was out of earshot.

"So much idyllic storytelling tonight," said Owen. "Bon appétit."

Gabe took a bite. "So good. I was afraid the lavender would be overpowering."

"Me too," said Owen. "I wish I'd met you before."

"There always seems to be a before," said Gabe.

"Kevin and I never had this."

"But we didn't meet before."

"No."

They ate in silence for a while.

"Food this good? No words," said Owen.

They continued to eat in the comfortable silence of easy friendship.

"So," said Gabe when he was done, "we've talked of your sexless open relationship and my fucked-up family. What's your fucked-up family like?

"Well... I embody what most of the world loathes. I went to a fancy boarding school and had legacy admission to an Ivy League college. After I graduated, I was a victim of nepotism with plenty of seed capital from family money, old money, of course. I learned how to sign an *x* for a country club tab before I could write my name. You've met my personal assistant, and I've confessed to having had a cook growing up, which implies an even bigger staff. There's nothing much more to tell. I come from old-money and privilege."

"I guess I come from no money and no privilege."

"Gabe, you *are* the privilege. I'm an only child. And my parents don't approve of my dreams of being a sustainable heirloom tomato farmer, but like Kevin, they're humoring me until I come to my senses and return to the law office, which I never plan to do. One reason I love farming is that most of my privileges have no value in the soil."

"That's a lot to take in." Gabe admired him even more. "This date has gotten very real very fast. Do we ever get back to small talk?"

"Power and trust-issues small talk?" asked Owen.

"No. Surface-things small talk," said Gabe. "Shouldn't we be comparing favorite movies or shows we streamed last?"

"Yes. On a real first date, you want to keep the conversation light and polite. You focus on data gathering. There's a lot of information on where people get their news."

"Fox—kidding. NPR, of course. Pacifica if I want the real truth. Next question?"

"We don't want the date to start sounding like an interview," said Owen. "I turn the data gathering into a game. I have a few favorites."

"Go for it," said Gabe.

"Do you have a theme song?" asked Owen.

"Don't be ridiculous."

"Humor me. If your life were a movie—"

"Like a rom-com?" asked Gabe.

"Even better. Your life is a rom-com, and you enter a room; what song is playing?"

Gabe took a moment but drew a blank.

"The go-tos," said Owen, "are 'Stand By Your Man' or 'The Way You Look Tonight'—depending on what your agenda is. All rom-com characters have theme songs."

"What's yours?"

"Right now? 'Take a Chance on Me' by Abba." Owen sang the title to Gabe. "Next week when you're gone, 'What'll I Do.'" He also sang.

Not a bad singer. "I see how this works. How about 'But Not For Me'?"

"Too evasive," said Owen. "How about 'Our Love is Here to Stay'?"

"Your agenda is showing."

"Seriously...you never had a theme song?" asked Owen.

Gabe took a moment. "Do you know the song 'In Dreams'?"

"Roy Orbison? Great song. Open for interpretation. Interesting choice. Are you implying there's a modicum of hope for us?" asked Owen.

"Anything's possible," said Gabe as the server approached them with two small plates. Gabe took a mental note: add the theme song game to the Oliver Armstrong storyline.

"Tonight's dessert is a deconstructed brownie served with creme fraiche." The server placed the plates before Gabe and Owen before returning to the kitchen.

They waited until he was gone before bursting into laughter.

"First of all," said Gabe, "why deconstruct the perfection of a brownie? Everything else tonight has been flawless, but this is pretentious."

"There's no way this brownie could match ours. Ready?"

They each grabbed a fork and took a taste.

"They skimped on the chocolate," whispered Gabe.

"Mabel and Amelia's recipe is without peer."

As they left the restaurant, Gabe was impressed that he never saw money change hands. "Thank you," he said when they were both in the SUV. "That was a special night."

"It's not over. The evening now needs redemption from the

deconstructed brownie disaster. We still have the movie portion."

As they drove to Gabe's house, Owen teased him with a guessing game about which movie he had picked.

"Hint: it's a perfect date movie," said Owen.

"*Fatal Attraction? Psycho?*" asked Gabe.

"Funny. Think: classy film."

"*Wild at Heart?*"

"That's classy?"

"Art house classy."

After going beyond twenty questions through a long list of rom-coms, from *Roman Holiday* to the latest Netflix *Kissing Booth* adaptation, Owen gave him one last hint. "It has been called the swooniest movie ever made."

"I'm drawing a blank."

"Open the glove compartment," said Owen.

Gabe pulled out a DVD. *In the Mood for Love.*

"Wong Kar-wai's masterpiece," said Owen.

Gabe was speechless at the coincidence. He was about to let him know *In the Mood for Love* was one of his favorite movies, but he could see how excited Owen was to share the film. "I don't know this film." Gabe's first big lie of the night.

"This is essential viewing. Oh, you are in for a treat." Owen's joy affirmed that Gabe's lie was the right decision. "I don't remember where all the televisions are in your house."

"There's one. In my mother's bedroom. She liked to watch in bed."

"We're watching this romantic film in bed?" said Owen as Gabe unlocked the front door. "Warning: there will be cuddling."

"Cool." Gabe turned on the light downstairs.

Owen took in the living room. "What's different? Oh, my God! It's really gone!"

"Thanks for that."

When they got to his mother's bedroom, Gabe took over tech duties. "I think I still know how to set up the DVD player."

As Gabe fiddled with his mother's DVD player to play the film, he could hear Owen slipping off his loafers and fluffing a pillow pile against the headboard. Gabe was still feeling vulnerable from everything he had shared over dinner. When he turned around, he caught Owen staring at him in a way that made him feel objectified, yet empowered.

"What?" asked Gabe, throwing the remote to Owen.

Owen grinned and patted the bed next to him. "Let's watch the movie, you gorgeous man."

Gabe took off his shoes and climbed next to Owen.

"Aren't you hot in that cashmere?"

Gabe stripped the sweater off and tossed it to the side of the bed. His Oxford shirt came untucked in the front revealing a delicate line of hair below his navel disappearing into his pants.

"Look at you with your sexy treasure trail."

Gabe untucked and pulled up Owen's shirt. "You have one, too, I see." Gabe wanted to caress Owen's navel.

"Focus on the movie, dude."

Owen immediately enveloped him with one arm and pulled him into his chest while his other hand clicked the remote to start the DVD.

"I can hear your heart beating," said Gabe, comforted by the steady rhythm.

Owen put the remote aside and held Gabe's hand. He looked him in the eye. "You good?"

"Oh, yeah."

While the mandatory FBI DVD warning screen about copyright infringement and opening credits played, Owen gave Gabe enough context and background on Tony Leung and Maggie Cheung's characters so he would have the inside scoop.

"Her dress is gorgeous," said Gabe as soon as the first camera shots lingered on Maggie Cheung's beautiful couture.

"They're Cheongsam dresses from the early 60s in Hong Kong. Each a work of art," said Owen. "She never wears the same one twice. The costume designer must have been annoyed," said Owen.

"Costume designers live for this kind of project," said Gabe, quickly adding, "I assume." He did not want to sound like an industry insider.

When the couple in the film first crossed paths, Owen whispered with warm breath into Gabe's ear, "Meet cute, like us."

Gabe was getting turned on in Owen's arms. He did not want to pop a boner in front of him. He shifted slightly.

"You okay?" asked Owen.

"My arm was falling asleep." He didn't want Owen to feel any tumescence coming and going. Gabe was aware his lying increased dramatically around the movie. His rationale was self-preservation.

"Gorgeous score," said Gabe.

"Shigeru Umebayashi's 'Yumeji's Theme'."

Gabe was impressed how well Owen knew the film. "Their theme song," said Gabe. "It gives the film a dreamlike quality."

"Very Roy Orbison," said Owen.

"That and the repetition of shots and use of slow motion," said Gabe as if he were in the production room at work. "It's astonishing... It's beautiful."

"You're right." Owen pulled him in gently. "I'm glad you're enjoying this."

"It casts a spell."

They sat in stillness and let the film wash over them as art and meditation. If every night ended in his arms like this, Gabe could get used to life with Owen.

"What's Nat King Cole singing? I don't speak Spanish," said Gabe.

"'*Quizas, Quizas, Quizas*.' Perhaps, perhaps, perhaps."

Midway through the film, Owen's hands casually landed on Gabe's wrists, which Owen began to caress. Gabe did not pull back.

A few minutes later, Gabe had a major realization and pushed up on an elbow. He looked directly at Owen and said, "Spouses fooling around on the side, the leading man wants to be a writer, she acts like a kind of consultant to him, and they don't end up sleeping together. Many similarities. Is that why you picked this film?"

"How do you know they don't sleep together? You said you hadn't seen it."

Gabe took a breath. In a split second he had to decide whether to cop to his lie and potentially ruin a perfect night or bullshit his way out of this moment.

Gabe chose the latter. "The integrity of the story demands they not sleep with each other. The premise is based on the fact that they're better than their adulterous spouses. We're rooting for them not to have sex. Glances and passing caresses, a hand on a lapel—that's all we need for them. Their yearning is what makes this—what did you call it—the 'swooniest' film ever."

"That makes them similar to us too. Sorry, I had no agenda. Consciously, anyway. Trust me."

Gabe responded by putting his head on Owen's chest, lightly caressing a shirt button near Owen's heart.

"That was insightful," said Owen. "You should think about writing film and television."

"I took a film class once... Sh..."

Near the end of the film, Tony Leung has to accept the fact that Maggie Cheung won't leave her husband. Gabe didn't need to bring up more similarities. When Maggie Cheung responds that she didn't think he'd fall in love with her, Tony Cheung says he didn't either, but feelings have a way of creeping in. Owen took the remote and paused the film.

"I had forgotten this scene— I don't want you to think any of this was premeditated. I haven't seen the film in years. But I need to confess something to you."

Gabe sat up.

"I lied to you," said Owen. "Yesterday, when you asked me why I hadn't texted you, I said I was busy. I was—busy obsessing about what to text you. Every time I would start a text, the same words came out. I chose to practice restraint instead."

"What were the words?" asked Gabe, remembering the chat bubbles with no messages.

"I wanted to tell you I have fallen in love with you. But I kept chickening out."

"Better to say something that important in person."

"I agree."

They stared at each other to see what the other would do next.

"Feelings do have a way of creeping up on you," said Gabe.

They continued to stare at each other, looking for a clue as to what to do next, until they both moved in at the same time in slow motion and melded their lips together, not like their earlier kiss, but a mutual moment of agreement. Lips parted and gentle kisses became more forthright and determined. They had pushed beyond the swoon. The dreams of yearning had become a waking reality. Kissing time can sometimes languish, but both men's desire for more lacked patience. Their hands explored and drifted, first to their faces, and then down their necks. They had not defined boundaries.

Gabe unbuttoned one of Owen's shirt buttons, and his hand fell to Owen's waistband to the hair below his navel, where he had yearned to touch since he had discovered it. Owen caressed the same place on Gabe, who gave out a soft moan, the first sound either had made since they started kissing.

Owen stopped. "I want to make sure this is okay."

Gabe was breathless. "What part of the fake date are we on?"

"There is nothing fake about this part of the date. Are you all right with us doing this?" asked Owen.

"Very."

"You trust me enough to know I would never hurt you?"

"I trust you, Owen."

"We can stop at any time."

"The integrity of our narrative demands we keep going," said Gabe, going in for more kisses, unbuttoning Owen's slacks as Owen did the same to Gabe's khakis. They worked with the curiosity of children finally discovering the treasure they were after.

"They grow them big on the farm," said Owen.

"You're nothing to be ashamed of either."

Owen looked deeply into Gabe's eyes as he kissed his chest, undressing him as he went down his body. Gabe tried to do the same, but the physical logistics got too chaotic having both go at each other at once.

"You'll get your turn," said Owen. He pinned him and stripped him of everything but his underwear. "You are a beautiful man. I can think of nothing hotter than you in those tighty-whities." Owen kissed his chest and once more worked his way down.

"Wait. My turn." Gabe surprised Owen with his power as he flipped them both. He unbuttoned the rest of Owen's shirt with his teeth and smothered his chest with kisses.

"Mmm. You are full of lovely surprises tonight, Mister," said Owen.

"Kevin and Maddy are going to be extremely pleased."

"Yeah, they will." Owen pulled Gabe up to his face. They returned to their kissing, going even deeper now. Both men, stripped of everything but their underwear, were enjoying the feel of each other's body against their own. Despite their rock-hard erections, neither was sure how to make the next big move.

"I have an idea," said Owen. With one smooth move, he got to his knees and lifted Gabe into his arms.

"Where are you taking me?" asked Gabe.

"Trust me."

Gabe surrendered to Owen's strength.

The still shot of Tony Leung at the beginning of the Angkor Wat sequence remained frozen on the television screen as Owen carried Gabe out of his mother's room.

"There's a much better place for what we're about to do."

Owen crossed the hallway and moved Gabe's body at a diagonal across the threshold of Gabe's bedroom.

"No more erasing Gabe Hartman," said Owen. "After tonight, this is his bedroom where he has sex with whoever he wants, however he wants. It's time to regain control of your room."

"Fuck, yeah," said Gabe. He kissed Owen with a newfound depth of passion as Owen lowered him onto his bed. The double bed was a tight fit for sleeping side by side, but just enough room for two grown men coming together as one. Owen lay on top of him, as the two men matched each other's passion.

Their lust rose with each kiss as the friction of their bodies could no longer be contained. They clawed off each other's underwear, unable to restrain themselves from the inevitable.

"How exactly do you see this working, Mister?" asked Owen, kneeling between Gabe's legs. "We both claim to be versatile."

"Wasn't the point of this date to let you in more?" said Gabe. "Why don't we keep going with that idea? For starters."

Gabe raised his hips to give Owen more access to his desire.

"Looks like everything is falling smoothly into place," said Owen, self-lubricating and adjusting himself, intent on fulfilling the promise of their first meeting.

"Boy gets boy, boy gets all of boy." Gabe whispered in his ear as he set aside his inhibitions.

They continued their date all through the night.

Chapter Six

The next morning, Gabe awoke disoriented. He recalled being carried into his bedroom. It took him a second to remember why he was completely naked. He stretched out his hand to where Owen had been sleeping.

No Owen.

The clock said 7:00 a.m. Waking up, his synapses were firing faster recalling both this morning and the events of the night before. Gabe and Owen had gone many imaginative rounds. The memories of last night were making his groin get tingly and stiff.

Where had Owen gone? No signs of his clothes. Owen had been the one complaining no one spent the night anymore. Had there been a walk of shame? Gabe didn't take the abandonment personally. However, he was disappointed he wouldn't get to start the day a la morning sex with Owen.

Gabe was fine being alone, happily exhausted after a night of great sex. The best sex in a long time, maybe ever. That's what didn't track about Owen's leaving without a goodbye. Maybe he left him a note downstairs.

Gabe was suddenly struck by regret. *Damn! This is what happens when you fall for a married man. He will ultimately let you down. Abandonment will be the expectation. Best not pin too much on it.*

Dehydrated and in need of a glass of water, Gabe also had too much work ahead of him to linger between the sheets. He got out of bed and put on his tighty-whities.

"Where do you think you're going?" asked Owen, coming through the door in only underwear and a grin, carrying a tray with breakfast for two.

"I didn't think you were still here."

"I'm not done with you, Mister. Back into bed you go." He gave Gabe a loving nudge, sending him onto the bed. "In dreams, you're mine all of the time; we're together in dreams," Owen playfully sang as he set up the breakfast picnic in bed. "Don't even think about getting dressed yet. I hope you're into morning sex."

"Twist my arm." Gabe's underwear was starting to tent as he pawed Owen's crotch.

"You want some more of that, huh?" asked Owen. "Slow down, cowboy. There's plenty of time. Let's get fueled up first."

"Look what you made us!"

A beautiful breakfast lay between them: two plates of poached eggs on a piece of toasted sourdough bread with a drizzle of olive oil and a sprig of Italian parsley. On the side, he had cut apples to look like flowers.

"Your mother had everything here," said Owen.

Thinking about Owen snooping around downstairs made Gabe nervous. He was glad he hid the *If Tomorrow Never Comes* envelope in the liquor cabinet. He was even more delighted Owen had stayed to make breakfast and no telling what else to come.

"Drink some water." Owen handed Gabe a glass of water. "Replenish the bodily fluids we exchanged last night."

"We shared all kinds of DNA. Such fun."

"We *are* versatile. No doubt about it. Bon appétit."

"It's too beautiful to eat. If you ever tire of heirloom tomatoes, you can always open that restaurant."

"How about I open a restaurant when you have a *New York Times* bestseller," said Owen, giving him a kiss.

"Fair enough."

"I don't know if you have plans for later," said Owen, "but I wouldn't mind hanging. Like tonight."

"I wouldn't mind, but I do have some work to do." Gabe was happy to have a sexy new sequence for the Oliver Armstrong storyline. He would have to tone the sex down significantly for the network censors.

"I guess I should do some work today too," said Owen. "My heirlooms are thirsty."

"They're not the only ones."

As they ate, they stared at each other, smiling through each bite, two people who couldn't believe their good fortune.

"There's coffee downstairs," said Owen, moving the tray off the bed, "but you need to earn it first."

Gabe pulled Owen's underwear down with his teeth and proceeded to show off his ability for earning merits.

After they were both perfectly satisfied, after they had showered together, and after they had cleaned up both bedrooms, they got dressed and went downstairs for coffee.

"I hate to take off like this," said Owen, looking like he did at the beginning of the date, only more wrinkled, "but I need to get home before Maddy shows up. No telling what that would set spinning. I'm not ashamed, but let's spare us all that nonsense."

"She can know after probate settles," said Gabe.

"That might be a while. You still have the end of *In the Mood for Love* to watch. I highly recommend it."

"When do you need the DVD back?" asked Gabe.

"It's a gift," said Owen. "And look over those recipes; see if there's something we can make together."

"How's after seven?" Gabe didn't want him to cross paths with his favorite express delivery gal.

"Sounds good."

Owen planted a deep kiss on Gabe's mouth, now more knowing and warm than exciting and new. They were settling in. Gabe found comfort sexier than novelty.

"Remember, boy doesn't have to lose boy a second time," said Owen.

As soon as the SUV drove away, Gabe made a beeline to the liquor cabinet for the ZipExpress envelope. He looked over the pages and added notes to add some sexy spice: formfitting tops for one of their sexier actresses and one of their blander leading men going shirtless or getting out of the shower wearing only a towel. Overall, the pages seemed fine. He annotated minor redundancy tweaks, suggestions for possible cuts, a later start to one scene, and a more suspenseful ending for another before a commercial, assuming the actor would say the line as written.

The revision pages took less than an hour. He would drop them off at his stealth overnight drop-off before lunch. Next, he added to the Oliver Armstrong story arc, which had become a coded mirror of his relationship with Owen. He wrote in the fake date, the theme song bit, watching the movie, and cuddling that led to passionate sex.

Gabe's mind was easily distracted by memories of the night before: Owen's warm smile, his moan during intense sex, his infectious laugh, his tender kindness. He had never had this with anyone. Was he falling in love? When Owen confessed he had fallen in love, Gabe had held back. Owen couldn't have expected him to respond in kind.

When Gabe took the breakfast tray into the kitchen, everything had already been cleaned up. All Owen had left for Gabe were some plates and glasses. Owen's stock continued to rise.

Gabe flipped through the recipe cards. He recognized a lot of favorite treats from his childhood. One particular card caught his eye, maybe twenty or thirty years old and written in his mother's best cursive: a recipe for a galette. He had seen many recipes for galettes recently, but he had never known his mother to make one. The recipe was in two simple parts: dough and fruit filling. What caught his eye was the phrase "his favorite" under the title in parentheses.

Gabe opened his computer and added to the document he sent to Jessica. "His" must have been his father. In no time, Gabe composed the story he had shared last night with Owen. The words flowed like a stream of consciousness. When Gabe reread what he'd written, he was amazed his words formed such a cohesive, deeply felt narrative, full of forgiveness and admiration for his mother's strength and resilience.

A faint *ding-a-ling* came from the phone he left in his mother's bedroom. He sprinted up the stairs in hopes of hearing Owen's voice on the line. He was disappointed to see Cohen's number on his phone.

"This is Gabe. Good morning."

"Morning. Roger Cohen here."

"Is everything okay?"

"Great. That Greene is terrific."

"Yeah, he's pretty amazing," said Gabe, smiling.

"They set up your trust documents fast. And we threw a few extension monkey wrenches at the property tax people. Hopefully, that will prevent the government from putting a lien on your personal assets."

"Great news!"

"It's happened faster than we've ever seen. Now we need to put the funding documents in place. That way, the property can be transferred to you once probate is settled."

"I understand probate timing is unpredictable."

"Everyone agrees we want to get your ducks in a row for when that happens. I spoke to Greene's assistant."

"Maddy? She starts work early." Gabe tried not to betray his worst fears with his voice.

"She's dropping off all relevant documents in a few minutes for us to look over. Can you stop by this afternoon at, say, two o'clock?"

"I'll be there."

Gabe tried to imagine Maddy taking in Owen as he arrived home this morning, still wearing his clothes from the night before, only a more wrinkled version of them.

He texted Owen.

Gabe: *All good?*

Owen: **thumbs-up emoji* *heart emoji**

The colorful vermillion DVD case for *In the Mood for Love* caught Gabe's eye. A few unwatched minutes remained before the final credit roll. Gabe found not completing a great film completely unsatisfying, even one he'd seen several times. He grabbed the remote and clicked the On button.

Tony Cheung materialized, meditating in an Angkor Wat temple by a tangled banyan tree. In an earlier speech in the film, Cheung's coworker tells him how secrets used to be kept in the old days: find a tree, carve a hole in it, and whisper the secret into the hole before covering it with mud. Leave the secret behind forever, which Tony Cheung does with the help of a banyan tree in Angkor Wat. One of the last shots is a muddy patch of grass covering the hole in a banyan tree.

Gabe admired the elegant poetry of the gesture. He grabbed a sharp knife and went out to the aspen tree in the backyard. His mother's ashes were still clearly visible as there had not been much wind and no rain. Gabe was careful not to step on any as he made his way to the tree. With the knife, he hacked a small hole in the side of the aspen where he whispered all the secret lies he had told. Then he took a handful of moist soil and packed it into the hole. His mudpack was messier than the film's, but he had faith it would secure his secrets.

Gabe was now living a paradox. He had surrendered to the one tenet he vowed never to break: he got involved with a married man. Owen had proven to be the safest presence in his life, and he was clearly smitten with him. Why walk away? The comfort that enveloped him in Owen's arms, by his side, across the table from him, navigating the kitchen with him... Gabe understood how his mother could stay with her married man.

When his phone rang, Gabe assumed Owen was calling. "Hello, you." His tone oozed with sexy warmth.

"Good morning?" Erin's voice was a splash of cold water.

"Oh, hey."

"I don't have time for a dating update right now," said Erin. "Work stuff."

"Shoot."

"They're filming the farmers market sequence tomorrow. Barrett's rehearsing with Suzy today."

"I'm not worried about Barrett, but that's a lot of lines for Suzy to learn in a short time."

"She'll paraphrase most of the lines anyway," said Erin. "Second, the Douglasses are making the official announcement about moving to LA tomorrow sometime."

"How did you find this out?"

"I taught them how to do push-notifications. They asked me to 'proofread' it."

"Did you just put air quotes around proofread?"

"Of course. Do boomers not know about the invention of AI editing apps?

"At least they're no longer using pagers. Everything is coming along. I'd better write the second and third sequences."

"One tiny suggestion."

"Shoot."

"Your outline says Suzy gets legal advice from Oliver. Legalese can be a snooze unless you write it as double entendre."

"Like, I want to see what's in those briefs?"

"You're way ahead of me."

"I've got your deposition. No objections? Overruled!"

"Yeah, yeah. You got it."

"I'll overnight the Friday pages. Mostly notes on where we could lean into more sex."

"The whole show could use some sexing up— Wait! Does this mean...you had sex with Mr. Handsome Married Lawyer last night?"

"You'll have to wait until I send the script pages."

"You dirty dog! I wish I could see you happily postcoital. Good for you."

"I'd love to stick around and share the details, but NSFW is real.

And you're at work."

"Bitch."

"Let me know how the rehearsal goes."

The *If Tomorrow Never Comes* set designers didn't have the resources for a Victorian interior, but they had done basic contemporary farmhouse sets. Gabe cranked out another five days' worth of scenes for Suzy and Oliver in record time. He added a male Maddy-type into the scene as an under-five. The suits put no restrictions on how many under-fives he could add. If the actor performed well with under five lines, they would sometimes make him a recurring character or give him a day player contract. But for now, he kept male Maddy's line count to under five.

Gabe's phone buzzed a message.

> **Owen**: *Miss you. Can't wait for tonight.*

> **Gabe**: *Now that we're having sex, no more inappropriate memes? If I'd known, I never would have...*

A cow meme appeared in seconds.

> **Owen**: *"Studies show farmers have more sex than any other profession."*

> **Gabe**: **Ha-ha emoji**

A rusty tractor meme arrived next.

> **Owen**: *I may be old, but you can still ride me.*

> **Gabe**: *K, K, we can still have sex. Don't you have a conference call or something?*

> **Owen**: *Later (CMBYN reference)*

> **Gabe**: *Yeah, yeah, Elio.*

Eleven o'clock was closing in. Gabe grabbed his laptop and headed to his mother's bed to watch *If Tomorrow Never Comes* in broadcast time, multitasking as he wrote.

Today's main Harmony Hills storyline was a sequence about a minister who was addicted to porn. Gabe had stolen the story from a Concord Valley minister addicted to video games. Addiction storylines provided the classic tale of redemption. But the actor playing the minister had been on the soap for decades and had become a hack. He couldn't pull off the erotic or the pathos to make the story work. Gabe turned down the volume when this porn-addict sequence came on. He needed to write in peace.

He concentrated on punching up the legal language in Oliver's dialogue to make it sexy: "This case had fallen in my lap."

"It's not a big case. Does size matter to you?"

"I don't want to strip you of your profits, adversely impacting your...bottom...line."

"We might have to erect a constitutional wall."

Gabe wove enough fast-paced double entendres into the dialogue to make the lines feel like a screwball romantic comedy. The actors would enjoy playing this scene.

As the show's credits rolled, Gabe was pleased with his work and grateful his relationship with Owen made for good story structure. He shared the document with Erin and included an invite for notes. He then headed to the ZipExpress office the next county over.

"Hey, confidential George Sample," said his least favorite ZipExpress clerk. A woman at the store's only copy machine glanced casually in his direction before returning to her printing project. The ZipExpress woman's casual disregard for his anonymity worried Gabe.

"Can we keep that information between us?" asked Gabe.

"You betcha, boss."

He would have to find a new ZipExpress store.

"Off to Manhattan it goes," she said, securing a new mailing label and tossing the envelope in a bin behind her. "I looked you up, George Sample," she said with a loud whisper. "Very impressive."

"Thanks."

He would definitely be finding a new ZipExpress office.

On the way to his meeting with the Cohens, his phone buzzed a text.

> **Owen**: *Me judging every gay boy's Instagram. There was a meme of Meryl Streep as a sarcastic Miranda Priestly. Mykonos? For summer? Groundbreaking.*

> **Gabe**: **Ha-ha emoji**

When he parked the car in the town square, he texted Owen back.

> **Gabe**: *We're already at Meryl memes? This is getting serious.*

> **Owen:** **heart emoji**

> **Owen**: *Yep.*

As Gabe was getting out of his car, Arthur approached him with a woman he didn't recognize.

"What a nice surprise!" said Arthur. "Gabe, I'd like to introduce you to Lenore."

"Nice to meet you." Lenore was a lovely woman about Arthur's age with gray hair in a short, sensible haircut. She was smartly dressed.

"Gabe here is indirectly responsible for our getting together," said Arthur. "We are coming from our first coffee date."

"So the app served you well," said Gabe.

"Gabe helped me sign up for one of those dating apps," he told Lenore before turning to Gabe. "I deleted that app when I realized all those women wanted to get in my boxers. But being on the app gave me the confidence to open up and immerse myself in the dating world again. And look who showed up."

"We met at the smoke shop," said Lenore. "We both like to smoke pipes."

"After you and I spread Amelia's ashes, Gabe, I got a craving for some new cherry-scented tobacco, so I stopped by the smoke shop.

Lenore happened to be there at the same time buying tobacco too."

"What are the odds?" asked Gabe.

"It's better," said Arthur, "when two people meet over something they have in common. Other than sex."

"I couldn't be happier for you," said Gabe. "But you'll have to excuse me. I have a meeting with the lawyers."

"Of course. And if you need any help closing down your mother's house, don't be a stranger." Arthur took Lenore's arm and led her away as Gabe headed to the Cohens.

"Right on time," said Roger with a handshake as Gabe came through the door.

Gabe gave his phone a cursory glance. Another text from Owen must have arrived when he was with Arthur and Lenore. He'd look at Owen's text after the meeting.

"We're set up in the back," said Roger. "This won't take long."

To his surprise, Gabe found Bethany and Maddy sitting at the conference table with signing documents laid before them.

"Hi, Gabe," said Bethany with a firmer handshake than her husband's. "You know Maddy."

Maddy shook his hand. "Gabe and I go way back."

"Good to see you and thanks for everything," said Gabe as they all sat down. Owen had warned him not to trust Maddy, especially if she had figured out Owen spent the night at his place last night.

"Maddy wanted to be here in case you had any trust filing questions," said Bethany.

"The legal paperwork is almost done," said Roger.

"Great," said Gabe.

"We filed the trust on Monday," said Maddy. "Probate is in play. Great suggestion about the banana bread. You want to return to your job in the city soon, right?" asked Maddy.

Gabe smelled an agenda. "That's the idea. I have limited time off for bereavement."

"That's what we figured," said Bethany. She moved a document in front of him. "This is called a Funding Document. It allows the property to be transferred to you once probate is settled."

"Sign and date at the tab," said Roger, handing him a pen.

Gabe signed and dated under the yellow "sign here" tab.

"What else?" asked Gabe.

"That's it," said Roger. "Greene gave you Cadillac service."

Gabe imagined Maddy hiding a smirk.

"There's still plenty of the retainer left," said Bethany. "So, we're square."

"The paperwork is all in place," said Maddy.

"If anything else needs signing, we'll do it via electronic signature," said Bethany.

"I think you're free to head back to the city," said Maddy.

"Every obstacle we discussed last week has been cleared," said Roger.

"Your timing couldn't have been better," said Bethany. "There's nothing legal keeping you here."

Gabe wasn't ready for this moment. And he certainly wasn't ready to say goodbye to Owen yet. Where was he on the *Death for Dummies* to-do list? "When can I legally deal with an estate sale and sell the house?"

"You shouldn't put the house on the market until probate settles," said Roger. "Think after Labor Day. We can connect you with realtors at that time."

"But you can have an estate sale whenever you like," said Bethany.

"I may stick around and interview a couple estate-sale companies," said Gabe, "while I'm here."

"You might also get a lockbox for a key and keep it on the backdoor," said Roger. "For logistics."

Maddy offered an expressionless nod. She wasn't giving anything away.

"My experience with estate-sale people," said Bethany, "is you want to get on their calendar ASAP."

"And get one who will do the broom sweep," said Roger, "so you don't have to worry about getting rid of what doesn't sell."

"I can send you some referrals," said Maddy.

"I appreciate how hard you all have worked on this," said Gabe.

"All Greene's doing. His work was superb," said Roger. "You might want to find a special way to thank him."

Gabe made it a point not to make eye contact with Maddy. He nearly choked on his tongue to keep from laughing.

Outside their office, he checked his texts.

Owen: Maddy will be at your meeting. Heads-up.

Gabe: !!!

Gabe: All good. See you around 7?

Owen: I'll bring Chinese takeout.

Gabe: I picked a great recipe for us to make for dessert. And while it's baking...

Owen: Is this when you send me a dick pic?

Gabe: After last night my dick should be indelibly etched in your psyche.

Owen: And my throat and my... He attached a meme of Meryl Streep raising a martini glass in a toast.

Gabe's phone rang as he got home after picking up ingredients for the galette and a good gewürztraminer.

"I don't know where to start!" said Jessica.

"Was my writing that bad?" asked Gabe.

"Stop begging for a compliment. A memoir with recipes through the lens on homegrown feminism—and you never say the word feminism. Brilliant! We need to get you an agent."

"So I should keep writing it?"

"No. Publishing isn't like film and television. No more writing on spec. The pieces you wrote are good enough for writing samples. Now we need a winning book proposal."

"I don't have the bandwidth right now."

"I knew you'd lead with an excuse. That is why..." Gabe could hear her typing something on her computer, "I took the liberty to... Go ahead and check your email."

Gabe swiped to his email and opened the attachment Jessica sent seconds ago.

"I went ahead and generated a draft of a book proposal," said Jessica. "If you could take a pass and make the words sound more like your voice. When you send it back, I'll pitch it to my bosses."

"Oh, my God. I like the title: *My Mother's Recipe Cards: Unveiling the Heart of American Cuisine*. You are fabulous!"

"Thank artificial intelligence. I'm looking into the expense of printing actual recipe cards readers could pull out of the book."

"That would be amazing! You sure I don't need a full draft first?"

"That's not how nonfiction works. Book proposal and sample pages only. The publisher always has notes. No more writing the book until you have a contract with an advance."

"I don't know how to thank you."

"Don't dawdle with the revision. I have to tell you, Gabe, the quality of your writing on those two pieces was beautiful and deeply moving. You get to tell your mother's story from the heart. Who else ever gets to do that in life?"

"Her recipe cards woke something up in me. They're oddly inspiring."

"This is the perfect way to leave her a legacy. Oh, I forgot to ask. How was the memorial? I'm sure you crushed the eulogy."

"Never believe your reviews," said Gabe. "And I may have salvaged my mother's finances."

"You must be exhausted," said Jessica. "Wait! What's wrong with your sex life?"

"Nothing..."

"Your hookup app hasn't gone off once this call. Wait—did your hot married loser make a reappearance?"

He wasn't sure he wanted to tell Jessica about Owen.

"Oh, my god, he did!" said Jessica. "Boy meets boy again. Rom-com destiny at work!"

"Yes, he reappeared. But it's still in the nascent stage."

"Better nascent than none at all. I'm happy for you. I know how you feel about married men, but I'd rather you have a tawdry affair with a class act than a dozen zipless fucks with toothless meth heads."

"I'm sensing some class bias."

"I'm happy you have someone to comfort you on Grief Island."

"I don't want to jinx it." Gabe's phone announced a call from Erin. "I have a call coming in."

"Liar."

"I'll take a pass at the book proposal and get it to you tomorrow."

"Not tonight?"

"I have a date. Gotta go." With a single click, he said, "Hey, Erin. What's up?"

"Great rehearsal today. Suzy and Barrett have phenomenal chemistry. We shoot tomorrow. Here's the funny part: Barrett learned his lines as written which must have freaked Suzy out. She memorized her lines as written, too, instead of improvising like usual."

"I love it."

"And you are on a roll, dude. The new scenes are even better than the last. The other reason I'm calling... Put me on speaker."

A knock at the front door led Gabe to find his favorite ZipExpress gal.

"How do you manage that every time?" asked Gabe.

"She has our tracking app," said his favorite ZipExpress delivery gal.

"Don't give away my secrets," said Erin.

"What's with Miss Loose Lips at the ZipExpress office in the next county?" said Gabe signing for the envelope.

"She's a hot mess. You should check out our shop in Anderton. It looks far on the map, but the scenic drive makes it go by in a blink."

As soon as the door slammed, Erin continued the conversation.

"The Douglasses asked me when you're coming back. From the 'long night of wild sex' additions to the story arc, I assume your stay isn't the only thing that keeps extending."

"It partly depends on what happens after the LA announcement," said Gabe.

"Are you acting out more potential scenes for the storyline tonight?" asked Erin.

"Maybe."

"What if he figures out he's a prototype for a soap opera?"

"The man brought me *In the Mood for Love*. He's not watching *If Tomorrow Never Comes*. But he'll be here soon, so I'd better get ready."

Gabe went to the kitchen to organize the ingredients for the galette. He had found blackberries and plums for the center. He got out brown sugar, corn starch, vanilla, an egg, and raw sugar. For the dough, he got out flour, sugar, and salt, but kept two sticks of butter chilled. In his secret fantasy world, making dough with Owen would devolve into making love, the flour flying everywhere.

He uncorked the gewürztraminer to let it breathe.

He got a text at a quarter to seven.

Owen: *Parking.*

Gabe: *You're early.*

Owen: *I couldn't wait.*

Gabe: *Same.*

Gabe had a pang of anxiety when the ZipExpress envelope on the dining room table caught his attention. He hid it away in the liquor cabinet, set the gewürztraminer on the coffee table, and headed to the front door where he found Owen, holding a brown bag of Chinese food.

"There he is," said Owen, reaching out for a hug, trying not to smush the Chinese food.

"A hug?" Gabe countered with a kiss.

"That," said Owen, "was what I've been remembering all day. More, Mister, more."

Gabe put the Chinese food next to the wine on the coffee table and sat Owen on the sofa. "We need to decide how the night is going to proceed."

"At some point we have sex," said Owen with another kiss.

"We also have to eat Chinese food," said Gabe, kissing him back.

"Maybe after we have sex," said Owen.

"I like cold Chinese food," said Gabe, unbuttoning Owen's shirt.

"Then we should definitely have sex a few times," said Owen, working on Gabe's buttons.

"And in different rooms," said Gabe.

"Starting here," said Owen, ripping off Gabe's shirt and kissing his chest.

"And we need to make time...mmm...to cook something," said Gabe.

"Fuck yeah. I want to bake your fucking brains out," said Owen, taking off Gabe's belt and pulling down Gabe's pants and underwear. "We can bake later... First, aperitifs."

Owen's tongue made circles down Gabe's chest to his navel, following the treasure trail to its pot of gold. The more Gabe squirmed, the more committed Owen was to satisfying him. It didn't take Gabe long to come to full satisfaction.

"My turn," said Gabe and soon matched Owen's every move. At one point, he gently placed Owen's hands on the back of his head. "Guide me," he whispered.

"How did you get to be so sexy?"

"Shh." Gabe pressed Owen's fingers to grab him by the hair. "It's all about you, babe."

It didn't take long for Owen to finish, both men tasting like the other. They pulled up their pants and put their shirts on. Gabe handed Owen the opened bottle of gewürztraminer.

"They say gewürztraminer pairs well with spicy, salty food," said Gabe. "Share? Or do you need wine glasses?"

"If you're worried about getting my germs, that ship has sailed," said Owen, before taking a swig. "Hungry?"

"I can always eat," said Gabe with a devilish grin.

Owen set the Chinese food out on the coffee table on top of the magazines and newspapers while Gabe undid the lids.

"I haven't had sex like this since—" said Owen. "I don't think I've ever had this much fun with anyone."

"Not even Kevin?"

"The Kevin sex was always fine. We met vacationing in Provincetown—in a bar—and all that comes with that. Where's the closest gay bar around here?"

"Albany, when I was growing up, anyway."

"Kind of far."

Gabe was impressed by the Chinese food he brought. "Nice choices."

"I figured last night was a bit rarified. Tonight I'm managing expectations. Good, normal food, but still delicious."

They both opened and halved a pair of cheap wooden chopsticks.

"Bon appétit! How was your day?" asked Owen.

"You first," said Gabe.

"Well, I had the most fabulous morning with a lovely gentleman."

"What a coincidence. Was Maddy already at your place when you rolled in?"

"Seconds later."

"You know what I'm asking."

"If she was looking for scandal, she could have inferred one. I mean, she made the dinner reservations. But she doesn't do my laundry, if you know what I mean."

"She was at my meeting with the Cohens this afternoon."

"Completely unnecessary. How did it go?"

"Everything is in place. In fact, there's nothing keeping me here," said Gabe.

"You're hurting me," said Owen.

"Financially. Cohen kept saying I could head home to New York if I wanted. And Maddy kept asking me what I was going to do. More than once."

"What did you say?" asked Owen, eating kung pao chicken from a carton, hiding his vulnerability.

"I told them I was falling for a local tomato farmer and the sex was too good to walk away from right now." Gabe was happy to see a smile on Owen's face. He leaned in and kissed Gabe. "That's some real heat on the pork dish."

"I got your heat, babe," said Owen. "You should have told them your farm consulting gig is still in play. If you have time tomorrow, I might need your help with staking the tomatoes."

"I can help you with that. You should try out cages and simple stakes. Tomorrow morning?"

"You don't want me to spend the night?"

"Of course. If breakfast and morning sex are involved. But two nights in a row?"

"I know. A codependent red flag. What else happened at your Cohen meeting?" asked Owen.

"They told me I couldn't move forward with selling the house until probate closed."

"Correct."

"That I should do something special for you to thank you."

"Which you have done ten times over," said Owen, bringing his foot to Gabe's crotch.

"There's one other piece you might find interesting."

"I find all of you interesting." Owen moved in for a kiss.

Gabe met his kisses with more kisses while continuing the conversation. "I asked about setting up an estate sale. The Cohens said I could move forward with one since I technically own the contents of the house."

"That's a good reason to stick around for a few more days." Owen's kisses increased in intensity, and Gabe matched them.

"Maddy had some referrals," said Gabe.

"Of course she did," said Owen. He stopped kissing him. "Two questions. What will Maddy do with all this information? But more important, how do you see you 'n me settling in?"

"Can we continue this conversation in the kitchen?" asked Gabe.

"I was hoping our next stop would be Gabe's bedroom where he has amazing sex with dudes."

"Sounds good. Last one naked gets to decide who tops!" Gabe leapt off the sofa and sprinted up the stairs, ripping off his clothes while he ran.

Owen was right behind him. "We didn't have a consensus on the rules. Not fair."

"Life is not fair."

Gabe was naked except for his socks by the time he flew onto his bed. Owen tripped over the clothes at his ankles getting out of his pants as they both lay almost naked on the bed.

"I win," said Gabe.

"Socks are clothes," said Owen, ripping off his socks to be the first one completely naked. He snuggled up beside Gabe. "I win."

"On a technicality. Well? Who's the top?" said Gabe, finally removing his socks.

Owen looked him deeply in the eyes. "I know I'm selfish, but I enjoyed being inside you, like <u>really</u> enjoyed it. Mmm," he purred. "And from what I could tell, you did too."

"Maybe more so," said Gabe as he wrapped his legs around Owen's hips. "We switch roles after we bake."

"Equity is fucking hot."

"Almost as hot as you are, Mister."

They devoured each other. They were still learning each other's body as Gabe discovered Owen's ears to be super sensitive. Blowing, whispering, licking—anything he did only added to Owen's pleasure. And Owen had plans for how he wanted Gabe to feel too. "Let's come together at exactly the same time. I want to be looking in your eyes when we blow."

Gabe did everything he could to make that happen. He found Owen even sexier than the night before. Gabe loved experimenting with ways to explore new places on his body. They found an easy rhythm. Owen had no trouble getting Gabe to the edge, and Gabe let him know how effective his technique was. Owen wanted to last longer, but after about fifteen minutes, he could no longer contain himself. Gabe paced his release so they were perfectly in sync.

When they had collapsed into each other, Owen was still on top, damp with sweat and semen. He caressed Gabe's sides.

"That tickles," said Gabe.

"That after-sex sensation..."

Gabe squirmed more with each gentle touch. He tried to tickle Owen back, but Owen was much stronger when he was on top.

"You're terrible," said Gabe, loving every second. "If this were a rom-com..."

"We are way past boy meets boy. Even way past boy eats boy and boy breeds boy."

"Uh-oh. We're due for a boy-loses-boy moment."

"Didn't that already happen after the dump?"

"That was the first one. If this were a rom-com," said Gabe, "we would definitely be headed for a crisis and a climax."

"Didn't we both just experience a pretty great climax?" asked Owen. "That was far beyond any sex I'd ever had. Maybe we get to skip the crisis part." Owen gently kissed his shoulder. "Are you saying this won't last?"

"I'm saying if this were a rom-com, we would be technically in the blissful fun 'n games time right before something terrible happens. Great sex and getting-to-know-you can't sustain. Reality is a bitch. How do you see this settling in?" asked Gabe.

"That's not up to me. I know you have to return to your vaguely unsatisfying, all-consuming job at some point. I hope you'll drive up here once in a while. Get away from the City."

"If you're around, yeah. My mother's estate will be in play for a while. And I'm extremely concerned you'll overwater those heirlooms. Do you ever make it to the City?"

"Everyone I know is there. I try to avoid visits to the City. I came here to get away from all that. But if you're there... Neither of us has done the open relationship long distance dance before. How about if we take it one weekend at a time?"

"Sure, but if we are following the rom-com template," said Gabe, "it's all going to come crashing down soon. None of this matters in the end." Gabe glibly changed the subject with a kiss. "Shower time?"

"Nope. I want you all over me all night. But if you need to, I understand," said Owen.

"I want the 'you' part to stay, but I need to get rid of the 'me' part." Gabe grabbed a few tissues from the nightstand and gave his stomach a good wipe. Owen grabbed a few more and helped him before giving his belly a loving kiss.

"Let's go cook something," said Gabe.

They found their abandoned clothes as they headed downstairs.

"From the mise en place," said Owen when they were both fully dressed again in the kitchen, "it looks like you prepared some kind of fruit tart."

Gabe handed Owen the recipe card.

"I love a galette! Have you ever seen the public television video about making a peach galette?"

Gabe had seen the video a few times.

"It was amazing. There's that moment when the chef folds away the leaf of a peach to show how it faded the peach skin."

"I weep watching her fold the galette dough," said Owen. "Her fingers are gorgeous."

"This recipe calls for plums and blackberries. Did you read the parenthetical at the top of the card?"

"'His favorite.' Who do you think?" asked Owen.

"The card looks older than me. There's a strong chance 'his' means my dad's favorite."

"I am honored you are sharing this profound event with me."

"I have never made a galette, and I don't remember my mother ever making one."

"It might have brought up too many memories for her."

"Have you ever made a galette?" asked Gabe.

"A few," said Owen. "One of Luisa's specialties. I see everything here except the butter."

Gabe got two sticks of butter from the refrigerator.

"Chilling the butter. Good boy." Owen set the oven at 400 degrees. "I'll start the dough while you mix the fruit filling. Then we can both fold the outer rim together. How does that sound?"

"As long as I have the easy part," said Gabe.

They worked in silence. Gabe marveled at how adeptly Owen had learned the geography of the kitchen, like he'd lived there his whole life. Owen moved with elegant grace and blissful concentration. Owen caught Gabe staring at him.

"What?" asked Owen.

"I know I've said this before, but watching you in the kitchen…"

"How did we end up at the I-should-open-a-restaurant conversation again? I'm sure it's a lot less fun with a dining room full of entitled diners, a kitchen manager shouting orders, and not one of the staff looking as handsome as you."

"Nice deflection," said Gabe. "I'll shut up."

Owen resumed with the preparation of the dough. His rhythms were soft and orderly as he cut the butter into perfect cubes and then sprinkled cold water on the flour while kneading the butter into the flour, treating the salt and sugar as incidentals to the main event. Owen was a man who understood portion and care. The only other time he had seen this level of attention from Owen was when they were making love.

"How do you know when to stop adding water?"

"Luisa always said to look for blueberry-sized clumps. See," said Owen, pinching two small clumps together before forming a large ball of dough. "With pastry dough like this, you need it to hold together."

Owen opened a drawer and got plastic wrap to cover the dough.

"You haven't asked once where anything is," asked Gabe.

"Where else would the cling wrap be?" he said, putting the dough ball in the refrigerator and the plastic wrap away in the drawer under the silverware. "I love this kitchen. We'll let the dough set for a bit. How's the fruit coming along?"

"I don't trust this recipe. Fruit, sugar, cornstarch, and lemon juice? It seems too simple. I feel like the dish wants something special, like lavender or sorrel or something."

"Don't overthink it. If this was a thirty-year-old recipe, a simple galette would have been special enough. Maybe a dollop of something for a topping, but the beauty of a galette is in its simplicity."

"Like life," they said in unison.

"Cooking is such an intimate act," said Owen, brushing past Gabe as he worked.

"And a great way to find out if we're compatible," said Gabe.

"Checking in: How are you feeling about getting involved with a married man?"

"How are you with falling in love outside your open relationship?"

"I disclosed that, didn't I?"

"The number one rule as I recall."

"We're two hot messes compromising our value systems, aren't we? I figured why lie?"

Gabe didn't think this was the time to untangle some of the other lies he had told. He trusted the aspen tree to keep his secrets safe for now.

"I'm sorry I didn't say it back to you last night," said Gabe.

"I should apologize. It was too soon."

"I'm not used to saying it. That's all."

"If you're in a long-term relationship, it pops out, like, 'How's your day?'"

"And when you've haven't been...in a long, long, looong time...it feels awkward and somewhat performative. But..."

"Yeah?"

"I think...yeah...this must be what love is." Gabe went in for a kiss to the side of his cheek. "And that scares me."

"The best parts of life are always scary. That's how we know they're important. Ready to fold our gazette? I'll bet your mother had a pizza pan." He pretended to be a kitchen psychic. "And she kept it...?"

"I have no idea," said Gabe.

Owen opened a lower cabinet door to reveal a circular pizza baking pan resting on its side with a couple of cookie sheets. "Voila! Too bad this will be someone else's home by the end of the year. What kind of fold does the recipe call for: rustic or not too rustic?"

"'Fold' is all it says."

"We should dust it with flour. Don't want it to stick." Owen tossed a handful of flour onto the pizza pan and got the dough out of the refrigerator. "It's perfect. Not too hard, not too soft. No sex jokes, please, we're working in a sacred space here."

Gabe wanted to start taking notes for the next Oliver Armstrong scene, but Owen kept interrupting his thoughts.

"Do you want a rolling pin?"

"The best galettes are made with loving hands," said Owen, placing the dough on the pan. "Come here." He put Gabe in front of the counter, his hips facing the dusted pan. Owen cozied up behind him and guided his hands from the back. "We're doing this together." They spread out the dough until it overlapped the edges of the pan, Owen's hips pushing into Gabe's backside in rhythmic rocking.

"Sorry. It can't be helped," said Owen apologizing for his rising hardness.

"When do I get to top you?" asked Gabe.

"Keep your pants on, Romeo."

"You're no fun."

"For now."

When the dough had been pressed out evenly, Owen stepped back.

"You should do the honors with the fruit filling," said Owen, "but leave most of the juice in the bowl. Or you know what might happen?"

"Soggy bottom!" they said in unison.

"Which you personally experienced earlier tonight," said Owen.

"I still am..."

"*Ba-dum-tss.*"

Gabe evenly placed the fruit in the center of the circle of dough and spread it out a bit.

"Perfect," said Owen. "I'm coming in for more."

"You can't get enough, can you?"

"Nope."

Owen took Gabe's hands and, this time, taught him to fold the edges of the dough up and over to prevent the fruit from leaking out. Their hands moved in a dance. All Owen had to do was gently nudge his fingers in the direction Gabe folded the dough. The movements of their hands flowed and caressed like primal erotica. When they got to the end of the circle and folded the last pinch, they were breathing in unison.

"That's beautiful," said Gabe.

"Hence, 'his favorite'."

"He had great taste."

"Obviously," said Owen. "The only problem with galettes: they don't last."

"How fitting."

"You want to prep the egg wash?"

"Let's see if I got this." Gabe cracked an egg on the counter and whisked it with a fork.

"So teachable. But I knew that."

"Do we need a brush?"

Owen shook his head and dipped his fingers into the egg wash. He spread it around the edges of the galette. Gabe followed, at first treating the egg like fingerpaints. The moment his hands crossed Owen's, it became foreplay. When they ran out of egg, Owen gave Gabe a kiss.

"That should do it," said Owen.

They rinsed and dried their hands at the sink.

"It's gorgeous," said Gabe at the galette.

"Do you need a pic for your Instagram account?" asked Owen sarcastically.

"Put it in the oven."

Owen opened the oven and centered the galette on the middle rack. "What does the card say for a bake time?"

"Fifty-five minutes."

"About an hour," he said, setting the timer on his phone. "Hmm, what can we do to fill an hour?"

Gabe approached and put his arms around him. "I know I said I wanted to top, but I'd rather cuddle on the sofa."

"You sure? I am all about equity between the sheets."

"How about I take my turn tomorrow?"

Gabe took Owen's hand and led him to the living room where the Chinese food and gewurztraminer were still on the coffee table. "It feels like a week ago you showed up with Chinese food."

"Can I tell you something I admire about you?" said Owen. "You understand how life must be weighed and measured." Without prompting, they cleaned up the cartons and wine, putting everything in the refrigerator. They also cleaned up the galette fixings. After giving a good wipe down to the kitchen, they went to the sofa where they held each other. They were in sync like they had lived together for years.

"The galette smells even better than the brownies," said Gabe.

"I enjoy you so much," said Owen. "Who knew not having sex could be this satisfying?"

They kissed each other softly until they both drifted off to sleep. The timer on Owen's phone dinged, disorienting them out of their slumber. They stumbled into the kitchen to take the galette out of the oven.

Owen went directly to the drawer with the potholders. "I can't tell you how much I love these." Gabe rolled his eyes at his ridiculousness. "Would you like to do the honors?"

Gabe took the potholders, pulled the pizza tray from the oven, and put the galette onto a small baking rack on the counter. The pastry crust had browned beautifully but the purple and black fruit was less than appealing.

Gabe grabbed a pizza slicer.

"We should let it cool for a few minutes," said Owen giving Gabe a backrub.

"It's kinda ugly," said Gabe, looking over their creation.

"I'm glad you said that," said Owen. "It's hideous."

They both burst out laughing at their visually disgusting treat.

"I'm now remembering why Luisa preferred apple and peach galettes."

"I hope it tastes better than it looks."

"It can't not."

"We could hide the fruit and cool it down with some ice cream," suggested Owen.

"Good idea," said Gabe.

Owen took up the pizza slicer while Gabe prepped ice cream, spoons, and bowls.

"Bon appétit!" said Owen, and they blew on the galette so as not to burn their tongues.

"Oh, my god," said Gabe.

"Except for the appearance, that right there is a winner."

They devoured the contents of their bowls but agreed to split the rest and reheat it for breakfast.

"Another perfect night," said Owen at the front door with half of the remaining galette wrapped in tinfoil.

"It can only go downhill from here," said Gabe, giving him a warm kiss.

"I still need you to stop by tomorrow morning sometime before eleven o'clock."

"Tomato stakes and cages, right?" asked Gabe. "And I'll be collecting my sex equity sometime tomorrow night."

"Of course. Can't wait."

With another kiss, the night came to an end, the house still smelling of sweet baked pastry and fruit.

Chapter Seven

Gabe woke Wednesday morning to the realization he preferred having Owen by his side in his bed to waking alone. He would suggest he spend the night tonight.

In one week, Gabe had established a rhythm to his life as a Concord Valley orphan. Breakfast, notes on the latest overnight soap pages, updates on the shared Jessica document, write Oliver Armstrong script pages, and off to ZipExpress. Today, he would check out the Appleton store and get home in time to see the broadcast of *If Tomorrow Never Comes*. He was no longer worried about finances, but now he was always looking for time to squeeze Owen into his day. Today, he needed to check in with Erin as soon as the email announcing the move to Los Angeles was pushed out.

Right now, he was hungry for breakfast.

Owen had suggested heating up the leftover galette for ten minutes at 325 degrees, but "manage all expectations and enjoy your soggy bottom." When the galette was warmed, he put a dollop of yogurt on top and took a picture that he texted to Owen with a "Sorry, that was meant for my socials." He would have phoned but he didn't know if Owen was an early riser when he woke up alone. The galette still tasted wonderful, which may have been woven with the memories of the night before.

Gabe got the shooting script out of the liquor cabinet and breezed through annotating cuts and punch-ups. With the notes on the shooting pages easily completed, he headed to the new ZipExpress office in Appleton.

His favorite ZipExpress gal was right: the road to Appleton came with a glorious scenic view. A quiet rain shower in the early morning hours had left all the leafy greens and green yellows extra vivid. Meandering streams and quaint bridges wove through fields and forests. Even though it took longer to get to Appleton, the gorgeous views made up for the lost time.

The Appleton ZipExpress store was small. No business center with random strangers making copies and overhearing conversations. One clerk worked one counter, making sure t's were crossed and i's dotted on forms. No intrusive small talk or threatened boundaries. Exactly what he wanted.

On the way back, Gabe searched for his phone but couldn't find it. He must have left it at home. Not being attached to technology, however briefly, was liberating. He stopped off at an Appleton nursery and picked up a few tomato stakes and cages. He preferred the cages but would let Owen decide for himself.

When Gabe got to Owen's place, he parked next to an expensive-looking car in the driveway. Gabe assumed it belonged to another legal client. As he got out of his car carrying the tomato stakes and cages, he saw a man he didn't recognize coming around the side of the house, also carrying tomato stakes and cages. He was a handsome man, dressed like he'd stepped right out of a high-end, farm-themed fashion catalog spread. Owen came up behind him not quite able to catch up.

"Hey, Gabe. I texted you, but," said Owen, trying subtly to project subtext.

"I left my phone at home," said Gabe. "You already have tomato stakes...?"

"That part of the quirky, rural, anti-tech eccentricity around here?" asked the stranger.

"Gabe, this is Kevin," said Owen.

Kevin? Oh, my God! That Kevin! Of all days to forget my cell phone.

"Oh. Nice to meet you," said Gabe. He wasn't ready for this moment. *It doesn't have to be awkward,* he tried to convince himself.

"I've heard so much about you," said Kevin warmly. Kevin maneuvered the stakes and cages for a handshake. Through nervous giggles, Gabe did the same for a goofy handshake.

"All good, I hope," said Gabe.

"I'm glad Owen was able to make a good friend up here," said Kevin.

Kevin presented as a nice fellow, the kind of man who was secure being himself. He was a touch shorter than Gabe and Owen by a half inch or so, not Wally Shawn short a la *Annie Hall. Of course, Owen had married someone well put together who could charm anyone he needed to.*

"I wondered what kind of man Owen would marry," said Gabe. "Lots of heavy lifting with this one."

"Tell me about it," said Kevin.

"I'm standing right here," said Owen.

"What a nice surprise," said Gabe. Gabe was aware of how carefully he was choosing words as part of him was shut down.

"I had a client cancel two days of meetings, and I missed this big guy. I figured I would surprise him with an overnight visit," said Kevin, bumping his shoulder into Owen's, an act of establishing territory.

"He missed you too. Looks like great minds think alike," said Gabe, holding up his tomato stakes and cages, also implying territory.

"He mentioned tomato issues when we chatted," said Kevin, "so I stopped off at a nursery. Owen claims you're his farming consultant." Scolding Owen, he said, "You didn't tell me how good-looking he is."

"I was about to say that about you," said Gabe to Kevin.

"Get a room, you two," said Owen.

Kevin gave Gabe a look that said, "Maybe we should."

"So what do you think?" said Gabe to Owen, holding up the stakes and cages. "I know you were set on stakes, but they get labor intensive as you have to tie them and adjust the ties as the plants grow. I know they're more expensive, but I recommend you go with the cages."

"Money is no object when it comes to his farming dream," said Kevin with a thumb pointing to Owen.

Gabe could hear their history in the sarcasm of Kevin's tone.

"I told you, Kev thinks this is a phase I'm going through," said Owen.

Kevin shrugged.

Gabe was fascinated at how Kevin and Owen kibitzed, half performance, half conversation, more like siblings than a married couple.

"If you want one of either for each plant," said Gabe, "you should get Henderson's to order them now. Once the growing season starts, they're nowhere to be found, and you'll have to order them online, which will take forever."

"Thanks," said Owen. His smile was full of gratitude.

"And thank you for the galette," said Kevin. "Owen said you made it last night?"

"No soggy bottom?" asked Gabe.

Kevin cracked up like he was hearing a soggy bottom joke for the first time. "That galette was baked to perfection. Listen, I'm only here for an overnight, but I'd love to have dinner, the three of us. How's the Italian place on the town square?"

"Lucentio's?" asked Gabe. "It's an institution, but the food is mediocre on a good day. Old school Southern Italian red sauces that have been cooking all day on the stove."

"Fried mozzarella sticks and eggplant Parmesan? Love it! Shall we say seven o'clock?" asked Kevin.

"That's late for Concord Valley," said Gabe. "Let's meet a little after six."

"Do we need reservations?" asked Kevin.

"Never," Gabe said with a grin, checking his watch. "I know Owen has his standing meeting at eleven. I better head out."

"Can't get in the way of that," said Kevin.

Owen gave him a gentle shoulder slap.

After some quick "nice to meet yous" and "see you tonights," Gabe headed home. This was the life his mother had warned him about. The spouse got priority while the third was always at a disadvantage. Gabe hadn't been there when the rules were set up. He only consented to follow them. At least the third had the agency to walk away, sooner more probably than later. Why had he agreed to dinner tonight? He would cancel as soon as he got to his phone.

In another context, Gabe would have befriended Kevin. He had a charming sense of humor, a sexy-fun energy, and was very good-looking. Kevin obviously had figured out Gabe and Owen were sleeping together but was practicing discretion. Kevin being a class act made the situation all the more challenging. If Gabe were someone else, he would have been rooting for Kevin. Maybe dinner wouldn't be a complete disaster. The Owen situation was definitely shifting.

When he got home, he was overwhelmed by the number of unread text messages. He could barely find the first.

Owen: *Kevin made surprise visit. Abort morning plans.*

Checking his emails, he saw the news was official: *If Tomorrow Never Comes* would be moving to Los Angeles at the end of the month. Erin (and everyone at work who had his number) had messaged him a follow-up.

"It's been cuh-razy around here!" said Erin when he called.

"Catch me up," said Gabe.

"The actors—talk about drama! Several are threatening to quit."

"The ones still paying 300 dollars a month for a rent-controlled apartment in the West Village, no doubt. In the end, the actors will go where there's work. But they do like to make a scene. What are the others saying?" asked Gabe.

"Most everyone was more interested in who knew and when."

"In a dysfunctional work environment, information becomes the currency. Blame the Douglasses."

"Speaking of, they want to talk to you. They've had a few cocktails but are still in their happy place. You up for it?"

"Might as well."

"I'm walking to their office right now."

"Are they still shooting the Oliver farmers market scenes today?"

"Of course. Barrett's been great. He's better than good. And did we discuss Cam and Barrett as a couple?"

"Why do you say that?"

"I observed them checking out long-term vacation rentals to share together in the Hollywood Hills."

"Speaking of information as currency..." said Gabe.

"You already knew, didn't you?"

"I had a hunch. They were in that play together in the Village."

"I'm at the Douglasses' door. Ready?"

"Might as well."

Gabe heard a knock followed by a muffled "Come in" followed by "I have Gabe on the phone."

Then he heard a loud "Gabe!" from Doris.

"A helluva day around here," said Thomas.

"Very exciting news," said Gabe. "Your email was excellent. Perfect wording."

"Thank you," said Thomas.

"He means, thank AI," said Doris. "Love, love, love the pages you have written for Oliver Armstrong!"

"Some odd hyphen usage from time to time," said Thomas, "but..."

"Tweak them as you see fit," said Gabe.

"Now that the cat's out of the bag," said Doris, "we need to drop running."

"How much longer are you taking bereavement?" asked Thomas.

"Well...I still have some unused time," said Gabe. Even though he was getting used to the rhythm of his life in Concord Valley, the appearance of Kevin was nudging him to make an earlier departure. "I still need to line up someone to run the estate sale, but after that, I'll head back."

"A few more days are fine," said Doris.

"We'll be direct," said Thomas. "The suits want to take advantage of this transition for a few other moves. One of which is to promote you, give you a long overdue producing credit."

"Congrats!" Erin whispered.

"Thanks," he whispered back.

"And we'll make sure this gold nugget, Erin, moves up too," said Doris. "As soon as everything settles. She's learning where all the bodies are buried."

Gabe hoped this was true and not the alcohol talking.

"Before the move, we want to do something tricky," said Doris.

"This is a highly confidential conversation," said Thomas.

"Of course," said Gabe.

"We need to complete all the current storylines, if we can, before the move," said Doris. "Get them all in the can."

"This must be done with complete discretion," said Thomas. "We're looking for a clean start in LA."

"It will mean everyone will be working double maybe triple time for a month," said Doris. "But everyone agrees this is for the best. *Everyone*, of course, means the suits."

"The network. If you do the math, not everyone's coming to Los Angeles," said Thomas. "But those decisions have not been made yet."

"Lots of moving pieces here," said Gabe.

"No shit," said Doris.

"We'll need you to fly to LA sometime next week," said Thomas, "to meet with our future production facilities people to plan and organize the layout for how pre, post, and production can flow together. We already have a great studio space in the Valley picked out."

"Does Wednesday work for you?" asked Doris.

"I can tie up loose ends before then," said Gabe.

"We'll have Erin here get you some blueprints of the space," said Thomas.

"Congratulations on your promotion!" said Erin, outside their office when the call was done.

"I'll believe it when I see a contract," said Gabe. "Something's amiss here. They could have promoted me years ago. And they haven't been replacing the last few producers who left. How were the latest ratings?"

"Worse than last week."

"That's why I'm suspicious," said Gabe. "We're not getting the whole story. Why shoot all storylines to a conclusion?"

"Insurance? Moves always take longer than planned?" asked Erin.

"I guess. Best proceed with caution," said Gabe. "Some long overdue housecleaning would surprise no one. But how much exactly?"

"They just spent money on an expensive new hire. They'll keep Oliver and Suzy at least."

"Good point. The first Oliver scenes premiere on Monday, right?"

"If the editors keep to schedule."

"Then I better write the next section," said Gabe. "Oliver's going to teach Suzy how to make a galette."

"I see hot action on the countertop and lots of flour flying. But do you think our audience knows what a galette is?"

"They will after they see this sequence."

After his phone call with Erin, his phone buzzed at the arrival of a text.

Owen: *You were great with Kevin.*

Gabe: *I told you the world would fall apart, #rom-comrules I *heart* Kevin.*

Owen: *He *hearts* you too. But if you need to cancel/resched tonight, I understand.*

Gabe wanted to cancel, but Owen would figure out a breakup was not far behind.

Gabe: *Bad form. C U @ 6*

Gabe crawled into his mother's bed and got to see the last few minutes of *If Tomorrow Never Comes*. The bed still smelled like her, earthy and warm, especially her pillow, but a little less than before. These quiet moments in Concord Valley would be coming to an end soon. The estate-sale people would clean all evidence of their lives from the house, and he would get consumed with the business of the Los

Angeles move, which would make any future plans with Owen difficult to manage. Gabe's life was clearly at a crossroads. *Death for Dummies* had not prepared him for this.

Jessica phoned him as the final credits rolled.

"Did you get representation yet?" she asked.

"For what?"

"The book proposal. Heads up: legal is sending you a Deal Memo this afternoon. The team loved your proposal."

"Everything is happening too fast." Gabe pulled the covers over his head and made fake baby crying sounds.

"This should be an exciting time, no? Congratulations are in order."

"Can't I represent myself?"

"Legal will screw you six ways to Sunday. They're paid big bucks to make sure you won't get yours. Surely you had a literary agent when you got the soap job."

"She died and I never replaced her."

"Call your guild for a referral. Or ask a lawyer. It's pretty boilerplate. A modest advance, and the rest on completion, points where appropriate. You need someone who knows the legal-ese and can figure out what needs negotiating."

"I don't know..."

"No sabotaging. You're at the finishing line, Gabe. You'll have a year to write it, and a decent lawyer will phrase the contract to make sure there's no late penalty. I am so proud of you. Don't present as an amateur. My reputation is also on the line."

"I'll do my best. I have to go write soap pages."

"Get a rep, dude!"

He turned off the television and went straight to his laptop in the kitchen to write the galette script pages. He got the rest of the galette out of the refrigerator and propped the recipe card against his screen as a good-luck totem.

It must have worked its magic. The galette dialogue spun easily from his imagination: part fond memory of baking with Owen, part fantasy of a bodice ripper. Gabe wished life were as predictable as a rom-com. He would also have loved to linger awhile in Concord Valley getting to know Owen without Kevin or Maddy around. Owen was easily the best part of the last week: the easy conversations, the spontaneity, the honesty met with deeper trust and intimacy. An unexpected growing up. Yet last night seemed far away and fading. Today had become about moving to Los Angeles and his first book contract. The velocity of life was moving at a blinding speed. With the arrival of Kevin, Owen had been relegated to "tying up loose ends." He could already imagine Concord Valley disappearing in the rearview.

Gabe shared the completed draft of the galette scenes with Erin. She must have also been feeling overwhelmed; at six o'clock, the nightly visit from his favorite ZipExpress gal was not met with a call from Erin.

"You broke up with your girlfriend?" she asked, handing him the envelope and the digital signature device.

"Clearly something's up," said Gabe. "Thanks for the Appleton tip."

"Who doesn't appreciate discretion?"

Gabe was about to hide the envelope in the liquor cabinet. Instead, he tossed it on the kitchen table to work on in the morning as there would be no visitor tonight.

He got dressed for dinner, wearing exactly the same outfit from his fake date.

"Cashmere never goes out of style," said Kevin, giving Gabe a friendly hug at their Lucentio's table.

"We got here a minute ago," said Owen with a similar hug.

Lucentio's had been around for a couple of generations. It was opened by an Italian immigrant family who refused to make Rieslings, the only profitable varietal in the Upstate region. Gabe's mother saved Lucentio's for special occasions like graduation and birthdays, but the restaurant was also a go-to for the more affluent locals and always much busier than Gabe expected.

"Great place. Tres twee," said Kevin. "I hope you don't mind. We took the liberty of ordering a bottle of the house Chianti." Kevin poured three glasses from the straw-covered bottle.

"That's all he has on the menu, right?" said Gabe.

Kevin chuckled at the provincialism.

"*Cin cin!*" Owen toasted, attempting a little Italian accent.

"Cheers," said Gabe as they all took a sip.

"Ow! We should let that breathe," said Kevin. "Like for a year."

"So. What have you two done today?" asked Gabe.

"This one," said Kevin, "was getting ready for tomorrow's farmers market."

"Thursday already?" asked Gabe. "The week has flown by."

"The house smells like his famous banana nut bread," said Kevin.

"I'm only selling banana bread this week," said Owen.

"Great idea. Wait for the tomatoes before you return to produce. Were you helping in the kitchen?" Gabe asked Kevin. "He's fun to cook with."

Kevin and Owen exchanged an awkward look.

"Kevin doesn't like it," said Owen. "We don't cook together."

"I had too many work calls," said Kevin.

"I set up a room for his Alpha Male Call Center."

Gabe definitely had the upper hand over Kevin when it came to cooking with Owen.

"What do you do, Gabe?" asked Kevin. "Owen hasn't told me much about you."

"I'm not exactly sure what he does, Kevin," said Owen. "Some kind of admin."

Gabe was aware Owen was tightly wound when Kevin was around.

"I tried to look you up, but you don't have a presence on social media," said Kevin.

"No," said Gabe. He went directly into his lying and evasion mode. "I work for a multi-national management consulting firm with a focus on top-secret defense and energy contracts. I'm a glorified admin assistant. Because of the nature of our work, my contract includes a confidentiality agreement. That's all I'm legally allowed to say."

"That answers that," said Owen with a look to Kevin.

"Have you ever looked yourself up online?" asked Kevin.

"Drop it, Kev," said Owen.

"I don't have much of an online presence. Part of the confidentiality agreement." Gabe shifted this conversation to safer topics. "But can I share some good news I got today on another front? Did Owen tell you I dabbled as a writer?"

"I mentioned it," said Owen.

"I wrote a book proposal, and it looks like I'm getting a Deal Memo for an offer to publish it," said Gabe.

"That's great news!" said Owen.

"Congratulations!" said Kevin. "What's the elevator pitch?"

"It's a cookbook-memoir-biography mash-up. I'm taking my mother's recipe cards and telling her story through her recipes."

"That sounds...amazing," said Owen, genuinely impressed.

"Thanks. Now I need to find someone to rep me," said Gabe.

"Owen can hook you up. You know people in contract law, right, Owe?" said Kevin. "Maybe John?"

"He'd be great. He should be able to make sure the publisher does right by you," said Owen.

"Thank you," said Gabe, genuinely moved and relieved to have one less item on his to-do list.

"I have a good feeling about this," said Owen.

As Kevin and Owen read the menus, they operated as a couple, speaking in shorthand, often communicating with only a glance. When Kevin asked for any recommendations and Gabe suggested going somewhere else, they all shared a good laugh. Gabe was surprised how easily the evening flowed. Owen showed a more cautious version of himself when he was around Kevin. Gabe didn't trust Kevin, but he enjoyed his energy and humor. And he enjoyed watching a long-term couple banter.

"How long have you two been together?" asked Gabe once their food had been ordered.

"I've lost count," said Kevin.

"Over a decade since Provincetown, right?" asked Owen.

"One of the reasons I wanted to have dinner," said Kevin, "besides getting to know you, is to put all our cards on the table. I think Owen's told you about our arrangement, yeah?"

"Open relationship," said Gabe. "Are you going to invite me into a threesome or something?"

"No," said Owen.

"That is not who we are," said Kevin. "I wanted to give you a chance to ask us—me—any questions. Before you jump into anything."

Gabe silently looked from Kevin to Owen and Owen to Kevin. He was getting some good dialogue for a future Oliver Armstrong scene.

"Well," began Gabe, "how long have you had an open relationship? And I'm curious how all this came about."

"Fair enough," said Kevin. "Same-sex marriage was amazing and landmark. And long-term gay relationships start off great: you fall in love, and there's lots of great sex and romance. And you make the decision to get married. Well, *we* did anyway. You may have seen our wedding announcement in the *Sunday Times*. Remember print newspapers? Owen and I were one of those boy-boy couples the gays loved to make fun of but secretly envied."

"The *Times* piece was how my parents legitimized our union," said Owen.

"That and the prenup they made me sign," said Kevin.

"He doesn't need to know all that," said Owen.

"I think he does," said Kevin.

"He's not a transactional guy, Kev."

"That's not who I am," added Gabe.

Interrupting their awkward exchange, the server arrived with their food. Their plates all had a similar look, topped with red sauce, melted cheese, and the thick heavy warmth of Southern Italian comfort food. Gabe enjoyed watching Kevin's amusement at the unapologetic kitsch as the server circled the table with obligatory twists from a long pepper mill.

"So, here's what the heteros didn't tell us," said Kevin, picking up where he left off. "Once you're married, you can't use sex and dating rituals to distract you from the realities of married life—sustainable married life. They say all couples devolve into either Lucy and Ricky or Fred and Ethel."

"I'm Lucy to Kev's Ricky," said Owen.

"Correct. And of course, the sex peters off—"

"Terrible pun, Ricky," said Owen.

"Other rituals and commitments kick in. Busy boys like *us* travel a lot," said Kevin.

"Like *you*," said Owen.

"Like you used to. Cut to the chase: we drifted apart. Now that you're a farmer, we are lucky to be in the same state half the year. We still love each other, but we're no longer 'in love.' And it's 'Could you take care of the plumbing in the Manhattan place?' and 'My family wants to stay in the Malibu place for the holiday. When was the last time it was cleaned?' And a decade goes by, and you're lucky to have sex maybe four times a year."

"How is the sex after a decade?" asks Gabe.

"Funny you should ask," said Kevin. "About a year ago, we realized our sex life had devolved to appointment sex."

"We were literally checking our calendars," said Owen.

"And the sex was getting fairly ritualized and downright vanilla," said Kevin.

"*Your* therapist suggested we spice things up in the bedroom," said Owen.

"Like adding sex toys and edible underwear?" asked Gabe.

"After a decade...that's not our style. Relationships change over the years. These days, it's more about shared vacations and companionship over meals. We needed to shake things up a skosh; hence, the open relationship. My therapist walked me through how it worked, rules and boundaries and all—and we agreed on some things so neither of us would feel like we were cheating. Rules are designed to prevent resentments, right? So far, it's worked out. And here we are."

Gabe looked at them both. "That's it?"

"Kinda. Yeah." Kevin got out his phone and clicked on an app. "You do hookup apps, right?"

"Yeah?" said Gabe.

"Are you Gud2Go? I like the pun. Quick and satisfying."

"How did you know?"

"It says Gud2Go is zero feet away," said Kevin showing him the app on his phone. "If you can trust the algorithm."

"I guess I am still on it. I haven't gone on since I turned the sound off."

"Nice obligatory headless torso shot," said Kevin, sharing Gabe's profile pic with Owen, "Does he look like this up close and personal?"

"Where are you going with this?" asked Owen.

"Send me a dick pic," said Kevin.

"No," said Gabe.

"Did he send you one?" Kevin asked Owen.

"No. Kevin..." said Owen, his anger starting to show.

"I keep that world separate from...this one," said Gabe.

"I get it. It's slim pickings out here. Do you know this guy with the mullet?" Kevin held up a picture of Joey Dakota and showed the table. "He's the cutest guy around, and one of the few willing to chat with me."

"Isn't that the dude you hooked up with...?" asked Owen.

"Good for you," said Kevin.

"I don't kiss and tell," said Gabe.

"A man of morals. I like that," said Kevin. "He said he was only available when his wife was at work."

"You didn't tell me he was married," said Owen.

"He didn't tell me he was. He wasn't wearing a wedding ring." Gabe could feel Kevin studying him. "His wife must have been out of town that one time we hooked up."

"What about this one?" said Kevin, holding up a picture of a man dressed like Elphaba from *Wicked*.

"Too weird for me," said Gabe.

"Me too. Unusual, right? I have to confess. 'Elphaba' and I chatted a bit. Who knew there's this whole cult, kind of like furries. They get off while dressed as characters from Broadway musicals."

"Why are you even on that app?" asked Owen. "You're here to see me."

"I am, sweetie," said Kevin, patting Owen's hand. "This is the closest

I could get to learning anything about Gabe, aka Gud2Go, online. His profile says he's HIV negative and on Prep. Comforting. Versatile?" asked Kevin with a suspicious look. "Tribes..."

"Enough! I'm not going to participate in this!" Owen got up from the table and stormed off.

"Where are you going?" asked Gabe, hiding his panic.

"He's fine. He'll go to the bathroom to stew. After that, he'll realize he can use this as an opportunity to pay the bill when no one is looking. Owen loves to pick up the tab. And he'll chat with the cashier and tell her to compliment the chef. The cashier will see he overtips and take him to the kitchen where he and the chef will exchange recipes. You'll see. Look, we have a couple of minutes to ourselves. I'm only here to fly reconnaissance. I was wondering if Owen was slumming it with you, but that's not the case. Nice cashmere. And I didn't come here to break you and Owen up, if that's what you're worried about."

"We're not a couple," said Gabe.

"But you've slept together, and the sex was fabulous." Gabe was about to tell another lie, but Kevin interrupted it. "Don't deny it. You are clearly accustomed to lying your way out of tricky situations, Mr. Gabe Hartman. I figured it out when you said you were a lowly admin assistant at a military consulting firm. I know those guys. They're assholes, and you are clearly a cut above. That's when you revealed your 'tell' for lying, by the way. And for some reason, you didn't tell Owen what's-his-mullet was married. That's when your 'tell' was confirmed. How'd you get so good at lying?"

Gabe had never been confronted about his lies by such a bright, attractive man. He found this uncharted territory frightening and exciting.

"Growing up in Concord Valley, lying and hiding in plain sight saved my life."

"You talk about this place like Stonewall never happened," said Kevin.

"You obviously haven't been here long. One thing I'm not clear about," said Gabe. "If a lying scoundrel like me can be a threat, how strong can your relationship be?"

Kevin appreciated Gabe's honesty. "That is the question, isn't it? I like you, Gabe. You're smart. You're game for whatever's in front of you. And you're sexy. If this evening weren't about this, I might have been tempted to see what versatile means to you, but unfortunately, I'm here to protect my husband's peace of mind. I wish I'd found something about you online, but I'm not about to hire a private investigator. This way is more efficient."

"Do you do this with all the guys Owen hooks up with?"

"This is the first time he's taken advantage of our open relationship. So, yes."

"What do you want from me?" asked Gabe.

"The question is, what do you want from Owen?" asked Kevin. "Some good sex, a sweet companion as you lay your mom to rest? Or something more nefarious?"

"You're acting like I went after him," said Gabe. "I initially told him no, but he kept pursuing me."

"He's hard to resist," said Kevin, "and, by the way, he's falling in love with you."

Gabe shook his head in disagreement.

"There's your tell again. He's falling in love with you hard, Gabe. I can see it in the light in his eyes when you walk into a room. He hasn't been in love in a long time. And that's the problem. You hold the power in the relationship."

"You think I'm some gold digger?"

"Having met you, no. You seem like a perfectly nice fellow who has more than enough in life. But you haven't bothered to see this through Owen's eyes. I don't want to be around if and when you break up with him. The amount of pain he will experience will be in direct proportion to the amount of power he gave you in this relationship. That's all I'm saying."

"I'll be heading back to the city in a few days. When that happens, our circumstances will change."

"Our marriage may not look like much, but I still care deeply about him. Please don't hurt him. That's all I'm asking. Shh. Here he comes."

"I got the best tiramisu tip from the chef," said Owen, returning to the table with a small plate of tiramisu and three dessert forks. "Swap out egg whites for whipped cream. Try some."

Kevin gave Gabe a "told you so" look as they all took a taste of the tiramisu.

"Mm-mmm," said Kevin. "It's good."

"Shall we split the bill?" asked Gabe, mid-bite.

"Your money's no good here," said Owen.

Gabe and Kevin exchanged another knowing look.

"Oh my god, this is delicious!" said Gabe.

"Right?" said Owen.

"I like your new friend," said Kevin to Owen. "You chose well."

Gabe got home with plenty of time to get some work done. He opened a document and jotted some notes for an Oliver Armstrong sequence where the wife comes to visit, channeling Kevin as he wrote.

His text message buzzed.

> *Owen: Kevin's leaving after the farmers market tomorrow. Take up where we left off?*

Gabe wasn't sure how tomorrow would work, but he gave Owen's message a thumbs-up.

> *Gabe: Take him to the dump.*

> *Owen: He'll be long gone.*

> *Gabe: As will your amazing banana bread. Bet the house smells great. I like Kevin. Super smart. Hope to have a BF someday who cares as much for me.*

> *Owen: You already do.*

> *Gabe: *heart emoji**

One last text came in.

Owen*: Forwarding contact information for John Thornton. He's the best contract lawyer I know. He'll do right by you. I'll let him know you'll be contacting him.*

Gabe sent another heart emoji. He was grateful Owen had his back. Owen was making it hard to break up with him.

Gabe checked his email and found the email from the legal team at Jessica's publishing company. He opened the attachment, immediately getting lost in the legal jargon. Negotiating for himself would be impossible. The advance was modest, as Jessica had told him. Hopefully, John Thornton would take care of it.

When Gabe graduated from college, a book contract at a major publishing company had been his dream. He wished his mother had been alive to witness his successes. Would she have approved of Owen? He might have kept him a secret from her, which made him sad.

Each day after his mother's death, he had been asked to step farther and farther outside his comfort zone. Gabe fell asleep sure of one simple fact: tomorrow would certainly bring more surprises.

Chapter Eight

Over breakfast, Gabe called Erin. Together, they needed to look over the spreadsheet she had created.

"I cross-referenced their storylines and a possible shooting schedule for the next month," said Erin.

"Brilliant! This is going to make our lives much easier," said Gabe. "All we have to do now is assign each story to a staff writer and give them outlines and deadlines. These are going to be shot fast and loose."

"Wouldn't it be ironic if the ratings went through the roof?" asked Erin.

"Highly unlikely. Our staff writers are mostly hacks," said Gabe.

A banging on the front door surprised him.

"Someone's at my door. Hold that thought."

Gabe found Kevin on his porch, with Owen in his SUV running idle in the driveway.

"Morning," said Kevin. "I hope I'm not interrupting anything."

"A work call," said Gabe, "Did you catch my tell that time?"

"Nope."

Gabe didn't invite him in, not with the table filled with paperwork from the soap. He didn't want to risk it.

"Listen," said Kevin, "I didn't want to leave town without saying goodbye and all that. I'm glad Owen found a good friend."

"That means a lot."

Gabe initiated a hug.

"Don't be a stranger. And call John Thornton today. He's amazing. And versatile. You might like him."

"Stop."

"Jus' sayin'. And Owen wanted you to have some of this." Kevin handed Gabe a couple of wrapped pieces of banana nut bread with new labels. "Broken bits from what he's selling today."

"Thanks. Fancy labels." Gabe held up the bread and gave Owen a wave. Owen gave him a thumbs-up and warm smile.

"Who was that?" asked Erin when Gabe returned to his work call in the kitchen.

"Oliver's wife came to town."

"Shut up."

"You know Michelle's Yeoh's character in *Crazy Rich Asians*?" Gabe said as he bit into the banana nut bread. "I'm kidding, but not entirely."

"Someone attempting to break up the couple is a traditional rom-com trope."

"Breaking up may be my wisest option right now," said Gabe. "I think we're approaching boy loses boy for good."

"Don't end what you've got until the Oliver Armstrong arc is written," said Erin. "I'll set the writing deadlines on the spreadsheet."

"And I'll send out the email to the staff writers. Right now, I need to get the next Oliver Armstrong sequence down. It's the fake date."

Gabe couldn't pinpoint the exact moment he understood the situation with Owen had to end. The Kevin meeting complicated things. Kevin's ability to see Gabe for the liar he was made him recalibrate many of his assumptions. Gabe was used to getting away with his lies. At some point his liar's luck would run out, and Kevin would find out he wrote for *If Tomorrow Never Comes*. Kevin would tell Owen, and Owen would learn he had used their story for the Oliver scenes. Gabe didn't want to hurt Owen. Best cut his losses. Time to break up.

Gabe sat at the kitchen table, first taking a pass at the daily shooting draft pages that needed more sex and punched-up dialogue. He underlined an occasional operative word to cue the actor on the best line reading. The staff writers had gotten lazy working from home. Cleaning house in the writers room would certainly include letting go of some of the more pedestrian scribes. The suits would want to let go of as many cost-cutting positions as possible once the move was in motion.

When the shooting script notes were done, he started on the fake date sequence. The joy of writing the Oliver pages was getting to relive his favorite Owen moments. Owen's kindness and care re-emerged. He *was* irresistible. He included their theme song dialogue but checked copyright laws for the number of words in a lyric he could use before it became a copyright infringement. The "fair use" laws were vague: thirty seconds. *Not helpful.* Gabe settled for song titles with no lyrics to save the legal department any headaches.

Gabe's text buzzed.

> **Owen**: *A meme appeared: "Marriage lets you annoy one special person for the rest of your life."*

> **Gabe**: *We moved onto crazy spouse memes? Fuck, yeah.*

> **Owen**: **heart emoji**

Gabe sent Owen a picture of Freddy Krueger and Michael Myers in bed together.

> **Gabe**: *It could be worse.*

> **Owen**: **Ha-ha emoji**

With the ZipExpress envelope sealed and ready, he headed off to Appleton. The scenic drive was great for clearing his mind.

His text buzzed with a generic marriage "be right or be happy" meme. Gabe could only give it a thumbs-up press and click because he was driving. He would miss the constant texting and calling. He would miss the sex and loving attention. This was the price he would pay to get out from under the pressure of his house-of-cards deception.

He considered the scene he would have with Owen tonight. He had several options. Maybe a knee-jerk goodbye: "It's over." Too harsh. A gentle fade-out followed by a ghosting period seemed more civilized. He would prefer a situation where he manipulated Owen into being the one to break up, but that was outside his bandwidth right now.

In the empty parking lot at the Appleton ZipExpress outpost, Gabe sent Owen a text.

> **Gabe**: *Good luck at the farmers market today. Don't bring home leftovers.*

> **Owen**: **heart emoji**

Guilt about leading Owen on overwhelmed him, but he had written enough breakup soap scenes to know about the power of surprise.

On his way home, an unknown 212 number appeared on his phone.

"I have John Thornton for Gabriel Hartman," said a cool professional female voice.

"This is Gabriel."

"Hold, please."

Hearing his full name aloud made him giggle. Gabriel Hartman, professional author. Much more legit than Gabe/George Sample, pseudonym for the head writer on a soap. Before he could stress about talking to a hotshot contract attorney, a friendly male voice came on the line.

"Gabriel! John Thornton here. Our mutual friend Owen Greene said you needed someone to look over a contract."

"What all did he tell you?"

"He said you have a contract for a book deal. Congrats! I'm going to assume that means a Deal Memo?"

"Correct."

"He also said you're a brilliant writer who is going to be big, and I should beg to rep you."

"That's sweet—and overly generous of him."

"That's our Owen. Listen, it sounds like you're driving. When you get to your computer, forward everything you've got to my assistant. I'll have her contact you, and we'll take it from there."

"Thank you."

"Thank Owen."

"It should be fairly boilerplate," said Gabe.

"Not how this works, my man," said John Thornton with swagger. "The publisher expects a negotiation. We start with more money."

"Great! Do I need to arrange a retainer?"

"Owen took care of it. He said you might be returning to the city next week. Let's do a meal or something. He said you were good people."

Breaking up with Owen was getting complicated. Owen made his life feel charmed. He would miss the Owen magic.

"You're still here?" said Arthur when Gabe popped into the Quinn & Ink. "I hoped you would say goodbye before you took off."

Gabe was tying up as many loose ends today as he could since he would be hunkering down this weekend to crank out Oliver Armstrong script pages.

"I'd like to take you up on your offer to help curate the house," said Gabe. "I'm taking off sometime next week. But before I go, I'll be setting up an estate sale, and I need a point person."

"Count me in."

"I'm putting a lockbox on the backdoor. Do you have a favorite number I can use for the passcode?"

"2020, as in hindsight."

"Nice. I'm going to go through the house this weekend and set aside things I want but be sure to take whatever you want."

"All I want from your mother already lives right here." Arthur pointed to his heart.

"How did you and Lenore turn out?"

"Lenore!" said Arthur, waving to someone behind Gabe. "You remember Gabe?"

Gabe turned around to see Lenore behind the counter at the cafe, foaming milk.

"Your mentor," said Lenore. "Hey, Gabe!"

Gabe waved back.

"Fun fact," said Arthur, "Lenore was part of the first wave of baristas to come out of the Portland coffee movement. I was able to convince her to come out of retirement."

"Just when I thought I was out," said Lenore, pouring the steamed milk into a latte, "they pull me back in."

"You never know what a person is going to bring to your life," said Arthur.

Outside the Quinn & Ink, Gabe could see the farmers market. He tried to spot Owen, but the crowds were thick. A large group surrounded one particular booth. He imagined Owen and Maddy selling out banana bread faster than expected. Owen would get by fine without him.

Gabe bought a lockbox at a home goods store and set the lock at 2020 as Arthur had instructed. As soon as he got home, Gabe forwarded John Thornton's assistant the Deal Memo documents and let the legal department at Jessica's publishing company know who his rep was. In a matter of minutes, Jessica called him.

"You don't fool around. John Thornton!"

"Have you heard of him?"

"He's the guy you get to negotiate major corporate mergers, not a rinky-dink Deal Memo for your first cookbook memoir. Oh my God! He literally just merged two top talent agencies in Hollywood. I just looked him up online."

"He was a referral."

"From whom, Gloria Allred? Legal was impressed; that's all I'm saying."

"You asked me to get representation."

"And you did not let me down."

"I asked my trust attorney."

"Your trust lawyer must be part of the gay legal mafia. Wait! Wait! Are you dating your trust attorney, the married man?"

"Nothing gets past you."

"Wait! Wait! Wait! Is your trust attorney also the hot married loser? The great equivocator lives!"

"Too bad I'm breaking up with him tonight."

"After he gives you John Thornton? That would technically make you a little shit."

"Not new information."

"Way to sabotage! Didn't you try to break up with him once before? The rules of rom-coms won't allow it."

"This is the opposite of a rom-com. I had dinner with him and his husband last night. What rom-com trope is that?"

"All I'm saying is, if you're dumping a guy who introduced you to John Thornton, he might not be the hot loser here."

Gabe fought hard not to believe in rom-com destinies and good fortunes, no matter how much Owen had improved his life in one short week.

At 5:59 p.m., Erin checked in. "I saw the first edit of the Oliver sequence. It's too good for the soaps."

"I know you didn't call just to tell me—"

Someone knocked on the front door.

"Put me on speaker," said Erin as he opened the door to see his favorite ZipExpress gal. "I love her."

"My friend missed you," said Gabe to his favorite ZipExpress gal.

"Hey, girl, where were you last night?"

"It's been crazy at work," said Erin.

"Tell me about it. I had to deliver about 100 tomato cages to some rich gay dude who thinks he's gonna be heirloom tomato king. My aching back."

"I feel your pain. Probably for some lawyer-farmer," said Erin. "Will I be reading about this in future pages, Gabe?"

"But the worst part was," said his favorite ZipExpress gal, "he and someone I took to be his spouse were in the middle of a heated

232 | Tom Diggs

discussion. I usually enjoy eavesdropping on domestic squabbles, but this fight made even me uncomfortable."

"I thought you were about discretion," said Gabe, signing for the envelope.

"That only applies to present company. You have to earn my discretion," said his favorite ZipExpress gal. "Mañana?"

"Mañana," said Erin, getting off the phone.

Gabe immediately texted Owen.

Gabe: *lmk when I can stop by.*

Owen: *I'm all yours.*

On his way to Owen's, Gabe rehearsed his breakup speech. He was no longer obsessed with not getting involved with a married man. And he didn't want to let on that Kevin had any influence over the decision, although their one-on-one may have been the turning point. Gabe was simply trying to be realistic about what his future might bring. He would tell Owen his company was sending him to Los Angeles; he didn't need to know what company. He would lie and say they had casually floated the move but hadn't made an official decision until today.

Halfway to Owen's house, Gabe was stopped at the town's only railroad crossing as the one cargo train made its weekly journey through Concord Valley. It was the custom for citizens of Concord Valley to turn off their engines for the few minutes it took the train to pass.

Gabe got out his phone to check his messages. Nothing new.

He scrolled through Owen's messages in reverse order. The last ones were now a rune for the Kevin visit. The crazy spouse memes could be seen as incited by Maddy's attendance at the Cohen meeting. The sophisticated postcoital Miranda Priestley and Elio memes preceding the "I've fallen in love with you" day of silence. They had developed their own relationship language with interrobangs, convo boundaries, and noisome behavior.

The train kept moving. Could he have told Owen he wrote for a soap from the start of their friendship? Too risky. Owen might have a hard time keeping a secret from the locals. Who wouldn't feel betrayed by Gabe stealing their lives for soap storylines? And he wouldn't have been able to use theirs. Too late now.

Gabe returned to the texts, smiling through dumb house pets and farming memes. The infamous Chairvana, Mrs. Henderson, and his heirlooms loaded into his SUV. The whole "crying not crying" debate and thirty slash seventy. Gabe had never been pursued by someone as charming and sweet and affluent and good-looking as Owen. How wrong were his first impressions?

Gabe could see the caboose about to pass by the railroad crossing, and he turned over his engine. *No matter what happens tonight.* Gabe put away the texts. *Owen has been great for my confidence and self-esteem.* He continued on his way to Owen's.

The moment Gabe saw Owen come down the steps of his front porch to welcome him, he forgot everything he had rehearsed. Owen gave him a warm-honey kiss and a butter-melting hug, the kind of care and comfort that made Gabe weak and defenseless. When he let go, Gabe searched for the strength to make the breakup speech, but he got too distracted by Owen's loving blue eyes.

"What?" asked Owen.

"Nothing," said Gabe, his love for Owen washing away his plans.

Owen lifted Gabe into his arms and carried him up the stairs.

"Someone's getting stronger," said Gabe.

"It's from toting tomato cages and fending off rabid banana nut bread customers. More likely, the latter."

"How'd you do?"

"Three times the inventory and sold out twice as early."

Owen kicked open the front door and carried him inside the house.

"Where are you taking me?" asked Gabe.

"Tonight, we will reinvent *my* bedroom," said Owen.

"Oh my God, what's that wonderful smell?" asked Gabe.

"For later," said Owen, carrying him up the stairs.

"Don't strain anything. You don't want to reinvent your bedroom as a convalescent center."

On the landing, Owen stopped. "The only way I know to get you to shut up..." He put his lips on Gabe's and continued the climb.

Gabe pulled away briefly. "I can think of a couple of other ways to shut me up."

"All in due time, Mister," said Owen at the top of the stairs heading to the bedroom.

"I'm capable of walking."

Owen kissed him again to shut him up as he carried Gabe to the bedroom at the end of the hall. He gently placed him on the king-sized bed, never letting his lips leave Gabe's mouth. They immediately got out of their clothes and proceeded as if there had been no visit from Kevin to interrupt their intimacy momentum.

Owen made sure Gabe's cock was at full attention before he slid in under him.

"Your turn, Mr. Versatile" he said, lifting Gabe above him, raising his own legs into the air. Gabe didn't protest and skillfully fulfilled Owen's wish. The shift in power dynamic was as much a turn-on for Gabe as the sex itself. He was about to pull out right before he came, but Owen knew the look in his eyes and pushed Gabe deeper inside him. He was intent on them coming together at exactly the same moment Gabe surrendered his desire.

When they were done, they lay there blissed out for a good long time.

"I missed you," said Owen.

Gabe wanted to say, "It's only been a day," but that wasn't the truth. "Same."

"Does this make me one of your regulars?" asked Owen.

"You're my one and only regular," said Gabe.

"Correct answer."

"In Concord Valley."

Owen gave his earlobe a playful flick.

"No one," said Owen, "has ever made me feel the way you do."

"And to think I was going to break up with you tonight," said Gabe, feeling safe enough to tell Owen anything. Almost.

Owen got up on an elbow, "Did Kevin get to you?"

"I like Kevin," confessed Gabe. "Besides his being a dick... Anyone who cares about you that much can't be all bad."

"Did you get the 'Don't hurt my husband' speech?"

"A very effective speech."

"I'm glad you changed your mind," said Owen. "About breaking up."

"You're hard to resist. Nice bedroom," said Gabe, taking in the well-designed, somewhat familiar room. *I got laid in the bedroom pictured on my vision board.*

"It's generic, too bougie. I prefer your place," said Owen.

"My bedroom is a postage stamp."

"But it has character. Seriously, this place feels more camera-ready than a home. My mother hired an interior decorator when I bought it— as a gift. I'm embarrassed to say the house was featured in some magazine. At least it got my mother off my back."

Owen's embarrassment about being in a design glossy made Gabe love him even more. He planted a long kiss on Owen's mouth.

"Happy to reinvent your space with you," said Gabe.

Owen got up and went to the en suite bathroom to grab some towels. "I'm usually a fan of minimalism, but I need a place to put all my paraphernalia for sex, a detail my mother forgot to tell the designer." Owen rejoined Gabe in bed. "I wonder...tell me if this is too soon, but, um, what do you think your mother would have thought of me?"

"She would have liked you. She would have bought your banana bread by the loaf every Thursday."

"No, I mean, what would she have thought of us?"

"Aside from the married man part...it's hard to say."

"Not what I was expecting."

Gabe could see Owen was a little put off.

"The essence of my relationship with my mother was 'you 'n me against the world.' I never introduced her to anyone I was dating. If she had known us as a couple, the dynamic of our relationship would have changed. I came out to her, of course. To her, having a gay son was an intellectual concept she quietly accepted. She never asked about guys I liked, and I never told."

"What about that guy—your last boyfriend a million years ago?"

"I never told her about him."

"You really don't think she would have liked me?"

"Of course she would have liked you. Here's how I would have handled it, Concord Valley Style. I would have broken her in gently. I would have told her I have a new friend in town, maybe let it slip you were gay. I'd bring you around to meet her. You could ask for cooking tips—not that you need them."

"We'd still be having sex though, right?"

"Fuck, yeah. As often as we could. There's nothing hotter than sex you keep secret from your mom."

"That last time was pretty hot."

"Every time has been pretty hot. But we would have had to sneak around until she was ready for the truth. No telling how long that would take."

"You have incredible patience, Gabe."

"With a fucked-up moral compass and a lot of trust issues."

"I trusted you to help me reinvent this space. It's now officially the room where I have sex with men I have fallen in love with," said Owen, giving Gabe a peck on the cheek.

"Not that it's any of my business, but...no sex last night?" asked Gabe.

"It wasn't on the calendar. Unless you count fighting as foreplay. We had lots of that."

"Sorry."

"Not important." Owen kissed Gabe. "You know what I want even more than having you inside me?"

"You inside me?" asked Gabe.

"Later. First, I want you inside my kitchen. I made you supper."

"Thank God. I haven't eaten since breakfast. Busy day."

Gabe reached for his clothes.

"No. sir. We're not ready to get dressed yet."

Naked, Owen opened a walk-in closet full of clothes and emerged carrying two plaid robes that probably came from a high-end men's apparel shop. "Which one?"

Gabe pointed to the green tartan robe.

"Good choice."

Owen tossed it to him.

Owen donned the red plaid robe, and they headed to the kitchen.

"Smells great," said Gabe. "What did you make?"

"Do you know what a daube is?"

Gabe shook his head no. "A Luisa recipe?"

"Of course. French sailors invented it. They were usually single men—as women didn't like men who smelled like fish and bait. They would put all their leftovers in a pot and boil them all day with a whole bottle of wine over a slow heat while they were at work. When they got back, they would have the most wonderful stew waiting for them."

Owen ladled two portions into bowls, and they sat eating at stools in the center by the work table in Owen's spacious kitchen.

"Bon appétit!" said Owen.

"Oh, my God, this is delicious! What are the flavors? Orange?"

"Good call. Olives and cloves too. It's one of my favorite dishes ever. I'm happy you like it."

"You have to admit, this is a great kitchen."

"My favorite room in the house. My mother's architect didn't get her mitts on this space."

"Where's the Alpha Male Call Center I heard about?" asked Gabe, taking another spoonful of the daube.

"Upstairs at the far end of the hall. Kevin becomes an obnoxious New Yorker when he's advocating for clients. It's what they pay him for. I bought the place hoping Kevin would want to have a weekend getaway Upstate. But he hates Concord Valley."

"He strikes me as more of a Sag Harbor gay."

"What do you think of that space?" said Owen, pointing to a room off the kitchen.

"It looks like you renovated the original maid's quarters," said Gabe.

"Correct. I had that area built out a bit. I don't think the maid did much in the space but sleep. You think you might be able to write in that space?"

Gabe wasn't exactly sure what Owen was suggesting.

"I know you'll be returning to the city soon," said Owen, "and your mom's house will eventually sell. You'll need a place to stay...and work from when you come to visit." Owen leaned in and planted a kiss on his forehead. "I have a fantasy that involves farming and cooking for you as you work in your writing room."

Owen exuded such happiness, Gabe didn't feel this was the time to tell him about his imminent Los Angeles move. "My God, that's generous of you."

"Incredibly self-serving. Trust me."

"It's nice to know there's always a place for me here in Concord Valley."

"It *is* your home."

Gabe was never comfortable with the word "home." But this wasn't the time for a philosophical conversation about never belonging to a place. Gabe didn't want to indulge Owen's romantic fantasies either. "It looks like I have to head out on Tuesday."

"That gives us four lovely days to fill," said Owen, not letting any sadness show. "I do have one favor to ask. When we're done with...whatever the night brings, could you please spend the night?"

"Sure..."

"I want to normalize your being here. I want Maddy to see you having breakfast with me in the morning. Take some of her power away. Are you comfortable with that?"

"Absolutely," said Gabe as he took another spoonful of the daube. He was looking forward to the next four days, probably their last together.

The cadence of those days had a steady rhythm with few aberrations. Gabe was surprised how much he enjoyed waking up next to Owen, both men ready for more sex and affection the moment they were conscious. Owen insisted on making breakfast for them. He was as skillful whipping together a frittata as he was preparing a homemade granola parfait. Their time together was like a perpetual honeymoon. Gabe was scared how happy he was in the role of Owen's lover and sad their time was coming to an end.

After breakfast and showers, they would separate to go to work. Gabe was careful to hide anything remotely connected to his job in his liquor cabinet. Owen was not afraid to pop into Gabe's at any time for a minute-visit and a kiss, which would usually devolve into more than a few minutes and much more than a kiss. Gabe was good about eventually sending him on his way. He needed to resume his work.

The ride to Appleton remained a good midday head clearer. Gabe made it a point to get home in time to watch *If Tomorrow Never Comes* from his mother's bed, knowing he would never be interrupted as Owen's standing meeting kept him conveniently occupied. A check-in with Erin let him know all systems were "go" on Project Overtime. Also, Monday's broadcast would now officially include the meet-cute farmers market scene, introducing Oliver Armstrong to the world and Harmony Hills.

Friday's rhythm was interrupted briefly by a call from John Thornton.

"My assistant sent you over a fairly iron-clad contract for your book proposal. The first one was loaded with all kinds of problems. I got them to find you some more money up front on the back end. They'll pay for any hard cover book tour. And they are no longer screwing you out of film and TV rights."

"Thank you," said Gabe, feeling like a deer in the headlights. "But I don't see this as a film or television show."

"*I Love Dick* was originally published as a critical theory text, but it ended up as narrative fiction starring Kevin Bacon, produced by a major studio. You never know. Best to have that in your pocket. You'll get an EP credit, when that time comes. That means Executive Producer."

"Good to know," said Gabe, playing dumb. "Let me know how you want to do the billable hours."

"I told you, our mutual friend has taken care of all that. Take him out to dinner or do something special for him."

Gabe came up with a few naughty ideas on the spot.

"Now, all you have to do is complete the electronic signature form and write the damn book. By the way, I negotiated half a year more to complete it."

"They went along with all this?"

"Demand bestselling author rates, and they'll treat you like one."

Gabe opened the new contract to sign. From what he could tell, John Thornton had doubled his advance and his royalty points, and tripled the free copies.

Back in the rhythm of his workday, Gabe's afternoon was set aside for more writing. At around six, Erin called to announce the arrival of his favorite ZipExpress gal with a snarky retort or two, followed by the ritual hiding of the ZipExpress envelope and a dash over to Owen's or Owen arriving at Gabe's, depending on whose turn it was. They were all about equity.

Variety was the hallmark of their sex: always something new to try, to explore, to enjoy. Nothing too kinky, boundaries always clear.

"You know what surprised me most about you?" said Owen on Saturday night, still sweaty from their predinner romp. "I thought getting to know you would be all about building trust. But that hasn't been the case at all. Has anything about me surprised you?"

"I thought," said Gabe, straddling Owen's chest, "you would be a pedestrian, boring lover. And that has not been the case at all either."

Owen raised his hips and proceeded to disprove that case even further.

They eventually found themselves in the kitchen where Owen had prepared one of his "greatest hits" dishes, usually something Luisa had taught him or from a recipe card he had secretly borrowed from the Amelia pile.

Owen dashed off a Sole Africans with a banana-onion sauce, dazzling Gabe with its flavor notes. Owen warmed up a summer squash lasagna, "an old *Gourmet Magazine* recipe. Boy, I miss *Gourmet*." And one night, he warmed up a special surprise for Gabe.

"Close your eyes," said Owen.

"Is this some kinky *9½ Weeks* moment? I'm all for some spice, but I don't think I can get it up again for at least another half hour."

"Keep you tighty-whities on...until after dinner anyway. Close your eyes."

With Gabe's eyes shut, Owen fed him a mini-piecrust in the shape of a cupcake, but filled with barbeque beef, topped with melted cheese.

"This tastes...familiar," said Gabe. "It's definitely a flavor from my childhood."

"Good," said Owen. "Open your eyes. I got it from here."

Owen handed Gabe the recipe card.

"Bar-bee Cups!"

"She wrote 'Gabe loves these' on the card," said Owen.

"I did. I do. You nailed it. How hard are these to make?" asked Gabe.

"The recipe calls for pre-made dough and sloppy joe mix with melted cheese on top," said Owen.

"But this is not that. Did you deconstruct a Bar-Bee Cup? " asked Gabe. "Is nothing sacred with you foodies?"

"'Fraid so. How are they?"

"Amazing! And I reserve the word 'amazing' for stuff that actually amazes me."

"I can't wait to read what you write about this card in your book," said Owen, trying a Bar-Bee Cup for the first time. "Mmm. These *are* amazing."

Saturday afternoon arrived with a visit from the estate-sale woman. She wanted to get a tour of the place before she signed a contract.

"I need to know what I'm getting into." Bonnie was a crusty Upstate native who took no guff and knew the ins and outs of her world like nobody's business. "First off, there will be armies of people here. And early. First thing I do, I look at the parking situation. You have plenty of room in the driveway." She leaned to peer out the window. "Looks like there's easy off-road parking. Otherwise, I charge you for valet and security. Estate sale bargain hunters make the Black Friday shoppers look like Rebecca of Donnybrook Farm."

Gabe took a note to self: *Bonnie shows up in Harmony Hills at some point.*

"I was going to tidy the place up before the sale," said Gabe.

"Don't you dare! Do not throw anything out. Used Kleenex box? I can get a quarter for that. Old magazines? A dime apiece. Old newspapers are as good as kindling. One man's trash, another man's poison, and all that. How old was your mother?" asked Bonnie.

"Young. Late sixties."

"Was she hoarding yet? Nothing like the old ladies who super-stash everything away after a superstore run. The 'greatest generation' and the 'boomers' have more junk than you can dream about. I see she had a few antiques. The black furniture doesn't sell right now. Can't explain estate sale trends, but trends are trends."

"What do you need from me?"

"You're going to give me a quick tour of the place. After that, I'll work my magic, take photos of valuables for the site and notes on what I think the place is worth. We need to make a thousand dollars for you to cover my fee, everything after that, we split. I make sure the house gets a broom sweep and we call it a day."

After Gabe showed her the house, he left Bonnie alone to do her job.

Gabe: *The estate sale woman is here. Omg! I couldn't keep a straight face if you were here.*

Owen: *Come over when you've done.*

"Oh, hon," said Bonnie when she was finished. "Do you know where the true value of the house is? The kitchen. Your mother had one of the best preserved collections of mid-century modern kitchenware I have yet to come across. All in mint condition. The tacky mid-century crap you once couldn't pay to get hauled away now commands outrageous prices. Do you know how much you get for *one* of those mixing bowls? You're destined for a great sale, kiddo."

After a handshake and a wet signature—no electronic signatures for crusty Bonnie—they set a weekend for the following month. "It can't conflict with anybody's holidays, and that includes the high school sports season around here. The coach's wife assists me whenever she can."

Gabe gave her Arthur's contact information and the lockbox combination. "I'm heading to the city next week. I most likely won't be here for the sale," said Gabe.

"Good," said Bonnie, "because I don't allow family members within a mile of the house on the day of. Sentiment kills sales. Be sure to take everything you want before the sale. Take a couple pieces of that kitchenware. I'm sure your mother would have wanted that."

As soon as Bonnie was gone, Gabe went through the house inventorying the items he wanted. The recipe cards, of course. A couple of bags of the remaining fancy chocolate stash for the drive back. He'd leave *Death for Dummies*; he hadn't picked it up in days. He didn't want much from his bedroom, except the cashmere sweater that now held new sentiments. Gabe's attachment to his childhood home was diminishing. A wave of grief attempted to peak, but he easily deflected it with memories of Owen.

In the kitchen, he stood in front of the cupboard with the well-known and well-loved dinnerware. His mother had collected at least two dozen pieces over the years, one pile of pastel yellow and one of light blue, both with cheerful graphic design patterns. He grabbed one from each pile and held them like ancient pottery. They were always beautiful, but now they were also valuable. He grabbed the rest of the homemade potholders from a drawer and headed to Owen's.

At Owen's house, Gabe told him all about Bonnie's visit.

"It makes sense," said Owen, holding one of the mixing bowls. "They would eventually be worthy of the Smithsonian. Museums are filled with pottery of basic kitchenware from different eras. This mid-century modern would eventually earn its icon status. Look at that detail."

"For you," said Gabe, offering Owen the second of the two bowls.

"I couldn't possibly."

"And you need the whole set of these too," said Gabe with the pile of homemade potholders.

Owen let out a near-orgasmic sound at the gift of potholders. "These are everything!"

Nothing could have come between Gabe and Owen. In fact, the latest phase of their fling was going better than Gabe could have imagined. *So much for everything coming crashing down via the tenets of rom-coms.*

Crossing paths with Maddy in Owen's kitchen as they finished breakfast, still in their bathrobes, was the new normal. Navigating the guilt of not telling Owen about writing for the soap and his future move was Gabe's only real challenge. Since Owen was resigned to Gabe's taking off midweek, Gabe considered his slow fade away a winning strategy. He might even satisfy Kevin's request for no heartbreak. Gabe's current plan was to enjoy the ride, live in the moment, and get as much writing done before returning to the distractions of his New York City workplace.

Sunday evening, while everyone slept, a rainy windstorm pelted Concord Valley. The elements themselves didn't do any damage, but the combination of low winds and fast drench had a cleansing effect on the town. Of note, the aspen in Gabe's backyard tree was sprayed clean of all dirt and soil.

Monday morning at Owen's place, after some lovely sex upon waking, Owen showed off his extraordinary culinary skills with his ebelskiver pan, a first for Gabe. At the heirloom tomato planters, Gabe helped Owen add a nitrogen, phosphorus, and potassium mix to his fertilizer before spreading it over the topsoil. All the plants had taken successfully to their planter soil.

Gabe said his goodbyes after the arrival of Maddy, per Owen's request. Owen made a specific effort to give him a full-on romantic kiss goodbye in front of her, no ambiguity, which Gabe received gladly before heading home. They had plans for a nice, quiet, but wild evening at Gabe's later that night.

Gabe was excited to get home to see the first scenes of the Oliver Armstrong sequence as they aired. He was curious to see how the editors had spliced the Oliver Armstrong scenes into the rest of the show that had already been shot.

As eleven o'clock rolled around, Gabe climbed into bed one last time as the cold opening started. The show led with the first Oliver scene. That was a good sign. The suits must have been impressed with the storyline. Barrett projected sexy confidence in his work shirt over a tank top. His tight jeans left little to the imagination. He moved sensuously even as he tended his farmers market booth.

Suzy appeared and approached his booth. "What do we have here? First off, these are not heirloom strawberries. Where did you pick them from?"

"The side of my driveway."

"These are common weeds."

"No wonder nobody bought them."

"You're not from these parts, are you?"

"Maybe I should pack it all up and go home."

"Not so fast. What else have you got in the van?"

Oliver brought out the rhubarb.

"This."

"Rhubarb. You're charming, and you have a gorgeous smile. Do you have something I can make a sign with?"

Oliver handed her poster board and a sharpie, and Suzy instantly produced a small sign. "Here. Best Rhubarb in the State."

"Thanks."

"Oh, and it's such a warm day, I'd lose the work shirt and stand there with your best country boy 'aw shucks' grin. Just a suggestion."

Suzy walked off-screen as Oliver took off his shirt, revealing what the soap opera trades would likely proclaim as "the sexiest new torso in daytime."

The camera faded to the opening credits and theme song. Gabe immediately dialed Erin.

"Barrett makes Suzy look great," said Gabe.

"The set not too tacky?"

"As long as his nipples are at attention, who's looking at the set?"

The next scene was the meet-cute. He had substituted orange juice for the iced coffee. He thought about changing the wild strawberries and rhubarb. Too late now. *If Tomorrow Never Comes* hadn't seen this much chemistry...ever. Oliver and Suzy might develop a significant following if they played their cards right.

The meet-cute was well staged with the spilling of the orange juice all over Oliver. He had no problem taking his shirt off onscreen and acting topless. Most of the men in the cast would have balked, but Barrett led with his assets. He had obviously put in some precise upper body gym time. Gabe's dialogue was having a hard time competing with Oliver's six-pack.

At the commercial break, Erin immediately called.

"Still on track?" asked Erin.

"Exceeding all my wildest expectations," said Gabe. "The rom-com structure was money, Erin. Thanks."

"It's a shame they have to play the other storyline sequences today. This would have made a great eighteen-minute set."

"No shit, but this is all good news. They have one more scene in this show, right?"

"The kiss and the reveal. We'll see you in person tomorrow, right?"

"That's the plan."

The other sequences in the Monday show were less exhilarating. The other actors were fine, but no one had Barrett's spark. Suzy had to be savvy to match his magnetic charisma—or fade into the background. This was some of the best work Gabe had seen on a daytime drama in years.

The editors had cut the lines explaining why Suzy was helping Oliver empty the trash at the farmers market. The setup for their final scene didn't fully make much sense. As long as the whiff of sex and romance was in the air, the audience would go along with anything. The set was a darkly lit dumpster in an alley. The change of location was immaterial as long as the chemistry between Oliver and Suzy kept sizzling. As the actors said their lines, Gabe savored reliving the visit to the dump with Owen.

"You grew up here?" asked Oliver.

"We can spot an outsider when we see one," said Suzy.

"Am I that much of a cliche?" asked Oliver. "City slicker tries his hand at farming."

Gabe enjoyed Barrett's aw-shucks Oliver, but he preferred his own real-life, less-mannered Owen.

"We should probably throw the garbage away," said Suzy. "That's the job we volunteered for."

They both tossed different bags into the dumpster, then simultaneously reached for the last one, which was on the ground between them.

"Let me," said Oliver.

"I've got it," said Suzy.

They both grabbed the last bag of trash and tossed it into the dumpster together. The near close-up camera shot demanded the scene be staged with tight precision. When the final bag was tossed, their lips naturally met in a close-up, and they did not separate. Their kiss would likely be labeled the soap Smooch of the Year. The audience couldn't tell who initiated the kiss, but they could see both sides consenting not to end it.

"You need any help back there?" an off-screen voice yelled at them.

They separated long enough for Oliver to respond, "We're fine."

"Couldn't be better," said Suzy.

"There's something I better share with you first," said Oliver. "I'm in a relationship. I'm married."

"Of course, you are," said Suzy. "Of course, you are…" and Suzy ran off, fraught and crying, leaving sexy Oliver, alone on-screen, heartbroken.

Gabe immediately dialed Erin. "You didn't warn me about the kiss."

"Oh, my God! I was not prepared either. If that kiss doesn't help the ratings, nothing will."

A loud knocking came from the front door.

"I gotta get the door. Did you send more pages?"

"No. When are you leaving?"

"Tomorrow after breakfast."

"I hope breakfast is a euphemism," said Erin.

"Stay tuned," said Gabe.

More banging sounded at the door.

"You're not getting any more express delivery pages."

The knocking at the front door got louder.

"I better get the door."

Gabe ran down the stairs to find Owen there holding a folded piece of paper.

"Hey, Owen. —I wasn't planning to see you until later—"

"What the fuck, Gabe! What the fucking fuck! When were you going to tell me—" Owen stormed past Gabe, brushing him aside with more aggression than he had ever seen from Owen. "—about this!?"

Owen unfolded the paper to reveal a printout of Gabe receiving his Daytime Emmy this year in Los Angeles. "Were you ever going to tell me your real name is George Sample?"

Being unmasked was the liar's equivalent of a gut punch. Gabe took a step back.

"Mr. I'm-A-Glorified-Administrative-Assistant. You're a professional television writer. No wonder your eulogy was flawless. As head writer for *If Tomorrow Never Comes,* you must have written dozens. Yeah, I read the credits. Kevin was right about you. How could I have been so stupid?"

"Did Kevin send you that?"

"Kevin doesn't waste his time on soap operas."

"Where'd you—Maddy?"

"*I* watch *If Tomorrow Never Comes.* Me! I watch the show every day at eleven o'clock. Religiously."

"That's your standing meeting?"

"Fuck you! Yes. I can't have a guilty pleasure? I have been hooked— since the first time I stayed home sick with Luisa. Yes, I have followed the comings and goings of the good people of Harmony Hills for as long as I can remember."

"I had no idea."

"Obviously, George Sample. Of course, you had no idea. I can't tell you how exploited and betrayed— What did you do? Run home every time we met and write everything into a script?"

Gabe was ashamed. That was exactly what he had done.

"So George Sample is your pseudonym, and that was why Kevin couldn't find anything online about Gabe Hartman? One of you has been exploiting the good people of Concord Valley for a long time."

"I have no idea what you're talking about," Gabe couldn't let go of all the lies at once.

"Cut the crap! When I first moved up here, I wrote off all the similarities as a coincidence. I should have figured something was amiss when the minister in Harmony Hills got arrested with a prostitute, and I heard the same gossip at the grocery store here. The love triangle similar to Gertie, Phil, and Concetta, Mildred's story and the woman who runs the diner—"

"Please don't say anything."

"I would never. Can you imagine how hurtful that would be? Or how hurtful this is! To me! I'm not a garbage person like you. People can be despicable in many ways, but the worst is to be oblivious to other people's feelings. Obviously, you lack that empathy—"

"Owen, if I had known you watched—"

"Would that have mattered? You warned me early you had trust issues. I didn't suspect you would be the one who couldn't be trusted, not the married man. This feels like deliberate cruelty. How can I trust anything you told me? You tricked me into thinking you were letting me in."

"I was. But—"

"No, Gabe, there's no 'but.' You exploited me for professional gain. You convinced me you were better than that. We were bringing out the best in each other. How beautifully you played me! Did our intimacy mean nothing to you?"

"Of course, it did."

"So tell me this. Where exactly is this new Oliver's storyline going? Will he be growing heirloom tomatoes and cooking brownies with Suzy? Will there be legal expertise that reunites them? Please tell me there's not a galette recipe or a fake date that ends with a movie cuddle, hot sex, and the theme song 'In Dreams.' Oh yeah, I see exactly what I meant to you."

Gabe stood there in deep, silent shame. He had been caught. He had taken every wonderful detail about their relationship and put them into the Oliver script pages. Now he was paying the price.

Owen continued, "You sucked all the good out of what we had. How else was I deceived? Did you pretend you had never seen *In the Mood for Love?*"

"You were having such a good time sharing it with me—" Owen shook his head in disgust. Gabe could no longer look Owen in the eye. "It's one of my favorite movies," he confessed.

"You broke all the good we were creating. We had the best connection I ever had with another man, and I know you've never had anything nearly as good. What do you think Kevin and I were fighting about—he had never seen me this happy. He knows our marriage is a charade. It has been for the last five years. We agreed to stay married to avoid fortune hunters who would only want me for my wealth. Once he figured out that wasn't you and we were actually in love— But, no, you had to fuck everything up. For good."

"I wish I could say something—"

"Say goodbye, Gabe. It's over. I have no more affection to offer you. Don't bother getting in touch with me. Ever. For the record, all I wanted from you was to make a glorious, joyful, wonderful life together, not to prototype rom-com storylines for Harmony Hills. What a fucking fool I was. I never want to look at you again. Whoever the fuck you are. Boy loses boy. For good."

Owen stormed past him and slammed the door, leaving Gabe alone.

Owen Greene was no longer a part of Gabe Hartman's life or George Sample's.

Chapter Nine

Under normal circumstances, Gabe would have been devastated, gutted, and immobilized by such a dramatic breakup, but Gabe was too skilled at compartmentalizing his life. Now that his mother's estate was settled, he didn't have time for a good sob or a goodwill attempt to correct his mistakes with Owen. His to-do list was all about moving to California next month. In the end, Owen breaking up with him had been the most expedient solution. To an outsider, Gabe's "game face" may have seemed downright sociopathic.

As soon as Owen stormed out of the house, Gabe gathered his wits and recalibrated his day. He went to his computer and created a new document named, "Oliver/Suzy/Breakup." Still shaken, he jotted a few of the most dramatic lines from Owen's tirade while they were still fresh.

It was time for Gabe to say goodbye to his childhood home. He gathered the recipe cards, his *If Tomorrow Never Comes* paperwork, the cashmere sweater, several containers of gourmet chocolates, and all the clothes he'd brought with him. At the last minute, he grabbed the *In the Mood for Love* DVD. Even though the aspen tree had failed him, he still wanted a memento of his Owen time. After all, it was one of his favorite movies.

Gabe gave the house one last look, double-checked the lockbox, and headed out. He didn't even stop at the Quinn & Ink on his way out of town. The situation demanded a clean break.

When he got to the offices of *If Tomorrow Never Comes,* he discovered a beehive of activity, with filming scheduled to the quarter hour.

"Welcome back! Major events are happening at warp speed around here," said Erin on their "walk with me" briefing before meeting with the Douglasses. "The creative energy at this place is unbelievable. Even the staff writers have returned to the office. There's a rumor going around that not everyone is going to California. The quality of the work in this last sprint will be a determining factor. So everyone is bringing their A game."

"Sounds like a well-placed rumor," said Gabe.

"I read your latest Oliver/Suzy pages. You broke up with your dude?"

"The inevitable surprise ending."

"For now," said Erin. "I mean, if you're following a standard rom-com format."

Erin knocked on the Douglasses' door.

"For now, for Suzy and Oliver. For good, for me and Owen."

That was the first time Gabe had mentioned Owen's name aloud since the breakup. Shame and regret overtook him.

"Enter!" yelled Thomas.

Gabe was first struck by the tidiness of the office. No highball glasses in sight. He had returned to a significantly different world.

"How is the grieving process?" asked Doris with an empathetic hug.

"I'm good," said Gabe.

"He's a professional, Doris," said Thomas. "He never stopped working."

"Isn't that Barrett Hodges something!" said Doris. "You're giving him such great material. Can't wait to see the numbers tomorrow."

"He doesn't need smoke up his shorts," said Thomas. "He's won an Emmy. Listen, we need to talk LA. You're still going tomorrow?"

"That's the plan," said Gabe. "Taking the red-eye."

"You're a better man than I," confessed Doris.

"Heads up: the Hollywood stagehand union and the New York stagehand union are two different animals," said Thomas. "Hollywood is the most passive-aggressive place in the world. It's all 'I love you, kiss, kiss' to your face, but don't expect to hear from them again."

"Don't trust anything you see in LA," said Doris. "Everything is an illusion. It's something about how the sun bounces off the hills that makes the place feel like no one has to work for a living there. Everything is a deception."

"I got him all our current blueprints and facility needs requests," said Erin.

"I'll make sure everyone has a comparable place to land when we resume shooting there," said Gabe.

"When you're in LA, whatever you hear," Thomas's tone got serious and conspiratorial, "if it sounds even a smidgen off, run it by us before you jump to any conclusions."

"Don't scare the boy," said Doris. "Have a good trip. Keep in touch. And we'll check in the minute you get back."

Outside the Douglasses' office, they bumped into Barrett Hodges on his way to hair and makeup.

"Are you George Sample?" asked Barrett.

"Barrett!" said Gabe. "And please call me Gabe."

"I heard about your mother. If there's anything I can do..." said Barrett.

"Thanks. Nice to finally meet you."

"And I wanted to thank you for such great scenes."

"We're lucky to have you."

"I'm the lucky one. Your words are so easy to internalize. The dialogue feels fresh, like real people talking. I wish it was that easy to fall in love in real life." Barrett's star wattage was impossible to deny. His gestures and facial expressions reminded Gabe of Owen. *Owen was such a lovely man...* Mental pictures of Owen clung to Gabe's imagination as Barrett walked away.

"Star struck?" asked Erin.

"Something like that," said Gabe, shaking off all mental pictures of Owen.

"What was Mr. Douglass on about in there?"

"Don't know, but something's definitely up with the move."

"You should head home to pack," said Erin. "I've arranged your curb-to-curb car service."

"You're the best."

Gabe had a special place in his heart for Los Angeles. Every Los Angeles vista was a backdrop from some iconic film or TV show.

The freeway traffic was mercifully light. He was meeting with three members of the production team at the network's main facility in Studio City. Three burly men—Mark, David, and Larry—showed up with a carton of coffees and a pink box of pastries. The meeting took place in a large, empty sound stage, somewhat dusty but well lit. The four men sat around a large conference table set up specifically for their meeting.

After a few initial pleasantries, Gabe expected the meeting to move into the facilities conversation.

"Is this guava cream cheese?" asked Mark, more interested in the pastries.

"You swing by Porto's for these?" asked David.

"Some new Cuban bakery in Silver Lake," said Larry. "Not quite the Tropical, but what is?"

"What do you think, Gabe?" asked Mark.

"Delicious. But—"

"I hope you aren't lactose intolerant," said Larry. "They only make con leches."

"All good," said Gabe. "Do you guys want to take a look at the plans I brought?"

Mark, David, and Larry looked at one another blankly.

"Sure," said David, as if out of obligation.

Gabe spread out all the documents before the three men. He

explained what each of the departments needed in terms of studio and office space. The men listened politely but did not take notes. They were extremely polite and quiet, except for one moment in the middle of Gabe's presentation about storing the many set pieces. That's when David began to cough, like his pastry got caught in his throat.

"Sorry," said David. "Went down the wrong pipe." But he cleared his throat and was fine in no time.

At the end of his presentation, Gabe handed them each a one-page Erin had drafted. "What do you think?"

Mark, David, and Larry looked at one another once more, blankly.

"Big picture question here," said David, who had taken on the role of spokesman. "Are we 100 percent sure this is happening?" Mark and Larry nodded in support of his question.

"The New York office," said Gabe, "is fairly confident *If Tomorrow Never Comes* can start producing out here sometime within the next two months."

"But it's not official yet, is it." David's words didn't sound like a question.

"Hopefully, after this meeting, it will be," said Gabe.

"Of course," said David. Mark and Larry nodded in unison.

"Do you doubt *If Tomorrow Never Comes* could move out here?" asked Gabe. "There seems to be plenty of space."

"No, no. The real estate isn't the problem," said David. Mark and Larry shook their heads. "If—when—*when* it happens, we will be ready."

"Is there something you're not telling me?" asked Gabe. "Are you aware we're currently shooting double episodes in the New York studio to give us well over a month's worth of content for the transition? It's designed to be seamless."

"Moving a dying soap to LA must sound like a great idea to the suits in New York," said Mark.

"Look," interrupted Larry, "we are bottom feeders on the food chain. We know nothing."

David jumped in. "Moving an entire daytime soap operation from the East Coast to the West Coast has never been done before. It's going to be expensive. I haven't met anyone out here who thinks it's going to be worth it."

"But it's a better business model, and we're moving forward with the plans..." said Gabe.

"Yes. It looks that way," said David. "Here's the reality. Hollywood is a city of accountants, not artists. Accountants follow the numbers: production costs, salaries, ratings. The numbers never lie. Think like an accountant, and you'll never be disappointed in LA. My advice: pay attention to every detail. There are too many ways to sabotage this. That's all we'll say."

"Nice to meet you," said Mark, standing up.

The three men rose for farewell handshakes. The meeting was over, and they were gone.

"I don't know, Erin," said Gabe on his way to the airport. "Something's up. My meeting was weird. The union dudes were nice enough, but I got the feeling they didn't believe we would actually be moving the show out here."

"Are you going to tell the Douglasses about your meeting?"

"Like they're to be trusted. How were the Oliver ratings today?" asked Gabe.

"A nice uptick."

"Some good news for the accountants."

Gabe couldn't resist the warmth of Los Angeles light and the proximity to the beach. He had a few hours to kill before his flight. He asked his driver to take him up the Pacific Coast Highway well into Malibu. He had read somewhere all beaches were public in California and had downloaded an app that pinpointed access to the best hard-to-get-to beaches. After the driver parked the car by a wooden stairway hidden between two houses on the ocean side of PCH, Gabe took off his shoes, rolled up his pants, and headed to a stretch of white sand and smooth pebbles the app referred to as one of Malibu's best kept secrets.

Strolling the length of the beach and back, admiring the affluent homes on stilts above him, he imagined living there and waking up to the Pacific Ocean. The warm sea air filled Gabe with endless possibilities of life after Concord Valley, New York City, his mother, Owen. *How could someone I have known less than a couple of weeks take up such significant space next to my mother?* He regretted letting Owen into his life so easily. Gabe filed away all recollections of Owen and continued his walk.

He played in the tidepools at the far end of the beach. Sea anemones and mussels competed with starfish for his attention. He wanted his move to California to be a kind of rebirth, a fresh start. He would finally shed his perfect little boy identity, the kid who never got to live for himself. He would reinvent himself in California, sacrificing whatever it took to get on with his life.

For starters, he would do away with any false belief systems ruled by rom-com tropes. *Owen and I built a life based on a fantasy, a distraction to get through my challenging time of grief. Now that my grief has passed, I no longer need the sleight of hand a loving, generous boyfriend could offer...* For a moment, Gabe missed Owen's kindness. Gabe couldn't escape his regret at how their relationship had ended. At some point, he would have to find a way to make it right with Owen. But not today. Today was about new beginnings and not clinging to old ideas. Today was not about Owen.

Owen was taking up too much real estate in his head. Hopefully, his feelings for him, like his grief for his mother, would eventually be relegated to an occasional poignant memory.

*

The next month, Gabe's life at *If Tomorrow Never Comes* had the velocity of a runaway train. If he wasn't making final edits to shooting script pages, he was writing out Oliver Armstrong pages. The week after his LA trip, they would be shooting the big breakup sequence. Any chance of scrubbing Owen from his imagination was a fool's errand.

"Did the end of your relationship really play out this way?" asked Erin after reading the breakup scene.

"More or less," said Gabe.

"It must have been devastating. For both of you."

"Falling out of love is harder than I thought."

He regretted attending the table read with Barrett, Suzy, and the director.

"This is great writing," said Barrett.

"I find their destiny absolutely...tragic," said Suzy.

"He's such a shit," said Barrett.

"How so?" asked Gabe, trying not to appear defensive.

"The week before," said Barrett, "he goes to her house to break up but ends up sleeping with her. He's either greedy, lazy, cowardly, or head-over-heels in love with her."

"Or all of the above," said Suzy.

"Loveable assholes," said Barrett, "are the most fun to play."

"And the worst in a real-life relationship," added Suzy.

"Juicy scene," said the director, more focused on cameras than content.

"Our ratings have risen incrementally," said Gabe. "That's a testament to the great work you two have been doing. When we get to Los Angeles, we're going to find a way to make you the new Luke and Laura."

"The way you talk..." said Suzy.

"Is next week going to be a big apology scene?" asked Barrett.

"Absolutely," said Gabe, who hadn't yet considered an apology scenario with Owen. *Maybe writing an apology scene will be the closure I need to shake Owen once and for all.*

Gabe studied the schedule. He figured they were shooting enough scenes to cover the one-month move, maybe even a two-month move. "In case there are unpredictable hiccups during the transition," said Thomas Douglass. "There always are a few."

The last week of shooting, Gabe got a call he didn't recognize from the Concord Valley.

"Is that Gabe? Arthur Quinn here."

"Arthur! How are you?"

"Good. I want to give you an update. The first day of the estate sale went off without a hitch."

"That was today?" said Gabe. "I've been swamped. I completely forgot."

"That gal Bonnie will be giving you a call tomorrow when it's all done, but she did a crackerjack job. She wanted me to tell you that you made your nut before noon. The rest is gravy."

"That's great news."

"How's New York treating you?"

"Keeping busy," Gabe made every effort not to ask about Owen. "And Concord Valley?"

"Same ole, same ole. Any plans on a visit?"

"My company may be sending me to California for a while."

"That's something."

"When I get back, I'll plan a trip to Concord Valley."

"Then I won't ask you to be my best man."

"Lenore?"

"Looks that way."

"Congratulations!"

"We haven't set a date yet, but it's definitely headed there. Neither one of us wants to die alone."

"Hopefully, that won't be for a long time. Congratulations. I hate to cut this short, Arthur, but I'm still at work. Better run."

"Don't be a stranger."

All the talk of death and loneliness made Gabe consider going onto his hookup app, but he would only be distracting himself. Out of an old habit, he checked his texts instead. He didn't know what he was hoping to see. A new text from Owen? An old one that had never been erased? Nothing.

Instead of obsessing about unfinished business or swiping left for a hookup, Gabe attempted to write the apology scene. This would be his first Oliver Armstrong fictional scene. Gabe had no experiences or memories to draw from. He initially drew a blank. Erin suggested he set up a collaborative meeting with Barrett and Suzy in a conference room.

"Before I jumped into the apology scene," Gabe told them, "I wanted input from you both. The apology scene needs to feel intimate and personal."

"Cool," said Barrett.

"She absolutely feels betrayed," said Suzy. "When a woman gives herself freely to a man, I don't think a simple apology will heal the hurt."

"I agree," said Barrett, "but I think he needs to say the words 'I'm sorry' at some point. He is. Clearly, he loves her. But there can be no justification for what he did. That would be worse than no apology. He can't undo the gaslighting."

"Do you think healing and forgiveness will ever be possible for them?" asked Gabe. "I'm trying to imagine what kind of future story arcs they could have."

"Hard to say," said Barrett. "Right now, Oliver needs to take full responsibility for the harm he caused her."

"Do you think they should have a reconciliation?" Gabe asked Suzy.

"It's a soap," said Suzy. "Whatever you write, we'll sell it, kiddo."

"If this were real life," said Gabe, "what are the odds she'd give him a second chance?"

"Only time will tell," said Suzy with a shrug and a twinkle in her eye.

Gabe placed the apology scene at the Harmony Hills Airport. Their paths crossed as Oliver was sneaking out of town to return to his wife and Suzy was escaping the town gossip with an extended South American vacation. They bumped into each other under the Departures sign. Gabe's dialogue paraphrased most of what the actors had said during the meeting.

During the filming, Oliver was earnest and forthright. Suzy cried real tears and let her makeup run. Their talents were perfectly matched.

At the end of the scene, Oliver took her chin in his palm and wiped away the tears. "I wish I could unsay every lie and start from scratch. But that's not how life works."

With that, he kissed her cheek and walked away as the credits rolled.

As each of the soap's sequences wrapped, the sets, props, wigs, and costumes were packed into shipping containers to be sent to the West Coast.

Erin was selected to stay in the New York studio until everything was shipped out. "This is when events might start to run amok," said Gabe to Erin. "Pay attention to everything."

A week before Gabe's move, he packed up his place. He hated giving up his rent-controlled apartment, but leaving it behind was a symbol of hope for new beginnings.

"When are you going to start writing the book?" asked Jessica.

Jessica had wanted to hang out with him once more before he took off. She insisted on bringing pizza and beer for a classic moving party.

"As soon as the soap settles in on the West Coast," said Gabe, "I'll find the time."

"I'd hate for you to have to pay back the huge advance."

They sat on boxes in his bedroom, finishing the last of the pizza.

"I'm going to write the book," said Gabe. "The last months here have been crazy. A regular old work schedule is going to feel like a vacation."

"I can tell you're busy," said Jessica, folding up the greasy cheese-stained pizza box to fit in the garbage. "I haven't heard your hookup app go off once since I've been here."

"Been a while..." Gabe hadn't had sex since his last night with Owen, but he didn't feel like going into all that with Jessica. "There's one last closet to pack."

As Jessica opened the closet door, a rolled up poster board fell from the top shelf onto the floor.

"What is this?" She unrolled it to reveal Gabe's vision board.

"Put that away."

"Let's take a look at what all came true."

They stood over the flattened vision board and took inventory. Owen's home in Concord Valley took center stage, surrounded by snippets of the lovely kitchen, the bedroom, and the parlor. Looking over the world he had sabotaged pained Gabe. The vision board also had many pictures of books: individual books, books on shelves, antique books, cookbooks—symbols of his new literary success. At the top of the vision board was a random picture of a temple in Angkor Wat covered by a banyan tree, not unlike the last scene of *In the Mood for Love*. Gabe had also glued a beach sunset onto the board, not exactly his favorite Malibu beach, but definitely a Pacific Ocean reference.

"It's uncanny," said Gabe, taking a step back.

"That was the guy's house, right?" asked Jessica.

"Yep. Much of what I experienced happened right there," said Gabe pointing to a picture of Owen's house.

"That's how vision boards work," said Jessica. "Magic."

Gabe tore the vision board in half.

"What are you doing!?" asked Jessica, horrified.

"I'm not taking this with me. No room."

"You shouldn't tear up the vision of your life. Bad karma."

"Don't be superstitious. I'll make a new one when I get to California."

"Right..." Jessica knew he never would.

The day before Gabe's flight west, he got a call from Bethany and Roger Cohen.

"We've got some good news," said Roger.

"Probate closed!" said Bethany.

"That was fast, right?" asked Gabe.

"Phenomenally," said Roger.

"You're a lucky guy," said Bethany.

"So what's next?" asked Gabe.

"You can either pay off the debts on the place and maintain ownership," said Roger, "which we do not advise."

"Or you can put it on the market," said Bethany, "and hope the place captures some sucker's—I mean, some buyer's imagination, which we *do* advise."

"Let's do it," said Gabe. "One caveat: I can't be there to interview realtors. I'm literally moving to California for work tomorrow."

"Bethany has a cousin up here who's a realtor with a solid track record."

"Sounds great. Have her take a look at the place and let me know.

The lockbox should still be on the backdoor. The passcode is 2020."

"We'll take care of it," said Bethany.

"Traveling mercies!" said Roger.

Gabe was astonished at how swiftly his life had changed. One day, he was walking the streets of Manhattan, hustling to get shooting pages ready, collaborating with soap stars about a forgiveness scene; a few days later, he was navigating the freeways of Los Angeles, prepping for the first ever soap production company's move west. The networks had rented him a car and a Studio City apartment close to the studio, which looked more like a three-star motel than an apartment building.

Gabe met Mark, Larry, and David every morning at the empty studio space. One of them would bring treats and coffees for the four of them. After pontificating on the merits of the treats du jour, they then all headed to different parts of the empty cavernous studio with their laptops where they waited (or pretended to wait) for the arrival of props, wigs, costumes, and set pieces for Harmony Hill's big move west.

Every day a shipping container Erin had signed off on would depart from the New York studio, headed to its new home in LA. Erin said the New York studio was a ghost town. The actors were at home awaiting news of who would be heading west. Even the Douglasses' office had been emptied. Erin was the only permanent employee holding down the fort.

Most of Gabe's LA day was spent seeing how successfully he could battle his obsession with Owen. Regrets lost to memories of the good times they had shared. Fears of dying alone fought with the reality there would always be plenty of men in the world. Gabe was a personification of Kevin's "proportion of pain to power" theory.

Gabe's stint in Studio City showed little variation. No one was exactly sure how long the containers would take to get there, but someone had to be there to meet them when they arrived. The smaller ones were put on trucks and expected in two to three weeks; the larger ones were sent via rail, and their arrival was anyone's guess. Gabe was extremely nervous about the timing of the show's transition West. Thanks to the extra scenes they had shot, the calendar was still in their favor.

Every day, Gabe would stream *If Tomorrow Never Comes* during its real-time broadcast. Whenever an Oliver Armstrong scene came on, Gabe relived his favorite Owen moments. He hoped Owen still tuned in. Gabe's nostalgia for Owen only grew with seeing each episode.

"Why not start building the layout for our production company's requests?" asked Gabe one morning over Mexican pan dulces and flan.

"When everything is here," said David.

"You still think this isn't happening?" asked Gabe.

"I'll believe it when everything has arrived from the East Coast," said Mark.

"We need to see how everything fits in the space first, especially the sets," said Larry.

"You might want to start bringing a project with you," said Mark. "It can't be easy living inside your head all day while we wait like this," said Mark.

About two weeks into the move, Erin announced that all the containers had been shipped except for the sets. The freight weights with the railroad they had originally contracted were creating a headache. Erin didn't understand the details exactly, but the Douglasses had shown up at the New York City office the day she shared this. They had been in closed-door meetings all day with the suits, figuring out alternatives to getting the set pieces to California.

Gabe was becoming skeptical, but he didn't want to share the set piece information with Mark, Larry, and David. He didn't want to believe they had been right all along. Instead, he created a makeshift office with some furniture in an empty corner of the studio where he could work. There, he organized his mother's recipe cards and worked on his book. To Gabe's great relief, on the afternoon he was separating cake from cookie recipe cards, the first smaller container of wigs and hats arrived.

"Where shall we put them?" asked Gabe.

"They're all marked, right?" said Mark.

"Beautifully labeled if I know our costume people," said Gabe.

"Let's keep them in the middle of the studio until everything else arrives," said David.

It wasn't how Gabe would have organized the containers, but since they would be doing the literal heavy lifting, he didn't want to make waves. There might be other more important hills to die on later.

Several days went by before the next shipping container arrived, but Gabe was relieved they were at least trickling in. More costumes. Mostly shoes. Mark, Larry, and David made sure the accumulating pile of shipping containers would be organized and easily accessible when it came time to open and unload everything.

Gabe spent most of his days organizing his book. He was making good progress with the recipe cards, jotting notes as he went. His obsession with Owen had been relegated to an occasional whisper.

Mark, Larry, and David had their own rituals. After the morning treats, they would go off to play their favorite computer games, only interrupted if a new shipping container arrived.

By the end of the first month, Gabe had arranged all his mother's recipe cards in a way that lent itself to a graceful narrative flow, organizing them around a system of well-orchestrated ideas. Sometimes the concepts would organically expand to anecdotes about his mother and her friends. Other times, he would have to research a culinary ingredient or historical gastronomy reference that didn't exist anymore. When he wasn't fretting about time running out on the move, he was having a great time organizing his book as a celebration of his mother's life. His obsession with Owen had all but disappeared.

By the Friday of the fifth week, all the containers Erin sent had arrived. They were just waiting for the sets. Gabe was now visibly worried as Oliver Armstrong's forgiveness scene would be broadcast that day. There would be only one last week of unaired, prerecorded work left. After that, they would have to play reruns, something unheard of on a soap.

Erin didn't know what was going on with the set. On Thursday, she had mentioned a visit from Aurora Helms to the New York office. No one in the network office had returned his messages yesterday. In fact, Erin hadn't returned his calls that day. Everything went straight to voicemail. Something was definitely amiss.

As the broadcast of the show began, Gabe streamed it from his computer. He had forgotten his earbuds, so the theme song must have attracted Mark, Larry, and David's attention, and they gathered around Gabe and his computer.

"You know," said Mark, "I've never seen this show."

"Our housekeeper watches it," said David.

"My mom tried to get me hooked when I stayed home from school sick," said Larry, "but it wasn't for me."

"It's usually awful," said Gabe, "but there's one scene today. The actors are terrific."

"You mind if we join you?" asked Mark.

"Please," said Gabe.

They each pulled up a chair around his laptop.

"That's me," said Gabe when the name George Sample flashed across the credits.

"I thought your name was Gabe something," said Larry.

"I use a pen name," said Gabe.

"Not everyone can write for a national television show," said David. "You should be proud."

"I'm sure he has his reasons," said Mark.

The final Oliver Armstrong scene began with Suzy and Oliver under the Departure sign at the Harmony Hills airport. The acting was vibrant, present, and alive. The men were compelled to lean in.

"This is pretty good," said David.

"Too good for a soap," said Larry.

"The actors are phenomenal," said Gabe.

"What's the big deal?" asked Mark. "What's he apologizing for?"

"A litany of lies," said Gabe. "He kind of exploited her."

"Women hate men who lie," said Larry. "Men hate men who lie. It's almost impossible to restore trust once it's been betrayed."

"I don't know," said David. "Those two actors, maybe it's their chemistry, but if it's meant to be, they'll reunite one way or another. Rom-com-style."

When the final credits rolled, Mark said, "That was not a waste of time."

"I'm proud of that scene," said Gabe.

"You should be," said David. "Oliver may be a heel, but I'm rooting for him."

"In spite of the tacky airport set," said Larry, "Maybe it's for the best those sets are not—" Mark interrupted Larry's sentence by clearing his throat, and David gave him a conspiratorial look, shaking his head. Larry pivoted. "That couple is meant to be together. It's undeniable."

"The sets...?" asked Gabe.

A memory of Gabe's first meeting with Mark, Larry, and David came into focus. When he had originally mentioned they needed a lot of space to hold all the sets, David had a coughing fit and claimed his pastry went down the wrong pipe. "You tried to warn me...didn't you?" The truth had been right in front of him, like Owen's eleven o'clock standing meeting. If only Gabe had paid attention and asked the right question. "They never had any intention of sending the sets, did they?"

"What makes you say that?" asked Mark.

"There's one week left of material to air, and the sets haven't left New York. They're not sending them, are they?"

"You didn't hear it from us," said David. "It was one of a lot of moving pieces."

"That's how they're canceling the soap?"

Larry, Mark, and David didn't need to respond. "They had no intention of sending the sets out West... This was the endgame all along."

"I don't think they knew exactly what was happening," said Mark. "But, yeah. Did you notice, they only sent the stuff the network could repurpose on their other shows?"

"Sorry, dude," said Larry. "You clearly have a lot of talent, Mr. Sample, but *If Tomorrow Never Comes* is never coming to California."

The floor had disappeared under Gabe. Erin must have figured it out, and the network had asked her not to contact him until they got to him first. The shock wasn't that the soap was being canceled. The elaborate ruse created to deceive everyone was the true outrage. Now Gabe was the one betrayed and lied to.

When the HR team eventually contacted him via video conference, they told him the network no longer considered *If Tomorrow Never Comes* a viable concern and apologized for any inconvenience. The conversation was detached and businesslike. They offered him six months of severance, which seemed slim after a decade of loyalty, but Gabe had his book advance, and there would be some unemployment at some point, which gave him enough financial security to accept the payout terms. They reminded him of his non-disclosure agreement, and they would only be paying for his apartment and rental car through the end of the week. "If you want the company to pay for your return ticket, please contact the travel office."

As soon as the meeting ended, he called Erin. She picked up this time.

"What was your severance?" she asked.

"Six months."

"I got three. I would have called, but they asked me not to, and I didn't know if they were monitoring my calls. Can they do that?"

"No. And you were wise not to reach out."

"You knew all along."

"I couldn't see how exactly. The Aurora visit must have been the tipping point. It's shitty no matter how you slice it. What will you do now?"

"I have a producer friend at *SNL* who's been begging me to start climbing the food chain there."

"Work those contacts, girl. Much better job security."

"You gonna stay in LA?" asked Erin.

"The only people I know here are three burly stagehand union dudes who have a sweet tooth and a penchant for enigma. I need to find a place to write a book. I'm sorry this happened, Erin. Promise me you'll stay in touch."

"How can we not? The world of television is a small town," said Erin.

If Gabe had Erin's ambition, he would have taken advantage of his time in Los Angeles to pursue other television gigs, instead of trying to get over Owen. But he had gone to work, waited for shipping containers, and hunkered down both day and night focused on his book. He wasn't sure he even wanted to work in television anymore. Organizing his book had been more satisfying than he had imagined.

He drove along PCH to clear his head. Something was drawing him to his favorite Malibu beach. Maybe the sea and the tide pools would reveal what he should do next.

As he was walking barefoot along the beach, he sensed his name being carried on the ocean breeze: "Gabe, Gabe, Gabe."

At first, he wrote it off as the chatter of gulls, until the volume and cadence changed.

"Gabe! Gabe? Ga-abe!"

He turned toward the direction of the voice, looking up. Someone vaguely familiar dressed in shorts and a loose T-shirt was waving at him from a glass balcony facing the Pacific.

"Gabe! It's me! Kevin!"

"Kevin? Hey, Kevin!" said Gabe, trying to shout over the waves.

"Come on up!" said Kevin, pointing down to an open door at the base of the house's stilts that led to stairs.

When Gabe got to the top of the stairs, he was met with a tanned, relaxed, and more handsome Kevin than he had met in Concord Valley.

"There he is!" Kevin welcomed him with an awkward hug. "I was pretty sure I recognized the man on the beach."

"What are you doing here?" asked Gabe.

"I live here. When I'm not in New York," said Kevin.

"You live on my favorite beach. This place is fabulous!"

"What you see is what you get," said Kevin, making a grand 360 degree gesture around the open-concept space.

Gabe took in the fullness of the home: a study in glass and steel, 2000 square feet of gorgeous, clean modernism with all the furniture designed to reflect either the sea (blue) or the light (white). The bedroom and bathroom seemed to depend on billowy track curtains for privacy. Gabe was visibly in awe of the sheer beauty and spectacle of the place and its pin-drop silence.

"Having a Pemberley moment?" asked Kevin.

Gabe nodded.

"You had no idea what kind of money you were walking away from, did you?"

Gabe didn't take the bait. "This interior is dead quiet, but PCH is right there..."

"Triple-paned glass. It's beyond fabulous. I got this place in the breakup." Gabe didn't know how to respond to Kevin dropping this nugget of news. "Owen's mother made sure this place appeared in her favorite interior design glossy—before I was officially granted the deed in the divorce papers. Owen refused to fly in for the photoshoot. I won't miss all that nonsense."

With two mentions of their breakup, Kevin must have been inviting some inquiry from Gabe. "When did you and Owen decide to split up?"

"Not too long after you left Concord Valley. Someone wise suggested if a lying faux admin assistant talk-show writer was a threat to our marital bliss, the marriage had most likely run its course."

"Soap opera writer."

"I can see why you kept that a secret," said Kevin. "Kidding. Not really."

"How did you recognize me on the beach?" asked Gabe.

"You're still Gud2go, right?" said Kevin, holding up his phone to reveal the app.

"I haven't used that app in ages." *Not since...before Owen.*

"If you didn't delete it, you're still online."

"How is Owen doing?"

"Dunno. My lawyer advised me not to have contact with him until after all the divorce crap settles."

"Maddy doesn't keep you updated?" asked Gabe.

"She moved, lives in New York. I hear he put his place on the market. He may have already sold it."

"What about his dreams of being an heirloom tomato farmer?"

"I heard he lost interest in gardening. It's kind of his pattern."

Gabe was sad to think Owen might have lost interest because he had left town. With news of their breakup, Gabe also thought Kevin might have another agenda inviting him into his home. Kevin was looking too sexy for an afternoon at home alone.

"Did Owen leave Concord Valley?" asked Gabe.

"No idea. Who knows where he'll end up next? Owen never has to worry about work or money like the rest of us. He has the luxury of obsessing about whether his life has meaning and purpose. He can do that anywhere. You should call him and catch up."

"He doesn't want to hear from me."

"I doubt that."

"He said as much when he broke it off."

"Obviously, a regretful moment of passion. I'd never seen him happier than when you were around."

"Not in the end. I don't think he wants to have anything to do with me."

"That doesn't sound like Owen," said Kevin.

"It got ugly. At least you got what you wanted: I didn't break his heart."

"You didn't hear that heart of his shattering under his angry fit?" asked Kevin. "The way he looked at you... He never lit up like that when I entered the room, even at the beginning."

Kevin was making him sad. Gabe would never love anyone like he had loved Owen.

Kevin's phone gave off a familiar *drrroot*. Kevin checked it.

"So here's the deal, Mr. Gud2go. One of my hot Santa Monica regulars, a daddy married to a woman, is parking on PCH right now, and he would be delighted to no end to discover I had arranged a hot threesome with a handsome television writer."

Ex-television writer. But Gabe didn't have the energy to explain.

"Whaddya say?" Kevin's thumb caressed Gabe's cheek with affection. "Are you going to let me experience firsthand what all the fuss was about?" Kevin's other hand found one of Gabe's belt loops and aggressively made its way to Gabe's crotch.

"As tempting as that sounds," said Gabe, stepping back out of his reach, "I'm going to pass. Plane to catch."

The doorbell rang an elegant clang.

"I won't take it personally. But would you mind escaping down the stairs to the beach? I like to keep my hookups tidy for my discreet daddies."

Gabe left Kevin unencumbered for his afternoon delight. He continued his barefoot stroll along the beach, wading in the tide pools, delighting in a galaxy of starfish. Gabe liked the Pacific, but the Atlantic was his first love. On the horizon, Gabe saw a pod of dolphins, sleek, graceful swimmers, leaping out of the water, followed by pelicans as they all seemed to be making their way home.

Chapter Ten

All his life, Gabe had dreamed of the mythical life of being a New York freelance writer: sitting in front of a typewriter (that became a laptop as the years went on), tossing crumpled pages first into a garbage can (that became a trash can icon), and chain-smoking cigarettes (that became vaping). He showed up at his computer every morning with no days off. He hadn't been prepared for the loneliness, but he faced it down and conquered it. Within a few months, he was ahead of schedule. The first draft of the book was nearly finished.

In California, Gabe had brilliantly organized the recipes. He simply showed up every day at his laptop, followed his outline, and kept writing. Doubt and distraction were his biggest challenges. Even though his writing Emmy stood sentinel on the mantel, he wasn't always sure he was a "real" writer.

Since his serendipitous visit with Kevin, his Owen obsession had returned. Every morning, he was tempted to take a deep dive and look him up online. Every morning, his good sense got the better of him, and he cut that impulse.

After the debacle in Los Angeles, he made the choice to return to

New York City. He easily found a small one-bedroom sublet in Soho. His stuff fit snugly, and he adored the working fireplace but never used it. He found the exposed brick wall the perfect non-distracting tabula rasa for writing a book.

The neighborhood had the obligatory overpriced Greek diner where he ate breakfast and got a coffee to go before heading home for his morning writing session. Around one o'clock, he took a walk and ate lunch out before returning home for an afternoon of revising and editing the morning's work. Evenings were earmarked for a distraction break. He went to the movies, streamed whatever looked moderately interesting, and watched television, but never a soap.

He did not want to see friends. They would inevitably ask about the book, and he didn't want anything to jinx his creative process until the draft was complete. Except for the errant pangs of loneliness and battling his Owen obsession, he loved his writerly life more than he'd expected. With the cancellation of the soap, Gabe was empowered like a man who had cheated death. He couldn't imagine his current life without a chunk of money in the bank. *This is what Owen's life must be like, but with money that never runs out.*

As time went by, doing away with any remembrance of Owen was more of a challenge. He considered going to therapy or a support group, but he didn't want to sacrifice valuable writing time on an ex-boyfriend. *I'm not that pathetic.*

Obsessing about Owen was time wasted on a fantasy, but not without a payoff. Every time he replayed the breakup in his head, he was connecting to Owen. The obsession was his way of getting Owen back, one way or another. He re-streamed the Oliver/Suzy apology scene, hoping for the outside chance it might someday become real.

When he wasn't obsessing about Owen, he was pushing himself to write from the heart. He dug deep into the well of empathy for his mother. She had never been able to pursue her dreams of being a caterer. She sacrificed those dreams for motherhood. Gabe was learning to detach from his guilt and celebrate his mother to repay her for decades of kindness.

His discipline was admirable. He only answered the phone twice while writing the book. Early on, Jessica called to see how the book was coming along, Gabe clearly did not want to be distracted by small talk.

"Then why did you answer the phone?" asked Jessica.

"I thought you might be calling with some business issue," said Gabe.

"Pardon me for caring," said Jessica. "Call me when you turn in your draft."

The other call was from the Cohens.

"Good news!" said Bethany. "You've got a cash offer on your mom's house."

"And it's enough to cover all the debts with a little money left over for closing costs," said Roger.

"That's amazing! Who's the buyer?" asked Gabe.

"Looks like another New Yorker escaping the rat race," said Roger. "Someone with too much money and not enough common sense. Everyone's got a dream."

"The AH Trust," said Bethany. "AH is most likely someone's initials. I can find out if you want."

"No need. Grateful to be rid of it."

"You dodged a bullet," said Roger. "Look for a slew of electronic signature emails."

Gabe had taken the call in front of the mirror in his bedroom. *Who have I become?* he asked his reflection. The loneliness had added depth to his countenance. He hadn't necessarily aged, but he had matured.

The more Gabe committed to his writer's retreat, the richer his writing got and the more his creativity surged. He had imaginary conversations with his mother where she told him about the food, her life, and her community of friends, a group of noble farm women who were struggling financially but had traveled the world through their kitchen recipe cards.

On a Saturday afternoon in late winter, he shut his laptop and called Jessica.

"Don't tell me," said Jessica, ready to be annoyed anew. "You have writer's block."

"Sorry I was such a shit when you called before," said Gabe. "But I finished the book."

"Oh, my God! I am so proud of you!"

"What happens next?"

"You should send the draft to your publisher. They might have a few notes for you."

"Don't you mean 'our' publisher?"

"While you were hunkered down, I left NewLibrary and took a job at Bright Ink. It's my Big Five publishing dream job!"

"Oh, my God! Jess, I'm—"

"Surprised?"

"—proud of you?"

"Editing young adult fiction ends up being one of my superpowers. I should have seen it coming. YA books were all over my vision board."

"We should celebrate for us both!" said Gabe.

"I'm currently at a book buyers convention in the Bay Area. When I get back."

"Who have we become, Jess?"

"Successful. By the way, I'm dating someone, and it's kinda getting serious. A guy named Gus. I met him at the hot bar at the overpriced health food store down the block."

"Delish. Was he on your vision board?"

"It's the one thing he's not on if you know what I mean."

"That good, huh? Any dating advice?" asked Gabe.

"It's about time you asked. As your unofficial rom-com ally—and the ally always gets the dude first—let me say this: when life gives you your grand rom-com moment, you better take it, Gabe."

"I'm happy for you."

Gabe immediately emailed his manuscript to his editor's assistant, a young woman named Kim. When that was done, he did something he hadn't done in months: he went onto his hookup app. The sound had been turned off since his mother's memorial service. Before him were more horny messages than he cared to consider.

The last year of his life had been documented in lasciviousness. Several Concord Valley dudes, a few guys from Manhattan, an occasional "Hey" from an old regular, a countless number of Studio City "Sups." One shirtless torso that looked like it could have been Larry from LA, but on second look, no. He finally read Kevin's message, the one sent from the balcony in Malibu. It came with an impressive dick pic. Next, a ton of messages from New York sent while he was completing the draft of his book: some first-timers, some one-offs, and some regulars, all unanswered. Many persevered, but all eventually gave up.

Gabe turned on the sound for the app.

A *drrroot* arrived immediately. The dude's headless torso profile simply said, *Visiting*. Someone from out of town meant low-to-no stakes.

Gud2Go: Sup

Visiting: Looking

Gud2Go: Into

Visiting: Cooking

Not what Gabe was expecting. *Could this be Owen?*

Gud2Go: 4real?

Visiting: Cooking n fucking is hot

Gabe liked where this was going. Maybe he *was* messaging Owen. *Is this my big rom-com moment?* he thought.

Gud2Go: Pic?

Visiting sent several nude pics that did not look like Owen naked.

Visiting: Power bottom

Gabe doubted Owen knew what "power bottom" even meant.

Gud2Go: *Brownies?*

Visiting: *Host?*

Gud2Go: *90 minutes*

Visiting: *wya*

Gabe sent Visiting directions, ran out to the over-priced "provisions" store two blocks away for the ingredients, and came back to prepare the familiar brownies mise en place. Visiting soon buzzed. Gabe was looking forward to the intimacy of cooking as a precursor to elevating the sensuality of sex once more. He was nostalgic for Owen.

Before he let Visiting in, Gabe immediately knew the evening would be a disaster. The top of Visiting's head didn't reach the door's peephole viewer. Gabe checked Visiting's stats. He had conveniently left out his height. Gabe was rusty at the hookup game. He took a deep breath and opened the door. Visiting was barely five feet.

Gabe learned his name was Luther, not a name you make up. But when Gabe told him his name was Gabe Hartman, Luther didn't believe him.

"That some made-up shit? Sounds like a porn star name."

Gabe got out his driver's license to show him.

"Could be a fake ID."

Gabe hadn't been around a lot of people while writing his book, let alone someone this hostile. *Maybe he becomes someone different in the kitchen...or the bedroom. One can hope.*

"Let's make brownies," said Gabe leading Luther to the mise en place in the tight galley kitchen.

"How come you didn't buy a mix?" asked Luther.

"This is my mother's brownie recipe. She recently passed away. It would mean a lot to me."

"It's gonna take a while. At some point, we need to get to the bedroom. I have to meet some friends later."

Gabe strained to imagine having sex with Luther: lots of ineffective moving around, everything a touch off. *And what exactly did Luther think a power bottom was?*

"Why don't you start cracking the eggs," said Gabe, "and I'll melt the butter and chocolate?"

Luther cracked the first egg on the side of a bowl.

"In France," said Gabe, "they crack eggs on the counter, not the side of the bowl."

"We ain't in France," said Luther, reaching his fingers in the bowl to dig for pieces of eggshell.

Gabe wished they had washed their hands before starting.

"That's why— You can use the eggshell to scoop pieces of eggshell. It's easier," said Gabe.

"My fingers work fine," said Luther, still chasing the eggshell, eventually pinching one and lifting the small fragment out.

Gabe missed Owen very much at that moment.

Luther pretended to check his phone for the time, but Gabe could see him checking out his other hookup app options that had accumulated since arriving at Gabe's place.

"Why don't we forget about cooking and get down to business?" asked Luther.

"Instead," said Gabe, "why don't we cut our losses?"

Luther took a second to realize what Gabe was saying.

"Oh," said Luther.

"Yeah," said Gabe.

"No, man, I think you're hot and all. Me horny. You?"

"Sorry. Not feeling it."

"You want me to blow you?"

"I'm good," said Gabe, opening the front door with authority: Luther was no longer welcome. "Do you need directions to the Spring or Canal subway from here?"

"I'm ridesharing." Luther was already messaging someone else as Gabe closed the door behind him.

Gabe leaned against the door. His exhale was a final cleansing re-lease. He grabbed his phone and not only blocked Visiting Luther, but he deleted the app altogether. The phone's final question: "Are you sure you want to delete this app?" warned of a new finality.

Delete.

Gabe was now living in terra incognita. He was certain he would die alone, but he would die living the joy of freedom.

The remains of the mise en place caught his eye. Cooking with Owen had been a blip in a lifetime of microwavables, greenroom food, and takeout. He pushed through his loneliness as he melted chocolate chips and butter in the microwave.

Making his mother's brownies in a cramped kitchen sublet sad-dened Gabe. He wished he had a real home, but he didn't even know what home meant anymore. The soap offices had taken the role of his primary home, and his colleagues had been his extended family. His apartment had merely been a place to sleep.

Gabe prepped the brownie pan with butter and parchment before mixing the dry ingredients. He took half an eggshell and scooped out the broken pieces Luther had missed. The process made him feel connected to Owen. Next, he added the wet mixture to the dry. Making brownies from scratch alone was the opposite of the wonderful cooking experi-ence he'd had with Owen, getting to know Owen. Owen...

Putting the brownies in the oven, he understood cooking had made him horny. He considered rubbing one out, but it would be done more as a habit than organic sensuality. Instead, he checked his emails.

Kim, the assistant to the editor, had acknowledged receipt of the completed manuscript. She was impressed he had turned in the draft far ahead of deadline and had passed it along to the team. He should expect a few notes "within a fortnight." Gabe had to look up the length of a "fortnight." He was also curious to see their notes. The book had been a pleasure to write, but that didn't mean anything. He was hoping to avoid a page-one rewrite. He had been careful to unify the headnotes intro-ducing each recipe, explanations, and directions. The text of the recipe couldn't be copyrighted, the legal department had explained, as recipes were simply lists of ingredients and actions. The heart of every cookbook was everything written around the recipes. While Gabe was pleased with his work, he was the first to admit he didn't know what he was doing.

When the brownies were done, Gabe gave them a good whack! on the counter to give the surface sheen an artful crack throughout. His first thought was to send Owen a picture of the brownies. Kevin had intimated Owen might be open to a new conversation, but Gabe's instincts told him otherwise.

A year ago, Gabe would have phoned one of his dependable squad for a friendly telephone chat. But he wasn't sure he even knew where they were anymore.

"Erin! Long time!"

"Gabe! Great to hear your voice!"

"How is life at *SNL?*" asked Gabe.

"It is much easier to make one show a week—and only twenty-one shows a year. It's like a vacation."

"Much more sustainable."

"No shit. You taught me so much. I'm forever indebted. Listen. There's a line producer job opening up here you'd be great for, if you want me to put in a good word."

"I wish I could." Gabe lied. "I'm in the middle of drafting my book. I have to see this process through to the end. But thanks for thinking of me."

"I'll always owe you for giving me my first break. Did you hear Aurora Helms is starting a new soap opera cable network where reruns of her soaps will be looped in perpetuity?"

"I had not heard. Interesting," said Gabe.

"More than interesting, Gabe. Aurora was the one who canceled *If Tomorrow Never Comes*. She wanted the show exclusively for her new network."

"As long as the sherry keeps flowing, right?" said Gabe.

"The whole process was intentionally vague and drawn out for the sole reason she was waiting to get official authorization for her new network. The suits were willing to give the show a shot on the West Coast.

It was all Aurora's doing." Gabe listened and gave pause. The world of television was now a faraway memory, fading fast. "Look," continued Erin, "if you change your mind about the line producer gig..."

When the brownies were cooled, Gabe took a spoon to one corner. The brownies were delicious, but one ingredient was missing.

*

Gabe received the editor's notes long before a fortnight had passed. The publisher had surprisingly few notes, some style issues, a tonal shift in two sections, but the notes included very few suggestions for revisions. The level of respect and loving attention in the coverage made Gabe feel like an authentic, respected writer. The editor also mentioned how impressed everyone was with how strong his first draft was.

The book was being fast-tracked to hit the stores between Halloween and Christmas—hopefully, before Thanksgiving. After Gabe's second draft revisions were with the copy editor and proofreader, he was sent several hardcover dust jackets for consideration. Gabe requested a prominent photo of his mother for the front cover. He had one photo with all her friends, but it had nothing to do with cooking. He considered a sweet picture of the two of them cooking together taken when Gabe was about four, but Gabe didn't want to appear on the cover. He wanted Amelia to be the sole focus. He settled on a picture of his mother as a young woman in a kitchen he didn't recognize, dressed as a French chef, her expression sheer joy as she tasted something on the stovetop from a wooden spoon.

Printing the individual recipe cards was a more complicated issue. Initially, everyone was excited about putting them in envelopes attached to the pages of the book. That process would have priced the book at around seventy-five dollars, which would have made it a coffee-table book, neither the correct market nor the intention of the book. Also, some of the recipes were written in cursive, and not everyone reads cursive anymore. In the end, the consensus was the original recipe cards would simply be photographed and the recipes would be typed out legibly for all to read.

The day the galleys arrived marked the end of the drafting journey. Kim emailed him a document of protocols for how to edit galleys. He liked the cover: the photo had been rendered in a soft sepia reverse negative that gave the book a nostalgic feel.

When he was in the middle of the galley edit, he got a "I have John Thornton for Gabriel Hartman" call.

"Gabe! Word on the street says you're the man of the hour," said John Thornton.

"What's going on?" asked Gabe.

"Several insiders have already read the galleys, and there's strong buzz about your book."

"That's good," said Gabe.

"It's better than good. The publicists are saying the book should get some specific attention. You need to be ready. Do you need any media training? You should have five minutes of inoffensive, compelling, charming anecdotes for the morning talk shows."

"Like cable access?"

"Network, dear. Hoda, Gayle, Robin, whoever. They are going to be chomping at the bit. Cookbooks don't always hit the bestseller list, but we're hiring a top-notch PR person to see how far we can get at the *Times*. Minimum, a capsule review, but if they like it, who knows? There's also the social media piece. We're eyeing several influencers."

"How much is this going to cost?" asked Gabe.

"The publishing company is footing the bill for anything to do with the hardcover. I made sure every detail for that was covered in your contract."

"You're good."

"I have my moments. The publisher also wanted to know who they should get to blurb it? Who are your most famous friends who would be willing to read a galley and write a sentence or two for a cover quote?"

"Is Barrett Hodges famous enough?" asked Gabe.

"How do you know Barrett Hodges? He's a great actor," said John Thornton. "But not famous enough. Yet. And his fan base doesn't fall in the realm of our marketing strategy. You still in touch with Owen Greene?"

"Is he famous enough?" asked Gabe.

"Maybe not. He was doing farm-to-table something..."

"Heirloom tomatoes," said Gabe. "But he quit."

"He's a hot mess, but I love him. You think on it. Bottom line: We need to get on the radar of all food, cooking, and culinary magazines for Christmas book suggestions. And before the paperback comes out this spring. Sound good?"

"Sounds great," said Gabe, feeling like his life was changing before his eyes. He had Owen to thank for John.

"Before I forget: you're contracted to do a book tour. I think I negotiated a two-week tour, maybe ten days, nothing too inhumane. Mostly independent bookstores in hip cities, places where the publisher thinks the book will sell well. You'll get to meet all the right people. The publisher is paying. Save all your receipts to get reimbursed. You need to show up looking like a happy author, be on time, read a delightful excerpt, and sell, sell, sell, I mean sign, sign, sign books. You'll need some 500 to 750 word excerpts for public readings. It can't be from chapter one, and nothing untoward. Two or three short bits work best. No one has an attention span anymore. The publisher will be sending you an itinerary. You no doubt want to keep working on your galleys. Oh, one last item: I'll be sending over a contract this afternoon for you to look over."

"For what?

"Your next book. The publisher doesn't care what you write as long as they get to publish it. You're hot, new, with lots of buzz. This phase has a short shelf life, but right now, Gabriel Hartman, you are in the catbird seat!"

Gabe ate another spoonful of brownies. He should have been more excited. If only he had someone to share the good news with.

Reading the galleys, Gabe could see his mother fully as an extraordinary, strong woman, a woman who didn't care what the world thought of her as she independently loved the man she loved and created communities of care with her limited resources. As he read the galleys, he got lost in the writing and sometimes forgot he was the author. He was coming to understand what a compassionate writer the book had encouraged him to become. He appreciated the soap for its steady paycheck. But he was ashamed of his work there, and he was often stretched thin by its incessant demands. He had to leave the comfort of hack work to come into his own as a writer. Everything in his past had to be destroyed to lead him to this moment.

The publisher sent over his book tour itinerary as soon as they got a solid release date. Gabe couldn't have picked a better list of bookstores.

He started in the Northwest with Elliott Bay and Powell's, headed down the coast for City Lights and Book Passage, then to Los Angeles for Skylight and Book Soup. (He was delighted when Mark, Larry, and David showed up at Book Soup.) He then zigzagged east to Santa Fe, Denver, Minneapolis, and Nashville, when his book started to appear in social media videos. The conventional wisdom was that authors loathed book tours and would often develop carpal tunnel from all the signing, but to Gabe, his travels were pure pilgrimage. Sharing his mother's life and stories with strangers brought him great joy.

My Mother's Recipe Cards debuted at #14 on the *New York Times* Nonfiction Bestseller list, most probably thanks to mentions on social media. From that moment on, Gabe Hartman's name would always be preceded by the phrase, "New York Times Best-selling Author."

Gabe's biggest challenge was to navigate the sustained loneliness. He was tempted to reload the hookup app as a distraction to take the edge off his travel day, but memories of the Luther debacle and Kevin's cringy Malibu caresses stopped him. Instead, he sat and dwelled in all his discomfort until he transformed his loneliness to solitude. He had books to sell, and he didn't want to sully a good book tour.

Somewhere around Oxford's Square Books, the absurdist repetition of relaying the same anecdotes and reading the same passages settled in. Gabe understood why two weeks was about the limit for a humane tour. After a charming visit to the Blue Bicycle Bookstore in Charleston, Gabe got a call from a Concord Valley area code that was vaguely familiar. He answered, hoping it might be Owen.

"Gabe, Arthur Quinn here. Looks like your book has legs. My

goodness, number twelve this week. Well done, m'boy!"

"Arthur! Long time."

Arthur's voice was strained, a little older, but any voice from Concord Valley would have comforted Gabe.

"How are you?" asked Gabe, expecting to settle in for a friendly chat in his hotel room.

"I'm fine. Lenore and I visited the Justice of the Peace last week—mainly for tax purposes. But your mother taught me I could have a premium life as long as I had a companion by my side."

"Congratulations, Arthur. I should have put that quote in the book."

"Speaking of, I need to shift gears and turn this into a business call. My store didn't have the clout or sales volume to make the book tour your publisher set up, but I was wondering if you might want to pop up to the Quinn & Ink when you're done to sign a few books up here. For a friend. It's not often one of our own makes it as a writer in the real world. I gave your book a special spot at the front table."

Gabe had worried the town might have learned he had exploited them for *If Tomorrow Never Comes* storylines. His worries had apparently been in vain.

"I'm on the road for the rest of this week," said Gabe. "But no plans after that."

"It would mean the world to your mother's friends," said Arthur. "And I would love to see you."

It had been a while since someone had offered a warm welcome to Gabe. Gabe could hear the sound of home in Arthur's voice.

"Can we set something up?" asked Arthur.

"Let's do it!"

Arthur scheduled the reading for a Thursday in the late afternoon when the farmers market crowd would be thinning and folks from outside Concord Valley might be tempted to linger on the square to meet a famous author at the bookstore.

Arthur's invitation shifted something in Gabe. If he was ever going to find out what happened to Owen, he would learn it on this trip. He didn't want to troll Owen online, as he didn't want to pollute his mind with any misfortune via the untrusty internet. Any internet search would feel like stalking. Also, people have ways of finding out when you've trolled them. Gabe didn't want that to be part of their story.

After the final book signing at the Strand in New York City and interviews on the morning show circuit, including a "surprise" cooking demo of his mother's ciambellone tea cake recipe with their in-house celebrity chef, Gabe got word *My Mother's Recipe Cards* had finally cracked the Top Ten on all the major bestseller lists, usually at number eight or number nine, where it would likely linger for a few weeks before its run came to an end.

The next day, Gabe was filled with both terror and excitement as he headed up to Concord Valley. Outside town, he was greeted by the new "Entering Concord Valley" sign with its updated population listed at around 12,000, which meant the town was either growing or they had absorbed surrounding unincorporated villages into their population. Gabe was curious to see what the AH Trust had done with his old home and fearful they had razed it to build a mini mansion, but he was running behind. He would make time for sightseeing after the signing.

The farmers market was winding down as he drove into the downtown square area. He parked in front of McFarland's because the market patrons were taking up the best parking spaces near the bookstore. Through McFarland's open door, Gabe was glad not to see Joey Dakota at the bar. He hoped Joey had found some peace of mind.

Gabe didn't recognize any of the vendors at the farmers market. (Later, he found out from Arthur that Charlize had moved to an assisted living facility in Florida where she scootered along a running trail by the ocean every morning.) Gabe had once fantasized about seeing Owen at the farmers market, selling gorgeous heirloom tomatoes, but Kevin had put an end to that idea. Besides, only greenhouse tomatoes grew this late in the season.

A butcher-paper sign over the Quinn & Ink's permanent signage announced, "Gabe Hartman Book Signing Today." The sign was reminiscent of something high school seniors made for homecoming. The bookstore display window was a lovely shrine to his mother with several copies of the book prominently on display. Gabe was happy he had made the trip.

The bookstore was configured like the memorial service, designed this time as a celebration of Amelia Hartman's life. Her surviving friends who were mentioned in the recipe cards were in attendance. Gabe was met with hugs and "your mother would be so proud" comments. Arthur greeted him with fatherly affection. Lenore handed him a bottle of water and made sure the event began promptly at 5:00 p.m. Arthur moved more slowly now; Gabe was glad Lenore was there to watch out for him.

The reading was set up with a simple mic stand and a stool. As Arthur introduced him to the crowd, Gabe scanned the store wondering if Owen was hiding in the back. He got a wave from the Cohens, Bethany giving him a friendly thumbs-up as she held up his book. Arthur's speech was brief and down-to-earth: "local boy makes good" but "never take his dating advice."

"If my mother were around, she would be pretty angry she missed this event," said Gabe before reading from the book. "She left us too soon, but she left us a kitchen full of heart."

As Gabe read his favorite passages, he could hear the crowd listening in a different way from the other bookstores. Gabe was telling their story, and they were making sure he got it right. He usually didn't read the introduction to the holiday cookie section. However, since many of the women his mother had shared cookie recipes with were in the room, he thought it fitting. He could feel their pride as he read.

"Mrs. Abbott was there when I broke my arm. She drove me to the emergency room because she didn't want my mother to miss any work. Her Peppermint Snowball cookies should not be missed. Ms. Terwilliger, who always had time for a throw/catch when she'd stop by for a gossip with my mother, her Raspberry-Pistachio Linzer cookies are to die for. Mrs. Hamilton's Peanut Butter Blossoms are a local legend. I can't tell you how many petitions she had my mother sign. She always had a petition in her hand."

"Still do!" shouted Mrs. Hamilton from the side holding up a pen and a signature roster for a new recycling initiative.

Gabe's role was not merely to celebrate his mother, but to acknowledge the community that had supported and loved them both through the years.

After the reading, Lenore whisked Gabe to the signing table, which she had filled with pens, books, and another two bottles of water. Gabe was impressed by her efficiency and organization. While signing books, he got caught up on all the local gossip. Several people mentioned he should stop by his old house and that his mother would be pleased with what's been done with the place. No one gave him any specifics, but a drive-by was mandatory before heading off for the City.

Gabe didn't want to do too much driving at night, so he needed to head back to the City as soon as the signing was done. Everyone understood, and he bowed out early. On his way out of town, he took a roundabout route to get to his old house that also went by Owen's old place, with its Offer Pending For Sale sign out front. Owen's lovely house had once borne warm memories but now appeared empty and lonely. Gabe was tempted to get out to see what became of the heirloom tomato planters, but he was afraid of what he'd find and didn't want to get caught trespassing.

He had one last stop before heading back to the City to figure out his next steps in life. He had no problem finding his old house. Even though golden hour was at its peak as he turned down the street, extra brightness emanated from his old home. It was still standing. The front porch was now lit with a small neon sign. The closer he got, the letters came into focus: Amelia's Place. The thin neon tubing had been meticulously bent and crafted to look exactly like his mother's cursive handwriting on her recipe cards.

Gabe parked his car. *Let's hope the best parts of life really are the scary bits,* he thought to himself as he quietly walked toward the house.

The place had been cleaned up and renovated with a new front porch. The curtains on all the windows were open, making it easy to see the interior. Several smaller tables were positioned around a large community table in the center of the dining room, all adorned with a variety of tablecloths, place settings, and small bouquets of flowers. A young woman was writing an artful menu on a whiteboard on a side wall. He could make out Mushroom Lasagna with Smoked Mozzarella.

Gabe's heart leapt as Owen entered the dining room to speak with the woman at the whiteboard. Gabe could feel his pulse accelerating. A young man dressed in chef's gear approached Owen holding two peach galettes on pizza circles. Owen seemed pleased, and the young chef returned to the kitchen. Gabe waited for the girl at the whiteboard to leave the dining room before risking an entrance.

The interior doorknob had a string of bells around it. Owen's head pivoted around. "Our first seating isn't until— Oh...hey. Arthur said you were coming to town. I wondered if you'd— I didn't know what you'd—"

"Amelia's Place?" asked Gabe.

"You know you won the parent lottery, right?" said Owen.

"I had to go away to learn it," said Gabe.

Gabe didn't know how to escape the awkwardness.

"You look different," said Owen.

"I got older," said Gabe.

"No...maybe wiser," said Owen. "You still look good. Better. If that's possible."

This made Gabe smile. "You too. The Cohens said the AH Trust had bought the place."

"Cash offer," said Owen.

"AH?" asked Gabe.

"A—Amelia, H—Hartman," said Owen. "Creating a revocable trust in her name felt right."

"You had my back. Once again," said Gabe. "In spite of everything."

"Maybe because of everything... There was a lot to get over and unpack. Not important. You know how much I love this place."

"I love the upgrades," said Gabe. "And the community table." Gabe gave him a thumbs-up.

"Thanks. When you left, I did some soul-searching and made a list of everything I have loved most in life: cooking, farm-to-table, prix fixe restaurants, your mother's dessert recipes. This house. You kept telling me this is what I needed to do. I had to get over myself and listen. So far, it's worked out nicely."

Gabe was hoping *he* had made Owen's list of favorites. Even if he had, it would have been unearned to ask. "Growing heirloom tomatoes didn't make this list?"

"No," said Owen, "but I grow herbs in the garden by the aspen tree."

"Where her ashes are," said Gabe.

"She's a part of everything we cook."

"I'm happy for you." Tears welled in Gabe's eyes. He didn't bother hiding them.

"I make sure to feature her desserts every night. Tonight it's her peach—"

"—galette. 'His favorite,'" said Gabe. "Lovely."

"You were right about many things, Gabe," said Owen.

"I was wrong to lie to you. I didn't mean to exploit you. I'm sorry about all that went down. If I had to do it all over, I would have told you the truth from the start. I got scared. Lying was my MO."

"Oliver's big apology scene at the airport—that was for me, right?"

"Of course."

"I have to admit, I cried during the scene. I'm sorry the show ended. I was a mess the week of the last episodes," said Owen.

"We still had quite a fan base. But for me...it was for the best. I was stuck in a job that embarrassed me and burned me out. And now we're all free at eleven o'clock."

"That's now about when my local produce vendors arrive. I replaced one standing meeting for another. Did you go by my old house?" asked Owen. "I think the new owners are going to close in two weeks. I hear they're cannabis people. They liked the wooden planters."

"I don't understand. What happened to your passion for farming?" asked Gabe.

"The joy left town with my consultant," said Owen.

"I'm sorry I hurt you," said Gabe. "I wish we could start from scratch. There's no reason you should forgive me, but I wish you would."

"I regret the terrible things I said to you," said Owen.

"You came by it honestly," said Gabe. "You're the first person I ever let in. I was in over my head. But letting you in was never a lie."

"So where does this leave us?" asked Owen. "Considering we've never been here before. I mean, there's no more Kevin to mess with your moral compass. And no more job for you to lie about lifting storylines from loved ones."

"No more betrayals," said Gabe. "I promise."

"I'd say this leaves us in a pretty good place," said Owen.

"If this were a rom-com," said Gabe, "one of us would have to make 'The Speech,' like, 'I'm just a boy, standing in front of another boy, asking him to forgive me.'"

"Isn't that from the movie *Nodding Off*?" asked Owen.

"How about 'You had me at galette'?"

"That's from *Jerry MacTired*."

"'It doesn't matter if the two guys are perfect, as long as they are perfect for each other.'"

"That's *Good Will Punting*."

"You can do better than that," said Gabe.

"I'm not the writer," said Owen.

"For a sophisticated former, white-shoe lawyer, you know a lot of cheesy rom-com references," said Gabe.

"I was a cheesy white-shoe lawyer," said Owen. "And stop plagiarizing. You're a *New York Times* bestselling author now. It's a good book, by the way. It's one of our kitchen bibles. And getting her local friends to blurb it: so sweet. But I still want my big speech. Throw me something original."

"My version of 'The Speech'?" asked Gabe before clearing his throat.

Owen gestured, inviting Gabe to take all the room he needed.

"Owen, you woke up something beautiful in me, something wonderful that will never go to sleep. No one else enters a room and fills me with light like you do. The only time I ever feel like I belong is when I'm with you. Please make a life with me, Owen Greene. The rules of rom-com destiny say boy is inevitably going to get boy in the end. Why fight it? I look at you and I'm home. And I know that's from *Finding Nemo,* but I don't care."

Owen took in the fullness of the moment. "You're done?" He took a pause.

The possibility of Owen having second thoughts terrified Gabe.

"That was...perfect," said Owen. "I've been in love with you since the first moment I saw you. And I know they say that in every rom-com, but it's the truth. Loving you is what I was made for. Is this where we hug?"

"I hope so," said Gabe.

They met in the middle for a good warm hug, the kind of hug that says these two men cared deeply for each other. The kind of hug that says, "You have no idea how much I have missed you."

"So...where *does* this leave us?" asked Owen. "This feels kinda like a reboot."

"It feels like a new starting place. Boy meets boy, and a second chance begins," said Gabe.

Owen went in for another hug, but this time it merged into a kiss, a kiss that took up exactly where they had left off.

"How come," asked Gabe, coming up for air, "I always feel stupid when I'm with you? Good, but dumb."

"Maybe you are in love, Mister. Love makes everyone stupid."

They sealed their mutual stupidity with another kiss.

"I missed you so much," said Gabe.

"Me too. But right now," said Owen, "I have to get ready for the first seating."

"And I should be taking off."

The introduction to Eva Cassidy's "Somewhere Over the Rainbow" played softly through the restaurant's speakers. A smile spread across Gabe's face.

"You may be in for a few surprises around here," said Owen.

"Any Roy Orbison?" asked Gabe.

Owen shrugged. "We need to get you a new theme song," said Owen. "Something more cliched, like 'It Had to Be You.'"

"Let me think about it. I have to head back tonight, but when can I see you again?" asked Gabe.

"You're the jet-setting author," said Owen. "You tell me."

"Is my bedroom still available...if I come visit?" asked Gabe.

"Sorry, the room where you had sex with men you had fallen in love with is now the business office. The times are a changin', young buck."

"And my mother's room?" asked Gabe.

"You mean *my* room?' said Owen. "You would have to share the bed."

"I wouldn't mind one bit," said Gabe.

*

They were back, not as the wild, adventurous boys living with abandon as before, but wiser men, no worse for experience.

In no time, Gabe had packed up his Sullivan Street sublet, bought a sensible, pre-owned compact SUV, loaded it with his stuff, and headed to Concord Valley. Owen found Gabe a corner of the business office where he could write in privacy, but Gabe usually drifted downstairs, often to the kitchen, to be near Owen, or to the community table when he wanted privacy but to have Owen nearby. Sometimes they would work in silence and sometimes not. Owen would ask him to taste a dish, when he needed advice on a flavor note, always carried with the legendary potholders. Gabe wasn't ready to share what he was writing, and Owen never asked. At one point Owen gently suggested he hoped Gabe would someday tell their love story. He wasn't sure if Gabe had heard him, but he had learned to be patient with Gabe. Nothing mattered as long as they were a part of each other's life again.

"Close your eyes," said Owen, late one spring morning, coming into the dining room when Gabe was writing at the community table.

Gabe closed his eyes.

"It's one of your mother's recipes I hadn't tried yet." Owen fed Gabe the treat.

"Is that a popover?" asked Gabe. "With strawberries?"

"Heirloom strawberries."

Acknowledgements

Special thanks to my agent Jackie Kruzie at Focused Artists, to my first readers, Katrina Schroeder and Stephanie Shiflett, for always offering sound support, and to everyone at NineStar Press, especially my editors who helped make this story even better.

And finally, to Bill, for his love and support, and for always making sure there was a good coffeehouse nearby where I could write.

About the Author

Tom Diggs is the author of fiction, plays, and musicals. His fiction has been published in *The James White Review*. His play, FAIR AND DE-CENT, was developed by the Kennedy Center and nominated for the Pulitzer Prize for Drama in 2008. When he's not working on his own writing, he enjoys teaching middle schoolers to write. Outside of the world of letters, he bakes, bikes, and keeps up with the latest technology. A lifelong learner, he attended Brown University, the University of Washington, and NYU/Tisch. Once upon a time, he interned on *All My Children*. He currently spends his time between San Francisco and Santa Fe and is a member of the Dramatists Guild.

Email
TDiggs5555@me.com

Facebook
www.facebook.com/tom.diggs

X
@diggsyt

TikTok
@tomdiggs

Instagram
diggsyt

Website
www.tomdiggs.com

Connect with NineStar Press

Website: NineStarPress.com

Facebook: NineStarPress

X: @ninestarpress

Instagram: NineStarPress

BlueSky: NineStarPress

Threads: @ninestarpress